Praise for Adele Pa...

'Wonderfully plotted, moving and insightful . . . shot through with funny, tender and observant moments'
Daily Mail

'Full of emotional set-pieces and real insight into relationships between men and women' *Heat*

'A fabulous mix of comedy, real life and emotional depth'
Daily Express

'Dark, funny and observant' *Cosmopolitan*

'A wicked pleasure' *Woman & Home*

'She is a particularly acute observer of relationship ups and downs, and her stories are always as insightful as they are entertaining' *Daily Mirror*

'Guaranteed to keep you hooked until the end'
She magazine

'Parks writes with wit and a keen eye for detail' *Guardian*

'Compulsively addictive' *Elle*

'Funny, tender and observant' *Grazia*

'Deliciously down to earth' *The Times*

Adele Parks worked in advertising until she published her first novel, *Playing Away*, in 2000, which was the debut bestseller of that year. Adele has gone on to publish eleven novels in eleven years, and all of her novels have been top ten bestsellers. Her work has been translated into twenty-five different languages. Adele has spent her adult life in Italy, Botswana and London until 2005 when she moved to Guildford, where she now lives with her husband and son. Adele believes reading is a basic human right, so she works closely with the Reading Agency as an Ambassador of the Six Book Challenge, a programme designed to encourage adult literacy. In 2011 she was a judge for the Costa Book Awards.

For more information visit **www.adeleparks.com** where you can sign up to receive Adele's newsletter. You can also find her on Facebook **www.facebook.com/OfficialAdeleParks** and follow her on Twitter **@adeleparks**.

Adele
PARKS

LOVE
LIES

To Mackenzie.
The World's Best Intern!

love *[signature]*

x x

R
headline
review

First published in Great Britain in 2009
by PENGUIN BOOKS

This edition published in Great Britain in 2012
by HEADLINE REVIEW
An imprint of HEADLINE PUBLISHING GROUP

1

Cataloguing in Publication Data is available from the British Library

ISBN 978 0 7553 9429 6

Typeset in Garamond MT

Printed and bound in Great Britain by
Clays Ltd, St Ives plc

Headline's policy is to use papers that are natural, renewable and recyclable
products and made from wood grown in sustainable forests. The logging
and manufacturing processes are expected to conform to the environmental
regulations of the country of origin.

HEADLINE PUBLISHING GROUP
An Hachette UK Company
338 Euston Road
London NW1 3BH

www.headline.co.uk
www.hachette.co.uk

For Tracy Bradbery

Prologue
Scott

'Do I smell, Mark?'

'No.'

'You'd tell me if I did, right?'

'I would.'

'Is my hairline receding?'

'No.'

'You're sure I'm not going bald?'

'Yes.'

'Do you think I'll lose my teeth?'

'Only if someone punches you.'

'My nan got gum disease.'

'We've got great dentists. Scott, you are coming down and this is just another one of your irrational worry sessions. We can waste a lot of time doing this, mate.'

'Mark, do you think I'll end up broke? You know, blow it all.'

'No, we've sorted out your finances. You're never going to suffer from poverty – other than poverty of spirit. No matter how many TVs you throw out of hotel windows.'

1. Fern

I have taken a bullet. I live an ordinary life. I've almost accepted it. Almost.

I ought to clarify I don't always go around thinking big, profound thoughts like that. Quite a lot of the time I amuse my brain cells by thinking about which movie star is shagging which other movie star (and do they have better sex than us mere mortals), or whether I can get away with not washing my hair if I'm inventive enough with my up-do (thus securing an extra thirty minutes in bed in the morning). My idea of deep is wondering whether organic food is worth the huge price tag or whether it's all just a ghastly marketing con. But today I am twenty-nine years, eleven months and three weeks old. I can no longer keep the big thoughts at bay.

Let me clarify, when I say ordinary, I mean normal, average, run of the mill, commonplace. Mundane. Clear?

I know, I know. I should be grateful. Ordinary has its up-side. I could be some human mutant with skin stretchy enough to be able to wrap my lower lip over the top of my head, *or* an über-fertile woman prone to giving birth to sextuplets and now be a proud mother of thirty-six indistinguishable, media-loving brats *or* someone who really does train-spot. Then my life would be considerably worse than the one I am leading, but even knowing this is not as much comfort as it should be.

I live my ordinary life with Adam. My boyfriend of four years. I hesitate to refer to him as my partner because that would suggest some sort of equality or responsibility in the relationship and, frankly, both things are notably lacking. I organize the paying of all the bills (although he does cough up his share when prompted). I buy groceries, cook, clean, remember the birthdays of his family members, buy wedding gifts for our friends, arrange travel and accommodation if we ever do manage to grab a weekend away, I even put the pizza delivery people's number on speed dial. Adam alphabetically arranges his CDs and vinyls in neat rows, all the way along our sitting-room shelves.

Yes, we do share a flat. A two-bedroom flat in Clapham. Not the posh bit of Clapham, sadly. The bit where the neighbours think old pee-stained mattresses and settees, spurting their cheap foam innards, are acceptable alternatives to rose bushes in the front garden. Despite sharing a flat, I also hesitate to refer to Adam as my live-in lover because that would suggest an element of passion and that's notably lacking too, of late. Our relationship is more prose than poetry. It wasn't always that way.

We used to be wild about each other. We used to swing from chandeliers, or as good as. There was a time when we couldn't keep our hands off one another. Which led to some, er, shall we say interesting situations. I'm not trying to brag. I just want to paint a fair picture. We are certified members of the mile-high club and we have made love under canvas, in a swimming-pool and once in a botanic garden (Kew). We made love frequently and in many, many different ways; slowly and carefully, fast and needy. In the past we often came at the same time. Now, it's unusual if we both are in the room at the same time.

I used to think we were going somewhere. It looks like we've arrived. This is my stop. I have to get off the train and take a long hard look at the station. It's not one with hanging baskets full of cascading begonia and there isn't one of those lovely large clocks with Roman numerals. There's nothing romantic or pretty about my station at all. My station is littered with discarded polystyrene cups and spotted with blobs of chewing-gum.

Frankly, it's depressing.

We don't own our flat. We don't even have an exclusive flat-share. My best friend, Jess, also rents with us. Normally, I acknowledge that this is no bad thing. She is (largely) single and so we are each other's on-tap company on those nights when she doesn't have a date and Adam is at work.

Adam is in the music business. Don't get excited. He's not a rock star, or a manager, or producer, or anything remotely glamorous and promising. He's a rigger; which, if I've understood things correctly, is one step up from the coach driver on a tour but not as important as the people who work in catering. He freelances, and while he must be quite good at his job (offers of employment are regular) it's clear he's never going to be a millionaire. For that matter, he's never going to have so much as a savings account.

This didn't used to bother me. I'm a florist and work in someone else's shop: Ben's Bunches and Bouquets or Ben's B&B for short. Ben, who is as camp as a glow-in-the-dark feather duster, is an absolute angel of a boss but I only earn a modest wage. Jess works in a bookshop and, after thirteen years' service, she has just reached the dizzy heights of store manager. We're not the type of people to be motivated by money (one of my other great friends, Lisa, is married to a City lawyer and he's rich but we think he's nice *despite* that). I don't resent Adam's lack of cash. I resent his lack of . . . oh, what's the word?

Commitment.

His inability to grow up. To move on. It is Adam who has jammed our brakes at the ordinary station because he's a settler. He lacks ambition. When challenged, he says he's content and throws me a look of bewilderment that's vaguely critical. He thinks I'm unreasonable because I yearn for more than a tiny two-bedroom flat-share (all we can afford despite working endless, incompatible hours). I long for something more than Monday to Wednesday evenings in front of the TV, Thursday nights at the supermarket, Friday and Saturday nights at the local and Sundays (our one day a week off together) sleeping off a hangover.

Recently, I've been overwhelmed with despair as I've come to understand that not only do I currently have very little in my life to feel energized about but, with the exception of hoping my lottery numbers come up, I have absolutely nothing to look forward to in the future. This is it for me. The sum total.

When I was a tiny kid I once saw a deeply unsuitable sci-fi TV show where the goodies were trapped in a room and the walls were closing in on them, about to crush them to death. The same menace was used in *Star Wars*

Episode IV but Princess Leia had it really bad because she was knee deep in garbage too. I found the concept truly horrifying and suffered from nightmares for months. Lately, as I watch the (supposedly) best years of my life amble off into the dim distance, I've started to experience the same nightmare again. I wake up sweating with the taste of fear in my mouth. I'm going to be squashed to death by the walls of a tiny room.

In the beginning I was impressed by Adam's *joie de vivre*; his jaunty carelessness was part of the attraction. I loved it that he would find the time to listen to some demo disc from a yet to be discovered band. A demo disc that he'd scrounged from a no one and would pass on to Someone; not because of the lure of brash financial gain but just because he thought this band might be the next 'it' – more, he thought they *deserved* to be the next 'it'. I didn't care that I didn't actually understand what he was on about when he said something like, 'This band is totally thrashing with PJ Harvey-meets-Throwing Muses Fire, yet it's so completely purring with hectic pop.' I wonder if he cared that I just smiled and said nothing. Maybe my lack of knowledge about the pop scene has been interpreted as a lack of interest, because Adam's stopped urging me to listen to lyrics that are 'all about a breakneck chase through messy relationships'. I think he's accepted that my music tastes are mainstream. It's a shame in a way, because while I didn't understand what he was on about I did respect that he was on about *something*. I loved it that Adam had this extraordinary passion and I believed it would lead to something big. Problem being I never actually defined exactly what that something big might be – and nor did Adam. Yes, he pointed one or two promising bands in the right direction and they went on to greater things. But Adam's stayed still. Ground to a halt.

Thinking about it, it's a good thing that Adam has stopped asking me to join him at the gigs of struggling bands which take place in tiny underground bars that flout the no-smoking laws. I wouldn't want to go to those sorts of places any more. When you are twenty-five it's easy to be impressed by passion, creative flair, free spirits, etc. etc. When you are pushing thirty it's hard to resist being contemptuous about the very things that attracted you. Why is that? One of life's not so funny jokes, I guess.

On evenings like this one it's particularly hard to remember why I thought dating a gig rigger was ever a good idea. On evenings when Jess is out on a proper date (at some fancy restaurant somewhere) with some guy who has potential (a hot merchant banker that she met last Saturday) and I'm left alone with nothing more than a scribbled note (attached to the fridge by a Simpson's magnet which we got free in a cereal box), I struggle.

I'd especially asked Adam to stay home tonight. I'd said to him that I wanted to talk. Well, to be accurate, I pinned up a note to that effect on the fridge this morning; we didn't actually speak. Adam was working at a gig in Brixton last night and he didn't get home until three this morning. My boss Ben and I take it in turns to go to the New Covent Garden flower market each morning and today it was my turn, so I had to leave the flat by 4 a.m. I didn't have the heart to wake Adam so I left a note. It was clear enough.

We need to talk. Don't go out tonight. Don't accept any work. This is important. I'd underlined the words 'need', 'don't' (both of them) and 'important'. I thought I'd communicated my exasperation, urgency and desperation. Apparently not. Adam's reply note reads: *Got a sniff of a big job coming up. Lots of green ones, Fern-girl. Would love to gas tonight but no can do. Later. Luv u.*

When I first read the note I kicked the table leg, which was stupid because not only did I knock over a milk carton which means I now have to clean up the spillage but I hurt my foot. It's Adam I want to hurt.

I drag my eyes around the flat. It's a bit like rubbing salt into an open wound. If I was sensible now I'd just pick up my bag and phone a mate (or use any other lifeline) and I'd head back into town for a meal and a chat. It's a rare lovely summer evening. We could sit on the pavement outside a cheap restaurant and drink house wine. But I don't call anyone. Actually, I can't. Jess and Lisa are the only two people I could face seeing when I'm in this sort of mood and I know neither is available. I have other buddies but they are either friends Adam and I share (and therefore not useful when I want to let off steam about his inability to grow up and commit) or they are my good-time-only friends (also not useful when I'm steaming).

Jess is on her date and Lisa can never do a spur-of-the-moment night out. She has two kids under the age of three. A night out requires a serious time-line leading up to the occasion and military precision planning on the actual night. She grumbles about the lack of spontaneity in her life but Jess and I refuse to take her grumbles seriously; we both know that not only has she everything she ever wanted, she also has exactly what we want too.

So, it's a night in the flat with just the washing up to keep me company – the flat that epitomizes all that is wrong with where I am at, just one week before my thirtieth birthday. Great.

Jess and I have tried to make the flat as stylish as possible on our limited budgets. We regularly visit Ikea and we're forever lighting scented candles that we buy from the supermarket. However, all our good work can be undone in a matter of minutes if Adam is left un-supervised – in many ways he's a lot like a Labrador puppy. Because he, and many of his mates, work nights they often waste away a day hanging around our flat. When Jess and I leave for work the place usually looks reasonably smart. Not posh, I realize, but clean and tidy. When we come home it looks like a particularly vicious hurricane has dashed through.

Today the place looks especially squalid. The curtains are drawn even though it's a bright summer evening. My guess is that Adam and his mates have been watching DVDs all day. A guess that is confirmed when I find several discs flung across the floor, giving the flat the appearance of a bad dose of chicken pox. There is a collection of beer cans abandoned on every available surface. Most of the cans have stubbed-out fag ends precariously balanced on top, which I hate because our flat is supposed to be a non-smoking space. The scatter cushions have been well and truly scattered in messy heaps on the floor (men just don't get it – cushions are not to be used, they're for decoration) and I'm annoyed to notice something has been spilt on one of them (coffee, I think). The room smells of stale, male sweat; this might be a hangover from the numerous bodies that have been rotting here today, but more likely the hideous stench is coming from the pile of skankie trainers that are heaped next to the TV. Why Adam insists on taking his shoes off in the sitting-room, and then leaving them there for eternity, is beyond me.

I draw back the curtains, fling open the window and start to gather up the empty cans and cups. I work efficiently, as irritation often makes me noticeably more competent. Ben has commented that I pull together the most beautiful bouquets just after I've had to deal with a particularly tetchy customer. 'Darling, temper works so well for you. You are a true artist and these lilies are your brushes; this vase your canvas.' (Ben honestly believes he's a secret love great-grandchild of Oscar Wilde.) I throw the trainers to the back of Adam's wardrobe, I put the soiled cushion cover in the wash basket and while I'm there I sort out a quick load of darks and pop a wash on. I wipe surfaces, dust and drag out the vacuum cleaner. It is only once the room is shiny and clean that I allow myself a glass of wine. I think a large one is required.

I carry the goldfish-bowl-size glass of Chardonnay back into the sitting-room, plonk myself on the settee and start to flick through the TV channels. Annoyingly (and predictably, considering my tense mood) nothing grabs my attention. Maybe some music will help. I flick through my CDs. As I've confessed, my tastes are mainstream and my CD collection is probably identical to tens of thousands of other women, my age, up and down the country. In my teens I was an Oasis girl, who wasn't? I have a bit of Röyksopp and Groove Armada that I listened to in my early twenties, especially when I was in the mood for luuurve. There was a big loungy vibe going on at the time, or at least I think there was – there was in my flat. More recently I've bought CDs by the Arctic Monkeys, White Stripes, Chemical Brothers and Scouting for Girls. I buy these CDs on average six months after they've been big in the charts. Hidden in a box near our CD racks I also have Diana Ross and Dido, who I listened to approximately once a month throughout the first half of my twenties (whenever I broke up with my latest squeeze). I hate it that being with Adam has somehow made me apologetic about my collection. It's brought me hours of entertainment, consolation and fun. Surely that's what music is about. Half the stuff Adam listens to sounds trashy, loud and overly aggressive or just plain old depressing, if you ask me. But then, he doesn't ask me. Not any more.

I opt to listen to one of Scottie Taylor's CDs. Scottie Taylor is, in my opinion, the greatest entertainer Britain has produced ever, and the biggest pop phenomenon we've had since the Beatles. I'd never dare make huge sweeping statements about anything to do with the pop industry in front of Adam but I'm on fairly solid ground with this one. For one, Adam is not here (which is why I've been driven to drink and the imaginary arms of Scottie Taylor), and for two, this opinion is pretty much accepted as fact. You could ask any woman in Britain, aged between fifteen and fifty, and she'd agree.

Scottie is the man every woman wants to fix and fuck.

He shot to fame fifteen years ago when he was just seventeen years old. Women my age have grown up with him; he's an institution. He was recruited by a pop mogul to join a girl band, X-treme, an obvious publicity stunt when X-treme were battling for chart supremacy against the Spice Girls. Despite the gimmick of introducing Scottie to the band, X-treme died a death and no one can even name any of the other band members now. I think one of them (the redhead) is a presenter on a Sky shopping channel, I spotted her when I was mindlessly flicking once; she's put on a lot of weight. The other three are occasionally papped coming out of the Priory or Primark. But none of them have even dared threaten a comeback tour. It's generally accepted there wasn't a platform to come back from. It was different for Scottie. As X-treme became more ex-dream, Scottie became bigger and bigger. After just two pop hits with the band he was approached by a new manager and went solo. As Scottie climbed to number one, you could hear the nails being hammered into X-treme's coffin.

He's an incredibly talented songwriter and vocalist but besides that he's needy, sexy, beautiful and has the most filthy grin in history. Despite sleeping with pretty much every gorgeous woman in the pop world, plus a fair number of models and film stars, he is resolutely single and as such the perfect fantasy man. Just what I need right now to ease the tedium of being ignored by Adam.

I put on his latest CD and turn the volume up high.

The thing is, it can go either way with music. Sometimes it's life-affirming and uplifting; other times it can plunge you into the deepest, darkest doldrums. By the time I've downed two-thirds of the bottle of Chardonnay I'm beginning to feel horny and hurt; a lethal combination. Scottie is crooning some love ballad, or more accurately some hate ballad. Something about knowing when love has made a dash for the door and love not living here any more. I start to swirl the lyric around my mind with the same seriousness I would if I was grappling with the monumental questions like: Why are we here? Why don't you ever see a baby pigeon? Why are yawns contagious?

The hardest thing to bear about my live-in relationship with Adam is not the mess he makes, or the unsociable hours he works, or his lack of focus on his career. The hardest thing is I love him and I have to wonder, does he still love me? That's why I'm often grumpy and bored. I don't feel special. I think there's a serious danger that our love has made a dash for the door. I sometimes think Adam and I are more used to each other than mad about each other. How depressing. The orange glow of an August sunset fills the room with a pale amber hue and yet I feel distinct shivers scuttle up and down my spine.

2. Fern

I can't help thinking that if Adam loved me as much as I love him, or as much as he used to, or as much as I want him to, or whatever, then things would be different. Things would feel more exquisitely special, distinctly not ordinary. Plus he'd follow basic instructions. I mean he'd stay in on the one night of the week that I ask him to, wouldn't he? He'd occasionally squirt a bit of Fairy liquid over the dishes in the sink or put his smelly trainers in the wardrobe, wouldn't he? He'd ask me to marry him.

Wouldn't he?

There, I've said it. It's out there. I am that pathetic, that old-fashioned, that un-liberated. I want the man I love, who I've been with for four years, to ask me to marry him. Tell me, ladies and gentlemen, am I so unreasonable?

Part of me is ashamed that after everything the bra-burning brigade did on behalf of my sex, I still can't shift the secret belief that if Adam proposed my life would be somehow more luminous, glorious and triumphant than it currently is. I know, I know, it's an illogical thought. Since his inadequacies are stacking up like the interest on a credit card in January, it does not make sense that I want to shackle myself to him on a permanent basis. The fact that I am irritated he no longer looks me in the eye when he's talking to me (what am I on about? He rarely talks to me!). The fact that the very sight of his favourite old baggy sweatshirt now brings me out in a rash (and yet I'd previously considered it to be cuddly and snuggly – right up there with my baby blanket in terms of offering comfort). The fact that the way he chews his food, cuts his nails in bed and leaves the seat up in the loo makes me want to hold his head under water and wait for the bubbles to stop surfacing ought to add up to something other than my desire for a huge, floaty meringue number. But it doesn't.

No matter how annoying Adam can be I find I am irrationally besieged by a belief (which grips me with the same severity as religious doctrine grabs some folk) that marrying him will somehow change things for the better between us.

I know, I know. Once again the facts would point in another direction. I've never met a woman who can, hand on heart, say this is the case. The vast majority of women insinuate (or openly state depending on their level of inebriation) that marriage only leads to a deepening of cracks in a relationship. Where there was a hairline fracture, throw in a dozen years of matrimony and you find an enormous chasm, a veritable gulf. Even the very happily married tend to look back fondly at the days gone by, the days of dating, when the most monumental decision a couple ever have to make is which movie to see – as opposed to endlessly debating domestic dross. Can we afford a new mattress? Is it worth insuring the house contents? Is it stupidly irresponsible to go with the quote from the *first* plumber who turned up to look at the leaky radiator – after all, it's taken six weeks to get a plumber to show, can we really wait for two more?

And yet I want a proposal.

I think I need to make it clear at this point that I am not one of those women who always wanted to get married. As a child I owned Airhostess Barbie, not Bridal Barbie. I had no ambitions to endlessly re-enact a marriage between said doll and her eunuch boyfriend, Ken. Nor did I dance around the kitchen with a tea towel tied to my head and a sheet around my waist singing 'Some Day My Prince Will Come' (although my older sister Fiona did this until she was about fifteen). In fact I spent most of my late teens and early twenties avoiding any sort of proper relationship. I thought a guy was being unreasonably controlling and presumptuous if he insisted on knowing my surname before making a dishonest woman of me. I was a good-time girl rather than a good girl. I never bought into the nonsense that sex was in any way tied up with responsibility, disgrace, doubt, guilt or even love. As far as I was concerned sex was all about hedonistic pleasure and fun – lots and lots of fun. I suppose sexist propaganda would have it that I ought to hang my head in shame, wear sackcloth and frequently beat myself rather than own up to the fact that in my past I've rarely dignified any relationship with longevity. But I won't. I can't be that much of a hypocrite.

Then there was Adam.

I met Adam in the same way I usually met guys back then (he was the mate of a bloke I was shagging at the time). It wasn't love at first sight or anything really corny like that – it was laugh at first sight. Not that I was laughing at him, I wasn't; I laughed right along with him, everyone did. He was a riot. He's one of those walking bag of gags lads. He's full of witty one-liners, bizarre facts and decent jokes. No one delivers a punch line like Adam. We flirted from the word go but Adam kept me at arm's length until my fling with his mate drew its last breath. Then he asked me to go to Glastonbury music fest with him. And that was it – we were an item.

I never so much as looked at another man from that moment on. Seriously, he held me captive. I realized that I hadn't simply been a slut (as I believed and my mum feared), I just hadn't met the right guy. Simple as that. As nice and old-fashioned as that.

I've loved being faithful to Adam. It hasn't been a struggle. Having sown my wild oats it was a joy to sink into a relationship where it really didn't matter if I occasionally wore cotton M&S knickers rather than lacy thongs – he'd still want to rip them off me.

Adam and I laughed our way through the first couple of years and we laughed our way into this flat-share and for quite some months after that. But we haven't been doing a great deal of laughing of late. In fact there hasn't been so much as a chuckle, a guffaw or a weak giggle. Neither of us is the rowing sort, so silence and tension have become our staple.

I call Adam to find out what time he expects to be back so I can gauge whether it's worth waiting up for him. Even before I press the dial button part of me knows this is likely to be a pointless exercise. Invariably, even if Adam is able to give an expected time of arrival, he's about as reliable as a politician a week before elections; besides that, he often doesn't answer his phone anyway. He's either up a ladder rigging lights or down a cellar listening to a band and so he can't reach his phone or the signal can't reach him. It's an accurate metaphor for our relationship. I'm therefore pleasantly surprised when he picks up.

'Hi, I was just wondering where you are and what you are up to,' I say, trying to sound as friendly and non-naggy as I'm able.

'Hey, Fern-girl. I'm coming right back to you.'

'Are you?' A rush of excitement floods into my stomach, pushing aside the irritation I've felt all evening.

'Yup.'

The doorbell rings. 'Hang on, someone is at the door, hold the line,' I say.

I open the door and Adam is stood facing me, holding his phone to his ear and grinning.

'Lost my key,' he says as he snaps closed his mobile and then briefly kisses me on the forehead.

'Lost or forgotten?' I demand. The rush of excitement at seeing him is instantly drowned by a fresh flash of irritation. Living with him is a bit like sitting in a ducking chair. *Oh, I can breathe; everything is going to be fine. No, I'm under water once more. I'm going to drown.* If he's lost his key again then we'll have to pay for the locks to be changed for the second time in six months. It's such an unnecessary expense, all that's required is a little thought. But, if he's simply forgotten to take it out with him I'll be just as irritated. I mean, it's not rocket science, is it? You go out, you come in again, to do that you need a key, put key in pocket.

Adam shrugs. 'Think they are in my other jeans.'

'I hope so,' I mutter as I head for our bedroom to

check in his jeans pocket. The jeans are on the floor in a crumpled heap. Luckily, I do find his keys, along with a stick of gum and his Oyster card. I walk back into the kitchen dangling the keys off my finger; half triumphant, half vexed. Nowadays I often rage with conflicting emotions when I'm around Adam. I wish it wasn't so. I wish things were simpler.

I'm taken aback because I find Adam serving up a Chinese takeaway. From the smell of it I think I can guess that he's brought me king prawn foo yung with egg fried rice – my favourite.

'Have you eaten? I figured not, as there's no food in the flat, so I thought we'd go wild, Fern-girl. I've even bought a side of prawn crackers.'

Adam doesn't often demonstrate this level of planning so I don't grumble about the keys; I simply slip them down on to the counter next to his wallet.

Sometimes we eat in front of the TV off a tray, but today Adam has put the plates, knives and forks on the tiny Formica table in the kitchen. An action which indicates that he's aware I've requested a level of formality and seriousness tonight.

There's the usual kerfuffle of sitting down, then getting up again to get a bottle of beer, sitting down for a second time and getting up again to find the soy sauce and sitting down and then getting up again to get a jug of tap water.

When we finally settle, Adam asks, 'So what is it that you wanted to talk about?' There's a hint of nervousness in his voice.

I'm grateful that I'm fortified with the best part of a bottle of Chardonnay. I decide to dive right in.

'You know that I'm thirty next week –'

Adam drops his fork dramatically. 'Oh, Fern-girl, is this about your birthday gig? Don't worry, girlie, that's all cool.' Adam looks relaxed now; in an instant all signs of tension have sloshed from his face. 'Jesus, Fern, I thought you wanted *the* big talk. I thought I was going to be kicked into touch, or that you were up the duff or you'd found the perfume bottle I broke.' He starts eating again. Are all these things on a par? How does this man's mind work? Before I get to ask him he adds, 'The birthday thing is in hand.'

I'm torn. I'm delighted to hear that Adam has given my birthday celebrations any thought at all and I'm dying to ask him details but, on the other hand, I need to keep on track and I'd never planned to talk about the festivities – more the significance of the date.

'Yeah, girl, Jess and Lisa are all over this birthday gig. I'm not sure exactly what's going down but they tell me it's going to be one hell of a night. One to remember.'

My blood pressure zooms sky-high again. So, Adam hasn't put any thought into my birthday, my brilliant friends have bailed him out. God, the man is hopeless. I can't deal with that right now, I need to stick to the point.

'I don't want to talk about the celebrations. I want to ask you what being thirty *means*. You know, what it means to *you*.'

Adam looks a bit startled. 'Buggered if I can remember, girl. I'm thirty-two already. Too many drugs and too much drink have been imbibed for me to have clear memories of my thirtieth.'

'Stop being an arse, Adam. We both know you don't do drugs. I'm not one of your rock and roll buddies – you don't have to pretend to be zanier than you are when you are with me. And will you please stop calling me girl, girlie or Fern-girl! Fern will do nicely; it is my name, after all!'

Adam always talks like this. He likes to pretend he's much more hard-core than is actually the case.

'But Fern-girl is what I call you. It's like our thing,' says Adam; he looks injured.

'I'm not a *girl*. That's my point.'

'Oh fuck, this is about you getting old, isn't it?'

'I am *not* old,' I insist indignantly and then a nano-second later I add, 'Yes. It is about that. In a way.'

'Fern-gir – Fern, don't worry, you don't look your age.'

Even though I'm cross with Adam I can hear that he's being sincere and trying to comfort me. He's wide of the goal though. He reaches for my hand but I sulkily pull away. My point is he doesn't act his age, *that's* what's annoying me.

'You are beautiful, Fern. Really hot. All my mates want a piece of you. Mick was just saying what a great pair of tits you've got and he didn't qualify it with "for her age" the way he does when he's talking about Sharon Stone.'

I give myself whiplash snapping my face up to meet Adam's so I can glare at him. He blushes, realizing that at this moment in time I'm not going to think it's a compliment that all of Adam's boozy, lazy mates want to shag me and have obviously discussed the matter at length. Plus, Sharon Stone has twenty years on me. A lifetime ago I might have thought that his comments were funny.

Not now. A lack of judgement and an effort to clarify makes Adam stumble on, despite my glares.

'What I mean, Fern, is that you could pass for twenty-six or even twenty-five in a dark room. You haven't got flabby bits like other women your age. I think it's all that hauling around buckets of flowers. And your height works for you because tall, athletic-looking women never look hunched and old and stuff. Plus you should be happy you're not a kid any more. Young girls have gross skins, really spotty. You've got pearly skin; what's the word? Sort of opaque, that's it!'

Adam stops yakking and grins at me as though he's just wooed me with an arrangement of beautiful and thoughtful words, the like of which haven't been heard since Shakespeare put down his quill. He must be confused, then, when I glower back at him with all the resentment of Lady Macbeth.

'I was not asking you for a critique on how well I'm ageing,' I say.

'Weren't you?'

'No. That's not what this is about.'

'Isn't it?' Adam pauses; his fork is stranded between his plate and his lips. A grain of rice falls on to his lap. He doesn't brush it away. 'But you said you wanted to talk about turning thirty.'

'Yes, I do.'

'But you don't want to talk about your party?'

'No.'

'Nor about how hot you are?'

'No!'

'Well, what then?'

'About *us*.'

'Us? What have we got to do with you turning thirty?' Adam can no longer resist his pork chow mein with rainbow fried rice; he shovels the forkful of food into his mouth.

'Why aren't we married?'

I hadn't meant to ask this so bluntly, and I immediately regret doing so when Adam's rice makes its second appearance as he spits and splutters all over me. I pick grains from my hair as he downs his bottle of beer. Both of us are wondering what he's going to say next.

'Married? You want to get married,' he says finally. Sadly, it isn't a question.

'Yes. Well, maybe. Eventually.' I realize that it's far too late for me to be coy but I back-pedal a little all the same, since his initial response is not what any girl would describe as encouraging. 'I want us to talk about it, at least. I want to know whether it's what you want or something you might ever want.'

'Right,' says Adam.

We both fall silent for what feels to be about a week until I clarify, 'I mean I want to talk about it *now*.'

'Oh, oh, OK, right,' he says again. There's more silence. After seemingly another week or so Adam asks, 'And you want to get married because you are thirty?'

The silence has wounded me. The alcohol which initially fired me with enough confidence to broach the subject is now hurtling me towards sulky self-pity. I find I can't explain my thoughts properly. For weeks I've been endlessly pondering why exactly I feel a compulsion to marry Adam. I've considered the fact that we are no longer in the throes of initial lust and our sex life has already become a little predictable. I've admitted to myself that he's a messy bastard and has no real prospects and yet, somewhat irrationally, I keep coming back to it. I want him. I find my weeks of careful thought on the subject distilled into one sullen sentence.

'Everyone else is getting married.'

'Oh, right, so everybody else is doing it. That's a great reason to make the biggest commitment of our lives,' says Adam with obvious sarcasm. He shakes his head and asks, 'Like who?'

'Like Pete and Tanya, like Eliza and Greg, like Will and Zoë.' I reel off the list of names of our friends that have got engaged in the last *month*.

'Would you jump off a bridge just because Tanya, Eliza or Zoë did?' he demands, sounding just like a grade three teacher talking to a child. I ignore him.

'Like, just about every woman who walks into my shop. I could do the flowers for our wedding,' I wail.

I'm a little bit shamefaced to admit it but I have spent quite a lot of time day-dreaming about our wedding. I have not planned every last detail – not quite – but I've certainly drawn the broad brush-strokes. I've picked out a dress, a menu, and I know we'll be having fat pink peonies as the centrepiece flower to all arrangements.

'Jesus, Fern, we can't get married just so you can showcase your flower-arranging skills.'

'You're being bloody stupid, I didn't say that. I'm just saying that we could save some money if I did the flowers. Weddings are expensive.'

'This isn't about the money,' yells Adam. He throws

down his fork and pushes his plate away, even though his chow mein is only half eaten.

My heart dives to the pit of my belly. I'd rather hoped it *was* about the money. I was hoping that Adam had secretly given the idea of our nuptials as much thought as I had but just hadn't got round to popping the question because he was worried that we'd never have enough cash to do the whole wedding thing properly. Apparently not. The problem with it not being about the money is that it means his non-popping of *the question* must be motivated by something much more sinister and devastating.

Adam doesn't want to marry me.

Adam doesn't love me?

Having surmised this much I know I should now just clamp my mouth closed and retreat with the tiny shreds of dignity left available to me, but while my brain is calculating that this is definitely the best course of action, my tongue – the current impetuous ruling power – runs on unchecked.

'My mum always said no man ever buys the cow if he can drink the milk for free,' I wail.

'Oh, lovely,' says Adam with mocking tones. 'A gorgeous image, I can't wait to curl up with that one tonight.'

'Well, she was right, wasn't she?' Of course I want him to say that no, my mother was wrong, and I want him to take me in his arms, stroke my back and tell me everything is going to be OK. He doesn't, so I trample on. 'I want commitment, I want a wedding, I want babies. I want something to look forward to. Something to *happen*.' With every demand I make I can almost hear our relationship being

25

stamped to death underfoot. It's a big fat squelchy sound. 'I want a proper home. I want you to grow up. But you don't want any of that, do you, Adam? You want to piss about pretending to be some vital cog in the world of rock and roll, when it's clear that you are little more than a glorified runner.'

With that I finally shut my mouth but it's too late. Adam looks shocked and fatally wounded. He's staring at me as though he hardly recognizes me. Right now, I hardly care.

'Is that really what you think?'

'Yes. We're treading water and I don't have time for this any more, Adam. I'm thirty next week. I have a biological clock to reckon with. I'm telling you it's up to the next level or get out.' I hadn't meant to say as much.

'You can't threaten me. You can't put an ultimatum on a relationship,' he yells back at me.

'I can do as I bloody well like, and I'm telling you, Adam, if there's no big shiny rock presented to me on my birthday then it's the last birthday we'll be celebrating together. Marry me or move out.'

The last words spurt into our lives with the devastation of a tsunami. I pant with fury and frustration. I regret the words but believe in them at the same time. It's complicated. Besides, it hardly matters what I did or did not mean to say. The fact is I've just issued my boyfriend with an ultimatum. An ultimatum with a very short deadline and a dire 'failure to comply' clause.

I hastily pick up the plates and manically start to tidy up the kitchen. I toss rice and congealed leftovers into the bin. I wash up and I wipe the table. Anything rather than meet Adam's eye. It takes me twenty minutes to have the tiny kitchen gleaming; I even drag a soapy cloth across the floor. Throughout my frenzied activity Adam says nothing and he doesn't move.

He is truly petrified.

3. Scott

Some people think it might just happen. Fame and that. That you'll just stumble on it. Or that someone will hand it over, that's the Simon Cowell effect, that is. But I always knew finding fame took more than that. It needed plans, schemes and determination. It needed energy. When I'm pissed I don't have much energy and I forget plans. So I had to stop getting pissed. Because to lose it all now, well, it would be a damn shame. It would.

The other thing people don't realize is that it's a violent toil making art. It's far too easy to lose your nerve. People who aren't good enough rarely realize it. Others who are good enough don't believe it. You have to believe in everything. In luck, in your fans, but mostly in yourself.

When I was fifteen I got a Saturday job in a butcher shop. I needed extra money for clothes and records and stuff that makes life bearable. Nothing could be as ugly as chopping meat. For twelve months all I smelt was blood. Even when I was nowhere near the fuckin' shop I smelt of blood. The bloke I worked for was an arse. I had to wear green nylon trousers and a green checked dickie bow. There was no amity or fun. Nan thought being a butcher was a good trade: 'You never see a skinny butcher.' (Yeah, but who wants to be fat?) She thought I should suck up to the arse that was my boss so he'd take me on full-time after my GCSEs. Mum didn't disagree, she didn't have the energy. It was like we were living in a different century to everyone else by growing up in the north in the late 70s and early 80s. It was made clear to me that I was starting at the bottom and that was where everyone expected me to stay. No one believed I'd be anything. A lack of belief can break your heart; it breaks your soul. If you let it.

But I do believe in myself, except when I don't. I do when I'm up there on stage and women are flinging their bras and morals at me. Then I know I'm a god. Trick is, not to think too carefully about exactly what sort of god I might be because then you stop believing in yourself and it's possible you might drown in your own vomit (the default end for a rock star).

When I think back about how I got here, I am not surprised. People say, 'A lad from Hull, here with all of this! Who'd have thought?' They say that all the time and they are surprised. But I tell you who'd have thought. *I'd* have thought. The wall-to-wall open legs, the millions in the bank, the swimming-pool that I could fill with champagne if I wanted to, this is my proper place in life. The two-up-two-down terrace in Hull was the mistake; that was the angels' clerical error. I should never have been dropped off there among all that disappointment. In our house there were just two states of existence, both underpinned by a solid sense of disappointment (my mother's – never too happy to be married, heartbroken after my father pissed off). The two states of existence were basically TV On, TV Off.

TV On was the dominant state; it ran from about 7 a.m. all the way through to 1 a.m. the next day (and the next and the next). The thin curtains would be pulled across the window, shunning the bright daylight in the summer and offering no protection against the dreary black elements in the autumn and winter. The TV droned or blared and my family sprawled in front of it. My nan, small, neat and industrious, usually knitting booties for young girls on our estate that had come undone. The girls were never grateful for the old-fashioned booties, preferring Mothercare's finest, purchased with government clothing vouchers. My brother and me sprawled in front of the TV; legs getting longer, tempers getting shorter with every passing year. My mum rarely put her feet up but when she did, she liked the TV on for a bit of company. Because we all lived too close to each other and yet miles away.

The house wasn't aired enough. We didn't open windows. It always smelt. It smelt of the dog, the chip pan, of farts and sweat. Different types of sweat: my mother's honestly earned and nervous, me and my brothers' fetid and hormonal, my nan's perfumed with lavender. But the smell I hate remembering most of all, out of all those foul stenches, is the smell of alpine air fresheners. That smell epitomizes my mum's desperate, pointless grasp at middle-class respectability and it depresses me. Really depresses me.

The TV was only ever off for a few short hours, after me and my brother had finally slunk off to our rooms, ostensibly to catch a few zeds. The silence started to hum. I didn't sleep at night. I dreamt. Dreaming is what most empty and confused teenagers do. The difference being, dreaming is *all* that most of them do. Changing dreams into ambition, that's what sorts the men from the boys. It was in those short, quiet hours when the TV was not blaring that I made my plans to be great. I wrote songs and practised on my guitar and swore to myself that I'd do anything, anything at all, to get to where I knew I should be. I'd work hard, I'd audition, I'd move to London, I'd ignore the word no, I'd keep trying, I'd win people over, I'd screw people over if I had to. I'd do it all.

4. Fern

Flowers are romantic. That much is accepted by everybody, whether it's a newly engaged woman wondering about the structure of her bouquet or some sorry-assed adulterer that's been caught with his willy out and wants to try to make amends with his missus. Everyone knows flowers are a good place to start when dealing with matters of the heart.

That's why I'm delighted to be surrounded by them in the shop every day, especially at the moment. Adam and I are barely speaking to one another. I worked all day Saturday. He spent Sunday fixing up a gig somewhere, I forget exactly where, I'm not sure he even told me. Rationally, I know that he'd already confirmed this work before we had our row; irrationally I feel he's avoiding me. To be accurate, we're avoiding each other. Even when we finally fall into bed at the end of our gruelling days we do little more than exchange monosyllabic polite questions and answers, designed to learn precisely nothing about one another's state of mind.

Since Friday night the flat has been full of stress and silences, so I'm happy to rush to work and let the fragrances which perpetually float in the air soothe me. Ben's Bunches and Bouquets is my sanctuary. My haven. Flowers can be calming, reassuring, joyful and sexy. Currently, they provide me with everything Adam isn't.

I never wanted to do anything other than be a florist. I started working at Ben's B&B four years ago, just before I met Adam. I love my job. The shop is just a ten-minute walk from our flat and Ben is just a few years older than me and a fun boss who gives me plenty of creative scope and independence; he's become more of a friend than a boss over the years. Even as a tiny tot I used to love to bury my nose in the bright roses blooming in my gran's garden. I'd inhale the silky, sensuous scent the way some starlets inhale cocaine in the loos at China White; I couldn't get enough. My gran had a keen creative and romantic streak. She lived before web design or adultery became acceptable conduits for these character traits and so, as she had always been especially green-fingered, she found a more genteel outlet – she arranged flowers.

Gran grew lots and lots of flowers in her garden. Mostly I remember roses and sweet peas but I know that she grew delphiniums, lavender, marigolds and nasturtiums too, to name but a few. It was my habit to trail her as she mooched around the garden. Clippers in one hand, wooden trug in the other, she'd set off in search of the most beautiful stems available. She never rushed. She'd amble along the borders, stopping from time to time to stand in front of a bush, carefully considering which bloom to choose. It was painstaking. I almost pitied the flowers that Gran overlooked, the ones that she didn't think were quite perfect and beautiful enough for her arrangement; the ones insects had gnawed through or more devastatingly had been blighted by some plant disease. Then, finally, she would select one. Snap, the stem would be severed in a swift sure cut, the bloom picked up and laid with reverence in her basket. Move on.

I found the process at once strangely thrilling and heartbreaking; which, I've come to realize, is true of everything to do with flowers. A bouquet sent to a birth is definitely to celebrate but also to acknowledge that the poor mum has a bruised vag; a wreath at a funeral is sent to express extreme sorrow but sent with love and respect.

Flowers are big, you see, complex.

As a kid there was nothing I liked to do more than watch my gran arrange the flowers she'd chosen. I spent hours watching her weave her magic, trimming the leaves from the lower half of the stem (or they would rot in the water, leading to a hideous smell), fearlessly snapping off sharp thorns from roses with her hardy, plump thumb (see, a rose can be improved upon, take away the thorns), swapping honesty for baby's breath to create balance and harmony. Her displays were always moving. Some were refined, poised and taut. Others were jolly, vibrant and wild. They all seemed wonderful to me. My advice to everyone is never underestimate the power of a bunch of sweet peas tied up with a cheerful, colourful ribbon.

I am doing my best not to think about all the things I said to Adam on Friday and I'm doing a pretty good ostrich impression by throwing myself into my work. I've briefly told Ben about the row but I've insisted that we don't discuss and dissect the matter. Ben's happy to follow instructions; he doesn't really like thrashing out anything tricky. He's always saying that all he ever wants is for everyone to be happy, preferably all the time. Sadly, it's not a very realistic aim and he doesn't have a magic wand or an especially clear grasp on how that might be achieved (who does?). He's a good businessman though. Precisely because he knows the value of dreams and the comfort of luxury, he is able to make a decent profit on both at Ben's B&B. It's a busy flower shop. Ben has carved out a nice little market in a chi-chi part of Clapham just off Narbonne Avenue. There are lots of yummy mummies who think that spending forty quid on a big bunch of lilies is essential shopping on a par with having milk in the fridge.

Working as a florist isn't a bed of roses (excuse the pun). People think I spend my entire day drifting around in a soft-filter moment; in fact there are some aspects of the job which are genuinely gruelling. Early starts at the market three times a week, loading the van by myself and then driving back to the shop, through the morning rush hour, means that sometimes it feels as though I've done a day's work before we've even opened the shop door. Adam is right, being a florist has made me strong and fit – there's a lot of heavy lifting. Besides the physical aspect, being a florist demands tact and patience and sometimes a bit of mind reading; you wouldn't believe how many customers seem only to know what they don't want but have no clue as to what they do want.

Still, this week I'm grateful for the gruelling and absorbing aspects of the job. I volunteer to take Ben's turn to go to market, I lug endless buckets of water around the shop as though I'm performing some sort of medieval penance, I rearrange the stock every day, I bone up on the life span of exotic flowers, even those we rarely sell, and I leap on customers the moment they cross the threshold. I'd rather do anything than dwell on the impending birthday and the ultimatum I issued. Ben has been joking that he might as well retire somewhere sunny; his secret ambition is to have a year-round tan. I do a pretty good job of avoiding any form of brooding until Wednesday, when not one, but two brides-to-be visit the shop to place orders for wedding flowers. That's God's zany sense of humour.

The first customer is a slight, unassuming woman with a no-nonsense approach to organizing her wedding flowers. She compares the prices of roses and carnations for buttonholes. She dismisses lilies because the orange stamen stains. She listens as I reel off a few options for her bouquet. It takes just twenty minutes for her to make her selection. She plumps for tight white roses for everything. She places her order for her small, simple wedding: a bouquet for bride and maid of honour, half a dozen buttonholes, and a corsage for her mum and the groom's mum. She digs out a pen and a small note-book from the bottom of her handbag. She makes a neat tick in the margin next to the word flowers and notes down the figure I gave her as an estimate. As she leaves the shop I envy her restraint and contentment.

The second bride-to-be arrives with considerably more commotion. The overly tanned and loud woman is accompanied by her mum and two friends. All four women have strong opinions on what will be 'absolutely a must' or 'to die for' and loudly express them over and over again, seemingly unaware that they often contradict each other and themselves. Ben is in the back room doing paperwork, so I alone have to deal with Bridezilla.

I realize that the woman is unlikely to be a virgin and her insistence on a 'totally massive white do, with all the extras' is perhaps a tad hypocritical but what the hell, who isn't? I know it's the way I'm going to go – floor to ceiling flowers. I'm excited for her from the moment she walks into the shop, even though I have served hundreds of brides like her in the past and I know that designing, sourcing and delivering the flowers for her wedding will cause no end of stress for me.

The bride hurtles through dozens of ideas. She shows me pictures that she has cut from glossy bridal magazines. There is a dramatic picture of red gerbera with clusters of cropped beargrass and a beautiful organza bow, and another one showing traditional pale lilies and roses draped with garlands of pearls, and a third of a bouquet of exquisite orchids which are beautifully combined with minimal foliage to create a contemporary design. She wants it all.

After several hours of bouncing from one thought to another (during which time her mum ran out for sandwiches, I served eight other customers and Ben completed the paperwork for this quarter's VAT return), we finally settle on stunning pink tulips and exotic nerines combined to perfect effect in a stylish and contemporary bouquet. The bride orders two bouquets; one to keep (apparently you can have your bouquet mounted in a glass dome – Lord help us) and another to throw to the hungry pack of unmarried female guests, as is tradition. She orders flowers to drape around the church door, decorate windows, for the top and bottom of the aisle and for the pew ends. She orders flower pomanders, hung on pearls, for her four adult bridesmaids, and flower hoops for the four little ones. She orders flowers for the tables, chair-backs and the reception entrance, the top of the cake and her car. The list goes on. It's extravagant, unnecessary, profligate (bordering on showy), but I can't help loving the bride for her indulgence. Sod it, why not? It's her big day. OK, so strictly speaking every guest does not require a buttonhole or corsage, but wearing a flower is a damn fine way to celebrate two people publicly declaring their love.

When she finally leaves the shop, I'm exhausted and Ben has a six-thousand-pound order. In an effort to stop myself screaming with delight, frustration and jealousy, I have to put my hands over my mouth. I hear the scream echo inside my gut for over an hour.

5. Fern

'Darling, you are a wonder,' gushes Ben. 'I am so pleased with the gigantic order that Bridezilla placed that I'm giving you the rest of the afternoon off. I'm a marvellous boss, I know. Don't thank me,' he waves his arms theatrically. 'I'm embarrassed by my own generosity,' he adds with a wink.

I love Ben, he's such a laugh to be around and I know his offer is kind but I'm reluctant to accept it. I'm going out with Jess and Lisa tonight and if I'm not working I am unsure how to kill the time in between. Time alone and without tasks means I might have to think about the sorry state of affairs my life has become. Not a favourite option right now.

I definitely don't want to go back to the flat; the air there is stale with disenchantment and anxiety, and I'm too broke to waste time in shops. No matter how much I kid myself to the contrary, I know that window-shopping will lead to an impulse purchase today. No woman can resist the lure of a cheer-up top/pair of shoes/new bag ('it's a classic/basic/essential, will come in handy/be perfect for that special occasion/is in the sale and therefore a bargain'). The reality is, of course, it's an impulse purchase, bought in order to bring cheer, that just makes things worse. Then you're down *and* broke, with a constant reminder of your own financial and emotional frailty.

At the risk of Ben thinking I'm insane, I tell him I'd rather stay at the shop until it's time to meet my friends. I get through the rest of the afternoon by comforting myself with the fact that I'll soon be getting out of my head with Jess and Lisa. The bonus being that while doing so, they might offer me some sound advice – or at the very least a shoulder to cry on.

I love Jess and Lisa. I really do. I met them at tech college; our eyes met across a crowded registration hall. That was fourteen years ago. We hit it off immediately and have been proper mates to one another ever since. In Jess I saw a soulmate, a partner in crime. In Lisa I spotted a calming influence, someone who might help me fill out the forms correctly and get me into the right classroom at the right time. I needed them both. Need doesn't always turn to affection; often it sours. But we worked well together as a unit, a team. We watched each other's backs and still do.

Jess is funny, witty and careless (bordering on the reckless). She is the perfect person to call if you've ever done anything stupid that you regret (she can usually trump the stupidity or at least knows someone else who can). She is fabulously non-judgemental, which has been important to me throughout my twenties.

Jess chose to attend tech college rather than stay on at school because she was dating a boy who was also studying there at the time. The boy who gets the title 'Her First Love', but no more mention in this story because she fell out with him the summer before we started our courses, which was predictable but inconvenient. Jess changed vocation three times before the Christmas holiday that first year. She knew that she didn't want to be a beautician, a nanny or a dental hygienist but she didn't know what she did want to do. I was studying for my qualifications in floristry and working at the local florist at the same time. Jess envied my reasonably regular jaunts to Top Shop and the lure of the pay packet eventually became too much for her to resist. Actually, Jess isn't the resisting sort. Jess applied for a job at the bookshop chain in the high street and has worked there ever since. She really enjoys it. She's a romantic but her own love life is often a disaster. By working in a bookshop she gets to read about other disastrous relationships – like that of Cathy and Heathcliff – and she does this at a ten per cent discount. It's some sort of comfort.

Lisa is also funny and witty but she's altogether more aware of consequences than either Jess or me. She's always been great to have around to flash up a big amber light, if any of our single-girl antics threatened to get out of hand. Obviously, since I've been with Adam, Lisa hasn't had to play the role of babysitter with me quite so much, but Jess still manages to get into her share of scrapes. Lisa's common sense is as invaluable as her frequent cry of 'I told you so' is irritating. Lisa loves a plan. Even back in college she kept meticulous spreadsheets on everything – from her savings account (including target figures, short-term and for twenty years on) to number of sexual partners (she ranked performance and cross-checked against income – more of this to follow).

I've always hovered somewhere between total awe and absolute horror at Lisa's level of control in every single aspect of her life. Lisa studied secretarial skills and book-keeping. She is really sharp and she could probably have done A levels and gone on to university if she'd wanted to, but she had a game plan. She wanted a rich husband. And she wanted him as quickly as possible.

Lisa is not a natural beauty; she is a girl who makes the best of herself. Even fourteen years ago when she didn't have a spare penny to toss she always looked a million dollars. She works out, she's always immaculately dressed and I've never, *ever* seen her without makeup. Reportedly she didn't relax this rule even when she was fully dilated and the midwife was asking her to push.

Lisa's plan was to get a job in the City, as a PA. In the financial district there are about thirty men to every woman and every last one of them earns a salary the length of a telephone number. Lisa wanted one of them. There were times I worried she wanted *any* one of them – which isn't a nice thing to think about a pal – but there were occasions when I really had to question her quality control. She didn't seem too fussed if the guy was dark, blond, tall, short, fat, thin, funny or a git. She just wanted a large stone from Tiffany and ultimately a large house in Esher. There were loads of details in between about where they'd honeymoon and which restaurants they'd go to and stuff, but I used to tune out when Lisa itemized every single strategic particular in operation 'Bag a Rich Guy'. It was bad enough that Jess and I, acting as wingmen, had to trail all the way out to Docklands to visit noisy bar after noisy bar, night after night (just to be hit upon or patronized by turn).

Her plan came together. By the time Lisa was twenty-three she was the proud owner of an Amanda Wakeley wedding gown, Jimmy Choo wedding slippers, and a full set of Arthur Price cutlery (including grapefruit forks).

Charlie is a nice enough guy. Considering the lack of direction on the brief, I think Lisa did well. He's clearly intelligent (although a bit dry), he's handsome enough (the sort of looks my mum would approve of but not the sort of look that turns heads or flips stomachs). The important thing is Charlie clearly adores Lisa. He is always showering her with expensive gifts, especially when he's had to work late.

I ache to see both Jess and Lisa this evening. Although I share a flat with Jess, my early starts and her late dates have meant that we haven't had a chance to catch up since Friday. I need to tell them about my row with Adam. Jess will assure me that while issuing an ultimatum to Adam was a dumb idea, she knows someone who . . . oh, I don't know . . . who has done something even more silly to back their lover into a corner, causing him to growl and spit and claw. Right now, I can't think of exactly what might be sillier but that's the point of Jess – she will be able to do so. And Lisa will tell me to take a deep breath. She'll understand why I need a game plan. Why I ache to move this relationship to the next level and she will confirm that I am within my moral rights and in my right mind. She'll find me a solution. A dignified way of moving this on. That's what friends are for.

6. Fern

Lisa staggers back from the bar carefully balancing a bottle of Chablis in an ice bucket and three glasses on a tray. She weaves her way precariously through the boisterous crowd; her face is tight with concentration. I hope she's thinking about my dilemma with Adam but it's more likely that she's thinking about not upsetting the glasses. Not that we need more glasses – we already have them – as this is our third bottle of the night. Bugger. How many units is that? Too many.

'I've got to stop drinking,' I mumble.

'Why?' asks Jess, who rarely stops drinking until she falls over.

'Because it's not helping me think straight,' I say.

Plus I can't afford to do this. If I'd known we were going to drink this much I'd have suggested that Lisa come over to our place. You can buy this exact same brand of wine for less than half the price in the supermarket. But I always feel like a killjoy if I suggest a night in. Lisa looks forward to her up-town bids-for-freedom, as she jokingly calls our decreasingly frequent get-togethers. But then, Lisa has no concept of watching the pennies, although she does think the pounds look after themselves as her cash appears like magic. Charlie gives her an enormous allowance, plus he unquestioningly pays off her credit card at the end of every month. Lisa gave up her job as soon as she and Charlie got engaged and is entirely dependent on him financially. This can cause contention in some families but Lisa is delighted with the arrangement – she likes to see a plan coming together.

I remember Lisa pointing out that her job as a PA paid less than they'd have to shell out for a wedding planner, so there was no point in her working in the run-up to the wedding since she could save some cash by organizing the wedding herself. Lisa's reasoning seemed logical, once I accepted that real people actually have wedding planners. I thought they were something *Hello!* magazine had invented to torment brides-to-be who were suffering at the hands of their interfering mothers. Although the odd thing was that Lisa employed a wedding planner anyway, so that she had someone to discuss lace and stationery with (Jess and I had a very limited interest in the subject at the time). After the wedding Lisa was flat out remodelling the house (apparently managing interior designers demands a lot of time), and now they have the children no one would dream of suggesting that Lisa ought to go back to work, she's busy enough – even with the help of a nanny and a cleaner. And somehow, knowing all of this makes me a little shy about admitting to Lisa that I'm a bit short cash-wise; I don't think she'd understand.

'Plus binge drinking is V fattening,' I add aloud.

'Oh, don't worry about that, you'll lose weight without even trying soon,' says Lisa as she starts to pour the wine.

'Why, because Adam is going to leave me and I'll be too heartbroken to eat?' I wail, with a touch of melodrama that I just can't resist.

Lisa tuts. 'No, because as soon as you are engaged you'll turn into a weight-obsessed freak and go all "nil by mouth". Everyone does.'

'You think he'll ask me to marry him?' I ask excitedly. I want a confirmation from Lisa that my plan is on track.

'Probably,' she says with more honest caution than I want. Why couldn't she have said *certainly*? 'He should do, if he knows what's good for him. You're gorgeous, the best thing that ever happened to him. He'd be mad to let you go. You two are so brilliant together.'

'One of the happiest couples I know,' confirms Jess with a small hiccup.

'But?' I can hear the 'but' hanging in the air.

'Well, men . . .' Lisa trails off.

It's an articulate enough comment. Men don't know what's good for them. Men don't always recognize the best thing that ever happened to them. Men don't always do the right thing. Men make mistakes. We all do.

'It's not in the bag, is it?' I ask drearily.

Sadly, my best friends shake their heads. I know they love me enough to want to lie to me and enough not to do so. We all take another gulp of our wine and gaze around the bar. It's noisy and busy. The bar we are in is not the usual sort of place we meet up. Normally we grab a bite to eat at the local Italian. The waiters know us there; the service is perfect – attentive but not over-bearing. The Italian restaurant is always full of other groups of gossipy women, the music is piped out at a reasonable volume and the conversations are conducted at a reasonable pitch. Tonight we've tried War Bar in

Clapham High Street because Jess is newly single again (it didn't work out with the hot banker, she said he had protruding teeth that got in the way when they were kissing) and she wants to use tonight to scout for talent. Lisa and I are fine with this. We'd both do anything to help Jess in her endless search for the perfect man. Plus Jess is a great multi-tasker; she can talk to us and flirt with the man on the next table without anyone feeling neglected.

Besides, I fancied a change too. A minuscule part of my brain seemed to want to remind the rest of my brain what it's like being 'out there' again. Something was compelling me to take a cursory glance at the scene in case, God forbid, the worst came to the worst with Adam and the ultimatum. The War Bar is the perfect place to conduct a study of this sort. Jess assured me it's a 'cool and happening' bar. It might just be my jaded view of things right now, but while the War Bar may be cool and happening, it isn't a very happy place. At least not for anyone over twenty-five. Most of the punters look a little despairing or bewildered. I watch as people fight to be in one another's physical and mental space. No one wants to go home alone. It all seems feral and desperate. At least the place is well named; everyone does appear a little shell-shocked. Jess is always telling me that the competition is tough, 'out there'. She's always telling me that because I haven't been single for years, I have no idea.

Jess must be reading my mind because she asks, 'What will you do if he doesn't produce a ring on Friday?'

I shrug. 'Leave, I guess.'

It's hard to know if I mean this because my head is

morphing into lots of different shapes and my tongue feels bigger than it did at the start of the day. I must say no to that next glass of wine. I have that thought at the exact moment that I reach for the bottle and fill up my glass.

'Really?' my friends chorus, shrilly.

'Yeah, I have to.'

'No you don't, not because of some crazy ultimatum that you issued after you'd had too much to drink,' says Jess.

'Not because of the ultimatum, no. But because I do believe what I said to Adam. I don't have any more time to waste. I'm *thirty*. I want a husband and a family and a home of my own. I want the next stage. If he can't give it to me then I have to find someone who can. While I stay in this going-nowhere relationship I'm letting any other chances at happiness float by.'

'But you love him,' says Lisa. One of her eyes is wandering around the room. It's not because she's deciding whether there is anyone more interesting she'd rather talk to. It's just the effects of the Chablis; it really is time to get a cab.

'I do but I'm not sure it's enough.'

'Then what is?' asks Jess.

I don't know how to answer the question so I change the subject; none of us seem too comfortable with this one.

'Anyway, during our momentous row, Adam also let slip that you two have arranged something for my birthday. Thanks, girls. Obviously you knew he'd never get his act together.'

Jess and Lisa exchange wary looks. They seem unsure what to say. I know they both like Adam and would defend him if they could but they can't. Sensibly, they don't want to elaborate on the theme of what a jerk he's being either, knowing I'll remember their scathing words if we make up after this. Prudent but a bit annoying. Right now, I could do with some hard abuse of my commitment-phobic boyfriend in the name of female solidarity.

'So what's going down? What should I wear?' I ask. 'You might as well tell me now the cat's out of the bag.'

'Can't tell you what's planned,' says Lisa.

'Won't,' giggles Jess. 'But wear your dark jeans and get a really pretty top.'

7. Fern

I am thirty. It's official. It's here. The big day. The enormous so-this-is-what-you-amount-to day. I wonder how long I can keep my eyes shut and pray that the whole messy business will just vanish. What the hell made me issue an ultimatum to Adam? Sweet, sometimes sexy, seriously funny, if not a bit hapless, Adam. What was I thinking? Everyone knows a bird in the hand is worth two in the bush, etc. etc. He's not always a perfect boyfriend but he is *my* boyfriend. I start to hyperventilate. The problem with ultimatums is you have to follow through with them. Everyone knows that. Otherwise you're a joke. Will he have got me the big, glittering rock, or not?

Bugger.

I can sense that Adam is awake. He's lying on his side and watching me, waiting for me to open my eyes. Over the past four years I've been exposed to Adam physically in every way possible. He knows me. He's seen me blubber, howl and erupt into judders during sex. Two years ago he watched me haul my aching body through the 26.2 miles of modern torture that is known as the London Marathon. He was waiting for me at the end and he flung his arms around me even though I was sweaty, bloody and weepy; he didn't even seem to notice. He's heard me snore, burp, gargle, hiccup and worse – intimacy isn't always what it's cracked up to be. I'd never dare fake an orgasm with him; he'd call me on it. As he does now when I'm faking sleep.

'I know you are awake. Open your eyes. I have something for you.'

Slowly, carefully, I prise my eyes open. I feel sick. With nerves? Excitement? Fear? I'm not sure. This might be *it*. This might be the first moment of my grown-up life. The happily ever after I'm hankering for. I might just be about to receive the allatrope of carbon that makes every girl a princess.

Or I might be about to get the biggest kicking I've ever experienced.

Adam leans close and kisses me on my lips. He smells of morning but in a good way; a little bit salty, with a vague hint of last night's booze. A little jolt of lust flickers up through my body. Down, Shep. Let's see if he's come up with the glistening goods first.

There is a breakfast tray on the bed. He's tried: tea, toast and Coco Pops. There are no croissants, no freshly squeezed orange juice and no miniature jars of jam. I'm not in a bloody film. Some way from it.

I struggle to sit up and stretch out my arm to grapple to find my dressing-gown. It's on the floor next to the bed where I left it just before I nosedived between the sheets in the dark last night. I sleep naked and I don't want crumbs to stick to my breasts. Honestly? I don't want my breasts on show at all. They are not bad breasts. Away ye false modesty. They are really rather nice; pert, a bit on the small side but even. Most people who have been introduced to them have greeted them quite favourably but recently I've started to think of my boobs as superfluous, considering Adam and I rarely have sex any more. They are a bit like a decent bottle of vintage port at an AA meeting: out of place. I pull my pink towelling dressing-gown around my body without upsetting the tray (quite a feat) and then pick up a piece of toast and bite into it although I have no real appetite. I scan the tray for something that gleams and I don't mean a teaspoon. No sign.

'Happy birthday, Fern-girl,' says Adam as he leans in for another kiss.

This one is longer and more lingering than the last. I don't bat him away but I don't get what you'd call actively involved, not even when he does that really special thing of gently tugging at my lower lip. There was a time when I thought there was a cord attached to my lower lip that trailed through my body and fastened tightly around my G-spot. One decent smacker and I was putty. Today I need to see what he's going to pull out of the hat first.

'OK, Fern-girl.' I glare at him. He shifts uncomfortably and corrects himself. 'Fern, gorgeous, I've been thinking about everything you said last week.'

Is this the moment to describe what he looks like? I think so because at this fleeting point in time I'm suddenly very aware of him, all over again, as though we'd just met and I'm drinking in the details. Maybe it's something to do with a rare shaft of sunlight flooding (past the grime) through the window. Probably. Oddly, the heaps of dirty and discarded clothes that litter our bedroom recede. All at once I'm less bothered about the trail of half-empty coffee cups that decorate our place (a unique twist as an interior design feature – other couples have fresh flowers and jars of massage oil, I'm sure). Unexpectedly, all I'm aware of is Adam.

Adam has dark, longish hair. Not ponytail length – heaven forbid! – he's more scruffy surfer. It's great hair. I love losing my fingers in it. He has heavy eyebrows and dark brown eyes, thick, long eyelashes that even Bambi might envy. He used to have standy-out cheekbones and a strong chin – truth be known, he's all a bit fleshier nowadays. But still attractive. Worn in. Familiar but cute.

He's got great shoulders. He's not the sort of guy you'd ever hope to see down the gym (sadly) but his job is physical enough to ensure broad shoulders, upon which I love to rest my head when we are lying in bed, chatting, late at night (not as regular an occurrence as I'd like). He has enough hairs on his chest to make it clear that he's man, rather than boy, but not so many as to create the urge for you to reach for the Shake 'n' Vac. His stomach is rounder than a Calvin Klein model's but not as lardy as Chris Moyles'. Sort of average for a thirty-two-year-old guy. He's wearing black Diesel boxers – he fills them. His legs are long and thin and stick out of the end of our bed. Right now, he seems pretty damn perfect.

I've never loved him more.

'So I've given a lot of thought to all you said and I think you're –'

'What?' I nervously jump in.

'You're right,' he says simply.

'You do?' I want to kiss him, but I hold off for the moment. I want to hear everything he has to say.

'Yeah. I need to move on. Grow up. Offer you more than my share of the monthly rent in terms of commitment. In fact, I want you to know I've been thinking about this for some time. Before you, er, brought your frustrations to my attention.'

'Really?' Kiss me, kiss me. I silently will him to pull me tightly to him. But at the same time I don't want him to stop talking. I'm fizzing with excitement. This is it! This is the moment I've been waiting for!

'I've got something for you,' says Adam. He reaches behind him.

The ring! The ring! What will it be like? A diamond solitaire? Maybe not, that would be pricey. I'd settle for something semi-precious yet stylish and meaningful. My birthstone perhaps.

Adam hands me an envelope.

'What's this?' I battle to keep the fear and disappointment out of my voice. It's too flat to be a ring. But then a thought strikes me – house details? Possibly. Maybe he's done something über-romantic, like got details from an estate agent of a place we might buy together and he's going to take me there this afternoon. He was very insistent that I take the day off and why else would we be starting the day so early? It's only 7 a.m. Thinking about it, a couple of months back he did start to scan the property pages of the local freebie rag but he always made comments about how ludicrously expensive everything was – way out of our league – so I never paid much attention. My fingers seem to be incapable of following even the basic motor-skill instructions that my brain is sending to them. But eventually I rip the envelope open.

'Tickets?'

'To the Scottie Taylor gig.' Adam is grinning at me.

'But, but, I don't understand,' I stutter.

'Had you good, didn't I, Fern-girl? That whole thing I made up last April pretending I couldn't get any tickets for the concert, not even on eBay.'

Yup, I remember. Scottie Taylor is doing this major gig tonight in Wembley Stadium. The like of which has never been seen before. He's performing in front of a massive crowd of ninety thousand. It's the first time he's played a gig in over two years. He's playing for three nights in a row. All the tickets were completely sold out in forty minutes. From the moment the lines opened for sales, I repeatedly pressed redial to the ticket office. I was gutted when I didn't get lucky. I was furious when none of Adam's industry contacts could help us find tickets. I wanted to go to the gig more than anything.

But that was four months ago.

The gig seems insignificant now, in light of my ultimatum, in light of my clearly communicated desire to move things on. How could Adam imagine that tickets to a pop gig are a reasonable response to everything I said last Friday?

'There are three tickets for tonight's gig; one for you and one each for Lisa and Jess. They are in on this. They don't really have anything else planned, like I said they had. It was all me. This is all my idea.'

'All you,' I parrot, unable to trust my tongue with any sort of independence. Now I understand why my friends were exchanging wary glances. They knew this wasn't what I was hoping for.

'And that's not all,' adds Adam.

Glimmer of hope!

He reaches behind him and hands me another envelope; it's identical.

Another crash landing. I feel the shock shudder through my body just as though I have endured a physical impact.

Carefully, slowly, I start to open the envelope. I can't fake enthusiasm; it's all I can do to hide my face; bastard, telltale tears of hurt and disappointment are springing into my eyes. I won't let him see that. I open the second envelope and there are three more tickets, this time to Saturday's gig. I don't understand.

'Tadaa.' Adam pushes a third envelope into my hand.

'What?'

'Open it and see,' he says. He's grinning like the Cheshire cat. Why? What makes him think buying two sets of tickets to the same artist's gig is a good idea? Is he mad? Two sets, these things cost almost fifty quid each.

'Three sets,' I say as I open the third envelope.

'Sunday's gig,' says Adam with hideous zeal. 'Of course you don't need to take Jess and Lisa every night. Maybe Eliza might fancy it, or Ben.'

I stare at Adam in pure bewilderment. 'You've blown four hundred and fifty quid on this?' I demand. I'm so shocked I can't summon the necessary torrent of abuse. I'm not worried; I know it will come, just as soon as I start to breathe again.

'That's the beauty of it. I didn't have to *pay* for any of them,' he replies.

'What, they are knock-off?' The words are strangled by outrage.

'No,' laughs Adam. 'I'm working at the gig. These are freebies. I've got a job with Scottie Taylor. It's silly money. You couldn't guess. Like six times the amount I'd normally get for a similar event. Apparently Scottie has this thing about sharing his wealth. I've known about the job for a while but I kept quiet about it so as to surprise you today.'

Adam pauses, no doubt waiting for me to leap on top of him and tell him how marvellous he is. I want to pummel him to death with the soggy toast.

'Fern, you are looking at Scottie Taylor's assistant stage manager. I have a *team*, Fern. It's a promotion. A big one. We are moving forward, like you wanted.'

I shake my head. 'You didn't pay for these?'

'No. I said so, didn't I? They were free. How cool is that?'

No ring, no ring. Bloody gig tickets but no ring. *Free* bloody gig tickets but no ring.

I hate him.

8. Fern

I don't have much time to demonstrate the hate. There's no opportunity to huffily push him away as he makes stealthy sexual advances because he doesn't make any advances – stealthy or otherwise. *Even* though it's my birthday!

Instead he says we have to get up quickly, or at least he does because he has to be at Wembley by nine. He suggests I should come along with him because he has backstage passes and he says it will be interesting for me to see what he does.

'I know what you do,' I mutter grumpily. 'You climb up and down ladders, twiddle knobs and put bulbs in lamps.'

Adam looks hurt. 'There's more to it than that, Fern. I am part of a vital team. My contribution to this spectacular is valid. It's like being part of an orchestra; even the guy with the triangle thing is crucial to the overall symphony,' he says.

'Get over yourself, Adam. Being in an orchestra is like being in an orchestra. You are a rigger. You put up scaffolding,' I snap. He doesn't bother to correct me and point out that he's an assistant stage manager now. I think he knows it will be cold comfort.

'Come anyway, we always need an extra pair of hands to run to the catering hall for coffee and you are on holiday so you've nothing better to do.'

The truth of his statement is horribly shocking. It's my thirtieth birthday and I have nothing better to do than fetch coffee for a bunch of guys, most of whom aren't even on nodding terms with soap. I wake Jess and give her an update. She's as sympathetic as I could hope for, considering it's this early in the day.

'Can you skive off for the day and keep me company before the gig?' I ask, not bothering to keep the self-pity out of my voice.

'I'd love to, sweetie, but I can't.' She squeezes my arm. 'My area manager knows that Adam got us these freebies and is letting me leave the shop an hour before the end of my shift as it is. He'd smell a rat if I failed to turn up at all today. Plus I'd feel a bit of a cow since he's already agreed to give me the extra hour with pay. You understand, don't you?'

'Suppose,' I mutter, without any grace. My mind is whirling. Seemingly, I veer off on a tangent but in fact it's all related. 'Do you realize I've never been on a club 18–30 holiday? I can't now. That's a missed opportunity.'

'I'd hardly class that as a missed opportunity. Who wants to drink luminous cocktails with horny, desperate strangers until you puke or skinny dip?' asks Jess.

'I wonder how many other opportunities I've missed,' I muse.

'Very few, from what I remember of your misspent youth,' says Jess matter-of-factly. 'Do you want your pressie?'

Jess has bought me some fabulous Mac makeup brushes. They are really glam and grown up. I thank her and resist commenting that right now all I want to do is stick them up Adam's backside.

'I'll call Lisa and we'll see you at the gig. Once you're there, do a bit of a recce and then text me to arrange exactly where to meet,' says Jess, as she kisses her ticket.

I dress with little care and can barely summon the energy to wave a mascara wand or draw a slash of red lippy over my lips. I'd imagined that I would start the day with a long (post-loving) luxurious bubble bath. I thought I might sip champagne in muted candlelight and maybe even persuade Adam to rub a bit of body oil into my back and shoulders. Then, I'd planned to pop to the hairdressers on the corner, to see if they could squeeze me in for a trim and blow dry. My hair has so many split ends, running off in opposite directions, it could be clinically diagnosed as schizophrenic. *But* I hoped I was going to be celebrating my engagement. Now, I haven't got the necessary emotional energy for that level of indulgent pampering. I don't like myself enough.

'You look great,' Adam lies, as we set off towards the tube. 'The whole dishevelled look is very rock chic.'

I glare at him but don't answer. In fact I don't say anything all the way to Wembley. I'm not sure if he notices because he's reading the sports pages of his tabloid newspaper and even if I came up with a new tool to patch up the ozone and scientific data to prove little green men do indeed inhabit Mars, he'd probably just grunt.

Loads of London venues are being tarted up for the 2012 Olympics and you can't spit nowadays without hitting an imposing building (or at least the plan or crane for one), but I've heard it argued that Wembley is still the most impressive stadium on offer. Renowned architects started work on the project when Noah was a lad and I remember hearing on the news that at one point there were more than three and a half thousand construction workers on site. Of course the project was dogged with delays; ambitious projects always are. On arrival I vacuously gaze around the enormous venue, too wrapped up in my own concerns to bother to make a judgement as to whether the state-of-the-art creation was worth the wait. Adam, on the other hand, is brimming with enthusiasm.

'There are seventy-five thousand seats and there will be fifteen thousand standing tonight,' he says. He shakes his head, marvelling at the enormity of the upcoming spectacle that he's part of. The seats, arranged in a bowl, are all protected from the elements by a sliding roof. The stadium's signature feature is a circular section trellis arch which Adam informs me has an internal diameter of seven metres and a 315-metre span. The arch is not upright but (again Adam's geeky info) is erected some twenty-two degrees off true; it rises to a striking 140 metres tall. Everything is super-sized. Adam, oblivious to my moody silence, tells me that the new Wembley is the largest stadium in the world.

'There are two thousand, six hundred and eighteen toilets, more than any other venue on the planet.'

'Fascinating,' I mumble sarcastically. I wonder how much enthusiasm he'd show if I started to relay my own treasured statistics? The average age for a woman to marry is twenty-nine, for instance.

'The stadium has a circumference of a kilometre.'

'Right.' The average length of an engagement in the US is sixteen months; I'm still searching for the equivalent data for the UK.

'There are thirty-five miles of heavy-duty power cables in the stadium. Ninety thousand cubic metres of concrete.' The average number of bridesmaids is three. 'And twenty-three thousand tonnes of steel were used in the construction.' The average cost of a wedding is twenty-one thousand pounds, but you can do it for a couple of hundred quid.

Someone please give me a drink; a stiff and large one. While I can see Adam's point (yeah, yeah, the place is big), I'm finding it impossible to pretend I give a damn.

'Each of the two giant screens in the new stadium is the size of six hundred domestic television sets.'

Marry me. Those were the only words I wanted to hear today. Not this inventory of dull facts. Marry me. Why not? Why couldn't he bring himself to do it? Am I not his one? Am I just the current one? Or the fill-in one until the next one, who really will be the one? The thought hits me with such force I believe I might implode, right here, right now at Wembley Stadium. I sway slightly, like a cobweb in a spring breeze; there's a real danger I'll blow away. Adam reaches for my hand; a habitual gesture but I can't follow our routine. I don't take his hand and gently squeeze, I pull away. My heart is hard with thoughts of other *ones* and the one he might propose to one day.

'You are dumbstruck, aren't you?' he says with a wide, crazy grin. I stare back resentful and shocked that he can't read me better. 'I just knew that tickets for the Scottie gig would be the perfect present,' he beams.

OK, I suppose I can admit that normally going to a Scottie Taylor gig would be something I'd get excited about. It would have been the perfect present if it was any other birthday. I saw Scottie live once before, about eight years ago, and he was bloody amazing; I couldn't sleep for days, I was that high on the buzz he left me with. And yes, any other day than today – the day I'd hoped and hoped and hoped Adam would ask me to be his wife – I might have been thrilled with an 'Access All Areas' pass; as things are, the crappy little bit of plastic seems like an insult. Adam casually flashes his pass and a smug grin at the bulky guys on the door. They nod with respect and check out my legs; I glare back resentfully.

Inside the stadium, it seems to me that everything is set to go. Adam tells me that his recent late nights have all been spent here, setting up for rehearsals. Adam is flying high as a kite. He's giggling like a seven-year-old girl, flinging orders and cheery hellos by turn at the guys and girls who I assume are his team.

I am now familiar with what to expect behind the scenes before the razzamatazz of the show; I've waited in the wings often enough. I scan the endless rows of lights, the towering stacks of speakers, the white cyclorama, the heavy drapes, and the jet black front curtain which are all carefully suspended from complicated zigzag girders hidden in the roof high above. It looks complex bordering on the chaotic. I know that it does demand a lot of patience and skill to get the set-up spot-on and I know that it is crucial for Adam and his team to get every detail pinned down if the trademark Scottie Taylor attention-grabbing spectacle of a concert is to be nailed. I recognize that this stage is bigger than most; there are more dazzling lights and larger stacks of speakers than I've ever seen before. I don't doubt that the set-up has been arduous and that Adam being the assistant stage manager is a big deal.

The thing is – I don't give a toss.

A girl is meant to take an interest, isn't she? A good girlfriend should care about her boyfriend's job. But I don't. Not today. Whatever is going on here isn't as glossy and polished as a diamond on my third finger would be. I should be really pleased Adam's got this great promotion and his career is taking off but I'm not impressed. I wish I was. Adam whips off his leather jacket and flings it my way. He practically leaps up a ladder like some sort of stuntman because he's seen an out-of-place cable. I can't remember when he last gave me the same attention.

I kill time watching guys in black T-shirts scuttling like beetles to and fro. On the stage the instruments are already laid out. They are still, waiting for life to be given to them by Scottie's enormously talented band. The shiny red and silver drums are set up high on a platform, centre stage. There's not just one keyboard but a whole gaggle of them to the left and the right and there are racks of guitars hung all over the place.

On the outer reaches of the stage there's a horrendous confusion of wires and plugs that presumably make sense to someone. The maze of wires ultimately leads to chunky black cabinets and monitors. Smoke generated from machines drifts across the stage and hangs around at knee level, giving substance to the beams of continuously flashing lights that slice across the floor.

I check my watch – it's just after ten. Scottie Taylor won't be on this stage for another ten or eleven hours and yet it's as though he's among us already. His presence can be felt in everyone else's sense of self-importance; not one bod here can believe they are working with such an enormous star. There are so many dreams coming true on one stage, at this one point in time, that it is likely to be some sort of world record. I can see tension, fear and excitement in everyone's faces. There's probably enough energy to power an inner city if it could be harnessed correctly. This is a big gig. Enormous. It means a king's ransom to everybody.

With the possible exception of me.

My dreams are not coming true on this stage, or any other, come to that.

Adam is still up a ladder and doesn't seem to remember I'm here at all. I can see from the concentration on his face that he has a lot on his mind. I'd put money on it that he's not thinking about a princess-cut diamond versus baguette.

I check my phone. There are text messages from two of my four siblings and a voicemail from my mum. I sometimes think mobile phones were invented just so families could avoid talking to one another.

Whenever you tell people you have four siblings they offer up a brief prayer for my mum's slack stomach muscles and the lattice grid of stretchmarks which she must surely have, and then ask if we are all alike.

No, we are not. Despite the fact that we all have the same mum and dad, and we were brought up with the same Protestant work ethic in the same lower-middle-class semi-detached in Reading, we are pretty much opposed in every way. In an attempt to ensure a close family, poor

Mum went to the enormous effort of pushing out a kid every two years – which I find scarier than watching the movie *Alien* (actually, I imagine the whole experience was like *Alien*, a series of exploding stomachs). Therefore it must be a bit galling for Mum and Dad that ever since we could all walk, we've been walking in separate directions, doing everything we can to carve out a bit of space and individuality.

We are nothing like the Russian doll set that my parents imagined. One of my brothers, Bill, went to Cambridge University to read politics. He glided through exams without having to break into a sweat; he didn't even appear to break the spine of the cover of a book – he's just dizzyingly intelligent. He's gone on to be a trust fund manager. Please don't ask me what that is because I have no idea. I do know that he drives a top-of-the-range X5 BMW, which, as my dad put it, 'must have cost a bob or two', and he married an equally bright (and smug) lawyer and they now live in a huge, tastefully decorated pile in Holland Park with their three kids. The type of kids who watched Baby Einstein on TV from birth and now have an opinion on international current affairs. I'm truly intimidated by my young nephews and baby niece. I usually try to read the quality newspapers before I visit them so that I have topics of conversation to discuss with the eldest (he's four). Neither Bill, nor his wife, has sent me a text to wish me happy birthday.

My sister, Fiona, managed to get to Salford nursing college but, hell, did she have to work to scrabble together the grades. She's a dedicated (read knackered) nurse at some OAP hospital, up north somewhere. I truly admire her but just can't imagine why she wants to work with the smell of pee. She's incredibly busy, lives miles away and has two kids, so we rarely see each other. When we do meet up (Christmas, big birthdays and Mum and Dad's anniversary) it's always excruciatingly embarrassing. I get the sense that we'd both like to be close but we find we have nothing in common and we struggle for something to talk about. My attempts at small talk seem silly in light of the fact that Fiona is pretty much Florence Nightingale and Mother Teresa in one neat, determined package. I once commented how I always think of her when I have to deliver a bouquet of flowers to a hospital. She said that flowers were a bloody nuisance and nurses didn't have time to run around looking for vases, plus they set off sneezing among patients with hay fever. That sort of brought the conversation to an end. Fiona's text reads: HAPPY BIRTHDAY, FGR+D. She doesn't have thumb time to text her family's full names.

Then there's Jake. I didn't really expect a call from him since he's resting at Her Majesty's pleasure; nine months for some piracy crime. I don't know the details because I avoided reading about them in the local rag and I tune out whenever Mum starts explaining the circumstances of his arrest. Mum maintains my brother Jake suffers from middle child syndrome. He tried too hard to carve out a point of difference in the family. It's her excuse for him being a criminal; she can make as many excuses for him as she likes. He was a thieving bastard from the day he could walk and I'll never forgive him for selling my Barbie doll in the playground when I was seven; Airhostess Barbie was a difficult doll to come by.

Then there's me. I've resisted sending a text to myself or posting cards to myself, as though I'm some sort of Mr Bean saddo. My younger brother, Rick's, text reads:

```
:-) bday sis. mAk suR itz a gud l.
hav lots of SX w Adam while he
stil fancies u. jst kidding. hav a
gr8 dA.
```

It takes me a while to translate. Ha ha very funny. The chance of having lots of sex with Adam never arose, did it? Clearly, Adam has already reached the point of no return in terms of lusting after me.

If I had to pick a sibling I'd take with me to a desert island it would probably be Rick. Something to do with him being the only one I could boss around, perhaps. No one in our family has any idea whether Rick's naturally brilliant, like Bill, but we do know that he's not prepared to work like Fiona. All Rick wants to do, has ever wanted to do, is play video games. He discovered *Pac Man* when he was about three years old and has been surgically attached to buttons and screens ever since. Mum and Dad despaired. Mum regularly tortures herself by going on to the internet, late at night, and reading cases about psychotic murderers who listed video game playing on their otherwise blank CVs. Fortunately, and somewhat miraculously, Rick hasn't turned out to be a psycho (one jailbird is enough for any family struggling to appear respectable) and he's somehow managed to turn his obsession with games into a career; he's a games tester for Sony. He does conform to stereotype in so much as he does smell and he doesn't talk. Which is why his long text is quite thoughtful.

Still, that's the sum total of messages. Ben will no doubt call when he gets a minute but he's in the shop on his own, which he never likes; he's probably busy. Lisa will be dropping the kids off at nursery and the gym crèche. She'll probably call after her aerobics class. As I mentioned, nothing comes between Lisa and her being 'well turned out' – not even a thirtieth birthday.

I sigh. The low number of messages wishing me many happy returns is depressing. In my opinion birthday celebrations peak when you are about six and ever after there is an annual decrease in merriment (with quite a steep gradient). Rationally, I know that there are a number of people scattered across the country who will look at the calendar today and think, 'Oh, it's Fern's birthday!' A few of them might have popped a card in the post. Of course, I can't expect everyone I know to interrupt their busy schedules just to shower me with gifts and present me with balloons, cakes and lashings of champagne, but –

I blame the media, or books, or movies, or ten seasons of *Friends* or all of these things combined. Because, truth is, a little part of me does expect everyone I know to interrupt their busy schedules to shower me with gifts and present me with balloons, cakes and lashings of champagne because the media, books, movies and *Friends* – especially *Friends* – have conspired between them to somehow create the impression that life would be just a little bit *more* than this. Especially today.

I'm bored watching Adam play chief and decide I might as well take full advantage of my 'Access All Areas' pass by wandering into the catering hall. It's quite something; clearly, feeding the team is taken seriously by Scottie Taylor. There are two chefs and about six more staff cooking breakfast. There's a choice of bacon butties, eggs (fried, scrambled, poached, boiled), sausages, tomatoes, onions, mushrooms, even black pudding – who the hell eats that? Maybe it's an ironic nod at Scottie Taylor's northern roots; he's from Hull, a city that (as far as I'm aware) is famous for absolutely nothing other than Scottie – I've heard him joke in interviews that Hull is the new Manchester but no one believes him. Still, it's nice that he's proud of it. Besides the cooked breakfast there are yogurts, croissants, Danish pastries, mountains of fresh fruit and about a dozen cereals to choose from.

I'm not hungry, but like most women when I eat, and even how much I eat, has little to do with hunger. I eat because it's a mealtime, I eat when I'm fed up and when I'm in a really good mood, I eat loads when I'm premenstrual and often just because food is there. So far, this complete lack of discipline has had no adverse effect because I'm lucky enough to have inherited my father's metabolism. Honestly, he eats like a pig but looks like a whippet. It's the one thing worth inheriting (as one of five in a family that tends to 'make do and mend', I'm not holding out for any family heirlooms). Today I feel entitled to pile my plate with everything I can, except for the black pudding, and I wash the lot down with two huge mugs of tea.

I eat really quickly (again it's the result of being one of five kids) and so despite the mountain of food I find that by 10.35 a.m. I am once again twiddling my thumbs, or more accurately the cord of the weighty AAA pass which hangs around my neck. Idly, I wonder exactly how far it can get me. Maybe I could have a snoop around the dressing-rooms. I have no interest in what Adam is doing front of stage, but as an avid reader of glossy gossipy magazines I'd be lying if I didn't admit to being just a tiny bit interested in seeing what Scottie Taylor's dressing-room is like. After all, I'm flesh and blood. Yes, disappointed flesh and blood but all the same . . . I wonder what sort of riders and demands Scottie Taylor makes? Adam once worked on a gig for a very famous boy band and they all insisted on having their own dressing-room with en-suite bathrooms, which isn't so strange, except they all had their baths filled with M&M sweets. Total madness but I can't criticize. Who's to say what I'd ask for if I could have anything? I bet those guys couldn't believe their silly request had been taken seriously. Scottie and his band won't be arriving for hours yet. Usually the artist arrives by helicopter just before the gig starts; it's part of the theatre of the event. I think I could have a little poke around the dressing-room without disturbing anyone.

I follow my nose through a labyrinth of corridors. I hope that stars' dressing-rooms truly do have enormous glittering stars on the door or else I won't have a clue which door to open. I pass a few busy-looking people, all of whom are smoking, which is illegal as this is a public building. I don't think they care; breaking rules is what they do. Some are carrying clipboards or instruments, everyone nods at me but no one strikes up a conversation or demands to know what I'm doing aimlessly wandering about backstage. Other than the smoking, the people I run into seem to have little in common. They are not uniformly young and breathtakingly beautiful, as might be expected from a Scottie Taylor entourage, nor are they all decked out in fabulous designer clothes. They do have a higher than average hit of slightly weird and whacky hair styles but that is about all that defines them as rock and roll. That, and the fact they are all very focused on whatever it is they are supposed to be doing, and so no one bothers with me. I imitate their efficient and purposeful strides so as to blend in. After a while I spot a door with the words THE BAND emblazoned in large red letters. I reach for the handle but before I push the door open I listen to see if there's anyone inside.

I can't hear anything so I risk a sneaky peek. I can always say I'm lost if I do get spotted and questioned by anyone. The dressing-room is not as glitzy as I expected. There are enormous leather couches pushed against two of the walls and a huge low glass coffee table in between. On the table there's a nice arrangement of large white calla lilies; I check the tips and they are fresh, they've probably just gone in water. I hope whoever put the flowers here put a drop of lemonade in the vase too; it gets a good few extra days of freshness out of most stems. There's a wall of mirrors with high stools lined up like soldiers and trolleys full of makeup. There's a bar; it's well stocked with various brands of canned and bottled beer and water but not much else. There is nothing to indicate that the band backing the current rock god phenomenon dresses here; no baths of M&Ms, no baskets of Labrador puppies, no lines of clothes or coke.

A bit disappointed, I leave and continue down the corridor to the next room. On the door, in even bigger red letters than the first, is written, SCOTTIE TAYLOR **STAR**. I get the sense that the huge and bold letters are a bit of a joke. The sort of joke I imagine Scottie Taylor would make; a tongue-in-cheek prod at 'Don't you know who I am?' Grinning, I open the door and stride in.

The voice bangs through the air. 'What are you doing in here?'

9. Fern

I want to be forthcoming but my throat tightens and chokes my words; he's got these eyes, you see, green, sparkling, soul-slicing eyes. He flashes them at me and with one single glance he strips me naked. I honestly feel my clothes come away at the seams and land in a heap at my feet. The sensation is so real that I look down just to check.

It's the man himself. Scottie Taylor. It takes a fraction of a second for me to understand this and I acknowledge the fact between my ears and between my legs simultaneously; I feel dizzy in both places. Close up he looks much bigger than I imagined. When I saw him in concert, eight years ago, he was a tiny dot on the stage. OK, so I was at the back in the crap seats but his size is still a surprise. I mean, most stars I've ever seen in real life are much tinier than you expect. Although, thinking about this theory, I ought to confess now that the sum total of stars I've seen in real life includes Beppe off *EastEnders* (I saw him in Covent Garden once, he was just coming out of a shop selling jacket potatoes) and Patrick Duffy (you know, Bobby from *Dallas*; I took my nephews to a panto last Christmas and he played Cinderella's dad) – so my theory is not based on what you'd call a robust study.

Scottie has huge muscled arms and he's about six foot one. He became famous when he was practically in short trousers, so it's easy to think of him as boyish. But that was then and this is now. There's no element of boy any more. He's man. One hundred per cent. My palms start to moisten; oh my God, so do other parts of my body!

'What are you doing in here?' He repeats the question; his tone is suspicious and cool.

Finally, I find my voice. 'Being nosey. Look, I'm sorry, I'll leave,' I squeak as I begin to edge out of the door. While my reply is absolutely accurate I don't think it got to the heart of what Scottie was trying to establish.

'Who are you?' He doesn't sound rude but he doesn't sound charmed either. He sounds wary.

I am at a total loss as to how to answer even this, the simplest of questions. I don't know what to say or do. I am utterly without common sense or even a simple grasp at good manners. For a moment I can't remember my name. My mind is a spongy black hole. Oh my God, my nipples are becoming solid. Can he tell? I'm practically dribbling.

'I'm Fern,' I reply. 'I'm not a journalist, or a nutcase fan, or anything like that.' I try to smile and reassure us both. I want to summon my most megawatt smile, the one I use to attract barmen when I'm waiting to get served, but I don't manage more than a lopsided, self-conscious grin. 'Well, I *am* a fan, a big fan; I'm not saying I don't like you because I do. Loads. You're great,' I garble. 'In fact my boyfriend is always taking the piss out of me for how much I like you. He buys me your official calendar for Christmas every year, not as the main pressie, just a stocking filler, he's not that tight. But it's not like I have a crush on you and I'm some sort of mad stalker. I don't want you to worry about that. You're totally safe. I've never stalked anyone in my life. Well, who does? Well, some people do, I know that, but I'm not one of them. My crush isn't a serious one. That would be crazy at my age. Far, far too old for a crush. Not that I'm old. I buy my boyfriend Kylie's calendar. It's a couple thing, you know?'

Maybe I was in a better place when my mouth was clamped shut and I had a search party out looking for my tongue.

'I'm here with my boyfriend actually. He's your assistant stage manager,' I add in an effort to make myself sound normal. Then I realize I might have just landed Adam in a whole load of do-do. Who knows if this Scottie Taylor is some sort of megalomaniac control freak? 'He's not going to get into trouble because I'm wandering about, is he? He doesn't know I'm in your dressing-room. I was bored watching him do his thing on stage and I was just killing time. It's not his fault, so don't sack him because he'd be devastated. I didn't think you'd be here. I just wanted to see if you keep M&Ms in your bath or anything.'

I finally stop twittering. For which Scottie Taylor is probably offering up prayers of thanks to all the heathen and traditional gods. Have I ever behaved like such a total imbecile in my entire life? Was it absolutely essential to blab all that? I steel myself to look at Scottie.

He's grinning. My pathetic verbal incontinence amused him, at least.

'So the lucky guy is that dark, tall bloke. Adam Cooper, right?'

'Right.' I'm stunned Scottie Taylor knows the name of his assistant stage manager.

'Yeah, I know him. He's good. I won't sack him.' I risk a small smile as I am an itsy bit proud that Scottie has noticed Adam and rates him; maybe what Adam does is part of a great symphony after all. 'I'll expect you to have sex with me by way of recompense, though,' adds Scottie.

'Really?' I ask, part horrified, part delighted. Certainly more delighted than is respectable.

'No not really, you silly sod, what sort of place do you think this is?'

This time Scottie's face breaks into a really wide, genuine smile and I feel as though I've just nose-dived into a warm lagoon of beauty and possibility.

'Scott Taylor,' he says, holding out his hand for me to shake.

His gesture is sweet. There was never any doubt as to who he was. It's pleasantly self-effacing that he's pretending we're just a couple of normal people saying hi for the first time. I place my hand in his firm grip and bolts of sexual lightning fire through my body, scalding every single nerve ending. We lock eyes and I wonder if he felt anything too.

'Can you play cards?' he asks.

10. Fern

Scottie's room is considerably more impressive than the band's. The look the interior designer has gone after is nightclub verging on brothel. There's red flock wallpaper and thick red shag pile carpet so the walls and floor seem to meet, leaving me feeling deliciously cosy, irresistibly woozy. There's a purple suede chaise longue and a number of enormous gold leather beanbags. There are a lot of mirrors with ornate bronze frames reflecting my stunned image right back at me, and whichever way I turn there are masses of enormous vases of gallica roses; a rich, velvety, purple rose which gives off a particularly heady scent.

Scottie flings himself on the chaise longue next to a low purple smoked-glass coffee table and I grab a beanbag and sit down to face him. He starts to deal.

'What stakes shall we play with?' he asks.

'Well, it has to be coppers because even if you play with tenners, it's coppers to you but not to me which would make the game uneven,' I say, without thinking whether it's crass or not to mention that he's a squillionaire. But then this is the man who signed a multi-multi-million-pound deal with his record company and announced to the world's press, 'I'm rich, I'm obscenely rich. Isn't that fucking great!' At the time the tabloids and even a couple of the qualities had got sniffy and said that it was vulgar of him to be so publicly chuffed with himself but I thought he'd got it right. Being filthy rich must be exciting, and if he hadn't admitted as much people would have complained he was taking himself too seriously.

Scott stares at me; I think he's contemplating what I've just said about coppers versus tenners while I'm wondering what his lips taste like. I use every jot of common sense and common decency to cast the thought aside.

'Fair enough,' he agrees, nodding his approval. 'You know, no one has ever pointed that out to me before.'

Someone should open a window; it's really stifling in here. I can feel my cheeks flush with colour. 'Duh, isn't it obvious? Who do you normally play with?' I ask.

'My band, my crew, you know, the gang.'

'Well, I hope you're paying them well,' I say as I reach for my purse. I look inside; not unsurprisingly it's empty except for a serious stack of loyalty cards and a button which came off my jacket last week. 'Bugger, I haven't even got coppers. How about we play for matchsticks?' I suggest. 'That's what my family did when we were kids.'

Scott smiles. 'Did any of your family end up in prison on charges of arson?'

'No, but my brother Jake is doing bird for some dodgy deal he was involved in. He was distributing pirate DVDs,' I admit thoughtlessly.

Scott doesn't skip a beat but continues to deal the cards.

Oh. My. God. What made me say that? I never rush to reveal Jake's stock trade. It's hardly likely to impress anyone; usually this choice piece of family history has the opposite effect. Cards are a good idea. I can concentrate on hearts versus clubs, spades versus diamonds and stop with the moronic twittering and inappropriate reveals. I cannot believe that I am sat here with Scottie Taylor. We are sharing the same air, imagine that! He's a legend. A god. I wish to hell I'd made an effort this morning. What made me think it was a good idea to come to the gig without even a wisp of makeup? I must be clinically insane. He's pretty unkempt too but he's wearing it much better. He hasn't shaved this morning and his hair is dishevelled; he looks as though he's just got out of bed. The thought makes me ache with something horribly close to longing. No, it can't be. That's just not right. I have a boyfriend. I can't start to feel anything like longing for anyone other than Adam. I'm just naturally curious because Scottie Taylor is a pop star, that's all. Doesn't every woman want to know what Scottie Taylor's hair feels like, what his tongue tastes of, what his sheets smell of? Just theoretically, of course. I wouldn't dream of . . . I don't mean, I'd ever . . . I have Adam. Deep breath. Deep breath. Just concentrate.

I'm actually really good at cards and know loads of games, thanks to endless caravan holidays in Britain with my family when I was a kid. We used to waste away countless wet hours playing a hand. I suggest we play German whist, a good two-player card game. Scottie knows it and agrees. Scottie plays with an admirable and steady determination too. I wonder where he learnt. I'd guess working men's clubs when he was knee high to a garden gnome. I know from stuff I've read that his mum was a cabaret singer in pubs and he and his brother were dragged around with her from an early age. Scottie became an entertainer, his brother is an accountant. I guess his brother was watching the till as Scottie was learning to sing and play cards. We both concentrate on the game and say very little to start with. That suits me; I need to gather my thoughts. It's a good game, we're equally matched and each admires the other's skill.

'You bluffer,' says Scottie with delight as I successfully beat him with a fairly average hand because he folded.

I scoop up his pile of matchsticks with the same pleasure as I would if we had been playing for tenners – well, almost. As I scoop my booty, he deals the next hand and his fingertips accidentally brush the cuff of my top – causing a sensation similar to riding a white-knuckle ride at a theme park. All my body parts get confused; the bits that I keep in my pants leap into my mouth, my breasts defy gravity as they seem to chase him round the room and my eyes dart to his, even though I know the last thing we should do is make eye contact. Eyes are dangerous. We silently stare at one another for some time. I'm not sure how long. Maybe too long. Maybe not long enough.

'No one ever beats me,' he says carefully.

'I bet everyone throws the game, like you are some sort of five-year-old.' I try to sound playful; we have to let the sexual tension swill away – or I might drown.

He takes my cue and jokes to lighten the mood. 'God, I hadn't considered that. I just thought that I was really good, you know? The superior player. But now you've mentioned it maybe that's exactly what they do.'

'Oh, Scottie is a poor little rich boy,' I tease. I get the sense that he likes me gently taking the piss out of him;

it's probably a novelty but I don't like hurting anyone's feelings so just in case I've gone too far I add, 'Of course it might just be that you are the superior player to those guys you usually play with but you're just not as good as me.'

'Rematch. I demand it,' he laughs. 'And call me Scott, not Scottie. Only people who don't know me call me Scottie.'

We play on. OK, deep breath. So I described Scott Taylor as the perfect fantasy man; that didn't mean I expected to *like* him if I met him for real. Frankly, distanced from his lyrics and the airbrush I expected him to be a big let-down; an infantile tosser with an ego the size of a planet and a brain the size of a pinprick. But after just two hours in his company I realize that my preconceptions were totally, utterly, completely wrong.

Scott is not a manufactured, brainless bore. He's the real deal. I've heard it said that if a girl met some superstar in a supermarket she probably wouldn't even notice him. And, honestly, I think I would leave Justin Timberlake stacking shelves and it's possible that even Mark Owen would not cause me to get all flustered while squeezing my fruit and veg. But I'd notice Scott. He could take me even in the dairy aisle – and it's really cold there. There are no screaming fans buoying him up as we play cards, no sign of an enormous entourage, no photographers, and he's not wearing clothes embroidered with gold leaf or any outward sign of his colossal wealth, and yet he oozes that ephemeral star quality that only one person in ten million is lucky enough to be born with. He is breathtakingly compelling.

I realize that Scott has asked me to play cards on a whim. This is not the start of a lifelong friendship. This dream will end when he gets hungry and needs to call for food or when something else catches or demands his attention, so I squirrel away every last detail of this experience. I know that I'll want to savour each moment over and over again, on my own and with friends. Hell, I might throw a party to tell people about this. Although I guess I'd have to edit slightly for Adam's sake. Not that I've actually *done* anything wrong but I imagine he'd be less than happy to hear that I'm zapped with lust every time Scott so much as glances at me. I watch the way Scott stands, moves, talks, stays silent, sips from his water bottle and it is absolutely fascinating to me. I'm entranced.

We are joined by a mountain of a man who appears not to be accustomed to smiling. I assume he is a personal security guard. He doesn't have a uniform but he checks behind doors and in cupboards and he examines the phones before he finally sits in a chair, in the corner of the room. Even then his eyes don't settle but dart constantly from left to right. He asks if he can look in my bag. Scott says it isn't necessary but I hand it over anyway.

'What was he looking for, my hairbrush?' I joke.

Scott grins as he glances across to the bald-as-a-coot security guard. 'Tape recorder, drugs, a gun,' he replies with a shrug.

'You're kidding?'

'No. I'm clean at the moment and these guys are paid to help me keep it that way. The last thing I need is some sexy siren coming in with a stash of crack, then getting me to do and say all sorts of weird things that she's recording so as she can serve them up cold in the tabloids the next day.'

I'm crazily flustered because he's just indirectly referred to me as a sexy siren. I wonder what sort of weird things does he imagine I might get him to do? I try to stay on track. 'A gun?'

'Never happened yet. Least not to me. But two words, John Lennon. Lots of fans are really mixed up and get into that "if I can't have you, no one can" mindset. It's fucking scary.'

'God, it must be,' I shift in my beanbag. I had been quite resentful of the security guard interrupting our tête-à-tête but now I'm glad to have him here. I quickly return to the deck and deal again. Scott picks up his hand and stares at me over his cards. I swallow hard. I've worked out that if I don't look at him or think about who I'm actually playing with, I manage quite well. The moment I catch his eye I find I'm floored.

He is absolutely bloody gorgeous.

Besides his strength, and height, and dirty grin and soul-searing eyes, he has broad shoulders that reduce to a neat stomach, slim hips and the cutest bum. Anyone who has ever read a copy of *Heat* magazine knows that his weight and level of fitness tend to fluctuate depending on how much boozing he's doing at the time, but right now I'd put money on him having stomach muscles taut enough to climb up. He is wearing a pale grey T-shirt and some battered, low-slung jeans that threaten to slip – that is part of the allure – no socks or shoes. I'm not normally a feet sort of girl. I couldn't tell you what Adam's feet look like because I avoid them as much as humanly possible, but Scott's are large, neat and tanned and his nails are smooth and shaped. I want to swoop down and kiss them. I throw down my first card and he reaches to pick up; his hand brushes up against mine, directly, this time. Flesh to flesh, not just the cuff of my top. His touch burns. I actually flinch. Shaking, I lunge about for a bottle of water which I plan to throw over myself.

'It's hot in here,' I comment pathetically.

Scott stares at me and holds my gaze. 'Isn't it,' he murmurs. I know, know, know that he's a practised seducer. He is sort of Don Juan, Casanova and James Bond all at once. Of course, he will have looked at hundreds, perhaps thousands, of women in exactly the same way as he's looking at me now. And I know, know, know that should make him less desirable –

But it doesn't.

'Have you ever played strip poker?' he asks, flashing me his famous flirty-flirty grin.

'No. And I don't think I've ever been asked to, least not since I was about thirteen,' I laugh, nervously.

What a daft, obvious thing to suggest. How ridiculous. Like I'm going to fall for that. I have a boyfriend; it's inappropriate to even imagine that I might consider it. A live-in boyfriend. We are practically married.

Practically.

We're not married, are we? We're not even engaged. And this flirtation with Scott is just a bit of fun, it doesn't *mean* anything. It isn't *going* anywhere. Anyone would do the same. Kill for the chance to. No one is going to get hurt by this bit of fun. Playing strip poker would just be a bit *more* fun; a lot more, maybe. It's not serious. Besides, he's bare-footed, wearing jeans and a T-shirt, add in boxers (assuming he's not commando); that's just three items of clothes. I'm wearing pumps, a vest top, a skirt, a zip-up top, knickers, bra, belt, earrings and about a dozen bangles – plus I'm pretty damn good at cards.

'It's a laugh,' he says with another filthy, bold, irresistible smile. He speaks with great certainty and a hint of challenge, and his words slosh my common sense clean away. I'm high on his presence and the crazy red room; even though I haven't been drinking I feel as drunk as a sailor.

'OK, deal.'

11. Fern

We are evenly matched but I stupidly lose my advantage every time I consider the possibility of seeing Scott Taylor in his undies. It is a real possibility because he's not afraid of showing his crown jewels (there are a number of websites that prove my point here – by displaying photos of him flashing his bits), plus he often shows his ass to the press if they've irritated him. My distraction makes me careless and hasty in my betting decisions. He seems to be able to keep a clear head and plays a ruthless game. Before I know it my shoes, zip-up top, belt and jewellery are piled in a heap to one side and he hasn't lost an item of clothes.

'You are a hustler,' I say. 'You were shelling out matchsticks left, right and centre but since we've been playing for clothes you haven't lost a hand.'

He takes a deep drag on his cigarette and smiles at my charge; proud rather than chastised. 'I win, again,' he mutters, laying down his superior cards.

Bugger, now I'm in real trouble. Skirt or vest top? Shedding either is going to leave me very exposed. I offer thanks to the cellulite god for not having sent that plague my way just yet (it's due on tomorrow's bus no doubt, now I'm thirty) but in the meantime I could probably risk taking my skirt off and not scaring him. But, my knickers! They are cheap, faded, big and blue. Not worthy of an outing. I dressed in such a mood and hurry this morning I never considered wearing any cute panties. What a mistake. My mum is always saying make sure you wear decent underwear, you never know what might happen. Mind you, I think she's on about me being knocked down by a bus rather than being bowled over by Scott Taylor. I could just throw in my hand, call it a day, cite Adam as an excuse. I pick up my bottle of water and take a sip to buy time while I decide what to take off. Scott stays silent and doesn't hurry me. His very silence is driving me wild with desire, how can that be? This is all very wrong and yet I don't want this to end. I giggle, nervously.

'You are biting your lip,' says Scott.

'I do that when I'm nervous,' I admit. I hope the lip-nibbling is provocative rather than creating the impression that I'm entering a gurning competition.

'Shit, you've drawn blood.' His face instantly floods with genuine concern. 'Fern, Christ, it's not that serious, keep your top on. It's a game.' He leans close and carefully but firmly smudges his thumb across my lips; he shows me the smallest drop of blood on his thumb and then sucks the blood clean away. It is the most erotic gesture I have ever been fortunate enough to be on the receiving end of.

Good God, I've died and gone to heaven.

I quickly glance towards the security guy but he's seemingly oblivious to our floor show. He's reading a tabloid and has his back towards us. In a flash I put my hand up my skirt and drag off my baggy blue knickers. Triumphant at solving the immediate dilemma of which garment to shed, I fling the knickers to one side and say firmly (and I hope, very sexily), 'Deal again.'

I'm not a vain girl but I'm not stupid either. He has the most enormous boner straining at his jeans. Result. I win the next two hands in quick succession. Scott Taylor can't concentrate on anything other than *me* because I'm knickerless!

'I think we should call it a day now,' I say as he starts to unbutton his jeans.

'Really?' He pauses, fingers on his fly buttons, ready to snap and tug if I give the word.

'Really,' I say with quite some reluctance. On the one hand there's nothing I'd like more than to be buck naked with Scott Taylor. It's the stuff fantasies are made of but I can't go any further. I shouldn't. I mustn't. The room is hot and red and the plumes of smoke hang in the air, creating a vibe similar to that of the nightclubs of old. I can taste sin. It's delicious. But can I stomach it? I don't think I can.

But then.

He moves a fraction closer and our lips are just centimetres apart. If I kissed him now, he'd kiss me back. I know he would. It wouldn't mean anything, I realize that it's just the sort of thing rock stars do, *but* he would kiss me. Which would be fantastic, wouldn't it? What a story. What a way to celebrate my thirtieth birthday. That single kiss would snatch me from the jaws of normality. For just a moment I'd spit back at the ordinariness that suffocates my days. If I kissed this rock legend I would at least have something to tell my grandkids when I'm a wizened and ugly old woman. I lean a smidgen closer too.

Grandchildren.

Adam.

Fuck.

Adam!

I pull away from Scott a moment before our lips mesh. Bloody hell, what am I thinking of? I have a boyfriend. A boyfriend of four years who I've always been absolutely faithful to. I can't snog a man just because I've been playing cards with him for two hours and I have no knickers on. What in the world am I doing with no knickers on? Hot flushes of shame rush through my body, overwhelming the feelings of lust that have dwelt there all morning. How have I allowed this to happen? Why haven't I had any control? A fantasy figure is my birthright. A flirtation is understandable. An affair is downright nasty. I'm not nasty – although I am a disgrace! Being with Scott has made me forget Adam even exists. That's terrible. OK, this morning Adam disappointed me horribly, we clearly have a lot to talk about and sort out, but I can't just rush off and kiss another man. Even if the man is Scott Taylor. Even if it is my birthday. Even if . . .

His lips are rose pink, plump cushions. Slightly fuller lower lip. Cheeky. Up-turned. Tempting. I feel myself edging towards him again.

No! There are no *even ifs*. It's clear cut. I have a boyfriend. Adam. I have Adam. I have to pull away. 'It's my birthday today,' I blurt suddenly, jarring my head away from his. I don't know why I say this, a desperate attempt to break the tension I suppose.

'Happy birthday,' says Scott, jumping up and moving quickly away from me.

I fight a fleeting feeling of disappointment. What did I expect? That he'd demand I kiss him? That he'd be in the slightest bit regretful that we didn't play tongue tennis? How stupid. The man probably never had any intention of kissing me; it was probably all in my imagination in the first place. Or if he was going to kiss me it obviously meant nothing to him. No more than sipping on his water bottle – an impulse to quench.

'Your birthday, cool. How are you celebrating?' he asks as he lights another cigarette.

'Erm, well, I'm coming to see your gig,' I reply lamely.

'That's sweet.' He smiles and then he looks away. 'I'm hungry.' He turns towards the security guy. 'Bob, can you get me a club sandwich? But no tomatoes. I hate tomatoes.'

12. Fern

About eight members of Scott's entourage arrive with the sandwich and sadly, it's clear my moment is over. I hastily grab my zip-up top, jewellery and shoes but I can't find my ugly knickers. Sod it. I'll leave them. I feel truly miserable when I consider that there's probably a pile of other girls' knickers stashed in this room, under beanbags and the like. The intimacy I felt between us, real or otherwise, has now totally vanished. I make my excuses and back out of the door as quickly as I can.

Scott calls, 'Have a great birthday, enjoy the gig,' but he doesn't get up from his chair. A woman in black leggings with a tidy blonde bob is giving him a shoulder massage. Her fingers are thin and strong. She kneads his muscles as though she's baking bread and it's obvious that she's done the same thing for him on numerous other occasions. The familiarity between them causes a spike of irrational jealousy to poke my innards. I leave quickly.

I scuttle back to the canteen, where the riggers, sound engineers and other crew members are eating their club sandwiches. The hall, which I'd previously thought impressive, looks lack-lustre now in comparison to the cosy room where Scott is holed up.

I spot Adam. He's sat with some of his team. I wait for my heart to leap. Nothing. Yet all morning I've felt as though I've swallowed a box of frogs. I sigh and, resigned, I weave through the rows of benches and make my way towards him; what else can I do? He nods at me as I sit down beside him.

'All right, Fern-girl?' he asks, but he doesn't wait for me to reply. Instead he turns back to his friends and they argue whether Status Quo or the Rolling Stones are the greatest grey entertainers of all time. Scott has listened to me all morning, he's valued every word I've uttered; Adam can't even be bothered to wait for my response to his most perfunctory of questions. It's so disappointing. Adam is disappointing. I stare at him and feel nothing other than bleak, steely resentment. I resent his very existence. If it wasn't for him I wouldn't have had to pull away from Scott's kiss. I wouldn't have to be so eternally, boringly, bloody ordinary. And why did I pull away? Does Adam deserve my loyalty? What if I've just thrown away the most exciting opportunity of my life and Adam is indifferent towards me? He certainly didn't take my ultimatum seriously. I glower at Adam but he's oblivious. I might as well be invisible because I don't have cable trailing from my butt attaching me to a bank of speakers or lights.

Thinking about Adam makes me feel irritable and agitated so instead I choose to fall back into thoughts of Scott, which are comforting and exhilarating. I think about Scott's smile, Scott's laugh and the way Scott's brows sort of take a bow when his head creases up with concentration and I'm crazed with excitement. That was the heaviest bout of flirtation I have *ever* indulged in. I'm hot and sticky all over just thinking about it. Where the hell can

I buy knickers? I can't go commando all day; I'm wearing a skirt! I wonder if they sell any knickers in the merchandise stalls. They probably do, ones with pictures of Scott's face on them. I'm not the only girl who has fantasies of having him between her legs – not by a long shot.

The unexpected but deeply intense encounter is probably work-a-day for Scott, all part of the rock and roll handbook, but I've never played strip poker and I've never dreamt of playing it with Scottie Taylor. For the first time since I issued the ultimatum to Adam I feel joyful. As long as I can deliberately shove all thoughts of Adam out of my head, then I am profoundly happy; there's a chance that this will, after all, be the best birthday *ever*.

Although it's actually not easy to shove all thoughts of Adam out of my head, especially when he's sat right next to me, braying with his friends and doing ridiculous impressions of Russell Brand. I stare at him with frustration; annoyingly the frustration is peppered with something hideously close to guilt. I don't want to feel guilty on my birthday so I quickly start a little reassuring self-justification. I tell myself that I haven't got anything to feel guilty about. I pulled back, didn't I? I may have walked right to the edge but I pulled back when it mattered; not every woman would have done the same. I *almost* believe me.

'What have you been up to this morning?' asks Adam, finally turning his attention to me.

'Nothing much; just looking around,' I mutter.

All I want to do is talk about Scott but obviously Adam isn't the right audience. It's tricky enough having to convince myself that playing strip poker with Scott is nothing for me to feel guilty about but I think it will be a whole lot trickier convincing Adam. And yet there is no reason for Adam to feel jealous of Scott because nothing is ever going to happen with Scott. Scott isn't like an ordinary man. He's an A-lister legend. His ultimate inaccessibility gives me a free pass to flirt with him. Doesn't it? I wouldn't dream of doing the same with anyone else I'd met because it might lead somewhere, it might mean something. Flirting with Scott Taylor doesn't mean anything. He's not real.

I suppose I could tell Adam about this morning and just leave out the bit about me whipping off my knickers but something stops me doing even that much. Scott is a delicious secret to have. Sharing those moments with him has lifted me above the horrible deadening feelings of normality that have stained my life recently. My morning was fun and special at the same time and suddenly, I feel amazing, alive and very, very sexy. I have a sense that I'll spoil that feeling if I talk about it with Adam. I'm not sure if he'd be angry or incredulous or even dismissive. I want to hang on to the feeling that I'm special, even if it's just for the shortest time.

'Well, I'm pleased to see something has put a smile on your face,' says Adam. 'There was one awful moment this morning when I thought that you were disappointed by my birthday pressie.'

'Erm,' I hesitate. Should I tell him that yes I was, I *am*, disappointed that he didn't respond to my ultimatum and that I still want us to talk more seriously about our future? Or should I let it go? Before I can decide on the right words he stands up and starts to leave the table.

'Well, I've got to get back to work. Keep out of trouble, hey.' And he leaves without giving me as much as a peck on the cheek.

I'm very muddled, but one thing I do know for sure is that I'm glad Adam has gone back to his work; at least now I can call Jess and Lisa to tell them how I've spent my morning. I call them by turn and they prove themselves to be excellent friends when I tell them about my encounter as they repeatedly squeal, 'You lucky, lucky cow.' They both ask what he's like.

'Even more gorgeous, and hot, and clever and funny than you can imagine,' I say somewhat smugly.

I give them a great amount of detail about what the room looked like, what the flowers smelt like, what the security guy did. I describe what Scott was wearing and I tell them about his low, throaty laugh, his eyes, his broad arms and even his neat toenails.

I leave out the bit about the strip poker.

Never before have I censored any part of my life when talking with Jess and Lisa. I've never had to, but they probably wouldn't understand how or why I agreed to such a thing. I barely understand it. I might mention it later on, when we are face to face, but over the phone it's difficult to explain why it was so utterly impossible to resist anything Scott suggested.

'What did Adam make of it?' asks Lisa.

'I haven't mentioned it to him,' I say, regretting the fact that my voice becomes slightly squeaky and thin when I admit as much. I don't want to be defensive. Lisa makes a funny sucking sound that I recognize as part warning, part condemnation. She sometimes makes that sound when I reach for an indulgent second piece of chocolate cake. 'He's busy,' I add. 'Besides, he wouldn't be interested or impressed. Adam and his crew probably all see Scott every day.' I know I'm being evasive. I don't know how to tell Lisa that sharing the encounter with Adam would somehow spoil it, risk it. 'It's no big deal, it's not like I met some *real* gorgeous, hot, clever, funny guy,' I joke.

'Scott *is* real,' argues Lisa.

I don't say, true, when he sucked my blood off his thumb he did seem very real. I say, 'No, he's not. He's a fantasy figure.'

'He was a fantasy figure until you spent all morning playing cards with him and now he's real,' says Lisa.

'If only,' I sigh with obvious regret. Then I make an effort to turn the subject. 'Now, let's make a plan. You have to get here as soon as you can. When's your babysitter due?'

After we've made our arrangements I go to the merchandise store and buy a pair of new knickers; I choose a pair with the words 'Scottie Taylor, Deity' emblazoned in silver, glittering letters. Then I decide to pass the rest of the afternoon sitting and thinking about my glorious secret; Scott Taylor – legend – definitely had a boner for me. It all came to such a weird abrupt halt that I can't quite decide what Scott thought of the encounter. Not that I'm assuming he thought *anything* at all. As I say, this is all probably in a day's work for him. He was probably relieved that I said no to more poker (he did at least have the opportunity to order lunch). But then I can't help wondering would he have carried on playing – stripping – if I'd allowed him. Would he have stripped me?

If I'd allowed him? I give myself a few moments to indulge in the fantasy. I shiver with delight.

Despite the fact that it's my thirtieth birthday today I feel about fifteen. I feel pretty, so pretty, and fine and I want to leap about like some character out of a cheesy Broadway musical. My panties are twinkling with Scottie Taylor.

13. Scott

'Let's make this interview snappy, hey.' I stare at Saadi and she understands. She understands that I haven't got my rocks off, that I'm not even able to for another few days and frankly it's pissing me off. That Fern chick was cute. Very cute. 'Who am I talking to anyway?'

'*Dazed and Confused*,' Mark, my manager, informs me. He means that's the name of the publication, rather than my state of mind. Although that would be accurate too.

Dazed and Confused position themselves as anarchic, feisty, real, grungy, edgy. Easy. They'll want to talk about sex. Most people want to talk about sex with me. I've never been so vain as to believe my sex life is all-absorbing; unfortunately the western world disagrees with me.

'So how did Adam Cooper's bird wash up in your room?' asks Saadi.

'Fern,' I say.

'Yeah, Fern. She doesn't look like a headcase.'

'Why would you assume she's a headcase?'

'She's issued Adam with this effing insane ultimatum. He has to ask her to marry him on her thirtieth or she's going to walk.' Saadi, a confirmed bachelor girl, shakes her head in bewilderment as to why anyone would want this.

'It's her birthday today. Is he going to ask her?'

Saadi shrugs. 'Nobody knows. He's been with her for four years but he can't make his mind up. He keeps going on and on about her ultimatum. Should he propose? Shouldn't he? His team are placing odds. He seems to think the whole thing is a bit of a laugh.'

'Fucking idiot,' I mutter.

'Who?' asks Mark, always on alert to my mood and nuances.

'Well, she seems interesting. And I mean, four years, you'd know, wouldn't you?' I say.

'Yeah, and you're the expert, right? You've never managed a four-month relationship, let alone four years,' says Mark with a weary sigh.

He's getting a bit fed up with cleaning up my messes. Wherever I go, I am known for leaving behind me a bloody trail of broken hearts belonging to starlets, groupies and songwriters. At first, when I was really young, I would have sex with any girl that would let me. Soon they all let me, so I only had sex with really pretty ones. Soon they were all really pretty, so I had to find a way to make some other sort of selection. I once slept with a girl because she wore a trilby at a cute angle, and then another because she had more body piercings than I've ever seen before, another because she had a tattoo that started on her vag (it was a vine) and curled under and up all the way to her arsehole. She must have been on some serious drugs when she let the artist go to work on her; I thought she'd earned the attention. I slept with another because she said absolutely nothing at all and then I slept with another because she was there. That soon became the only reason I slept with someone.

Nearest to hand. I started to sleep with sisters, friends and random willing groups. My selection process broke down, I guess. But it's exhausting; hedonism is harder work than it looks.

'Our Scott is a true romantic under all that bravado. He believes in love at first sight. You'd want to know by four days, wouldn't you, Scott?' says Saadi with a grin.

'Well, who the fuck has four years to waste?' I mutter.

Mark stares at me for a very long time and I think he's going to say something important. He does, he says, 'She's got great tits, Cooper's bird. Now enough chatter, we better get on with this interview. There's a schedule to keep.'

To combine licentiousness with novelty takes genuine effort and a little bit of luck. I wonder is it possible that Fern is my little bit of luck? Could Fern be the antidote to all of that excess?

14. Fern

A helicopter thunders overhead. The air whooshes across the ninety-thousand-strong crowd, banners declaring 'We Love You' are raised and the chanting crowd move their plea up a level. 'Scot-tie, Scot-tie.' The assumption is that Scottie Taylor (Scott to his friends) has just landed. But I know that he's been here since before ten this morning. The secret inside knowledge bubbles in my stomach and fizzes a little bit lower, too.

'I've never seen anything like it,' says Jess; she's breathless with excitement and therefore looks even more amazing than she usually does – who'd have thought such a thing was possible? 'Adam has got us fantastic seats.'

It's true we are only metres from the stage. There are seats all around the stadium, but we are in ones closest to the action. We're sat with other VIPs, such as press and friends of the band. It's thrilling; on the few occasions I do attend music events I'm normally one of the squashed and jostled individuals, stood in the mosh pit. There's always a fantastic atmosphere down in the mosh pit but there's also the danger of being stamped to death by hysterical women or at the very least sustaining a serious injury from a bony elbow or someone who is body surfing. I have to admit, Adam's job has its advantages after all. Right now, decent seats to a Scott Taylor gig trumps private health plans and even a company car, the sort of perks Lisa's Charlie enjoys.

'You've really gone the extra mile tonight, Jess. Have you made all this effort because it's my birthday?' I ask.

Lisa interrupts, 'You're kidding, right? She's done up to the nines because after your brief encounter with Scottie Taylor this morning she's now harbouring a secret fantasy of her own.'

'I'm not adverse to sloppy seconds in this instance,' laughs Jess.

Jess looks like Snow White (and the magic mirror did say that Snow White was the most beautiful woman in the land). She is tiny, only about five two, and her similarities to a doll don't stop there. She has creamy, flawless skin, bright, deep cobalt blue eyes and jet black shoulder-length hair. She always wears ruby red lipstick – it's her trade mark. Despite (or perhaps because of) her exceptional beauty Jess is often single. I don't think I want Scott bumping into her because even the pink, glittering cowboy hat – that she insisted on buying off a tout – can't detract from her beauty.

Mentally, I punch myself. What am I thinking? It's none of my business who Scott Taylor talks to. I have a boyfriend. What do I care if Jess gets her chance to play strip poker with Scott too?

I'd tear her hair out.

Just kidding.

Sort of.

Suddenly, red lights start to pulse across the stage and the crowd's chant reaches almost hysterical levels; everyone is up out of their seats. The band members run on and take their places. As they pick up their instruments the screams of anticipation reach a near violent pitch. 'Scottie Scot-tie.' A sea of arms sway, claw and clap. The noise and the flesh become unrecognizable and indistinguishable; almost inhuman and yet utterly human in their basic longing for this one man. The lights go white and then green for go. And he's here; striding on with a warmth and confidence that grabs every single member of the audience by the throat.

He's wearing a dark suit which is lined with a red fabric – the devil's colours – an acknowledgement that everyone wants to get naughty with him. Everyone would sell their soul in an instant if he asked them to. And he's wearing sunglasses, which hint at a mafia connection that is somehow thrilling and the right side of dangerous. He takes off his shades and women start to literally swoon; paramedics slip between the crowds to rescue fainting damsels before they are carelessly trodden underfoot.

Then, in a flat northern voice, he says, 'Hello, glad you could all make it. I am Scottie Taylor. And I'm here to give you a good time. Are you ready for me?'

They are. They scream, and yell, and jump and weep. And I'm part of it. I'm not in the least bit cool. I'm screaming louder than anyone. Up out of my chair, I'm shrieking, leaping, swaying. The air is so charged with hope, excitement and lust that I can almost feel my body being thrown about. His first track, 'Funk Me', is a catchy number with a strong beat and a risqué lyric; the entire audience are bouncing up and down on their feet, clapping hands and enjoying the party. I'm surrounded by teeth and tits, they're all enormous. There is no sign of cynical boyfriends who have been dragged here by their lusty girlfriends. Nor any spotting of the 'yet to be convinced he's really special, I'm just here with my mate' types; everyone is already converted, we're all fans. The place is alive with a special sort of energy. Good will – uncommonly short on the ground nowadays – is suddenly everywhere; you can bathe in it.

After just one song no one cares that it will take them six hours to get out of the car park later on, or that the loos are awash with crap and the beers cost a fortune and are warm and flat. Everybody is happy. Every man wants to be him, every woman simply wants him. He weaves a special sort of spell across the entire stadium. Every single person there feels unique, despite the obvious – which is that they are thinking and feeling exactly the same as the eighty-nine thousand, nine hundred and ninety-nine others who are singing along. They all believe he is singing to them and just them; more, that he knows them in a way that they've never been known or understood before. Despite the enormous crowd he creates a feeling of intimacy. I'm sold.

His lyrics are amazing; truly clever and thought-provoking. They talk to the innocents, the celebrity whores, the lovestruck and the cynical alike. Everybody thinks they can solve him and save him. He doesn't let up for a moment. It's pure gold entertainment. He works the crowd into a near frenzy, demanding, 'Show me you love me,' which gets the response of signs and banners being re-hoisted into the air. They read, 'Marry me', 'Love me', 'Pick me' and list telephone numbers. It's weird. What do these women think he's going to do? Look at one of them and think, 'Oh yeah, you might make a great lifelong partner; I must make a note of your number and give you a bell to invite you to tea with my mum.'

Yes, that's exactly what they are hoping for. It's desperate but it's almost an understandable desperation. I can hardly comment; I played strip poker with the man a couple of hours after meeting him.

Scott challenges one half of the stadium to sing and then the other side; he says one was louder than the other and creates a healthy competition. He singles out a girl at the front of the audience to sing to; she bursts into tears, he blows another a kiss and she lifts her top up to show him her bra. The girl next to her, determined not to be outdone, whips up her top and takes off her bra. Her huge double DD babies are caught on camera as Scott laughs and thanks her. Seemingly impromptu, he jumps off the stage and runs around the barrier touching the hands of the girls who scramble to reach him there. He pulls one girl on to the stage, sings to her and kisses her. Lucky, lucky woman. Everyone loves him.

The sun sets during the concert and we're all bathed in a wonderful orange light as he takes the tempo down and sings the dreamy song 'Hurtful Regrets', which would make women leave their husbands on the spot if he gave them the nod.

Scottie works through his most famous tracks: 'Fall Apart', 'Come Back to Me' and my favourite, 'Bit of Rough'. The audience are like long blades of grass bending in the wind and he can breeze or storm.

'I can feel your love,' he yells. 'You are the best crowd I've ever had. You've made me so happy.'

The roar is deafening.

It's pitch black by the time he sings 'Feeling Fine, That's a Lie', his first solo number one and the song that is still synonymous with his enormous success, even after fourteen more number one tracks. The stadium is aglow with camera flashes, strobe lights and smiling faces. He changes the words to 'Feeling Fine, That's *No* Lie', and tells the audience, 'And that's because of you, and you, and you, and you.' He points randomly at gasping girls. With the last 'and you', he catches my eye and pours a massive grin my way. My knees buckle. It might have been a random act or he might have been truly delighted to have caught my eye. The moment was too fleeting to be sure.

And then that's the end of the show. He leaps into the air and we all cheer and yell, cheer and yell some more. He doesn't ask us to stop; he stares wide-eyed with amazement and cries, 'I don't know what to do. I don't know what to say.' He seems genuinely humbled.

Although he's left the stage the audience wait with bated breath knowing there will be an encore. He hasn't sung 'Stamp on Your Demons' yet and everyone is expecting it.

He bounces back on the stage and the confident, focused and devoted musicians start playing the chords we all recognize as 'Stamp on Your Demons'.

'Stop, stop. No, no, no,' says Scott as he shakes his head and waves his arms. 'I'm not singing that tonight.'

The crowd assume this is part of Scottie's show; he's chatted between songs, flirted and had a laugh all night but I can see the band look genuinely perplexed. Maybe this is an unrehearsed, off-the-cuff moment. The papers always report that Scott can be a loose cannon.

Scott turns to the audience. 'Today is a special day for me. This is my first gig for two years and you lot have just been amazing. Mad. I love you.' More cheering. 'So, I hope you don't mind if I just make tonight a bit special for someone else, too. You don't mind, do you?' Ninety thousand give him their cheer of approval. 'A really lovely someone else, actually.'

He nods at the pianist, who is at least in on the act, and then the familiar chords of 'Happy Birthday' start to ooze out into the night. Scott turns to me. His eyes bang the breath out of me. The intensity of the moment carves deep into my existence. I'm trembling. The noisy surrounding crowds blur into one irrelevant, indistinct mass. We are alone in an exquisite clarity. I'm aware of my pounding heart and knickers and nothing else matters. He blows me a kiss. In a confident, slow, sexy voice, with emerald eyes glistening, he sings the entire song.

'Happy birthday to you, Happy birthday to you, Happy birthday dear Fern, Happy birthday to you.'

To me!

15. Fern

'What the hell was all that about?' asks Adam, the moment the door slams behind him. Our entire flat shakes.

'I'm going to bed,' says Jess. She scrambles off the sofa. 'Night, happy birthday.'

Adam stands in the door frame to our pokey sitting-room and glares at me.

'What?' I ask, mock innocent. I know what he is talking about. Nothing else has been on my mind for the last four hours. It's all Jess and I have discussed. Scott Taylor sang 'Happy Birthday' to me, in front of ninety thousand people tonight. He called me 'really lovely'. He blew me a kiss. How exciting is that!

For me at least; maybe not so great for Adam, I suppose.

'How did Scottie Taylor know it was your birthday?' demands Adam. It's nearly three in the morning. He had to stay and work on some light sequencing or something after the gig, so Jess, Lisa and I left without him. Lisa had to go straight home and get to bed, the kids will be up before six tomorrow, but Jess and I have been drinking ever since. We've sunk a bottle of champagne that Lisa gave me for my birthday and a bottle of white wine; this is on top of drinking a few beers each at the gig. It's a good thing Adam came home when he did, otherwise we'd probably have started on the cooking sherry next.

We've had a marvellous, giggly, excited night. We talked nonsense; lovely, lovely nonsense.

Adam looks tired and drawn. He needs to take better care of himself. Maybe get a haircut or go to the gym. He looked so splendid this morning, but Scott's perfection and the alcohol I've consumed have somehow left Adam looking a bit blurry; I can't get him into focus.

'I met him backstage before the gig. Didn't I mention it?' I ask as casually as I can.

'No, you bloody didn't.'

'Didn't I? Well, it was just a fleeting meet.' Whoops. I've just slipped from being evasive to being a downright liar. The alcohol spins through my body and the fact that I told Adam a teeny tiny lie doesn't seem like a big deal. I hope that it still doesn't seem like a big deal in the morning; it's so hard to judge it after so much to drink. Anyway, it's my *birthday*, there's probably a custom somewhere that states you don't have to be a hundred per cent honest on your birthday. If not, there should be.

'Fleeting?' demands Adam sceptically. 'You must have made quite an impression for him to sing to you in the middle of his biggest ever gig. Quite an impression.'

Oh I hope so! Is that a terrible thing to think? It doesn't feel terrible but looking at Adam, all startled and anxious, I consider it might be. I swallow my excitement and try to appear calm as I comment, 'Scottie Taylor is a showman. He probably sings "Happy Birthday" to some woman every night of the gig. It was probably part of the show.' I say this to placate Adam but at the same time I cross my fingers and hope to hell this isn't the case.

'No, it isn't part of the gig,' insists Adam irritably. 'I

know the exact run of his show. The impromptu "Happy Birthday" was a surprise to everyone; the sound and light technicians were all having a fit.'

'Oh.' I try to sound neutral – not bothered either way. Inside I'm dancing a jig.

'How long, exactly, did you spend with him?' he snaps.

My good humour begins to wane a fraction; I don't want to row with Adam but I do resent his tone. If Adam cared so much how I spent my thirtieth birthday then he should have made more of an effort. 'I don't know, some minutes,' I reply evasively. One hundred and ninety-eight minutes to be exact, although this probably isn't the time to share that fact with Adam.

'And that was enough time for you to mention it was your birthday?' asks Adam doubtfully.

'It's been the first thing I've told everyone all day.'

I'm getting into this lying thing – one does seem to come quite fluently after another. I never knew that. I've never *had* to know it. Honesty has always been my policy. But I tell myself that my lies are only little lies. I don't want to hurt Adam, not deliberately, and I suppose I know that what I've done today would hurt and anger him. I have to think this through. It's all a bit of fun, isn't it? No one should get hurt by a bit of fun. That's daft.

And if it's more than a bit of fun?

Well, it isn't, is it? Least it can't be to Scott; impossible. But he did sing to me. Oh God, my head is spinning, this isn't the time to try to think about this.

'He was flirting with you,' says Adam in a tone that sounds rudely like disbelief.

His tone causes me to be icier than I planned. 'People occasionally do,' I reply, defiantly folding my arms across my chest. I've spent this evening hugging myself with excitement but that's not a casual pose; I'm likely to arouse Adam's suspicions further.

'Who does?' demands Adam with a surprising slosh of jealousy. Hah! That's got his attention. I revel in the novelty. He's never jealous. Until today, I hadn't realized just how neglectful Adam has always been. I'd thought his relaxed attitude was a tribute to our relationship, proof that we trusted and respected one another, but now I'm beginning to think that he's simply indifferent towards me and that he's only, finally, been stung to jealousy because he's been publicly embarrassed at work.

'Occasionally, men who come into the shop to buy flowers flirt with me.'

'Dirtbags! Men buying their girlfriends flowers have the cheek to hit on my girlfriend? What sort of blokes are they?'

'Sometimes they are buying flowers for their mums or sisters,' I point out. 'Anyway I'm just saying a bit of flirting – *if* that was what Scott was doing – means nothing. People do it. You should be flattered.'

'Flattered that my boss hits on my girl in front of ninety thousand people?' Adam is spluttering with indignation. I'm not sure when he metamorphosed into a caveman but I'm already beginning to be irritated by this macho act. It strikes me as too little, too late. My tolerance is soused; pickled in 13.7 per cent proof wine. My irritation is being cranked up. How dare Adam be so moody about Scott singing to me? Why is he ruining my special moment? If it wasn't for Scott my birthday would have been a big letdown. I mean, OK, Adam got me the tickets for the gig but I was expecting an engagement ring! The tickets were free, and as great as the gig was it would just have been a free show if Scott hadn't singled me out and sung to me.

Which he did because I played strip poker with him unbeknown to my boyfriend. Ouch! My conscience stings for several moments. Even the copious amounts I've had to drink can't soften the blow. Huffily, I push Jiminy Cricket aside.

Adam's contribution to my birthday was minimal. He hardly spent any time with me. He didn't buy me anything; he didn't so much as send me a card. He should be grovelling not yelling.

'It was just a bit of fun. It made my birthday special. *Really special* actually, but he meant nothing by it.'

I'm torn. Part of me wants to diffuse this situation. I want to calm Adam down so that we can put this incident away, perhaps in a beautifully carved wooden box somewhere deep in my mind; a box that, occasionally when I am alone, I will sneak open. I'll revel in this wonderful, terrifically exciting memory but the flirtation will be compartmentalized. It won't affect any other part of our lives. Adam won't become angry and jealous, I won't become deceitful and secretive, I won't be consumed by longing for something other, something more. If this incident is immediately parcelled up and boxed off, then we will be able to sit down and talk about our futures – sensibly without ultimatums.

'Can't you be pleased for me?' I ask, hoping that Adam

will understand my need of and delight in this shiny, wondrous occasion. Adam glares at me and then turns and kicks the wall. Very mature. I watch the small flakes of plaster from around the socket scatter and I think, lucky them – I'd like to scatter.

Because, truth is part of me wishes that Scott *did* mean something by the flirtation. Part of me longs to be given a swift exit from my increasingly overwhelming sense of disappointment. As Adam surreptitiously rubs his sore toe on the back of his calf I acknowledge that it's quite a large part of me that wants the latter. I rub my eyes with the balls of my hands. I really am too tired and drunk to think clearly; I need to sleep now.

I walk into our bedroom and start to get ready for bed. I undress and then put on pyjamas; something I only ever do if I'm in a mood with Adam. Normally we like to sleep naked with our bodies squashed into one another. Adam follows me into the bedroom; he's carrying a glass of water. I wonder if he's going to offer it to me as a sign of peace. He glugs it back. Sod him. I know I'm going to have a stonker of a hangover tomorrow but I don't get out of bed to get my own water, it would give him too much satisfaction.

Our bedroom is tiny; it was an unbelievable struggle to get the double bed in here when we moved in, so Adam has to sit on the bed to take his clothes off as there's nowhere else for him to go. I find his nearness unwelcome. He starts to undress. He flings his leather jacket, jeans, T-shirt, socks and boxers in a heap in the corner of our bedroom; the corner is so close that I can smell his clothes. They smell of summer evening and faint sweat, mostly masked by deodorant. This is Adam's usual (and not altogether unpleasant) smell. Tonight I don't like it. I sigh and wonder does he really believe they walk to the washing machine all by themselves? I'm bored of being the laundry fairy and the shopping fairy and the cleaning fairy; there's no magic in it for me.

Adam gets into bed and lies staring at the ceiling. He mumbles, 'The man's a slut, Fern. A dangerous, ruthless slut.'

'It's good to know you think so highly of the person who is at the very pinnacle of your industry,' I mutter back sarcastically, and then I turn away from Adam, ensuring I take a huge share of the duvet with me.

I don't care if Adam is sulking, or wounded or angry. He's being silly. He should be pleased for me. It's my birthday, for goodness sake. And Scott singing to me was the most wonderful present. The most exciting thing that has ever happened to me, *ever*. It doesn't mean a thing. Not to Scott. I was just part of his show. He's impulsive. And the fact that I really, really, really wish it did mean something to Scott doesn't mean anything either. Does it? Scott is just a fantasy figure, as he is to millions of women. I know couples who have jokes between them about which A-lister they would bed, given the chance, and those jokes often extend to a tongue-in-cheek free pass to do just that, if the occasion ever arises.

Everyone knows those occasions don't ever crop up. Do they?

I lie staring at the wall and instead of counting sheep I wonder if I could have played things differently today. Perhaps I could have called Adam when I was in Scott's dressing-room and asked him to join us in the card game. Not strip poker, obviously, that would have been a bit tricky, but the earlier games. Scott and Adam might have got on, they might have become good buddies and that would have been exciting – that would have lifted us out and above our normal humdrum existence. They might be interested in each other's record collection, they both have guitars. And Adam only described Scott as 'a dangerous, ruthless slut' because he's in a mood. We could get round that.

In the moment I let the thought into my head I boot it out again. Who am I trying to kid? I don't want Scott, Adam and me to be friends. My feelings for Scott haven't dilly-dallied around the platonic, they fast-tracked straight to something bigger and more overwhelming. What I feel for Scott isn't friendship. It's more than that.

And right now, what I feel for Adam is less.

16. Fern

The next day I call Ben from my bed and beg him for another day off.

'It's Saturday, darling, I can't do without you,' he sing-songs down the phone. I realize I'm asking a lot of him. Saturday is our busiest day and he'd have to manage basically on his own (as our dopey Saturday girl is often as much of a hindrance as she's a help – we only keep her on because her mum is one of our best clients).

'Oh please, please, please,' I beg.

'I'm guessing you had loads of hot birthday sex yesterday and now you want a repeat performance. You're just being a greedy girl.'

'Actually, things didn't pan out as I expected yesterday,' I admit glumly. 'Adam didn't produce a ring.'

'But he did have a surprise for you,' Ben interrupts excitedly.

'Free tickets to a Scottie Taylor gig. Not what I was expecting.' There's a silence. Neither of us knows what to say next. No doubt Ben is trying to think of something to say to comfort me – but what can?

Well, Scott singing to me did. Scott flirting with me did. Scott saying I was lovely really did!

Briefly, I wonder how much detail I should give to Ben over the phone. I'm aware that Adam is sleeping right next to me and I decide to save all the fun bits until we can talk face to face.

'Really? That's it? Just the tickets?' asks Ben eventually. He sounds disappointed, almost as disappointed as I was. Not one to stay downcast for long, he quickly jumps to the assumption that Adam will have arranged a compensatory treat for today. 'I see, so you're planning to do something special today and that's why you need another day off?' he asks encouragingly.

'Yes,' I say cautiously. *I* am planning on doing something special but not with Adam. I feel bad that Ben is under a different impression but I'll explain everything when I see him. 'I have tickets for tonight's gig too. We can meet there. I'll get Jess to bring over one of the tickets for you. Freebies,' I say by way of persuasion.

'Oh well, in that case, I can hardly refuse, can I? It would be too ungracious. Take good care of your hangover, try fizzy elderflower and greasy chips. I'll see you tonight and you can tell me all about your gorgeous gifts.'

'Thank you, you're a superstar.'

I don't bother to tell Ben that, surprisingly, I am not hungover – despite the enormous amounts Jess and I drank last night. In fact I feel wonderful.

You see, the first thing that hit me this morning when I woke up from my Scott Taylor dream-filled sleep was not the disappointment of Adam failing to propose but the excitement that Scott Taylor singled me out and sang to me! Me! That's monumental.

I jump out of bed, drag on a tracksuit and dash to the corner 7–11 store. We need milk and I need papers. When

I get back to the flat clutching a bunch of tabloids Adam has emerged from the shower and is stood in the kitchen hurriedly eating a slice of dry toast (we're out of butter and I forgot to pick up any). Our flat is so tiny I practically jump on his knee just by stepping through the door. He shrinks away from me, shooting me a cross look.

'Morning,' I smile breezily.

He grunts but doesn't go as far as returning my greeting. Really, he's going to have to try harder than that to ruin my day. Not only did I spend yesterday playing cards with Scott Taylor but the truth is Scott Taylor sang to me! Have I mentioned that? It's impossible to be anything other than thrilled with life. As Adam puts the kettle on to make mugs of tea, I start to read the tabloids. Scott's comeback gig is emblazoned all over the front pages. The reviews are great, which is excellent news. Britain's pop prince has a tempestuous relationship with the tabloids. Sometimes he's golden boy and other times he's public enemy number one. I imagine he'll love this coverage. He's described as 'dizzyingly vibrant', 'class entertainer', 'the show of his life'. I work my way through the *Mirror*, the *Daily Mail*, the *Express* and then the *Sun*. They are uniform in their praise.

'Look at this,' I squeal. 'The *Mirror* has mentioned Scott singing to me.'

'Fucking great,' says Adam. He's drinking from a carton of milk which he slams down with unnecessary violence; some splashes on the floor. I'm pretty certain it will stay there until it changes to cheese. 'Not only do ninety thousand people witness Scottie Taylor hitting on my girl but now a further several million get to read about it.'

I start to read from the newspaper. 'It says he sang to an "elegant, mystery girl and everyone wants to know who is this *lovely*".' I don't think Adam hears me because he reaches for his jacket and then charges out of the kitchen and the flat (this takes about four steps). The door slams behind him so I go to Jess's room. I think it's more reasonable to assume she'll be pleased for me.

17. Fern

Jess has a hangover and she doesn't appreciate my jumping up and down on her bed and pointing out that I'm not suffering from one because Scott Taylor sang to *me*! I think she may be a bit jealous. She's used to being the one that exciting things happen to. She's normally the one bursting into my room on a Saturday morning with a whirling head and excited chatter about new flirtations. For years I've watched her being wined and dined by a dazzling array of blokes, and although she swears she'd swap all the variety for a bit of consistency that's just because she doesn't know how disappointing consistency can be. Consistency that leads to wedding bells and babies has its advantages, I don't doubt. But consistency which amounts to little more than an encyclopedic knowledge of Saturday TV schedules and the menus of all the local takeaway services is not something to covet.

'What did Adam say about Scottie's impromptu sing-song?' she asks.

'Well, he was huffy about it, mostly because it screwed up his light sequence, I think.' Her question stops me jumping up and down. It's hard to think about Adam without feeling ... what? Sad? Bad? Mad?

'He must feel a bit threatened. No man would like Scottie Taylor making a move on his girlfriend.'

'He's not threatened. Adam just doesn't like me

having fun,' I say a bit sulkily and a bit unreasonably.

'That's not true,' says Jess gently.

'It seems that way.' I sit on the side of her bed. Still and serious now, I struggle to be clearer. 'Or rather, I'm beginning to think that Adam is just indifferent to whether I have fun or not, whether I am happy or not. After all, he didn't acknowledge my request for more commitment.'

'You mean your scary, demanding ultimatum,' she clarifies with a wry grin.

'Is the thought of marrying me so scary?' I ask with a sigh. 'You know, I'm getting the feeling that Adam has one foot out of the door. We're not going anywhere. If we were, he'd have proposed. Why didn't he propose?' Jess doesn't reply, she doesn't know how to. She just looks uncomfortable.

'Will you carry out your threat? Will you break up?' she asks.

Now *I* don't know how to answer *her* question. We fall silent. I get a feeling similar to that of being at a wake. I think we might be burying my relationship with Adam. I use the pause to think about what Jess first said.

'So, *do* you think Scott was making a move?' I try to keep the hope in my voice subdued to a reasonable level.

'Well, yes, he probably does fancy you but that's not important, is it?'

'No,' I lie. Actually, hearing that Scott might fancy me seems magnificently important, especially right now when I feel Adam has passed up the chance to be with me. A boyfriend of four years not wanting to get married is a weighty blow to a girl's confidence and Scott Taylor taking an interest is a mighty lift.

'I mean, it's not like he's going to actively pursue you, is it?' continues Jess. 'He'll have moved on today, probably slept with someone else last night.'

'Probably,' I mutter. My stomach is full of swiftly solidifying cement. I don't want to hear this.

'It was just a bit of fun, wasn't it?'

'Yes,' I mumble reluctantly.

'I mean, realistically, like you said yesterday, Scottie Taylor probably does this sort of thing all the time. Not so much a girl in every port, more a girl in every pavement crack. He can't take a step without some woman offering herself up. Even if you rolled out of a rug and fell naked at his feet à la Cleopatra there's no guarantee that Scottie Taylor would even recognize you today.' Jess catches sight of my face and stops blathering. Maybe I'm not hiding my disappointment as well as I'd like to. She reaches over and squeezes my hand and gently says, 'I mean you wouldn't want to be just yet another woman he had sex with.'

Oh God, it's terrible, but part of me wants exactly that. I can't look at Jess in case she can see my wantonness written all over my face.

'I wouldn't mind being asked,' I mumble. 'Maybe Scott could ask me to sleep with him and then, obviously, I'll say no. That way I'll have the undisputed joy of knowing that he wanted me but the comfort of knowing that I'm a good moral person who stood by my man. Maybe that will be enough. Maybe *that's* the ultimate fantasy once you hit thirty.'

Or it might just be letting him fuck my brains out and not getting caught, I don't know.

'Still, this little flirtation has cheered you up after the

disappointment of Adam not producing an engagement ring. The idiot,' adds Jess.

I nod but don't trust myself to say anything. I'm in turmoil. My confidence and ego have been on a roller-coaster ride. One minute I'm up, the next I'm down. I don't know how to feel or act, but I do know that when I crash it will be spectacularly messy.

'This might be the wake-up call Adam needs,' says Jess with a sympathetic smile. 'Now he's been reminded that his girl is hot enough to catch the eye of Scottie Taylor, he might just get his arse in gear and pop the question.'

'Do you think there's even the slightest chance?' I ask her.

'What, of Adam popping the question? Yes, I do.' Jess nods confidently.

And only yesterday this is exactly what I wanted to hear. *All* I wanted to hear. I was desperate for even the smallest glimmer of hope that Adam might propose; today everything is different. 'No, not that. Do you think there is the smallest chance of Scott noticing me if I roll out of a rug and fall naked at his feet?' I ask.

'Ha, ha, very funny,' says Jess.

'Deadly serious,' I reply. Suddenly it's clear to me; I'm going to have to move on. Adam doesn't want me. He had his chance and he tossed it away. Did I have a chance with Scott Taylor yesterday, a real chance? Did I toss it away? I hope not, I hate waste.

Jess doesn't say anything more; she just flops back into bed and pulls the duvet over her head.

18. Fern

OK, the rolling naked from carpet thing might be a stretch. What worked for an Egyptian queen thousands of years ago might not do the trick for a twenty-first century, ordinary girl, but this time I do at least take great care with my outfit. I consider buying something new but don't want to waste a morning trailing around the shops, so I plump for a high-waisted grey pencil skirt that I bought in Zara last year but have only had occasion to wear twice, a silky emerald green top with a pussy bow and high, round-toed, petrol blue patent shoes. The combination of spray-on tight skirt and stilt-height shoes means that I can barely walk but I don't care because I know I look as good as it gets. No pain, no gain.

I hop-stroke-hobble on to the tube and set off for Wembley. Jess said I should leave Adam a note, but I wasn't sure what to say. I can't think about it right now, it's all too strange and raw and unsettled. I do know that whatever I have to say should probably be said face to face. I tell myself that I'll find Adam at the stadium and talk to him there, but I have a feeling I might be lying to me. I think I might just go directly to Scott's dressing-room and avoid Adam like the bubonic plague. I don't share this choice piece of info with Jess; I guess I know my intentions are far from honourable. I know that I'm not behaving especially well towards Adam right now; the fairest thing would be to formally finish our relationship before I move on with Scott but I don't have the luxury of time. Scott is a once-in-a-lifetime opportunity and despite the nasty spikes of guilt jabbing my conscience for the entire journey to Wembley, I'm determined not to blow it. It's an odd thing, but *knowing* that I ought to be behaving better and *actually* behaving better don't seem to be at all sequential.

It's easy to find his room today. I still have a pass, and besides which I walk with a new confidence through the labyrinth of corridors. A couple of people catch my eye and nod to me. It's possible they recognize me from last night's gig and think I have a right and a reason to be mooching around the dressing-rooms. I've almost convinced myself of as much.

After just a split second of hesitation I knock on his door and then walk straight in.

He is there. We lock eyes and my heart stops. He grins and it starts again. He's detonated a bomb of sensations. Effervescent shards of excitement, desire, fear and lust ambush me. The muddles of emotions settle, almost painfully, in my head and knickers. I am freshly over-whelmed by his presence.

'Good morning,' he says, with a mock formality.

'Morning,' I mutter, my determination and confidence flooding out of me with every passing moment.

He is sat facing the door, as though expecting me, which is impossible – so expecting someone else maybe? Again, he's dressed casually in jeans and a simple blue T-shirt. He hasn't shaved or combed his hair. His crumpled, just-got-out-of-bed appearance is once more irresistible. His legs are splayed and I can't concentrate. I daren't move closer to him or else I'll be stood between his thighs, like some sort of lap dancer.

'What did you think of the concert?' he asks.

'I was glad we met before I went to it,' I admit truthfully.

'Was it that bad?' he asks with a grin, leaning forward hands on knees now.

I smile back. 'No, not at all. It was . . .' I search for a big enough word but can't think of one. I settle for 'Amazing. That's what I mean. I'd have been too overwhelmed to talk to you the way I did yesterday if I'd had any idea the power you have. You are so big. I knew it but hadn't seen what that meant up close. You're bigger than anything I could ever have imagined.'

'Now, that is no word of a lie. That's not just PR, that's true, that is.' He jokingly grabs his crotch, in case I miss his innuendo.

He's being obvious, just like when he humped the mike on stage last night. I'm not normally a fan of Benny Hill humour but I can't help but wonder if his crass bragging is true. I can't help but hope it is.

'I didn't mean that, exactly,' I say, although in a way I did. The sexual energy he oozes is meshed with the creative performance. I can't pretend I don't find it attractive; me and several million others. 'It was all those girls. I was quite taken aback,' I add.

'What do you mean?'

We haven't taken our eyes off one another since the conversation began. The door behind me is still wide open, which is disconcerting considering the private nature of our exchange. I daren't close it until he invites me to do so.

'The flesh, the bums, the breasts. Just everywhere. Abundantly offered up.'

He laughs. 'What about it?'

'I don't want you to think I'm like those other women in the crowd.' The admission is awkward, mostly because to some extent I am just like them and I know it. I played strip poker with the man, shortly after meeting him for the first time. I wouldn't have done that with anyone else or under any other circumstances, would I? Plus, I'm stood in front of him in my sexiest outfit. I'm wearing stockings for God's sake; I'm not playing what anyone could describe as hard to get.

'So how are you different from those women? You're made of flesh, you have a bum, don't you?' He lets his gaze drop down from my eyes, to my boobs, my legs, and slowly, oh so slowly, he drags his look of longing back up to meet my eyes. My cheeks turn scarlet.

'Yes and boobs but I'm not here to flash them at you.'

'Shame, I'd guarantee you an appreciative audience.'

I can't help it, I smile, but then I bravely get to the heart of what I'm afraid of. 'Yeah, just the once, I imagine you would.'

'That's not what you are after?'

'I have a boyfriend,' I say, pretty much avoiding a direct answer. 'And I've never been into one-night stands, they're pointless; that's why I left in such a hurry yesterday.'

Scott nods. 'So why are you back here?'

'Because you sang to me.'

'I did, didn't I.'

'And so I thought maybe —'

He interrupts. 'That you are different?'

'Yeah.' I stand on the knife edge, blade slicing my feet, waiting to see if I've got this all muddled.

'And so you are, Fern, so you are.' He beckons me. 'Close the door.'

19. Fern

We play cards again; this time we keep our clothes on and stick to matches. Yesterday our conversation was limited to small talk about the hand we held, the room temperature, which flavour crisps we prefer. Yesterday our flirting did not have a time-line. We had flirted in the moment, for the moment, and with no regard or expectations of what, if anything, might come after. Today, we have upped the ante. Our flirtation reaches a new level. It's not quite so glib. It feels a little more individual. It's the sort of flirting that definitely has consequences. Plus we talk without flirting at all, which in my mind is much more of a compliment, especially after watching the show last night. I know he can flirt with anyone, anywhere, any time. Talking is a big deal. He tells me normal stuff. Stuff about himself that demonstrates a confidence in me that fills me with pride and pleasure.

Scott tells me about what he did after the gig last night (he was whisked away on the helicopter and taken to a swanky hotel in West London). 'I fell asleep in the reception,' he says bright-eyed and amazed.

'I'm not surprised, you jumped around for hours on stage.'

'I know, but it's the first time *ever* that I've done a gig and then fallen into such a deep, relaxed slumber. No one could believe it. You see, I don't do relaxed. Saadi, my

PA, commented on it. You'll have to meet her. I'd been on tenterhooks all afternoon. So fucking nervous about the gig. Having not performed live for two years I was all sort of –'

'Scared?'

'Yeah, scared, and then it was all great.'

'That's why you slept so well,' I assure him. 'The slumber of a man who knows he's done a bloody great job.'

'No, it wasn't. I've had great gigs in the past and it's taken me hours to come down from them.'

'Is it because you didn't hit the bars? You mentioned you're clean.'

I resist adding 'at the moment'. I know he casually volunteered this information yesterday but I'm not sure how to handle myself around addicts and don't know what to say for the best. I don't want to say anything that sounds like I assume that he'll fall off the wagon but nor do I want to sound as though I think the job's done. I know enough to understand once an addict, always an addict, and that every day is a struggle. Life's just harder for people born with that gene. The way it's harder if you are born with the gene which gives you a terrible disease or a really ugly face, it's just that the ill and even the slap-arsed ugly get more sympathy than addicts. I don't want to seem like I'm having a go.

'Yeah, that might have helped, but I think it was because of you,' says Scott. The 'you' is dropped like an atom bomb. It mushrooms and eclipses everything that has gone before.

'Me?' I'm stunned.

'Yeah. Come on. You know what I mean. You make me feel happy. Relaxed. Right in my skin. I can't explain it,' he says shyly.

I know exactly what he means. We stare at each other a bit stupidly, unsure what to do or say next. It's almost a relief when there's a knock at the door.

Scott's entourage file in and out of the dressing-room all morning. He introduces me to everyone and I try to hang on to as many names as I can but it's tricky. For a start, it appears there's a uniform of scruffy jeans and black T-shirts and, another thing, I keep thinking, Oh. My. God. I can't believe this. I'm in the same room as Scott Taylor! I'm spending a lot of effort and energy holding in my stomach and trying to touch up my makeup covertly at every given opportunity. This is undoubtedly really immature of me but cut me some slack. Scott Taylor is hitting on me!

Besides Bob, the security guy, several runners, the occasional (carefully escorted) journalist, a photographer and the guys from catering, six or seven band members wander into his room at some point in the day. The band members all wrap Scott in elaborate hugs. Hugs that involve slapping hands, sticking out their tongues and even wiggling their bums. There are waves of affection flowing as everyone is pleased with yesterday's gig and excited about tonight's. I am not on the receiving end of hugs – thank goodness. I'd be freaked out if I was deluged with mwah-mwah air kisses from strangers – but I am treated to a number of grateful and genuine smiles.

There are two male guitarists, one female, a drummer, a pianist and a couple of backing singers. Surprisingly, none of the band members are classically good-looking. There's no sign of chiselled jaws or tight, defined abs, yet every last member is mesmerizing. They ooze commitment to their craft and joy with their lives and as such are totally exhilarating to be around. It's fair to presume they have all endured years of struggling as members of inconsequential bands at tiny gigs, waiting for the big break. Now they are Scott's band they have officially made it. It doesn't get any bigger. They are confident and focused. They glow with satisfaction – so elusive in the streets I normally pound. It's fantastic to be around so many realized dreams. My friends are all struggling, waiting for something great to happen to them or resigned to the fact that it probably never will.

The production manager and two people from wardrobe also visit Scott. They remind him that tonight the concert is being filmed for TV and DVD. The production manager steals a quick glance my way and then says, 'You can't do the "Happy Birthday" thing tonight, Scott. It won't work on DVD.'

Scott stares at his employee for some time and then says, 'It's not Fern's birthday tonight, it was her birthday last night, so there is no danger of me singing "Happy Birthday" to her tonight. That would be silly.'

The production guy looks relieved and slightly miffed at the same time. He realizes that Scott is being vaguely condescending. Nothing mean; he's just flexing his muscles. A shiver of excitement runs up my back as I realize that Scott is flexing his muscles for my benefit. It's just like some kid showing he's the big boy in the playground in order to get the attention of the little girl with plaits; the little girl who doesn't normally join in kiss-chase. Although truthfully, I always joined in kiss-chase; shrinking violet, I ain't. Before I can wallow in the good feeling the production manager throws a bucket of cold ice.

He turns to me and says, 'Adam said hi.' He leaves the dressing-room before I can stammer a response.

Scott catches my eye but sensibly says nothing.

Adam, bloody hell, *Adam*. He *knows* I'm in here. What a nightmare. It's as though the production guy has just thrown a hair shirt on me. I itch with a terrible sensation of panic and unease. I really haven't given Adam any thought since I entered Scott's dressing-room. I'm shocked at myself that I have forgotten him so completely, so quickly; it's as though I'm on another planet, one lit by a dazzling, brilliant star. My old world – the world I shared with Adam – doesn't seem to even be in the same galaxy.

I stare at Scott and silently will him to reassure me. He reads my mind.

'You OK?' he asks.

'I think so,' I mutter.

'I could sack him,' Scott offers, casually.

'Adam?' I'm horrified.

'No, the production guy.' Scott grins at me to show that he's just joking anyway. He then steps forward and wraps me in a big hug. He strokes my hair and his touch is both comforting and wild. I barely understand it. Our bodies throb as one. I am aware of every single muscle, sinew, nerve; his and mine but I don't know where one starts and the other stops. 'I'm sorry for Adam,' he whispers in my ear. 'To have held you like this and then to have let you slip away, how does a man live with a mistake like that?'

Oh. My. God. What is Scott saying? Have I slipped away? I think I have.

The woman with the blonde bob who massaged Scott's shoulders yesterday turns out to be Saadi, his PA. She coughs, taps Scott on the shoulder and tells him that the choreographer needs to run through small changes to the dance routine. With painful reluctance Scott and I break apart. Bereft, we stare at one another until the choreographer practically drags Scott away and Saadi frogmarches me to the other end of the room.

'You OK?' she asks me, clicking her fingers in front of my face.

She has an Australian accent. I always warm to Australians. I think they are all my friends because they are the one nation with a positive cultural stereotype. I like the fact that they are known for their easy-going temperaments and their no-bullshit approach to life. In Britain you can know someone for years before you get the same level of honesty that you can get from an Australian after just two beers. It's not that we Brits are intrinsically mistrustful; it's just we live in fear of saying the wrong thing and therefore prefer not to say anything meaningful at all. The best of us hide behind impeccable manners, the worst of us think like an angry mob and covet ASBOs the way other nations covet Olympic medals.

'Never better,' I reply with a broad, open grin. It's true. I feel like a winner. I have never felt more excited and exciting in my entire life. This blows away when I got short-listed for a Blue Peter drawing competition when I was eleven.

'Have you had sex with him yet?' asks Saadi.

The question startles me; it certainly causes me to focus on her instead of staring dreamily at the door Scott's just walked out through. Even for an Aussie, that question is upfront. She asked it in the same way the nurse who performs smears asks you to open your legs and relax; a clinical probing that seems cold and unnatural.

'No,' I stammer, hating myself for revealing so much. What has it to do with her?

'That's great,' she smiles. 'Do you mind holding off until Sunday?'

'Sunday?' I stutter, unsure why I'm having this conversation with Saadi. Surely this is a negotiation Scott and I should be having – if sex is ever going to be negotiated, that is, and yes, yes, yes I admit it, I hope it is. My body is throbbing for his after that tight hug.

'These gigs are really important to him. To us. To everyone. A lot of money is riding on them. *A lot.* More than you could imagine in your wildest dreams. Just one night of sex can ruin months and months of planning and hard, hard work.'

'Sorry?'

She smiles and pats my hand. Her hand is cool and makes me think of a strict and demanding schoolteacher. 'Look, I don't want to spoil his fun. Or yours, for that matter. It's just sex complicates everything, unnecessarily so.'

This conversation is surreal. 'In what way?'

'Well, think about it. If it is good sex then he stays up

all night and is knackered and then he'll be completely out of sorts the next day.' An image of Scott and me writhing all over one another explodes into my mind. I think I must be grinning because Saadi smiles at me, indulgently. 'Yeah, but a good performance for you means a crap one for the paying punters. Yet, if the worst happens and the sex is rubbish, then he'll be fighting demons the following day. No one needs their ego kicking just before they stand up on stage in order to make ninety thousand people happy, do they?'

'It would be great sex,' I assure her, hotly.

'No doubt,' says Saadi. She doesn't look as though she cares either way. 'I'm just asking for a little co-operation here. A bit of help. You can wait until Sunday, can't you? I wouldn't mention it if it wasn't in Scott's best interests.'

Saadi smiles, briefly, coolly. The conversation is over. In truth she isn't asking for my help; she's telling me how things are going to be. She picks up her plastic cup of coffee and clipboard and swiftly exits the room.

20. Fern

Scott returns but it takes about another twenty minutes before everyone else has left the room. Everyone except Bob, the security guy, that is, but I'm getting used to his constant presence. I can't ignore him the way Scott does – I feel the need to keep making small talk with him – but he's settled into his Sudoku now and it's almost as though Scott and I are alone. I'm still feeling weird about the conversation I've just had with Saadi and can't decide whether to mention it to Scott. If I do, I'm openly acknowledging the fact that everyone else (and therefore us, too) thinks sex is a natural next step. I'm not sure I'm ready for that conversation. I have to finish things with Adam first. Cleanly and properly.

Is it the next natural step? Is that why I am here? To have sex? Will it just be sex? I'm not sure. I'd be mad to hope for more than that and yet the way he looks at me, the way he concentrates when I'm speaking – if it was any other man I'd think there was more. Scott excites me, he delights me and yet he also lulls me and soothes me. It's practically a miracle but he manages to make me feel calm and lovely even when we are talking about my family and my schooling. He listens carefully as I tell him about my sister and brothers; he comments, 'You wish you were all closer, don't you? You have the same dream as your mum. One big happy family.'

I nod. 'Yeah, but I'm realistic now. I know that I have nothing in common with any of my siblings, with the possible exception of Rick. Even then it could be that I credit Rick with more feeling for me than he has because I want his silence to speak volumes. The odd thing is I know that we all love each other even though we don't like each other much. It's enough. It's got to be because it's all there is. What about you?'

'I have one brother. He's an accountant. I'm a rock star. What do you think?'

'I imagine he's screwed up with jealousy.'

'Or disgust,' adds Scott.

'Does he do your accounting?' I ask.

'No, I have a team for that.'

'You should ask him to be part of that team. Or to head it up. He might like to be involved,' I say enthusiastically.

Scott smiles at me the way some dads smile at their little girls; indulgently marvelling at their naivety and wondering why they wasted their money on school fees. My father never smiles at me like that. For one thing I didn't go to a posh fee-paying school and besides, if I do say something he believes to be gauche or ill-considered, he's more likely to mutter, 'You daft mare,' than he is to smile fondly at me.

'It's not realistic. My brother specializes in corporate accounting. I need accountants who specialize in royalty fees etc. Besides, he wouldn't like to work for me and I wouldn't like him to work for me. You can't be friends with people who work for you and while we're not what you call friends now, I live in hope that one day we might be. If he was to work for me that option would be closed down for ever.'

'Maybe we should introduce your brother to my big brother Bill, the trust fund manager, I bet they'd get on,' I say flippantly.

'Yeah, we should throw a dinner party.'

And while I know he's only joking I can't slow down the part of my brain that is visualizing the dinner party where our families meet. We'd be in Scott's apartment. I have no idea what his apartment looks like, how many he has or even where they might be scattered across the globe, but I'm pretty sure his apartment won't be anything like the flat I share with Jess and Adam. My family never visit me at my flat because it's hard to squeeze all the animals of the zoo into a bird cage. I'm certain Scott's apartment wouldn't feel claustrophobic, there'd never be stale milk in the fridge, dirty socks on the floor and the carpet wouldn't be stained with beer spills. There wouldn't be a carpet at all, there would be dark wooden floorboards and clean white walls, there'd be an entire wall of windows and the view would stretch out over all of London. The view from my bedroom window is of the back yard – not even a back yard we are permitted to use, as (illogically) it belongs to the flat upstairs. It's not a loss, as there are often used condoms and empty cans in the back yard, thrown over the brick wall. If I stand on the wash basket in the bathroom and crane my neck to the right, I can see a bit of green; it's someone else's garden. But the last time I did, I fell off the wash basket and banged my foot on the side of the loo. It really hurt. I bet Scott's view of London is of the Houses of Parliament, the Eye and the fabulous bridges criss-crossing the Thames. London at its best, not the depressing, flabby underbelly that is my London.

The families would all sit around an enormous trestle table, we'd eat elaborate, expensive food with difficult-to-pronounce names and even Bill would be impressed. Everyone would get on. We'd laugh all evening. My mum and dad would finally stop worrying about me. I'd be a success. It would be a tremendous moment.

I probably need to think about something else now.

Scott and I listen to music. It's a huge relief and a pleasant surprise that Scott does not ask me what I usually listen to but instead excitedly tells me about his favourite artists. I actively try to like the stuff Scott's introducing me to; I mean he must know a thing or two. Adam used to do the same but I never liked the bands Adam listened to and never tried to change that opinion. Oh God, I'm thinking about Adam in the past tense. It's over but he doesn't know. A brief flicker of shame licks my innards. I suppose I have to call him. But what can I say? He knows I'm here with Scott; he sent a message via the production manager. How pathetic, how typical, he couldn't even be bothered to come in person. He's not interested in fighting for me – just in embarrassing me.

I find it's more comfortable to be indignant than racked with guilt.

Scott and I talk as though we've known each other for ever but haven't seen each other for a very long time. Everything I say seems interesting to him, he seems to want to approve of me, he envelops me in an overwhelming sense of Yes. Yes, I'm funny. Yes, I'm sexy. Yes, I'm interesting. The result is I feel so utterly gorgeous that I physically morph in front of him. I swear I become taller, stronger, leaner. The blemishes on my chin vanish, my cheekbones become more pronounced, my eyebrows curve in just the correct arch and there are no stray hairs jutting out at unfortunate angles. My hair is shining, my smile is radiant and endless, and my brain has never been more alert.

He showers me with stunning compliments in a way that seems casual and yet authentic. Not insincere or creepy. 'You're enthralling,' 'You're remarkable,' 'You're gorgeous.' These compliments are unusual and enormous. They should jar or appear disingenuous but they don't; it feels natural and I don't doubt him for a second. With him, I *am* these amazing things.

Besides music we talk about movies, food, favourite smells, school, chocolate and TV. They're small, everyday subjects but everything seems larger than life as I wrestle to be clearer, more truthful and concise than ever before. I want to find the most true and perfect words, so that I can dignify this magic.

Scott asks, 'Where were you born?'

'Reading.' I pause.

'What?'

'I was wondering if I should pretend that I don't know you were born in Hull, just for conversational form,' I admit.

Scott starts to grin. 'That's the first time anyone has ever admitted to that dilemma. Mostly people think they know me really well and don't ask any of the pleasantries but dive straight in and ask the most intimate questions imaginable.'

'Such as?'

'About sex mostly. They ask me if I've ever blar blar blar and if not why not? Do I want to? For blar, blar, blar you can use your imagination. I've been asked about every weird sexual perversion you could possibly think of, largely by total strangers.'

'Right,' I nod, embarrassed for Scott, myself and the unimaginative idiots who have intruded on his privacy in the past. After a brief pause I ask, 'Did you walk to school, ride your bike, take a bus, or get a lift? Which?'

It seems a banal question but actually I think it tells you quite a lot about the person you are talking to. Nowadays, all kids seem to be driven to school as part of their parents' inexplicable quest to contribute to child obesity, but when we were kids most people walked. You only got a lift if you were posh and went to a private school miles away. You caught the school bus if you lived in the sticks and you rode your bike if you were cool.

Scott grins at me. 'I rode my chopper. You?'

'Blue Raleigh,' I beam back, knowing he understands the transport code. 'I went to a state school about five minutes up the road from where I lived and received just the sort of education you would expect if you only travel five minutes to get it.'

'Were you a good girl?' He can't resist a cheeky grin.

'According to my school reports I was the very worst sort of pupil. All the teachers believed that I was bright and just not giving my studies my all. *Could try harder* was as good as tattooed across my forehead.'

Scott nods. 'I had that same experience. Every new school year began in exactly the same way. Teachers were initially enthusiastic and smiley with me. They were hopeful, perhaps even determined, to be the one that would make a difference, to unlock and unleash all that I'd kept carefully hidden from other staff members. But, towards the end of the academic year, I was invariably greeted with frustrated sighs and weary shrugs from those previously keen members of staff.'

'A result of one too many missed assignments or rushed pieces of coursework, completed during registration on the day it was due to be handed in?' I offer helpfully. It's clear we had the same experience.

'I just didn't want to be there,' says Scott simply. 'We only did music for one hour a week and then only until we were about fourteen. I didn't go to the sort of school where prodigies were discovered and tutored. We didn't have a music department as such. Certainly not an orchestra. Prodigies were more like clipped round the ear and told to sit down, shut up.' He's laughing but I sense bitterness. Maybe not for himself. He's made good. He's made excellent. But how many more kids are overlooked just because they don't or can't flourish under similar regimes?

'They had me all wrong at my school too,' I acknowledge. 'I was not a bright pupil unwilling to try, I was pretty average and doing all I could to keep my head above water. I'd somehow managed to create the impression that I was hiding some sort of light under a bushel because I was generally smiley and polite and most teenagers simply aren't. Plus I had a curious but extended general knowledge about flowers.'

'Flowers?'

'They're my thing. I'm a florist. A passionate interest in anything, especially something a little unusual, tends to create an illusion of deeper intelligence. Often wrongly. Really people should have seen me for what I was – a flower geek.'

'Tell me about being a florist.' Scott sits on the edge of the purple suede chaise longue and he looks riveted. His interest is very flattering.

'Well, like I said, I'm the fourth one down out of five kids, so my parents were pretty worn out with the whole parenting thing by the time they got to me and they happily agreed to let me leave school at sixteen so as I could go to the local technical college to study floristry. It's a two-year course –'

'No, no, not all the getting qualification stuff. Tell me why flowers?' insists Scott.

So I tell him that being in the garden with my gran, picking flowers, was the nearest I've ever felt to perfect peace. I explain how flowers mystify, exhilarate and thrill me. I explain that I believe the scent of flowers somehow flows through my veins, as much my lifeline as blood. I use that exact expression and I'm not embarrassed or ashamed. This man is a creative genius. If anyone is ever going to get it – get me – then he will.

'What's your favourite flower?' he asks.

'Pink peonies,' I say without hesitation. 'Flowers heal. They are important. They are so much more than a cheerful, colourful pressie. Flowers are there when we are born and all the way through until we die. They offer comfort and assurance. Plus they articulate stuff most people just can't manage. People need flowers to say sorry, and thank you, and cheer up, and I love you, and all the difficult things we inadequate humans can't bring ourselves to say.'

'In that way flowers are just like songs,' says Scott, proving he understands completely.

'Just like songs,' I beam at him.

21. Scott

I've been to rehab twice. It's no picnic. Do not believe it if you read in the press that rehab is some sort of day spa for the rich and gormless. Rehab is full of people who've fucked up and that alone is enough to make me want to run a mile in the opposite direction.

I have an addictive personality. It took lots of eminent doctors (each with a string of letters after their name) a long time to come up with that. They could've just asked my mum. People with my condition find it difficult to relax, bore easily, rarely have successful relationships and they toe tap.

Keeping on the move, filling my day, just doing stuff was seen as a good thing when I was a kid. Uncles would pat me on the head and give me fifty pence, tell me I was keen and dedicated when I ran around the football pitch more than the other boys and practised harder at keepy-uppies. I was that fanatical about my training that people used to ask me whether I wanted to be a football player. Maybe. I didn't know for sure. What I did know is I didn't want to be still. Because still people aren't successful. The best a still person can hope for, the pinnacle of their career, is to end up in the middle of Covent Garden, painted bronze, pretending to be Rodin's 'Thinker'. A hat full of loose change at his feet for making like he's a statue; what's that about? How can that be a good way to use the life your mama gave you?

I find doing something over and over again makes me feel good, deep, deep in my soul. It makes me feel useful and purposeful. Am I the only one who has noticed that we are just one breath away from admitting that it's all futile? Everything. The busier I am, the less chance there is of that thought swallowing me up. Doing something over and over again is soothing. Some of my addictions, most actually, are harmless. No one minded when I became addicted to the game Uno or Ludo or even Four-in-a-Row. Clink yellow counter slips into place, two in a line. Clink red counter blocks. Clink yellow counter going for the diagonal now. Clink red falls. Clink yellow dropped so quickly it might not be noticed. Clink red thrown in randomly. Clink yellow four in a row and then *crash*. It was that crash I relished; the sound of releasing all the counters to start a fresh game. I still love to hear a game of Four-in-a-Row in play, it's so relaxing. No one cared much when I became addicted to records; as long as I bought them myself and I didn't steal to pay for them, I could have as many as I wanted. My addiction to learning the guitar was actively encouraged. But then it started to go screwy.

In my adult life I've been addicted to fags, wanking, running, alcohol, food, sex, drugs, work, fame, tattoos, coffee, playing dominoes, playing cards and playing the fool. This is not a definitive list. More off the top of my head. And, to be clear, the addictions aren't mutually exclusive, some run in parallel.

Problem is, while they say the devil makes work for

idle hands (and that might be true) it is my experience that busy hands are often doing the work of the devil too, to sort of save him the bother, like. From the list above it is apparent that most of my adult addictions have been bad for me. Moderation is championed by all who love me – which makes me think no one knows me at all. The funny thing about being an addict is that everyone feels sorry for you until you are obscenely rich and able to feed freely your habit; then they want you to get over yourself. I *can't do* moderation. So, what I have to do is get addicted to safe substances. Chocolate is not that. If I'm jowly I'm as good as dead. Fern is safe. No one can have a problem with a man obsessing about a girl. It's what makes the world go round.

In many ways I wish I hadn't ever found drugs, of course I do, I'm not insane. I prefer waking up in the morning and having a clear memory of the night before. I prefer waking up in the morning and finding that my clear memory of the night before doesn't paralyse me with shame and regret. Indeed, I simply prefer waking up in the morning. Taking drugs reduces my chances of any of these three things happening.

But, if you ask anyone who's ever been in love whether it is better to have loved and lost than never to have loved at all? They will confirm yes it is, even if they've been left with a big gaping hole where their shattered heart once beat. If they don't agree, I'd say they weren't really in love, probably in lust, more like. Drugs are the same; just as many people feel about a worthless lover, I can't help but regret that I'm going to have to spend the rest of my life without them. Everyone assumes drugs are always to do with escapism but they weren't, not in my case. I'm loved on the planet, truly adored. What would I want to escape from? Drugs and drink were a celebration, at least at first. The drugs and drink made things more vivid – me more vivid, at least for a while. They accelerated and accentuated my feelings of ecstatic giddiness, until they stopped doing that. You see, drugs are a lot like love.

Music is the same. Music makes things *more*. More meaningful, more true, more important. The difference is music doesn't stop. There is no come down.

But should I tell you the hardest substance to kick, the addiction that crawls through my body, pumped by my own heart into my bloodstream, to rule every fibre of my being? Success. Success is addictive. And relentless. And fruitless. And I'm hooked.

22. Fern

I had no idea that such total happiness was available to me.

Scott and I have spent all day together. On Friday I met the man and watched the myth perform at the gig. Now, having spent all day with him, I realize that the two are intrinsically linked. The bloke, who snacks on jelly beans and occasionally scratches his balls when he thinks no one is looking, is just as amazing to me as the man who entertains millions.

I'm attracted to his quick mind and quick tongue, his hard-man northern roots, his just-submerged vulnerability, his excessive power and his excessive personality. He is droll, magnetic, poised, unexpected. I glitter in his company. The whole experience is surreal. A dreamy, singular, shiny, irresponsible occasion.

It's fun.

Scott and I reluctantly say goodbye to each other at about 6 p.m. when I slip off to meet Ben and Jess. Lisa has gracefully bowed out of tonight's gig. She said the excitement of last night was enough to last her a year. Jess, known more for her opportunism than her graceful behaviour, simply assumed I'd be giving her one of the tickets again tonight. That suited me fine, as it meant she was able to meet Ben and hand over the spare ticket. Plus, Jess is bringing me a warm top and trainers to change into. The sexy siren outfit, while perfect for a day of seduction, isn't going to be much help tonight when the temperatures drop, and I can't imagine tramping back to the tube station in these heels.

Ben is delighted with the idea of free tickets for a Scottie Taylor gig; not because he's a particular fan but because he says all the dancers and half the audience will be gay, rich pickings.

'We're sitting *here*? Darling, your man is a genius,' Ben says. 'I hate rubbing shoulders with the great unwashed.' It takes me a moment to understand that by 'My man', Ben means Adam. It's not how I think of Adam any more. Like yesterday, the seats Adam has secured tonight are only metres away from the stage. In fact, they are so good even Scott said he couldn't swap them for anything better. I wish I could feel grateful. 'You must have been utterly thrilled when Adam gave you these tickets for your birthday,' gushes Ben.

'He didn't actually pay for them,' I point out, a little unnecessarily.

'Yes, but even so, it's great fun, isn't it?' he insists. 'You must be so proud of him getting this job. What's his title again? Stage manager?'

'He's *assistant* stage manager,' I mutter.

Ben tries to catch my eye and I try to avoid his. As the support band starts up he asks, 'Everything OK, darling?'

I beam at him, 'Never better.'

'Well, I thought that was the case when I first set eyes on you. You look radiant, Fern, I thought Adam had finally popped the question, as you'd stipulated, er . . . I mean, hoped. But the moment I mentioned his name your face turned to thunder, so I assume that's not the case.'

'You assume correctly.'

'Yet something has put a smile on her face,' chips in Jess. She pauses. 'Or someone.'

Ben raises his eyebrows theatrically. 'Come on darling, spill. What are you hiding from me? I know there's a story. What's the mystery?' he teases. Ben can't bear not to be in the know.

'She's the mystery,' says Jess, rolling her eyes. 'She's the mystery girl that Scottie Taylor sang to last night.'

'The one who's in all the papers?' Ben practically leaps out of his seat and on to my lap in an effort to get close. 'The one he called "really lovely"?' I grin and nod. 'Hell, how exciting!'

'It is, isn't it,' I agree, beaming broadly at Ben.

'Unless of course you're Adam,' says Jess, throwing cold water.

'Why should Adam care? It's not as though this is anything more than a fabulous bit of fun. Scottie Taylor isn't likely to whisk Fern away, is he? And it isn't as though Fern would even want that, is it?' asks Ben.

My beam falters slightly. I choose not to answer the question but rather to interpret it as rhetorical. Ben and I have worked side by side for over four years now and we know each other inside out. Working in a flower shop often leads to long discussions on many of the more profound aspects of life; it's not all 'Do you like the yellow ribbon or the gold on these sunflowers?' I know Ben's views on the afterlife, the holy sanctity of marriage, and

I know his pet hate is losing half a digestive in his cup of tea, mid-dunk. He refuses to simply fish out the offending biscuit and carry on drinking – disgusted by the certainty of finding a sludgy mess of biscuit when he finally drains the cup. Instead, he insists on making an entirely fresh brew. That's not deep, it's just an example of how well we know each other. He takes one look at me and knows.

'Oh darling, you haven't fallen for Scottie Taylor, have you? You're not taking this seriously?'

'We have a connection,' I say carefully.

'She's talking of leaving Adam,' chips in Jess. I can tell she doesn't approve.

Ben continues, 'My sweet girl, you have to remember Scottie Taylor is a practised seducer. Of course it's flattering but –'

'I think it's more than that,' I say tentatively. My friends look sceptical. I know it's hard to believe, I'm struggling with it too. I mean why should I be attractive to Scott Taylor?

My eyes scan the tens of thousands of glowing faces. It's pretty much as it was last night; an abundance of excited girls and women, a scattering of indulgent, patient boyfriends and a raw smell of desire.

'Look over there,' laughs Jess. At first I think she's changing the subject but then I see she's just making a point. I follow her finger over the mass of pink cowboy hats and skimpy vest tops adorning expectant, fully made-up beauties and find a washing line of identical pink knickers. There's a large letter sewn on to each. It spells out, SCOTTIE. MARRY ME. A dozen women are holding the line of knickers above their heads and from time to time they hoist it a bit higher and chant 'Scot-tie, Scot-tie'.

'I wonder which one wants to marry him?' muses Ben.

'They all do,' I sigh.

Scott bounces on to the stage; the cheer is breath-stealing. The moment I see him my heart leaps into my mouth and then, through some anatomical ambiguity, it leaps into my knickers too. While it's exactly the same run of songs as it was last night, I feel totally overwhelmed and surprised by the show all over again.

'He's a marvel,' says Ben in awe. 'I had no idea I could ever be this entertained by a straight guy.'

I nod with a level of enthusiasm I thought I was saving until someone complimented me on the intelligence of my firstborn. My cheeks are aching from grinning. Pride swills through my body, carousing with excitement and a sense of privilege. I *know* that man. I've spent the last two days with him. I am different from every other woman in this stadium. Me. Me. Who'd have thought it? Fern Dickson is different.

And I do feel different.

'I'm living the dream,' Scott yells from the stage. And for a brief moment, I am living it along with him.

Countless girls are on their boyfriends' shoulders. The guys can manage the burden because they know their girls are as horny as hell and they are going to get rewarded with the best sex ever tonight. Who the hell cares if it is displacement sex as long as it's good displacement sex?

While Ben is distracted by the gig and the cute blond guy sat next to him, Jess grills me.

'So where've you been all day?' she asks.

'With him.' I point over the heads of ninety thousand and towards the stage.

'Have you shagged him yet?' she asks.

'No.' I want to sound outraged. Me? Shag a man when I (technically) have a boyfriend? Unfortunately, I think I just sound regretful.

'Why not?' asks Jess.

'No opportunity,' I admit with more honesty than I'd been intending.

Jess raises her eyebrow. 'So nothing to do with the fact that it would break Adam's heart then?' she asks wryly.

I turn to my best pal. I've known Jess for years. I've never lied to her. I'm not going to start doing so now, I don't even want to. I want to tell her the tremendous truth.

'I think I'm in love with Scott,' I gush.

'You daft cow.' She splutters her beer down the back of the girl in front. The girl doesn't seem to notice, as she's so engrossed in the lyrics of 'Hate to Love You'.

'No, seriously, I am.' I'm a bit frustrated that she's laughing so much beer is coming out of her nose now.

'You and everyone else, sister. Take a look around you.'

'But I'm different from them,' I insist.

'Not to him,' she says calmly.

'I am. I know him. He talks to me.'

'Of course it's attractive,' she says more patiently. 'He's a rock star. He's oozing success and power.'

'That alone I could have walked away from. He's more than that. Much more than that to me.'

'And Adam?'

Right now, Adam's name is not synonymous with success and power. Or happiness. Or even sexual attraction. All I can say to Jess is, 'He's hanging on by a thread called loyalty.'

'You need to talk to Adam. You need to tell him how you feel.'

'Or more accurately how I no longer feel.'

'Be careful, Fern,' says Jess. 'Don't throw away a good man for a fantasy.'

'I keep telling you, Jess, what we have feels very real. I know it's hard to digest and accept but I'm sure he likes me.'

Jess turns back to the stage, just as Scott picks out a young girl from the audience and pulls her on to the stage. He folds her in his arms and I watch as the skinny brunette melts. The crowd goes wild as he sings the romantic lyrics, 'Come Back to Me', to this fortunate. Every one of the ninety thousand hates and envies the girl he's picked out but they love him all the more for making her dream come true. It's clear from her closed-eyed look of absolute contentment that the girl in Scott's arms is entirely unaware of anyone other than him. Jess watches me. I shrug.

'It's part of the act. He did the same thing last night,' I point out.

'It's all an act with him,' says Jess. 'It's not even his fault. It has to be like that.'

The girl he's singing to touches his bum – cheeky bint. I swallow hard as I know, from the gig last night, the next thing he does is kiss the girl – a full-on lipsmacker.

Yesterday, I'd watched with curiosity, I'd shared the heightening sexual tension that sluiced the stadium; today something in my stomach contracts with anxiety. I wonder how old the girl is? Young. Early twenties. A lot younger than me.

Scott quickly kisses the girl on the forehead and then releases her. I swear his eyes flick in my direction. I might be mistaken; the gesture was too brief for me to be certain, but . . . I stare at Jess to see if she's also spotted the change in his gig routine and whether she's drawn the same conclusions as me.

She gawks back at me, open-mouthed. 'Bloody hell,' she mutters, shaking her head with disbelief. 'I think you might be right. He *might* like you. I don't know if that's good or bad news.'

'Don't be an arse, Jess. If he likes me, how can it be anything other than good news?' I reply. I'm getting more than a little fed up with her gallons of cold water. I'd expect Lisa to preach caution and care but I thought I'd have one hundred per cent support from Jess. Jess does reckless and romantic. What's going on? Why isn't she being more supportive? We don't say much else to one another but watch the rest of the concert in silence.

Between the songs he tells the audience he loves us all. His voice sends shivers throughout the stadium; women close their eyes and let his horny, husky melodies wash over them. He's able to change his mood with every song. He's pensive, sorrowful, cheeky, noisy and rude by turn. He's an actor, with an elastic face and dozens of poses. Are any of them for real? Jess obviously doubts it and I don't know for sure. But right at this moment, I don't know and I don't care. Not knowing or caring scares and thrills me. I want to believe in him. I stare at his thirty-foot image played out on monitors by the side of the stage. I lift up my hand as though I can touch the deep creases around his mouth, evidence that he's yelled too hard, laughed too hard, drunk too hard. He looks lived in, and frankly what better place to dwell? I feel a bit foolish when Jess catches my eye and I turn the gesture into a general wave of arms as though I'm swaying along to the tunes, but I don't think she's convinced because she raises her eyebrows again and sighs dramatically.

He completes his set and then he returns to sing his encore. He fulfils his contractual obligations and sings 'Stamp on Your Demons' as agreed with the TV and DVD producers. He runs back on to the stage one more time and he jumps into the air and punches it. The ripples are, no doubt, felt in Scotland. The crowd go wild. Screaming and crying and begging for more, more. Scott gazes around the auditorium; he's a satisfied man. He'll sleep well tonight, I'm sure of it. There seems to be no sign of the crowd ever relaxing their screams of adoration until –

'I've had a perfect day,' he growls in a sexy, deliberately not-quite-singing voice. 'I'm glad I spent it with you.' Then he sings Lou Reed's full version of 'Perfect Day'.

This time there's no mistaking it. Scott is looking directly at me. His liquid green eyes glisten, sparking up a fire in my stomach that I am incapable of dousing.

Incapable and unwilling.

23. Fern

I don't have to walk back to the station, after all. When the gig finishes Saadi, Scott's PA, appears from nowhere and informs me there's a car to take me and my friends home. Before I even get a chance to squeal with excitement she adds, 'The same car will pick you up at ten a.m. tomorrow, OK?'

'OK,' I nod, not quite understanding what I'm agreeing to but happy to go along.

'It was a sublime gig, don't you think?' Saadi asks.

'Yes.' I beam, and hope she understands the depth of my delight as I seem incapable of actually saying much, not something I'm often charged with.

'You appear to be good for his music,' she says, drily.

She stares at me for a moment, clearly questioning how this can possibly be the case. She obviously regards me as part of the great unwashed and must be intrigued to discover the source of the magic between Scott and me. Then she shrugs and grins, a busy woman – she doesn't have too long to ponder. I think she's decided that she doesn't much care what the source of the magic is, as long as it keeps flowing.

'Tell Scott goodnight from me,' I garble.

She nods. 'Get a good night's sleep yourself.'

No chance.

My mind has never been so intoxicated. It's not just

the effects of the champagne that Ben, Jess and I find in the car, it's the whole adventure that's making me drunk. I'm drunk on the smell of the leather seats in the Merc, which swiftly cuts through the crowds and takes us home. I'm high on the memory of the sound of the ninety thousand voices crying out 'Scot-tie, Scot-tie' and his low, soulful voice singing to *me*, telling me I gave him a perfect day. My sense is smashed and splintered as I think back over today's conversations. I'm inebriated at the thought of his eyes that flash with the promise of something totally, irresistibly, irreversibly extraordinary. Nothing can affect my mood; not Ben's insensible, animated, garbling nor Jess's sulky silence. I'm separate from them. I'm cocooned.

When Adam gets home I'm sat in front of the TV, carelessly hopping from one channel to the next, not expecting to find anything that will hold my attention. How can anything on TV, or in my flat, or in my normal life hold my attention after a day like today? I've changed out of my stockings, pencil skirt and silky top, as I knew the sight of me in such a sexy get-up would certainly lead to a row. Sad really. Once upon a time the sight of me in such a sexy get-up was sure to lead to sex. But Adam is no fool; he'd know I didn't wear that outfit this morning for his benefit. Jess drank the best part of a bottle of champagne (through a straw) on the journey home and so staggered to bed the moment we stepped through the door of the flat. I stayed up to face the music.

But not to dance.

All day my stomach has been full of delighted trembling butterflies, but when I set eyes on Adam, I feel their tiny wings beat a final time and then die. Adam looks weary. Worse than yesterday. He's in pain. I hadn't expected that. I don't know what I had expected, but not that.

'Where've you been all day?' he asks. The moment he opens his mouth I'm hit by evidence of serious boozing. It must be very serious for me to notice, as I've had my ample share tonight. Adam's breath smells of whisky – such a depressing drink – and his speech is slurred. 'Where've you been all day?' he asks again, unsure whether I understood him the first time.

He knows the answer and I know he knows. I wonder if he wants me to lie so that we can limp on, ignore this thing with Scott and hope it will go away. Or does he want me to tell him the truth so that he can scream abuse at me and give our relationship a decent funeral.

'With Scott.'

'What, talking?' he sneers cruelly, jumping to the conclusion that the last thing anyone would do with Scottie Taylor is talk.

'Yes, actually, just talking.'

'And you expect me to believe that?' A tiny dot of Adam's spittle escapes because he's in too much of a fury to control it. It lands on my cheek and I have to force myself not to rub it away. The gesture would be horribly inflammatory and Adam is itching for a fight. I'm not so keen. I've never seen him this nasty and furious. He's normally a jolly drunk. He's normally a jolly everything. It's bizarre that the thought of his spittle on my cheek is distressing me. His bodily fluids repulse me. When did that happen? Overnight? Two days ago I wanted this man to ask me to marry him. I wanted his babies. That would have involved swapping more than spittle. Today, I can barely stand the fact that he's in the same room as I am.

I'm bored with him. I'm bored by the fact that this display of anger is the first real emotion I've witnessed in Adam in months. He's failed spectacularly to be charming, passionate, interested or interesting for quite some time now but, all at once, he's found his fire. I'm not impressed by this macho display. I can't help but think his fever is nothing to do with our relationship, it's not about Adam and me – it's about Adam and his ego. He didn't want me until someone else showed an interest. He's especially irritated that the 'someone else' happens to be his boss, happens to be a rock legend.

If Adam had truly wanted me he had plenty of opportunities to demonstrate it. He could have surprised me occasionally by running me a bath after a hard day in the shop or running the hoover over the carpets in the flat; it's not like we live in a mansion, it wouldn't take much. He might have noticed when I bought a new outfit or had my hair cut. Is there anything more depressing than spending ages trying to look pretty for someone, only to discover he hasn't even noticed? It's humiliating that I'm often forced to ask pathetically, 'How do I look?' especially as I only ever receive a disappointing. 'Fine' – delivered without him taking his eyes away from the TV. If he'd wanted me he could have shown me by taking me somewhere more interesting than the local pub – just once in a while. He could have helped paint the flat instead of leaving it to Jess and me. Hell, if he'd wanted me for real, we'd have our own flat.

He would have asked me to marry him.

The thought cuts through me, a blade of pure, un-diluted distress. I gasp for breath but it's hard to breathe, I'm choking on the stagnant stench of a dying relationship. It smells like an overflowing cesspit.

'And you expect me to believe that all you did was talk?' Adam demands.

'You can believe what you like, Adam.' I hope my tone communicates that I no longer care what he believes.

'Have you fucked him?'

The nasty word sounds as mean as it ever can. Adam's face snarls with impotence and fury. I almost wish I could say yes. It's what he expects. It's what I want. And, by saying no, I'll give Adam a glimmer of entirely false hope. But I haven't fucked Scott.

'No.'

'Liar.' More spittle. His face creases with disbelief; he's purple and unrecognizable. Normally serene, Adam has transformed from unassuming Dr Jekyll to a sinister Mr Hyde. 'You've been hanging around his room all day like some cheap groupie. He sent you home in his car. I understand he's sending another car to pick you up tomorrow, of course you're fucking him.'

Clearly the tom-tom drums have been beating among the crew. I suppose this gossip is too good to simply consume, it's the sort of gossip that has to be chewed and regurgitated.

Adam's unoriginal accusations are no doubt deserved. It's an assumption most would make, plus I've treated him quite badly in the past day or so, but at the moment I am more sober than he is so I have the opportunity to scramble up to the high ground. I like it there. Everyone does and I'm not keen to give it up. Adam ignored my ultimatum. He did not take me seriously. I have not so much as kissed Scott. On paper – I'm squeaky clean. There's only one way I can keep it like that.

'It's over, Adam. We're finished.'

'Don't be so fucking stupid, Fern. You don't mean that,' says Adam irritably. I stay silent, indicating that I do. After a pause Adam adds, 'You can't think you have a future with Scottie Taylor.' Now he sounds incredulous.

'Maybe I do, maybe I don't. The point is, Adam, you made it clear that I don't have a future with you.' I'm battling to stay calm, so it's distressing that a fat tear rolls down my cheek; I wipe it away impatiently. I'm doing the chucking, why am I crying? I shouldn't be crying. 'I told you what I wanted,' I add.

'Back to the fucking engagement ring!' Adam slams his hand against the wall. Up until the last day or so he wasn't one for swearing or violence, now he's like a pot of spitting oil that's going to boil over and scald everything it touches; I don't want to be around when that happens. 'You stupid, stupid woman, don't you see he'll let you down?' yells Adam. With each word he slams his fist against the wall; again and again. It must hurt.

'That's none of your business any more, is it?' I say coolly. 'I'm going to bed. Tomorrow we can talk about who is going to move out.'

'Oh, you don't need to worry about me,' he says in a sneering voice. He's no longer hitting the wall but he won't look at me. 'I'm sorted. You're not the only one who is full of surprises.'

I don't quite get what he means but then he probably doesn't mean anything, it's just blustering drunken bravado. I suppose as I've finished the relationship I'll have to move out, or at least offer to. But I really think Adam should go and leave Jess and me to it. He's just had a promotion, he can afford something else and, after all, Jess was my friend first. Suddenly my head aches as the realities of this split hurtle towards me. Who goes? Who stays? Who gets to keep the stuff we own? Who gets to keep the friends we've made? It's going to be a mess.

I grab the spare duvet from the top of the wardrobe and throw it at Adam, indicating that he's on the couch. I close the door and undress in silence. Then I lie on the bed, which suddenly seems vast, and I breathe a deep sigh. It's a sigh of relief. There, it's done. It's over. We're finished. The relief is faintly tinged with panic. What next? Can Scott be my next? I think so but I seem to be the only one who does. But I breathe deeply, then I start to allow the wonderful happenings of the day swirl back into my head. I replay our conversations, I recall his grins and I remind myself that he sang 'Perfect Day' to me. Slowly, the butterflies gently flap their wings in my stomach once again.

24. Fern

I wake up feeling slightly queasy. I can't work out if it's the effects of the champagne I consumed last night or the anticipation of seeing Scott again. I dismiss the idea that it might be guilt or regret that yesterday I finished my relationship with Adam. I shower and dress in virtual silence; I don't want to wake Jess or Adam – I can't face either of them. I know I promised Adam that we'd talk in the morning but now the morning is here I don't think I have anything else to say to him. I just want to get out of the flat and as far away as possible without another draining encounter. As I pick up my mobile I'm delighted to find a text in my inbox to tell me that the car is outside.

I spot the Merc with tinted windows that dropped me at home yesterday and fling myself into the car with the same relief as a robber diving into a getaway car after a heist.

'Morning, gorgeous.'

His flat northern tones, truly music to my ears, cause me to jump a foot into the sky.

'Jesus, you scared me. I didn't expect you –'

He cuts me short by leaning over and kissing me firmly on the lips. It's a good kiss. Fabulous actually, as you'd expect. He's practised more than most. The kiss is lingering but still. It is a warm kiss that is full of purpose and implication. His lips are firm and tender. Smooth, warm, clear. We fit. We both keep our eyes wide open to see what effect we have on one another. It's devastating. Our first kiss.

'I didn't expect you,' I mutter when we finally – achingly – pull apart.

'You should have seen me coming, baby,' he says, quietly.

'Yes, I should have.'

'I'm right on time.' He moves some hair from out of my eyes and tucks it behind my ear. It's a gesture which seems more caring and intimate than some of the sex I've had in the past.

'I think you are,' I murmur.

I also think we are talking about more than one sort of pick-up. I should have seen him coming; well, if not sex god, music icon Scottie Taylor exactly, then at least I should have seen the fact that someone was going to snatch me from the jaws of the routine romance I was having with Adam. And Scott is in the nick of time. If he hadn't come along when he did I'd still be relentlessly pursuing a proposal from Adam; a proposal Adam clearly doesn't want to offer up. How could I have thought that route would lead to anything other than heartache?

But where is this thing with Scott leading?

I didn't sleep well last night, I wrestled with my conscience, heart and the facts, in an attempt to understand where I'll be dropped after this whirlwind passes through town. I wasn't kidding when I told Jess that I think I am falling in love with Scott. Of course I bloody am; I'm only human. But what about him? What does he feel and where does he think this is going? A quick dash around the duck-down duvet? Or more? I have no idea if I can realistically expect this to go anywhere at all but I do know that I am absolutely powerless to resist the momentum. I am not vain, naive or even just plain dumb enough to count on the idea that Scott might feel the same about me as I feel about him and yet . . . I can't help but harbour the smallest hope that he might feel something out of the ordinary. All this that I'm feeling can't be one way. It's too profound. I need to go where the flow takes me. I only hope it flows into an enormous ocean of possibility and not down some filthy sewer of disappointment.

'I want to see your flower shop,' says Scott, interrupting my ever-decreasing circles of reason. I don't mind, my reason crumbles into longing far too easily anyhow. I'm happy to be distracted.

'It's closed on a Sunday. It won't look as lovely as it usually does,' I warn him.

'But it will be private,' he grins.

The word private has exactly the same effect on me as if he were inching down my knickers with his teeth.

During the week Ben's B&B is one of the most beautiful flower shops in London. I know there's a serious possibility I'm biased but I think I can safely claim as much. It's quite small, situated on the corner of a short string of shops, but you can normally spot it at a distance because of the large, over-hanging, stripy orange and pink canvas. This offers year-round shade and shelter to the buckets of various blooms that spill out of the shop and on to the street. It's a riot of colour. Today it will look less impressive. The canvas will be tied back and the empty aluminium buckets will be stacked inside the shop. Rather than vibrancy and cheer I'm expecting tumbleweed. But, as Scott pointed out, it's somewhere private we can go. Obviously I can't invite him back to my flat, for a chat or a coffee (read – damn good seeing to – all I can think of since his lips touched mine). I understand his place is surrounded by press twenty-four-seven, and so that's out of the question. We're never alone at the stadium and if we did just want to chat and drink coffee and we nipped to the local coffee shop we'd be mobbed by every woman and girl in the neighbourhood. My florist, even if likely to be bare and damp on a Sunday, is our best option.

The shop keys are on the same ring as the keys to my flat. I dig them out of my bag and dangle them in front of Scott. He treats me to another wide, sexy grin.

'Let's go.'

It takes about a minute to get to the shop, as it's just around the corner from my home.

'Bloody hell, look, the canopy is down. That Saturday girl is hopeless. She should have tied that back last night. If it had rained heavily it might have been damaged,' I grumble. 'Ben left her to lock up as he was rushing to your gig.' As the car starts to slow I take another glance. 'The buckets – the flowers –'

I don't understand. The shop must be open. The buckets are all over the pavement as usual. Although, not as usual. It's Sunday. Plus there are more buckets than normal and instead of them being full of various blooms – roses, tulips, chrysanthemums – there are only peonies. Big, fat pink peonies. My very favourite flower, as I told Scott only yesterday. Peonies range from red to white or yellow but I love the pale pink peony that reminds me of a ballerina's classic tutu. They have compound, deeply lobed leaves, long stems and large, fragrant flowers. They are beautiful.

Not quite understanding what's going on, I clamber out of the car. I turn to Scott; he's grinning like a cat that's just eaten a canary. He dangles another set of keys back at me; I immediately recognize the glittery heart-shaped key-ring as Ben's.

Scott opens the door and we squeeze into the shop. B&B is a small establishment, and today space is at a particular premium as the store is rammed with bucket, after bucket, after vase, after vase, of stunning peonies. I gasp and am bathed in their particular perfume, heady, excessive, tantalizing. I have been plunged into my very own paradise, my very own Garden of Eden. The dank sweetness seduces me.

'Did you arrange all of this?' I turn around and around, bewildered but trying to make sense of the excess and beauty.

'Ben was a fantastic help,' says Scott with a modest shrug.

'But, how? I didn't know you even knew Ben.'

'There's always a way. I had the idea and I arranged it via my driver last night. After he'd dropped off you and your mate at your place he got me on the phone and I talked to Ben. He was really gracious,' says Scott with a shy and self-effacing smile. 'I explained to him that I couldn't send a florist a mere bunch of flowers and yet how could I possibly court a florist if I didn't acknowledge flowers. He understood my dilemma.'

And fell for his charm, clearly. 'Court' – what sort of word is that for any self-respecting rock star to use? A cleverly chosen one, that's what it is. The perfect word to woo Ben, a lonely pseudo-cynic who is secretly harbouring a deep longing for someone to prove romance is not dead. I stare at Scott with genuine admiration. He's a bright man, there's no doubt – a force to be reckoned with. Someone who knows what he wants and how to get it. In my book, there's nothing sexier.

Enough chat.

I beam at Scott and then hurl myself at him. The relief. I leap into his strong arms and wrap my legs around his waist. He clasps hold of my bum and hoists me high and close. He slams me against the counter near the till, almost upsetting a vase as he urgently and repeatedly kisses me. I kiss back, just as hungrily. My hands discover his body, it's hard and solid and totally man. There is no shyness or false modesty. We cling to one another, cleave as though we share a life source. He perches me on the counter and inches me out of my light jacket. The cool, damp air of the shop caresses me. The jacket drops to the floor, in a heap, I don't care that I spent an age ironing it this morning. I only did it to impress him and by the way he's eating my face, I'd say job done.

I hurriedly flick off my shoes; my toes jiggle their own little dance. I'd had them freshly manicured with a ruby red paint just before my birthday – a rare treat and well worth every penny, since Scott has dropped to his knees and is sucking my toes. His kisses trail up my calves and linger on my knees; every one of them causes me to moan and slither. He gently, but firmly, pushes my thighs apart. His kisses are precise, bottomless, alert, inquisitive. I wonder how far up my legs those kisses are going to trail. He's still at my knees; I silently urge him, another inch, another inch, higher, higher. But then he changes focus. He stands up and kisses my neck, my collarbone. He inches open my shirt and kisses my throat and shoulders. He kisses my cheeks, my jaw and hair, my eyelids, my eyebrows and my nose. I kiss him too, and lick and taste and devour. I want him. I want him now. Hard and fast. And *now*. His body is leaning close into mine and it's scalding me with desire, the like of which I just haven't come across before. I will him to inch his hand up my skirt. To plunge his fingers into me. More than his fingers. That will do to start with but I want him to sink his cock deep inside me too. It's all I want. All I need.

I scramble for his fly.

'No.'

No? Did he just say no? Scott jumps away from me. His breathing is heavy. I'm actually panting – it's embarrassing – especially as he is shaking his head and he's just said no. No what. No nookie? Please God, anything but that.

'Wait.'

Wait is better. Better than *no*.

Scott closes and locks the door of the store. Just as he pulls down the blinds I see Bob take up guard outside.

'Someone might have followed us,' explains Scott. 'I don't think so. We were really careful but the rat pack can scurry into the most surprising places. You don't need your bare arse plastered across the tabloids tomorrow.'

No I don't. I rather liked the reference to the 'elegant, mystery girl' in the *Mirror* yesterday but I'm significantly less keen on the idea of encountering a headline like 'Floozy found frolicking in flora' or anything similarly dripping in attention-grabbing alliteration. My mum definitely wouldn't like it. The mention of the door-stepping tabloid journalists has the same effect as an icy shower. Even with the blinds pulled we don't re-launch ourselves at one another. A gentle silence falls between us but happily it's not an embarrassed silence, it's quite calm and comfortable.

Scott wrinkles his forehead and then runs his fingers through his hair. His simple gesture grabs me between the legs. He's a moving icon. I still can't quite believe it. I'm sat spreadeagled on the counter of Ben's B&B, panting from the exertions of a pre-lim, pash-sess, with one of the undisputed sex gods of the twenty-first century. How can something this amazing be happening to me? And hallelujah that it is.

'Have you had breakfast?' he asks tentatively.

'No, haven't been able to –'

'Eat. Me neither.' He grins at his confession that I've somehow disturbed him too. I'm delighted. I want to kiss him again. Kiss him and never stop.

'But now I'm ravenous,' I admit.

'Got just the thing for that.'

Scott nips into the back room where we do all our paperwork and make cups of tea. The room is not much larger than the average woman's wardrobe, and in terms of sustenance the best he can hope to rustle up is a couple of mouldy custard creams. The Saturday girl will have polished off the chocolate Hobnobs yesterday, as she does every week.

Scott returns carrying a tray laden with breakfast goodies: a flask of coffee, enormous croissants, orange juice with bits floating (suggesting freshly squeezed – rather than past its sell-by date, which is what floaty bits would suggest in our flat). There's a bowl of Greek yogurt, a small jug of honey and an enormous bowl of plump, ripe strawberries.

I think of Adam's tray of toast and coco pops – limp by comparison.

'Just a little something I prepared earlier,' he grins, self-consciously. 'Fern, tell me, am I trying too hard?' He glances around the shop, stuffed full of my favourite flowers. My eyes meet his searing green ones as he gives a cheeky wink.

'Yeah, you are,' I giggle.

'Coming on a bit too strong?'

'Yeah,' I laugh now. 'It's really off-putting,' I joke.

'Not the moment to pull out a wedding ring then? Or reveal the vicar I've hidden behind the foliage, come to that?' he asks.

I know he's just messing around. But my heart literally leaps into my mouth and I find it impossible to swallow. Oh God, the horrible irony of that. Imagine if I were to choke to death on my own happiness in this, my perfect moment.

I get a chance to pull myself together as he sets the tray on the floor. He produces (seemingly from nowhere, but actually from the trunk of the Merc) a beige cashmere picnic rug and matching scatter cushions. We flop on to them. I lie on my back and he feeds me strawberries and I know with every single fibre of my body that life will never be sweeter.

25. Fern

By the time the croissants and strawberries have been eaten and the coffee has gone cold, neither of us is wearing much. *Quelle surprise*. He's in jeans, but once again he's revealing his tip-top chest, and I'm in just bra and knickers (revealing my best-if-I-breathe-in-and-lie-at-a-funny-angle bod). Our clothes didn't come off in a mad passionate frenzy but – a little like when we were playing poker – we indulged in a slow, tantalizing striptease.

I barely noticed him undo the buttons on my shirt and I hardly registered the soft slither of fabric as my skirt fell down my legs. It was almost as if when his fingers fluttered across my shoulders and neck the buttons sprang open of their own accord. And, as he gently stroked my back, my shirt pretty much spontaneously combusted. As he touched my waist and dwelt on my thighs my skirt ran for the hills. It's odd; while I know he's practised in the art of disrobing women, the experience still feels completely individual and mine.

While it's very lovely that he doesn't rush the disrobing, truthfully my knickers are doing a full all-singing-and-dancing routine of their own and I am more than willing to fling caution to the wind if he'd fling me to the wall (or the floor or behind a big bunch of peonies – I'm happy to be flung anywhere really). I'm keen to seal the deal, he's the one who wants to loiter and withhold gratification. Don't get me wrong, I'm enjoying every lingering, luxurious second, but I've never been a patient girl and I'm fighting a growing anxiety that this will all vanish at the drop of a hat. Disaster. Particularly if I haven't dropped my knickers. There's a serious possibility that I'm dreaming and I might wake up without getting to the really good bit. Because doesn't that usually happen? Nothing has ever been safe since Bobby Ewing emerged from the shower in May 1986 and revealed that Pam had dreamt the previous *Dallas* series. I was knee-high to a grasshopper when all of this occurred (or more accurately didn't occur) but I remember the effect it had on my mum (still in shock, she burnt the toast at breakfast the next morning). You can't just invalidate an entire season of the country's most popular show and not expect some long-term scarring. Imagine, if we found out Carrie never really met Mr Big, Aidan Shaw just dreamt him up.

Even if this *is* for real, there's still the very serious possibility that it might end hideously abruptly. Saadi might storm the building. The press might track us down with sniffer dogs. He might get bored. Asleep or awake, I have no control.

Besides, despite the cashmere rug and cushions I'm beginning to find the shop floor an uncomfortable place to lie. The cement floor is cold and unrelenting and I only endure it by concentrating on his soft warm flesh instead. I trace my fingers over his tattoos. The decorated skin slightly less yielding than the rest of his body. I gently trail the tip of my tongue over his nipples; the gentleness becomes hard. At this point he still hasn't gone anywhere near my tits but I feel my own nipples spring to a responsive point through the silky black fabric of my bra. I snake my fingers across the arch of his eyebrows, over his cheekbones, marvelling at the fine almost translucent skin around the sockets of his eyes. The fabulousness of him creates a pounding deep in my stomach and below.

He's so attentive. He seems to be just as mesmerized by me. He dances around my breasts and the parts where my legs join. He kisses my stomach, waist, ribs, neck, shoulders and arms. He kisses inside the crook of my elbow and tells me the skin there reminds him of holding a baby bird. His endless strokes, his confident caress and gentle, sweet touch create an almost unbearable and aggressive longing inside me. I have to bite my tongue to stop myself yelling that I *need* him to get a move on. I *need* him to take me. I am soaked with my excitement. I long to feel his cool fingers inside me on my red hot flesh. I'm sure I'd come immediately, spurting out on to his hands. The exquisite release would send shocks somersaulting through my spine. I'd grab hold of his cock, move it up and down, swiftly and expertly, until he came on my stomach. That wouldn't be breaking my promise to Saadi, would it? Not by the letter of the law.

I've never longed for anyone quite so much. For God's sake this is *Scott Taylor* and he's lying semi-clad on top of me, next to me, sometimes underneath me. He manoeuvres me like I'm featherweight. It's inhuman to expect me to resist. Actually cruel. There are probably international laws against such torture.

But I did promise Saadi. What if we do go for it and he's knackered at the gig tonight? Ninety thousand people are expecting to be entertained. My needs suddenly shrink and are submerged by this enormous statistic. With reluctance I wiggle out from underneath him.

'We can't,' I moan. 'I promised Saadi.'

'You what?' Scott looks stunned.

'She says it puts you off your stride,' I admit with voluble sadness. 'Believe me, there's nothing I'd like to be doing more than –' I search around for the best word. It wouldn't be a shag. Not considering the immense sexual attraction that clearly zings between us. But it wouldn't be a fuck, not after the hours of conversation; it would be more passionate than that.

Scott helps me out. 'There's nothing you'd like to do more than me.'

'Exactly.'

'Me too, so what's stopping us?' He kisses my shoulder again and my resistance shivers like a leaf hanging by a thread from a tree. He kisses the back of my neck and a great big breeze threatens to blow that leaf right off. God, I want him.

'I'm scared of Saadi,' I confess with a whine.

Scott laughs but pulls back and tosses my top back at me. 'We've got more chance of behaving ourselves if you put those fantastic tits away. I'll get the cards.'

He looks momentarily reluctant but stands up and starts to hunt for the cards. I'm grateful he's moved away from me. The smell of him sends me weak with want. He smells of pheromone, not of a chemical aftershave. It's delicious. While he roots around for his clothes and the cards I hunt around for the will to pull my top on.

He deals. 'Well, it's not so bad. We only have to wait until after the gig tonight, right? That's what you promised her? You haven't promised her you'd take Holy Orders or anything, right?'

'Right.' I smile.

'OK, great. We get more time to get to know each other and that's a good thing,' says Scott.

'What shall we talk about?' I ask. 'We covered all the basics yesterday. I know that you used to shoplift for dares, you know that I padded my bra with tissue –'

'Until you were sixteen!' howls Scott.

'Yeah.' I'm beginning to regret telling him that bit. 'You prefer milk chocolate to dark.' I pull on my skirt.

'You like that hideous white stuff designed for kids.' He picks up his T-shirt and turns it the right way out but doesn't put it on immediately.

'Correct. You've never eaten an oyster.'

'Snot in a shell.'

'Agreed. You like football and I like flowers.' I run my fingers through my hair and try to appear less rumpled than I am.

'Why are peonies your favourite?'

Good question. A bit left of centre. I've never been asked that before, yet I do have an answer.

'I think they're a great mix of sturdy and exotic, which has to be something every girl aspires to. They smell so clean. The flower was named after Pæon, a physician to the gods, who got the plant on Mount Olympus, from the mother of Apollo. Once planted the peony likes to be left alone and punishes those who try to move it by not flowering again for several years. I like the idea that a plant has a sense of revenge,' I giggle.

'No uprooting. I'll remember that,' says Scott.

'Ah, but remember, once established, it produces splendid blooms each year for decades,' I mutter, just in case we're talking about more than the plant. I continue with my search for fresh topics. 'I know all about your family. You know about mine. Where do we go from here?'

'You could tell me a little more about your boyfriend.'

The word boyfriend hits me like a train. Hell, does he still exist? The thought that Adam is somewhere – anywhere – doing something – anything – floors me. I'd completely forgotten that he existed. It's easy to do when I'm cocooned up with Scott, away from anything remotely normal or expected; protected from any inconvenient truths and intrusions.

'Adam.' Even his name sounds alien. Yet he's been in this shop a hundred times. He's popped by to while away slow hours and help me lug round potted trees. He's dropped off sandwich lunches, he came to my rescue when we had a power cut and I struggled with the burglar alarm and the electric till. These things happened a millennium ago.

'Yes. This Adam, is it serious?' asks Scott.

'We broke up.'

'When?'

'Yesterday.'

'I see.' And he probably does. It's clear-cut, isn't it?

'What about you? Seeing anyone special at the moment?' I turn the spotlight.

'Dangerous question, Miss,' says Scott, deftly side-stepping; another skill I realize he must be practised at.

How many times has he been asked that by a nosy journalist? What was I hoping for, that he'd say something like, *At this exact second, yes. Generally, no?* In my dreams.

'Dangerous questions are part of getting to know someone,' I tell him. 'I don't imagine you usually go in for this, do you?'

I'm nervous, partly because I don't want him to affirm that he's a heartless, relentless slapper and I'm heading for disaster and, partly, I'm shy because if he does confirm that *normally* he's a heartless, relentless slapper but I've made him different, then I've definitely dug for that compliment, which puts me right back in the position I used to be in with Adam when I asked if he liked my new top.

'No, this is fresh stuff. In the past I've been a bit of a careless fucker. Literally. You know, I'm a rock star, I'm young, gorgeous. What can I do?' He stares at me and as our eyes collide, I forgive him. He's right, he'd have to be insane not to be sticking it up every girl available. What's the point of being who he is otherwise?

Scott lights a fag. He smokes way too much and Ben wouldn't like it in the shop but I can't bring myself to reprimand him. He takes a long drag and then eyes me nervously.

'Fern, anything you've ever read about me is probably true. In fact, however bad it was, double it. The really bad stuff doesn't even get into the press. When I am doing a lot of drugs and drinking far, far too much – I'm an animal.'

For the first time since we met he seems to be having difficulty in holding eye contact.

'I shag indiscriminately. I'm careless. Heartless. Yes to whisky, yes to cocaine, yes to that hole. I'm an aggressive, rude slag. I don't have a sense of humour. Or even a sense of where the bog is. I once pissed in my wardrobe. Ruined thousands of pounds' worth of suits. Big shame. I don't like the person I am when I'm drunk or high and I don't suppose you would. Christ, my own mum doesn't.' He pauses and looks really pained. 'But I don't know who else I can be.' He draws breath. The impact of his raw and gravelly honest words hits.

'Well, there's bound to be someone,' I say carefully.

'You think?' He turns to me quickly, hopefully.

'Yeah.' I want to cheer him up. He hasn't told me anything I haven't already read about him (except maybe the peeing in the wardrobe bit), but just because this stuff is often splashed all over the newspapers doesn't mean it's not deeply personal and difficult to talk about.

'Have you ever been around an addict?' he asks.

'No, not really. My auntie Linda is a bit too fond of a tipple but she hasn't started to sell the family heirlooms to pay for her habit yet. Well, she can't, we don't have any family heirlooms, but you catch my drift. I don't know anyone who does drugs. I've had the recreational swig of Calpol when I've been babysitting for my nieces and nephews, but that's it.'

'You're shitting me?'

'I'm not. My mates did that *Just Say No* thing that John Craven and the Grange Hill Kids peddled for years.'

'Why?'

'Well, I thought it was because we were all fine up-standing members of the community but the truth is probably that we were only offered anything once and it's easy to say no once. I guess you've been tempted more than most.'

'Very understanding of you.'

'I'm only this nice until you sleep with me then I turn into a bitch,' I joke.

Scott pulls me close to him. My goose bumps bang into his.

'Addicts are fucking terrible people to care about. They break your heart without even meaning to. And they don't even notice, let alone worry. Addicts don't give you a moment's peace, any respect and their apologies might as well be written on bog roll,' says Scott.

'Why are you telling me this? Are you trying to scare me off?'

'Yeah, I think I am.'

It won't work. Surely Scott has encountered enough women by now to know that every woman loves a cause. Every woman wants to save and fix. It doesn't matter if it's a broken toy that needs glue or broken skin that needs a kiss and a band-aid; we like to be needed. Pathetic or noble, I'm undecided, but it's where we are after eight million years of evolution. I think that's why some grannies and great-grannies look back on the Second World War with a certain amount of fondness. The bright side to the carnage and terrible bloodshed, they were at least allowed to fulfil their true vocations; make do and mend is a woman's battle cry. And there's nothing we like to mend more than a battered, vulnerable heart. Especially if it comes as a box set with a pair of emerald green eyes.

I trail a finger over his stomach. I think I might have

to ask him to put his T-shirt back on in a minute; visual arousal isn't solely a male thing. 'Why would you want to scare me off?' I ask.

'Because it might be easier if you go.'

'In what way?'

'Because I'm beginning to realize that if you stay, everything will be different for ever more.'

Yeeeeesssssssssssssssssss.

Is there anything a woman prefers to hear? *I'm* different. I'll *make* things different for *ever* more. I want to punch the air and hang out bunting but I tread carefully.

'Different isn't bad, necessarily,' I say gently.

'I know that. But I'm not sure I'm ready for it, what it all means, you know? I want to be. But I'm not sure I am.' He stares at me, practically begging me with his eyes to understand.

I think I know what he's on about. He's on about the *really* rude C word, Commitment; much more pugnacious to most men than the C word that rhymes with hunt. In the past I've had many a rough encounter with the male gene that makes blokes commitment-resistant (think Adam – he's a fine example) and I haven't always been that sympathetic. But I can see why Scott might think a change to his free and single status would be something to worry about; he's got a really fabulous life as is. Why would he look for anything different? I'm not up against the same problem. Personally, I hanker for something different and long for change; my life is humdrum. Or at least it was until Friday. Scott has more choice than practically any other man in the world. Fascinating that choice isn't the gift one would imagine.

As though following my thought process, Scott says, 'I've never been that great with commitment. I've never really had what other people would call a girlfriend.'

'Oh, come on. What about . . .' Without pausing for breath I name at least five starlets and pop stars that he's dated in the recent past.

'Yeah, all nice girls,' he says, explaining nothing at all. He finishes his cigarette and then elucidates a bit more. 'But they all wanted something from me, other than me. You know. They had a record or movie to promote and it was convenient to date me for a few months, so we could be papped outside the Ivy and Nobu. That's what happens.'

'You are not being fair to yourself. I'm certain they enjoyed every minute they were with you,' I say hotly, perhaps showing my hand a little.

I feel distinctly uncomfortable that I'm banged up this close to his lack of self-confidence and his vulnerability. It's so close I can smell it. I preferred the pheromones. Scott's inner turmoil and on/off search for true love has also been reported in the press and unofficial biographies, in exactly the same way his laddish antics have. I've never really bought into it. Surely it's not hard for a man like Scott Taylor to find true love. If he can't, then what chance do the rest of us have?

'Maybe, but it's hard to tell with actresses. They'd reach the same climax whether they saw their face in *Heat* magazine, I bought them a pair of Manolos or I shagged them raw.'

'Right,' I mumble, gripped with jealousy at the very suggestion that he's shagged someone raw.

'Anyway, I always treat them like crap in the end. Whether they turn out to be sincere or not, I usually find them stupid. I have what my psychologist calls intimacy issues.'

'You're warning me again.'

'I am.'

'OK, I consider myself warned. I'm not worried.'

'You should be. You have no idea,' says Scott, shaking his head with some sadness.

'How bad can it be?' I force a laugh because this conversation is uncomfortable and I preferred it when we talked about our favourite TV shows or even how we felt when our pet dogs died.

'It can be very bad.' Scott searches my face. I stare back. He must find whatever it is that he's looking for, because then he adds, 'And sometimes it can be very, very good.'

26. Fern

I don't use the ticket Adam gave me; I left all three stuck to the fridge. It seemed a bit immoral using Adam's perk to see Scott. I knew Scott would see to it that I had a seat and he has; someone else must have been evicted. I vaguely wonder who; a record producer? A journo? I clean forget all about calling my mates to ask if anyone wants to use the tickets for the gig tonight and so it's a pleasant surprise when I see Ben, Jess and my baby brother, Rick, filing through the throng of people and heading towards me.

I leap up and hug them all. I'm so excited by life and brimming with happiness that I hardly notice that my brother is mortified by this public display of affection; he practically bats me away.

Ben jokes, 'You only saw me yesterday, not a month ago – don't be sloppy, darling.' As he gently pushes me away he whispers, 'Did you like the flowers?'

'Oh Ben, the shop has never looked so beautiful. Thank you.'

'He's impossible to resist, your new man,' he says with a wink.

Jess allows me to wrap her in a big hug but she doesn't look happy, she's tight-lipped and grey. I can't decide if she's concerned or jealous. If she's concerned then I'll reassure her, if she's jealous she needs to get over it and quickly – she'll get lines if she keeps scowling. I decide to ignore her mardiness. 'Good initiative to hunt out the tickets and come along, Jess,' I say cheerfully. 'Sorry I haven't had a chance to talk to you today,' I garble.

'I didn't use my initiative. Adam asked me to come along,' says Jess.

'He called me too,' adds Rick.

'And me,' confirms Ben.

I'm suspicious. Is Adam planning on staging some sort of American-style 'intervention'? I didn't even know what an intervention was until I started watching *Desperate Housewives*. For the benefit of the uninitiated, allow me to explain. An intervention is where 'concerned' friends and family gang together to tell their loved one something their loved one doesn't want to hear; ostensibly for their own good. I watched the episode in an early series where everyone tried to tell Bree her drinking was spiralling out of control. Like she wants to hear that after discovering her current fiancé murdered her first husband, her son's gay and there's dust on her pelmets. You can imagine; it went down like a bucket of steaming vomit. Why wouldn't it? Who wants to be subjected to mass bullying by their nearest and dearest; it's bad enough being on the receiving end of unasked for advice on an individual basis.

Is Adam hoping to surround me with friends and family and convince me that Scott is a dastardly villain and I ought to cease contact immediately? Perhaps even go back to him? Idiot. For one thing, Jess has already tried and failed to do as much and for another, I can't imagine either Ben or Rick intervening to try to put me *off* Scott. Ben never judges and will be wild about even the remotest possibility of me hooking up with Scott because then he might piggyback his way to some fabulous parties. Ditto Rick. I don't honestly think he'd notice that I've changed boyfriends even if I do upgrade to a mega pop star and my picture appears regularly in all the glossy gossip mags. So sod off Adam. I'm a big girl now. And, pertinently, I'm not your girl. I wait for the onslaught of objections and the insistence that I do a reality check; none come. Maybe Adam didn't plan an intervention after all; maybe he simply didn't want the tickets to go to waste.

I don't know how Scott does it. For this is the third and final gig yet he somehow manages to scour up enough energy not only to pull off a show on a par with the previous two but somehow a show that is yet more glittering. A lesser mortal would be knackered by now and crying out for Lucozade. But Scott manages to take us all the extra mile, a mile I would have believed it impossible to travel. He has even more power than the previous two nights. He sings with a smidgen more depth and meaning. He dances with an iota more energy, he chats to the audience with a manner that's fractionally more relaxed. He's sensational.

'I don't get what you see in him,' says Rick with a shrug and an ironic grin. I smile back. I can tell Rick's impressed, he's aglow. The tens of thousands of fans jump, holler, cry, scream, clap, stamp and cheer throughout the two-hour gig. It's a storming concert and Scott is riding high in the sky. He struts around the stage, performing that magical mix of the sexual and personal that makes each girl think he's performing just for her. He invites the entire crowd to be his friend. They scream like frenzied devil-worshippers and pledge eternal devotion. The whole audience quivers with excitement or passion or (according to Jess) cold. But she's wrong, it's a warm night.

Scott eventually comes on stage to sing his final song and then the encore. He repeatedly punches the air; over and over again. With every punch the crowds indulge in yet more hysterical and harried antics; women swoon, men swear, kids promise themselves they'll grow up to be rock stars.

Scott takes in the view and treats us to a wide, unrepentant smile. After some time he holds up his hands in an effort to lull the audience into quietness. They take his gesture as a sign that he's requesting more adoration and a fresh surge of madness is pushed into the night. It takes a drum roll and his repeated requests before the crowd finally hushes up and listens to what else he has to say or sing. I now know the run of the show, almost like the back of my hand. He's already sung 'Fall Apart', 'Come Back to Me' and 'Bit of Rough', 'Hate to Love', 'Demons', 'Dead Love' and 'Tell Me Something'. I search my mind for an outstanding song that he's contractually obliged to deliver, I can't think of one. It was at this point on Friday Scott sang 'Happy Birthday' and at this point on Saturday that he sang 'Perfect Day'. I wonder if he's going to sing to me again. Oh God, I hope so. But what will he sing?

Scott's looking around the stadium; his eyes are glittering.

'Ladies and ladies and ladies and gents,' he says, acknowledging that the vast majority of the crowd are women. 'Thank you so much. Thank you. Thank you for loving me.' The crowd erupts again; again he has to calm them down. 'You are brilliant, you know that? You are my lifeblood. Have I made you happy?'

The response probably registered on the Richter scale.

'I'm glad. I want you to be happy. Do you want me to be happy?'

Again they surge forward. Women fling their bras in the air in an effort to demonstrate just how happy they want to make him.

'Boys and girls and girls and girls, you amazing people, guess what?' He pauses and the crowd calms, hanging on his every word. 'I think I've found a way I can be happy.'

After his well-reported fights with addiction to drugs and booze the crowds are ecstatic to hear this. They roar their support. I wonder what he's going to say. Is he building up to a joke? Is he going to tell them whist is his new passion? God, I hope he doesn't tell them about strip poker; my younger brother's here, he might be twenty-eight but in my eyes he's eternally a little kid.

'I think I've found *someone* who makes me happy. Someone who is a bit different from anyone before.'

For the first time the crowd does not respond with a cheer. They look confused and uncertain. They turn to one another for reassurance. Girls and women who have been diehard fans for years somehow immediately sense that this is the end of life as they know it. I don't sense it quite as quickly, I have no idea where Scott is going with this.

'I'm in love.' He yells. 'Fuck me, I am.' He is? There's

an enormous groan across the stadium and the sound of thousands of hearts cracking at once. The murmur instantly morphs from sadness to something more dangerous, more threatening; a grumble gathering momentum, growing into disappointment and frustration. The security guards look troubled. I see them dash to space themselves around the stage, in case there's an influx of girls clambering to beat Scott with their cowboy hats. The security guards' eyes seem to say, 'Get Scott off the stage, this is going to turn nasty. What the fuck has he done now?' But Scott holds his nerve. I daren't breathe.

'Aww, don't be like that,' he tells his fans. 'Celebrate with me. Don't be angry with me.' He pulls his face into the lost puppy look, which I've seen before on and off stage, and people around me immediately begin to offer up a reluctant smile. He's compelling. 'You love me, right? You want me to be happy? You said so.' The crowd are disinclined to agree but have to. They did scream that – just minutes ago. 'Well, I've found someone who makes me happy. So bloody happy.' Half the stadium starts to cheer, offering support. 'Come on Wembley, you can do better than that. It's Scott here. Your boy. Wish me luck.'

He offers up his most beautiful smile. All teeth and eyes. He's gleaming. He's overwhelming. He's irresistible. The crowd meet him. They cheer for him. This time they are loud and committed. He's turned them around, a full one hundred and eighty degrees, in just moments. Everyone is putty in his hands. He's happy. They want him to be happy; never before have they longed for someone's happiness with quite so much fervour. Ideally they'd want him to be happy with them but that was never really to be, so they settle for him being happy with someone else. They become wild as they comprehend. Scottie Taylor is *happy*.

I watch as he turns the tide and for a moment it's all too enormous for me. All I can think is this man is bigger than King Canute. He *can* turn tides.

Scott roars above the cheering crowd. 'I'll write even better songs because of her. I promise you. I'll be a better man because of her. I promise you. God, I hope she'll have me.' They writhe upon one another, spewing out the most tremendous roar of the three days. 'I'm going to ask her to marry me.'

I don't remember anything after that, because I faint.

27. Scott

Why the hell not?

28. Fern

The first thing I see when I come round is Saadi. Her large brown eyes are clouded with concern but the moment she sees my eyelids flapping, indicating I'm coming round, she manages to crack a joke.

'You're not going to be able to have sex tonight now. The doc said you have to rest up.'

I try to smile back but my body is still in that overly relaxed state where muscles feel like liquid play dough and I have no control.

'Where am I?' I mumble.

'Where is she?' The louder, more insistent question comes from Scott. He bursts through what I now recognize to be his dressing-room door and charges towards me, scattering the small crowd surrounding me and sending his larger entourage into a vague panic.

He swoops down on to his knees and stares at me with real anxiety. Even when his face is constricted with concern he oozes a sex appeal; the type which can't be imitated, simulated or stopped.

'Quite some upstaging you pulled off there. I'm going to have to watch you,' he says to me, joking to hide his concern. Then turning to the room, 'Can we have some space here, guys?'

The hordes of people, some of whom I recognize as members of the band and crew, others I don't know, oblige. Only Bob remains put. Scott doesn't seem to notice.

'I didn't mean to scare you,' he says as he strokes my hair. His eyes ooze concern. His lips are so close to mine that I'm overwhelmed by his proximity and my recovery is set back. My tongue is still behaving like a beached whale and won't respond to instruction, although the instruction is a little vague. I don't know what to say. Perhaps I want to say, 'Pinch me.'

'I shouldn't have sprung it on you like that. I'm a fucking idiot. I got carried away. I should have talked to you privately first. That's what I'd planned. I should learn to keep my big mouth shut. No self-control. That's my problem.' He drags his hands through his hair. 'Have I fucked everything up? Are you hacked off with me?'

'No,' I mutter.

'Really?' His face is a beacon of happiness once again. 'It's just the PR team are really pissed with me. They say I've created chaos. That I should have done things differently, but I couldn't, you know?'

'I know.'

'Who the hell can think about selling exclusive deals to *Hello!* at a time like this?'

'Who indeed,' I giggle.

'So that's settled then?'

'I'll marry you.'

29. Fern

We leave the gig via helicopter (it's so incredibly noisy my ears hurt but it's fast). I look down on the tens of thousands of fans swarming out of the stadium, walking back to their cars, or the tube or train, and I can't believe I'm not among those hordes. That is where I've always been. I thought it was my place. Within minutes we leave behind the marching crowd and are soon above black fields of countryside. We land in the grounds of a smart country house, one of those impressive Georgian things that pops up in movies of adaptations of Jane Austen novels.

Saadi practically jumps from the helicopter before the blades have stopped rotating; she's talking down her mobile to the person on reception just a few feet away. A number of staff in black rollneck jumpers and dark grey trousers emerge from the house and pounce on us with almost terrifying efficiency. Despite the fact that it's a balmy night they offer blankets to put around our shoulders as we make the short walk from helicopter to hall. Scott shrugs them away; politely but firmly. I follow suit, fighting the urge to collapse into giggles – it's not like I'm ninety.

'There are twenty-eight bedrooms here,' Saadi tells me. The word bed practically makes me come. I glance over at Scott; he's divine. I want him with such a heady ferocity. Saadi goes on, 'We've booked the lot so there shouldn't be any privacy issues.' *Privacy*, that word pokes and jabs me. I am sick with excitement that within minutes Scott and I will be able to enjoy some of that privacy; enjoy each other. Saadi, oblivious to my lusty thoughts, continues, 'We've changed hotel every night for the last three nights to keep the press from finding us, which has worked so far, although it's a pain having to pack up every morning. But if we stay longer than one night anywhere hotel staff always leak our whereabouts to the tabloids. It's frustrating.' Saadi shoots a lethal look at the bellboy who is currently scuttling past her and taking her bags upstairs. He looks terrified – trialled, hung, drawn and quartered in one look; I feel a bit sorry for him. 'This lot are under contract to keep their mouths shut so we can set up camp for a few days if Scott wants to. There are bedrooms in the main house, the coach house, the stable block and the lodge. I've put you in the coach house. Scott is in the main house. There's better security there.'

'But –' I look around for Scott so that he can back up my objection. Surely we are going to share a room. 'But –'

'Don't worry.' Saadi cuts me off by waving her long hand in front of my face as if pre-emptively batting away any objections I could possibly make. 'There's no security risk to you yet. No one knows who you are. Once they do we'll have to think about hiring a big burly bloke to watch your back. Scott's fans will hate you. There's bound to be trouble. There'll certainly be nasty threats, although I doubt any actual attacks, but you can never be too certain.'

'Right,' I mumble, suddenly feeling much more nervous

than I ever have before. 'But –' I want to say that besides the security risk I'd like to be with Scott, my fiancé. Before I get the words out Saadi starts talking again.

'Oh, don't worry. You'll have a lovely room. All the bedrooms are large, individually designed and equipped with the latest technology from Sony LCD screen TVs and Sony DVD players to wireless internet access. The bathrooms have stand-alone or sunken baths. Do you have a preference? Whichever it is I'm sure it can be arranged.'

'I don't mind, but –' But I want to tell her that since we were in the flower shop I've thought of little other than Scott's tantalizing caresses and kisses. Through clothes I've felt his throbbing hardness and now I want more. Or less, actually – less clothes.

'Good. Plus there will be a full range of Molton Brown bath products for you to use. I love their stuff, don't you?'

'Very nice, but –' I mutter, and before I realize quite what's happening I notice that Scott's manager, Mark, is shooing Scott up the mahogany staircase and Saadi is leading me back out of the reception and through the courtyard to what must be the coach house.

'The doctor did say you need a rest,' she insists quite firmly. 'And Scott has a lot to talk about with Mark. It's been quite a surprising night for everyone.'

'Yes,' I manage feebly.

Saadi looks at me with a peculiar mix of sympathy and envy. 'Especially you, I suppose.' I nearly squash a tabby cat that's sleeping outside on the warm gravelly forecourt; as I stumble Saadi shoves me over the threshold into a beautiful room. She hands me the key and says, 'Good-night, we'll talk tomorrow.' She speaks in a tone of voice that makes it quite clear that no further discussion is required, expected or permitted.

30. Fern

The room, or rather rooms, are more beautiful than any hotel rooms I have ever seen – let alone stayed in. I've clearly stumbled into a movie set. The place is decorated in dramatic contrasts. White walls meet black wooden floors, there's a snow white, inches thick, shaggy rug waiting for me to sink my toes into and a huge squashy white corner sofa (leather) waiting for me to throw myself upon. I only just resist doing this right away because I'm distracted by a circular, transparent plastic chair hanging from the ceiling like a swing. *That*, I have to sit on. For a moment or two I dangle my legs and try to make myself go backwards and forwards but it doesn't really swing, more just hangs there, so I hop off and wander through to the bathroom where there is a free-standing bath and, as promised, shelves of beautiful-smelling products. Then I wander up to the mezzanine, where there is an enormous bed.

That I'm supposed to sleep in all *alone*. I recall his fingers skittering across my groin and his deep, passionate kisses, his tongue touching mine. Aaghh, I can't believe we're expected to sleep separately.

What a waste.

I flop on to the bed but I'm not in the slightest bit sleepy. In fact I am more awake and alive than I have ever been in my life. Scott Taylor has just asked me to marry him and I've just agreed! Oh. My. God. It does not seem possible. I have to talk to someone, anyone, who can confirm that this is all happening. I reach for my handbag and scramble around for my mobile.

Who to call?

Not Adam. Usually I turn to him before anyone but that clearly wouldn't be right under the circumstances. I can hardly ring Adam and say, 'Hey, honey, am I really engaged to another man, a man other than you that is?' Undoubtedly he could confirm or deny but it might be a tricky conversation. I shove Adam out of my head and determine not to think of him for as long as humanly possible. As soon as he comes to mind a lick of something disturbingly like shame engulfs my body. I guess there are kinder ways to show you've moved on from a relationship than getting engaged to your new beau, within twenty-four hours of splitting up and in front of an audience of ninety thousand. Still, at least there's no room for confusion and no one likes mixed messages.

I could call Jess. Where the hell is Jess? The last I saw of her was before I fainted in the stands at the concert. Why didn't she come backstage with me? Why didn't Rick or Ben? I can't believe they just buggered off and left me to all this insanity without so much as a by your leave. I'd have expected Ben to come along for the ride at least.

Lisa? My mum and dad?

These are the people I do generally turn to in moments of extreme happiness or pressure. Normally, between them, these people congratulate, support, guide or yell at me and I feel somehow validated once they have done so. Mum and Dad endorsed my whooping and cheering (almost gloating) when I got the best marks in my year in the floristry exams. Lisa sympathized with my blind terror at a (false) pregnancy alarm just four weeks after I'd met Adam. Jess and Adam and I celebrated together when we finally found our little flat with affordable rent and just minutes from the tube. Ben comforted me when my bag was snatched on Lavender Road and he instructed me to change locks and cancel cards while he put the kettle on for a calming brew. Part of existence is having experience substantiated, legitimized or authorized by your nearest and dearest. Eating a huge slab of creamy chocolate cake is fun but it is better if you do it with a mate. Finding a tenner in the street is a great piece of luck but telling your mates and buying them a drink is worth the same again. I'm the sort of person who likes to share, whether it be news, gossip, bills or heartache. I guess that's because I'm one of five. Secrecy is an alien concept.

But somehow tonight is different. I'm not sure who to call. I switch my phone on while I consider and it immediately starts ringing and beeping at me as though it's R2-D2 on speed. Apparently I have ten voicemail and twelve text messages. Congratulations pouring in already, I'll bet. I dial in for my voicemail. It's Jess.

'Er. Hi Fern, I hope you are OK. Sorry I couldn't stay with you. Give me a bell, huh. As soon as you can.'

And that's it. No congratulations. No shrieks of excitement. Actually, she sounded quite subdued. What's that about? I thought that now it's clear-cut that Scott is as crazily in love with me as I am with him Jess'd stop worrying. I press three to delete the message and listen to my second one.

'*What the heck is going on? This is wild. Call me the second you get a chance,*' insists Lisa. That's a bit more like it. This *is* wild. Wildly exciting, wildly wonderful, wildly different. Again there are no actual congratulations, which is a bit weird. I whooped and hollered when she told me that Charlie had finally popped the question. Mostly out of relief; we'd been waiting for him to do so for months and I figured once he finally had, she would at least have a different topic of conversation from second-guessing where and when he'd do the popping (she did – she talked about where and when he'd take her on honeymoon). I'd have thought Lisa would be a bit more openly ecstatic though, not least because Scott is a zillionaire; that's her currency. Although I don't suppose she's heard that I finished with Adam last night; I suppose, even if she has, it's still bizarrely sudden. I can't blame her for not understanding our speedy certainty as it wasn't like this for her and Charlie.

'*Fern, darling, call me this instant,*' insists Ben excitedly.

'*Fern fella. What a mind blower. How long have you been secretly shagging Scottie Taylor for? Call your bro and give me the lowdown,*' says Rick. Well, at least he sounds impressed, even if he has got the wrong end of the stick. This is whirlwind and romantic, there haven't been any deceitful long-term shenanigans.

The fifth message is from Adam, '*You bitch.*'

I stop listening to my voicemail right there. The text messages are along a similar line. There's one each from Ben, Lisa, Jess and Rick, all insisting I get in touch. There are eight from Adam.

You bitch.
You bitch.
You bitch.
You get the idea.

I switch off my phone. I don't want to read or hear any more. The lack of congrats is disappointing; I'm not in the mood to call any of them.

I know! I need Scott. Of course I do. He's the one I should be turning to now. I'll call him and tell him that I'm feeling exhilarated, nervous, and confused all at once. He's my fiancé. He'll hold my hand through this. He knows about jealousies. I bet he went through this with his friends when he got his mega record deal. People aren't very gracious in the face of good fortune – at least not other people's good fortune. I pick up my mobile, but as I'm about to press the buttons it occurs to me that I don't know his number. We haven't exchanged mobile numbers. Damn.

I pick up the phone by the bed and press 5 for reception.

'Can you put me through to Scott Taylor, please,' I say in my most confident voice.

'I'm sorry, Madame, who?'

It's Miss actually but I don't bother to correct him. 'Scott Taylor.'

'We don't have a guest of that name staying with us I'm afraid, Madame.'

'Yes, you do, we've just checked in together. Oh – I get it. Sorry, Scottie Taylor, you'll probably know him by that name but in fact his friends and his fiancée call him Scott,' I say with just a smidgen of self-satisfaction.

'I'm sorry, Madame. We do not have a Mr Taylor staying with us. You are mistaken, goodnight.' The line goes dead.

Bloody cheek, why won't they connect me? I know he's in the hotel. Then it occurs to me that the receptionist is probably under strict instructions not to connect anyone for security reasons. But I'm not anyone. I'm his fiancée. I wonder if I should call back and spell that out to the pimply, pompous moron who is standing between me and my man.

I could go and look for him or for Saadi at least; I know they are in the main house. There can only be a dozen rooms at most. Didn't Saadi say that we've rented them all? I could knock on every door and insist on being told his whereabouts. I'd only be disturbing Scott's entourage and as his fiancée I must be entitled to do that, mustn't I?

Suddenly I'm overwhelmed with shyness. I'm not sure I want to knock on the doors of the band and crew and explain that I don't have the mobile number or even room number of my fiancé; it looks weirdly desperate. It isn't the way things should be.

I sigh and slip my feet out of my shoes. I rub the arch of one foot against the under part of the other. It's comforting, and oddly, I need comfort. How mad is that? I should be dancing a jig, cracking open the champagne, feeling those liquid gold bubbles on my tongue then shagging my fiancé until I drop with exhaustion. I'm newly engaged!

Instead, fully clothed, I slip between the sheets. All at once I'm very tired. Maybe it's the after-effects of the faint. Perhaps I ought to follow doctor's orders and get some rest. I'll feel right as rain in the morning. It's been a big day. Bigger than I could have possibly imagined in my wildest dreams. I ought to get some beauty sleep and tomorrow I'll get Scott's number. In fact from tomorrow I'll insist that we are never apart from one another, no matter what his manager or PA says. I'm his fiancée.

I'm Scott Taylor's fiancée.

Oh. My. God.

31. Fern

It seems as though my eyes have just closed when they spring open again. Light and about a hundred people flood through my door. I only have eyes for Scott. He is breathtaking. He bounds up the mezzanine stairs and nosedives on to the bed and starts to kiss me, seemingly unaware of the other ninety-nine people in the room. All of whom are carrying fresh flowers and fruit or clean towels and toiletries to replace the untouched ones in the bathroom.

His kisses are gentle and erotic at the same time. Excitement starts to snake in my stomach and I forget to worry about morning breath or what I must look like (a state, I'm in last night's clothes and makeup, my hair will be frizzy and knotty rather than tousled). Neither of us seems to care.

'Morning, gorgeous wifie-to-be.' A cool hand has slipped beneath the sheet and under my top. It's lying flat on my ribcage, just centimetres from the modest swell of my breast. I've never experienced anything so erotic in my life. 'Sleep well?'

I beam at him like some sort of crazy loon and only just manage to stammer, 'Great.'

'Good.' He kisses the corner of my mouth. It's a slow sexy kiss, a mooching kiss, a full-of-promise kiss which causes the hairs on every inch of my body to stand erect.

He edges a fraction closer towards me and I'm instantly aware of his raw want too. Wow. It's huge. Hurrah. I wish all the room service people would bugger off and leave us alone. They don't, so I have to force myself to stop thinking about the fact he's so clearly proud and eager and so, so close.

'Gorgeous rooms, aren't they?' I mumble.

He stops kissing, glances around, as if for the first time, and then smiles at me. 'Yeah, nice. Glad you like them.' He resumes kissing, this time my earlobe.

The kisses are utterly fabulous but I can't dissolve into them completely as I'm aware that someone is opening curtains, someone else is carrying in newspapers and two other people are setting up breakfast in the room downstairs. I can't seduce or be seduced or even discuss the detail of our sleeping arrangements in front of an audience. Scott must sense my inhibition; he pulls away from me and says, 'I thought we'd eat breakfast together and make some plans.' He claps his hands together with excitement. 'Sound good?'

'Sounds perfect.'

It is official I am the luckiest woman on the earth. If I was in any doubt (which I'm not), it says so in all the newspapers. The tabloids have gone wild. Every one of them headlines with Scottie's proposal. Most play with the title of one of his songs

SCOTTIE IS FEELING FINE; THAT'S NO LIE
SCOTTIE FINALLY *LOVES* TO LOVE
SCOTTIE SAYS COME BACK AND MARRY ME

Not that it's clear where I'm supposed to have been in order to 'come back'. The accuracy of the headline seems to be irrelevant. Attention-grabbing is all. The tabloids dissect Scott's past love life, running mug shots of a variety of women (celeb and civilian) who have had the pleasure. I marvel at the array of stunning women he's dated.

'I never knew you had a thing with Madonna before she got with Guy Ritchie,' I gasp.

'Is that what the papers say?' asks Scott with a non-committal shrug.

Even the qualities cover the story. Although they tend to concentrate on Scott's creative and financial achievements rather than his sexual exploits.

Scottie Taylor (Grammy Award-nominated, 10-time BRIT Award-winning English singer-songwriter), whose career started as a member of the pop band X-treme, stunned his fans last night at his Wembley concert by proposing to a previously unknown girlfriend. Scottie Taylor is the second biggest selling British solo artist in history – Robbie Williams being the first. Taylor's album sales stand at over 50 million worldwide, and in addition he has also sold an estimated 12 million singles.

I'm struck again – in fact almost paralysed – by how strange this is. Scottie Taylor is sat in the same room as *I* am, and he's eating toast.

'I hate it that they always bring up Robbie. He hasn't brought out anything new for ages. Why can't they concentrate on me and the here and now?' says Scott peevishly. 'Oh God, look, he's made a comment in the *Observer*.'

'Who has? Robbie Williams?' I can't hide my excitement. 'What does he say?'

'He says, "Well, at least that's one thing Scottie beat me to,"' says Scott. Scott looks momentarily hacked off but then his frown lines dissolve and I almost think I imagined them. 'Well, he's right,' says Scott, smiling. 'Robbie might sell more records but only just, and I have you, which, you know, is my ace card. You're worth your weight in platinum albums.'

I bask in the compliment.

We slowly eat breakfast and paw over the papers. Scott jokingly comments which papers carry a photo that makes him look trim and hot. There are photos of the gig but, thankfully, there aren't any of me. I feared there'd be a shot of me passed out in a cold faint; green face and legs splayed ungainly. Luckily, not one of the hundreds of photographers present managed to get that shot. When Scott was proposing to me no one really knew who he was talking to, and while lots of cameras were pointing in my general direction, they were all directed at a rather busty supermodel who, coincidentally, was sat three rows behind me. She seemed a likely candidate for a Scottie Taylor proposal. I (a flat-chested florist from the wrong streets in Clapham) did not.

I let out a big sigh. Scott misinterprets my relief as disappointment.

'Fern, love, don't be disappointed. There will be hundreds of photos of you in the papers before you know it. Thousands. You should be grateful for the anonymity while you have it. It won't last long.'

'That's not why I sighed. I'm relieved not to have my

photo in the papers. I haven't talked to my mum and dad yet – which I need to do. This is all so big and fast. The tabloids are collaborating to launch a national search for the "blonde beauty", the "elegant mystery girl", the "luckiest woman alive".' I nervously glance at the windows, expecting journos to smash their way through, hanging on ropes and dressed entirely in black, SAS style. 'It's all quite overwhelming,' I add.

'That's what I thought, you need time. I said that to Mark and he worked hard last night to keep your name out of the papers.'

'I don't understand.'

'The rat pack know who you are already. I did sing happy birthday *Fern*. It's an unusual name so you were easy to track down. I imagine most of your ex's crew were rushing to spill the beans. No matter, we just struck a few deals to ask them to hold off announcing your name just yet.'

'Why? How?'

'Why? Because I thought you needed time to adjust to all of this. And how, we just pointed out that the story runs for longer if the details are revealed in dribs and drabs. They'll sell more papers. End of.'

'So they do know my identity?'

'Yes.'

'But they are offering a substantial financial reward to any member of the public that can identify me?'

'Yup. Rule number one. You can't believe what you read in the papers.'

'Ever?'

'No, not ever. Sometimes they print the truth but since

no one with any sense believes what they read in the papers it hardly matters. It's a clever double bluff.'

I must look perplexed, because Scott kisses the end of my nose and says, 'It's a mad world, I know, but you'll get used to it soon enough, more's the pity.'

For a moment he looks genuinely regretful at the thought that I'll be dragged into the media circus that is his life.

'You OK with your decision though?' he asks, tentatively.

'The one about living the rest of my days in wedded bliss with you?' I beam at him.

'Yeah,' he laughs, but he's too nervous for the smile to crawl into his eyes.

'Certainly am.' I pause and then bravely add, 'If you are.'

Say you are. Say you are. Say you are. I secretly plead.

He nods slowly, carefully. 'It struck me when I was hugging that girl from the audience the other night.'

'Which one, the blonde or the brunette?'

'I don't know. I didn't even notice one was blonde and one was brunette.'

'Friday was blonde, Saturday was brunette.' I remember with horrifying clarity. On Sunday he missed that part of his act, much to my delight.

'Yeah, well, whichever. I realized for the first time something that should have been obvious for years now. This is all too much for one guy on his own. I make or break dreams with the same regularity as other people make their beds. I've been overwhelmed by those audiences over the past few days; it seemed like I was entirely responsible for their happiness.'

Scott looks perplexed and vaguely alarmed. Somehow he wears even that look in a way which is knicker-ticklingly sexy. Consumed with lust, I am unable to answer. I just nod. It's true. It does appear that he can snap their dreams just as easily as if they were the matchsticks we used when playing cards the other day. Scott continues.

'But who is responsible for my dreams and my happiness?'

I almost answer, Saadi, Mark, the enormous entourage that follows him around twenty-four-seven, but I bite my tongue. I don't think that's what he means.

'It's a big responsibility making all those people happy,' he adds.

'Huge,' I agree.

'And I thought you might be the best person to, you know, share it with me.' I offer up an enormous unconditional grin. 'I've known for a long time that the world is a big place, almost too big. I think that's what the dependency on the drink and the drugs is about. Or at least that's part of it. But I've been thinking it might not be so lonely if you were, you know, hanging around it with me.'

'Why me?' I ask. Because I have no idea. Really, absolutely none.

He smiles. 'I don't know why exactly but I'm sure it is you.' We're sat opposite each other. He rests his bare foot on my chair. I fight the urge to kiss his feet and suck his toes. I shiver with the effort of restraining. Hell, he's magnificent.

'I'm not cool,' I warn.

'I like that in you. You're fun, and fun tops cool any day of the week. Besides, it's not all going to be palatial living and parties for you.'

'Isn't it?' I pretend to sound disappointed.

'I'm a bad man. Remember. I told you.'

'Yes, I remember.'

'Do you think you can make me good?'

'I don't even want to.'

Scott laughs so hard that he nearly chokes on his orange juice. He points at the enormous pile of papers now casually discarded and littering the shaggy rug. 'Do you think you might be able to forget who I am?'

'Do you want me to?'

'Yes.'

'Really?' I probe.

'No, not really,' he laughs again. 'Cos I'm a god out there.'

We laugh once more. Delighted in each other.

32. Fern

Some of the hundred people who invaded my room this morning brought with them a whole new wardrobe for me. Scott dismisses the rail of clothes as a mere trifle.

'Just something to tide you over until we –'

'Pick up my old stuff.'

'I was going to say until we get to the shops together.' Scott shrugs as though he doesn't mind either way.

As I start to look through the rail of stunning clothes I doubt that I will be bothering to pick up anything I own. More than likely it will all look shabby next to this lot. Carefully I trail my fingers along rows of chic skirts and shirts. There are at least a dozen pairs of jeans; boot cut, flare, straight, boy cut, high-waisted and spray on. There are piles of soft T-shirts in assorted colours and numerous floaty dresses in florals, stripes and block colours. It's as though a whole department of Selfridges has been shipped to my door. It's the first time since I've met Scott that I've stopped fantasizing about making love; now all I can think of is dressing up. I check out the labels surreptitiously. There are high-waisted pencil skirts and tailored jackets by Alexander McQueen, blazers by Viktor and Rolf, trousers by Chloe, tops by Miu Miu and Sportmax, dresses by Dior. I have never owned what you'd call a designer piece in my life – unless you count the copycat Hermès travel bag that Adam bought me last Christmas and tried to pass off as the genuine thing. I gasp as I finger the silky fabrics and admire the neat, precise tailoring. Scott grins and nods to a wall of shoeboxes stacked behind the rails of clothes.

'Oh wow!' I pounce on the boxes, flinging the lids aside like toffee wrappers, diving on the shoes, all carefully cosseted in tissue. Christian Louboutin, Kurt Geiger and Jimmy Choo heels, Escada pumps and Pied A Terre boots. Opium for shoe-holics.

I check the sizes. Everything is my size; top, bottoms, even shoes. I pounce on the frilly underwear; even the bra size is spot on.

'How did you know my sizes?' I gasp, amazed at the plethora of goodies at my feet.

'Saadi knows how to find out about that sort of stuff. She probably asked your friends.'

'Did she pick these out for me? She has exquisite taste.' I hold up a jade wrap dress and look at myself in the mirror. Just my colour.

'No. More likely one of Saadi's assistants or someone at the store.'

'How many assistants does Saadi have?'

'Not certain. Two at least, maybe three.'

My fiancé's assistant has assistants – two or three of them. This is off the scale. I can barely comprehend. I pull from the rail a pair of Diesel jeans and a pristine Agnès B T-shirt; mentally I toss away my high-street-purchased wardrobe at home. Once loved, all now seem slightly greying and fraying.

'I'll want to collect my photo albums and books from

the flat though. And my pink Roberts radio. I love it. Mum and Dad bought me it last Christmas.'

'Yeah, I like those too. I think I have one or two.'

'In pink?'

'No. I have a cream one, a powder blue one and Paul Smith did me a customized stripy one. But we can get you a pink one, no problem.'

'Like I said, I have one. I just need to pick it up.'

He looks at me quizzically. Obviously in Scott's world it's easier to buy new rather than go to the effort of retrieving an old anything. 'Fair enough. We do need to go back to your flat for your passport so we could pick up your other stuff then.'

'Passport?' I ask.

'Yeah, I was originally planning on flying out today but I guess we need to hold off a few days. I want to meet your ma and pa. And I want you to meet my mum but we have to be in LA by Friday latest. I've got to be in the studio by then.'

'LA?'

'That's where I live.'

Oh, yes. He does, doesn't he. I'd forgotten that. I remember reading about it in one of my gossipy mags some months back. Scottie found the press intrusion into his life unbearable here in the UK and so he took flight. Most enormous British A-listers end up living in LA because the Americans like success, whereas we British hate it or at least are so cripplingly jealous of it we feel an animalistic desire to destroy anyone who has achieved it.

I've never been to LA. To be frank, I haven't been

anywhere much. A few clubbing holidays to Ibiza and Greece when I was in my late teens and early twenties. Adam and I went to Edinburgh for a long weekend last year. I went with him to a gig in Hamburg once but it wasn't what you'd call a holiday; he was working and I almost drowned in the constant sheets of rain. Plus I developed a visual intolerance (bordering on repugnance) to frankfurters; seriously, I threatened that if I saw just one more I'd use it to batter Adam to death.

We kept talking about going to Paris but we never did.

LA is year-round sunshine, mountains and beaches, white teeth, tanned bodies and a load of shops. What's not to love? OK, so there's more than a bit of Botox; still, I can see myself living there. Yes. Why not? I take a deep breath.

'Can you send someone to pick up my passport and things, if I make a list? I don't want to go back into London.'

Scott grins at me. 'You're getting the hang of this rich and shameless thing, aren't you? Sure we can send someone to pick up your stuff, but as for your ma and pa, that we are going to have to do in person.'

33. Fern

Yes, my ma and pa, as he calls them.

On the one hand I'd like to believe that my mum and dad are going to be thrilled at my enormous good fortune, and yet I can't help but feel nervous they might not be quite as ecstatic as I'd like them to be; after all, Jess and Lisa haven't exactly bowled me over with their enthusiasm for my whirlwind romance. I tried to call both of them this morning but Lisa's phone went straight to voicemail (suggesting she was on the nursery school run and couldn't pick up) and Jess had her phone switched off. Ben's been the most supportive, even though he was with the cranial osteopath and couldn't talk for long. He isn't ill or injured, he just fancies the practitioner and makes up aches and pains every month. He had time to tease me about not working out my notice and told me to enjoy the ride; he then laughed in an especially mucky way which left little to the imagination in terms of which ride he was referring to.

But my parents?

Scott is keen for us to visit each other's parents as soon as. I say I'd rather put in a call and visit in a few weeks. After all, we haven't had that much time to ourselves yet (three and a half days and counting). Mark says meeting the parents is a PR opportunity and has to be managed with great care; we shouldn't rush things, and while I don't see meeting my future mum-in-law as a 'PR opportunity' I am grateful for the delay, which feels horribly like a stay of execution. Scott and his mum are reportedly very close. What will she make of his impulsive proposal?

'OK, my fabulous Fern, if that's what you want, I can roll with that but you ought to call your folks before the papers do.' Scott tosses my mobile at me. Although he's only a couple of feet away, I don't manage to catch it coolly with one hand, instead I drop it and have to scrabble on the floor to pick it up. He grins indulgently, delighted even with my gaucheness. 'I'll give you some space.'

I don't want space, I want sex. I can't take my eyes off his butt as he leaves the room. I'm consumed with the thought of it naked and honest, framed between my clinging thighs. Oh. My. God. He's lust on legs. It's horribly frustrating that Scott and I have yet to make love; I'd much rather do that than call my parents. If only we could get a moment alone; it never seems to happen. Still, I guess Scott's right, I can't let a tabloid journo break this news to my relatives. The thought of my parents dampens the lusty fire in my mind; suddenly I'm consumed with quite a different sort of giddiness.

Why am I so nervous about calling them? They'll be thrilled, won't they? Of course they will.

The phone rings about eight times before anyone picks up. I'd told myself I'd allow it to ring ten times before I gave up. In fact, I know that my parents are always losing the handset and when the phone rings, general panic ensues in their home as they turn the place upside down in a desperate bid at rediscovery.

'Hello.' My father sounds breathless. Why, I'm unsure.

They've lived in the same small three-bedroom house for forty years, how can searching a tiny, familiar place result in breathlessness?

'Hi Dad, it's me.'

'I'll get your mother.' So far so good. Situation normal.

'Hello love,' says my mum. 'Did you have a nice birthday? I've been meaning to ring you to ask if you got our card, there was a tenner in it. Did you get it? You can't be too sure when you send money through the post, can you? I was reading something in the *Daily Mail* the other week and it said that certain disreputable postmen target birthday cards and steal them because they often have money in them. That's why I wrapped your tenner in a piece of paper and then put your card in a brown envelope. No postman is going to spot that. Anyway I was intending to call but Mrs Cooper –' She pauses for a nanosecond to see whether I interject with the token grunt that will suggest I have a clue who Mrs Cooper is. I don't grunt in time so she launches on. 'You remember. Her from up the road who was married to the smiley bald man with glasses but he had a heart attack last Hallowe'en. Tragic. Well, she invited me over to look at her holiday photos. She's been on a world cruise. Can you imagine? A singles holiday at her age! Mind, I'm not knocking it, she looks marvellous. But she had album after album to get through and she's such a chatty sort I couldn't get a word in edgeways. So I'm glad you called. But I would have got round to it as soon as I'd finished with the ironing and wormed the dog –'

'Mum, I'm engaged.'

'Well, I'm speechless!'

This is a lie. Because no sooner does she mutter that sentiment than she starts to yell to my dad. 'Ray, Ray, our Fern and Adam are getting married. He's popped the question. At last.'

'No, er, Mum, that's not right actually. Adam didn't pop the question,' I interject desperately.

'Oh my God, Ray. She's gone all modern on us. Our Fern asked *Adam* and it's not even a leap year.'

'No, Mum. That's not what I'm saying.' I'm almost yelling in my effort to be heard above her excitement.

'But you are engaged?' she asks suspiciously.

'Yes. But not to Adam,' I say at last.

Now she *is* speechless.

Eventually she mutters, 'Then who?'

'Scottie Taylor.'

'I, I, I know the name.' My mum stutters, confused and unsure. 'Did you go to school with him?'

'No.'

'To college?'

'No.'

'Well, who the hell is this lad you are engaged to?' she questions.

'Scottie Taylor, the pop star.'

'Stop being a silly sod.'

'I'm not,' I insist.

The longest silence in our relationship follows and is brought to a close when Mum finally says, 'Talk to your father.'

I hear bewildered and angry snarls pass between the two but this isn't odd. Devoted as they are to one another, they haven't swapped a pleasant word for over ten years. I don't need to assume that my parents' bewilderment or anger is necessarily anything to do with the news I've just delivered. It might be that Mum has completed Dad's crossword – thus cheating him out of the satisfaction of entering the final letters – or it might be that Dad has hung the washing out in a way that does not meet Mum's exacting standards.

'What's all this bloody nonsense about you being engaged to a pop star?' demands Dad.

Or it might be my news.

I convince Dad that I'm serious. I refer him to his paper (he takes the *Mail* every day of his life; he swears it's just for the crossword) and I explain as best I can the circumstances of the proposal.

'So you've been carrying on with this Scottie fella behind Adam's back for a while now, have you?' asks Dad, not bothering to hide his disapproval.

'No!' I assure him. 'I only met Scott on Friday.'

'Last Friday?'

'Yes.'

'Stop being bloody soft.' I consider, should I fess up to an affair I haven't had? I'm sensing that my dad would understand that better than a whirlwind romance. 'Have you not heard of the saying "Marry in haste, repent at leisure"?'

'Well, yes, but I love Scott.'

'You don't *know* him. You live with Adam. Better the devil you know, I always say.'

'Dad, I'm thirty. Adam was never going to ask me to marry him.'

'Two wrongs don't make a right.' Dad is fond of quoting idioms. Until now, I've never noticed how fond.

'He's a multi-millionaire.' I'm hoping this will impress my dad or at least reassure him that I'll be looked after.

'Aye well, a fool and his money are soon parted.' I'm struggling to comprehend the relevancy of this particular idiom; I suspect my dad was just on a roll and it's not, in fact, relevant at all. 'Your mother is hyperventilating. I have to go. We'll talk about this later, Madam.'

I seriously doubt we will. When you have five kids a policy on non-interference has to be followed in order to keep sane. In fact, when we were teenagers, it wasn't unknown for my parents to lock themselves in their bedroom by way of disciplining us.

My father hangs up just as Scottie pops his head around the door.

'How did telling your folks go?' he asks.

'Good,' I smile. 'They're delighted,' I add. Although I have the decency to cross my fingers. There is no point in upsetting him by saying their reaction was one of disbelief and hysteria. 'You?'

'Yeah, great.' He nods and smiles enthusiastically, a little like one of those toy puppies that you see sitting in the back window of a Ford Escort. He's lying too, no doubt. 'I think, on reflection, there's no need for us to dash off to Hull at short notice. Better that we get to LA and then we'll fly the parents out for a longer more relaxed introduction, in a week or two. Like you said.'

'Fine by me,' I smile, happy to put that off for a while. Now, about the sex . . .

34. Scott

My mother has to be scraped off the ceiling; she maintains that this hasty engagement is the most stupid, *stupid* thing I have ever done out of the many, many, many stupid things she has to choose from.

'Is she pregnant?'

Since I was thirteen my mum has been scared the answer to this question would be yes. Then, once I turned thirty, she hoped it would be.

'No, Ma, she's not.'

'Oh.' I can hear her disappointment. 'Well, what's the bloody rush then?'

If Fern had been pregnant my mum would have given her some grudging respect as the mother-to-be of her grandchild; she would have approved of the speedy engagement. My mum is big into lads 'doing the right thing', which in her book is marrying the woman they casually and carelessly shagged, as opposed to avoiding a pregnancy in the first place. She accepts that sex is a rush and a fact. An unstoppable force. My mum's philosophy is based on the fact that she was four months gone when she and Dad tied the knot and that didn't turn out too badly, except for the divorce and everything. As Fern is not pregnant, Mum will assume Fern is a flighty gold-digger and 'no better than she ought to be'. I know, her reasoning is flawed, but hey, she's my mum. Fern is not a gold-digger, I've met enough of those to be able to smell their sweat a mile away.

'Everything resonates between us. We rhyme,' I say. 'Fern's going to be so good for my music. She's inspiring.'

I'm so fired up with ideas for songs that I'm jotting stuff on the back of fag packets and old newspapers that I find lying around; I even scribbled something on the hotel wallpaper this morning. It's great. It's a forlorn space, the place that's left where ideas used to be made. It's like a bed where love used to be made. Fern can fill that. I'm sure of it.

'Three days, you say. You met her three days ago!' The disbelief is biting at my mum's throat; I hope it doesn't choke her. 'Some would say it was a bloody silly thing to do to ask someone to marry you after just three days,' she says huffily.

'Why?'

'She might've said no.'

'But that's unlikely.'

'It's too quick. You don't know her,' she says, stating the obvious. 'She doesn't know you,' she adds with more alarm, voicing that which only she or I might worry about. Some say I'm a moulded pop product. Others say I'm a god. It's become difficult for us to know for sure.

'No one ever knows anyone anyway. At least this way we'll have plenty to talk about over the next fifty years.' Jokingly, I dismiss my mother's fears.

She'll calm down. My mum likes to pretend she's oblivious to my famous charm but in fact I honed my skills on her. Besides, it's not my mum who tells me what to do any more; it hasn't been since I was about six. Mark is happy with the engagement and my fans are too, now. The hype about the wedding is already growing; it's going to be cataclysmic. Right on plan. It appears I can do anything I want, as long as I don't grow up.

'Mum, somewhere along the line I lost the luxury of just being liked for who I am. And maybe that's no bad thing, because I'm not that likeable and if all I had to offer was me, naked, then who's to say anyone would want to hang out with me?' My mother sighs but doesn't comment. 'I'm impossibly cool and I mean that literally. It's impossible to be as cool as they want me to be and I'm exhausted trying. Then along came Fern. Fern likes me for who I am.'

My mum is not a romantic. She's been in love too often for that to be possible. Grimly she holds on to her anger and disapproval. 'Your problem is you've had such a splendid life that now you've become fascinated with the mundane. That's all that's left.'

I would argue, but she might have a point. What do I know? My mum worries about my success but then, if I was a failure, that would worry her too. She's one of the few who understands that if I'd never made it big it would have been good and bad in equal parts. Bad because I was born to be big. Convinced that I was a huge talent, that needed to find the light, she knows I would have died in the attempt to become great. But then, she knows I might die in the act of being great.

If I'd stayed in Hull I'd have been a cheeky rascal womanizer, with a few women crying after me and maybe an illegitimate kid I'd chosen to stand by. But now. Now, after this enormous and overwhelming unprecedented success, my influence has stretched too far. My opportunity to break hearts is too wide. There isn't a hole out there that isn't prepared to welcome me. Maybe my mum is thinking along the same lines, because she adds grudgingly, 'Well, I hope this Fern is firm with you. You need to hear "no" more often.'

'You'll meet her soon.'

'When?' Her curiosity can't be crushed.

'In LA.'

'LA,' my mum says with a tut.

Many Europeans are fucking snobby about LA because there aren't any ancient coliseums or lofty spires. They dismiss it as flimsy, gaudy and tawdry, but still, everyone seems to find the place irresistible. Funny that. I think LA is a little like a big plate of microwave lasagne; empty calories but tasty. The trick is not to gorge yourself, not to eat the whole thing – believe the whole thing – because you'll be left feeling sick. It's true there's a fair share of neon and plastic and broken dreams – I see them from my limo if I look hard enough – but there's splendour and excitement and magic there too.

My mum's dismissive tut has nothing to do with lack of spires. She doesn't like LA because it's a long way away plus there are lots of drugs there. Of course there are lots of drugs everywhere and she probably knows that too, but it's a thought that's too big and scary for her heart to deal with.

I think it must be torture being my mum.

I try to reassure her. 'LA is peaceful. My relatively low profile there means I can actually walk down the street without being mobbed. In the US only the European tourists bother me for autographs.'

When they do, I put on a hilarious (and no doubt inaccurate) accent and I swear I'm not Scottie Taylor but Zoran Obradovic from Serbia. I even offer to sign their autograph books as a lookie-likie but no one is ever interested in that, which is funny when you think at home women ask me to sign their tits with their lipsticks. In Europe I'm constantly met with hysteria: in Sweden my clothes are ripped from me, shops close for me in Germany, roads close in France. A police escort is essential in all the Latin countries. I'm often trapped inside a hotel room or TV studio. The screaming has become deafening.

'Oh Scott, love,' says my mum sadly. I think we both know the truth. The thing is, with each unhassled footstep I take in the US, I remember Paul McCartney telling me that the most important thing to all record producers, and to most artists too, if they are honest with themselves, is to break America. The thing is, without America you're nothing. No one. You're not even a Hasbeen. You're a Neverwas.

And that makes me enjoy the anonymity an awful lot less. I need America. I have to have America. Above everything.

35. Fern

Falling in love with a mammoth superstar is not ordinary. Yet in some ways it is.

Falling in love with Scott Taylor or even Scottie Taylor is exactly like falling in love with anyone else. I want to be with him every moment of the day. Everything he says is wonderfully profound, interesting and clever. I can't eat. Or sleep. I don't even want to. We can't stop touching one another. We both keep giggling. We forget that we're sharing this planet with 6.6 billion other humans.

But in other ways, falling in love with Scott Taylor is unlike anything I was capable of imagining.

Take flying, for example. Pre-Scott my experience in airports was an 'elbows out' affair; endless queues, ground staff who had spectacularly failed to graduate from charm school and barefaced jostling with other passengers in order to secure uncomfortable, unyielding seats – first in the waiting areas in the terminal and then on board. Every flight I have ever taken has been delayed by a minimum of three hours. Two hours fifty-four minutes of which I spend trying to resist purchasing one of the gigantic slabs of chocolate that are on offer in WH Smith. Chocolate bars the size of a mattress – intended for families of four to share over a two-week period. I always fold to temptation in the last six minutes and panic at the till as I hear my flight being called. I gobble the lot greedily as I run for the gate, thus guaranteeing I'm sick on the flight and spotty on holiday.

I had no idea there would ever be a situation where I'd be whisked through check-in and security and a nice lady from British Airways would usher me through the noise and chaos of the terminal, past the fraught and stressed, past the comfy-looking Club Class lounge and even past the prestigious First Class lounge, to finally lead me into the haven that is the secret waiting-room reserved for royalty (both pop and the more traditional variety). There, among plush suede couches, the aroma of scented candles and the relaxing chill-out tunes, I was offered champagne and elaborate nibbles, most of which I couldn't identify (but they tasted like little mouthfuls of heaven).

Scott, Mark, Saadi and I didn't even have to walk the ten metres from the gate to the aeroplane steps; a limo was waiting for us. At the steps we were met by a softly spoken guy with an Irish accent, gentle grey eyes and a calm smile. He introduced himself as the First Class Cabin Service Director and discreetly whispered that he and his staff would serve our every need. As professional as the crew were trying to be, they could not resist craning their necks for an extra peek at Scott. One cheeky, friendly crew member, Gary, informed me they weren't allowed to ask for autographs but he would never wash his hand again as Scott had touched his fingers when he accepted an orange juice. I giggled and promised Gary I'd secure him an autograph before we reached LA. Gary melted in front of me and had to be scooped back into the galley. He showed his gratitude throughout the flight by playing hangman with me when I was too excited to sleep but the others (more accustomed to the splendour) slept the full eleven hours.

I've read my share of *Heat* and *Grazia* and a whole bunch of other glossy, gossipy magazines and I thought I had developed a reasonably good idea of how the other half lives, but it turns out I had none. I had no comprehension about how it feels to no longer need to carry a bag or a brolly or even money; someone else deals with that stuff. I had no understanding that everyone, *absolutely* everyone is overwhelmed by Scott's presence and simply cannot act normally in front of him; many are overly solicitous or gushing, some are brash and hostile. It appears no one can just be normal in the presence of such wealth and success. From the glossy mags I could not grasp how scary it is when crowds of fans clamber on the car bonnet or lunge at Scott with a pair of scissors in an attempt to cut off a piece of his hair or clothes, to keep.

But then, I had no idea how much fun it could be to sit with Gary, in First Class, playing hangman while drinking champagne at two in the afternoon (or six in the morning – if you go by US time). It's all surreal.

Gary has now dropped all pretence of being aloof and professional. Away from the eye of the Cabin Service Director his effervescent personality bubbles uncontrollably.

'You are a lucky, lucky lady,' he says affectionately, not quite hiding his jealousy however much he wants to; it ekes out of the corner of his mouth as he tries to force a smile – I've seen that expression a lot recently. I guess being Scott Taylor's fiancée is going to attract envy with the same ease as a magnet attracts filings. I'm prepared to live with it. Gary's form of address might seem a little presumptuous, as we've only known each other for six hours, but I find his camp, hush-hush, off the record, you're my new celebrity best friend attitude refreshing. After days of people staying a respectful distance away from me I welcome the closeness, even if it is somewhat sudden.

'I know!' I admit indiscreetly. 'I never thought I'd be this in love.'

'Or this rich,' adds Gary.

I bristle slightly. I can't, hand on heart, say that I'm oblivious to the joys of Scott's wealth; this morning when I slipped on a pair of Paul Smith trousers, a Matthew Williamson shirt and a pair of Manolo Blahnik strappy green sandals I practically had an orgasm. But I can, hand on heart, say I'd have taken the man without his millions. I'm sure I would. His mind is like an enormous labyrinth of wonder. I'm continually surprised, delighted and amused by him. Plus he has the body of a Greek god and can hold a tune. What's not to love?

'What's he like then?' asks Gary, leaning closer, conspiratorially.

'He's really clever. Always thinking about stuff. And he has this lovely way of singing to himself all the time; he doesn't even know he's doing it. It's as natural to him as breathing is to us. Plus he's really firm but fair with everyone he comes into contact with. He makes an effort to learn the names of the guys who bring the room service. He doesn't like tomatoes. He –'

'I meant in bed.'

'Oh.' Despite the three or four glasses of champagne I've knocked back and the dizzying effects of the altitude I'm shocked at the intimacy of this question and I recoil, ever so slightly, from my new best friend.

'Well, that's erm –'

'Private,' says Saadi, suddenly appearing from nowhere.

Gary and I both jump a fraction. He grabs the empty glasses that surround me and disappears behind the blue curtain back into the galley where the other crew members hang out; Saadi clearly scares him too. I have no idea why I persist in being terrified of her – she has never been anything other than professional and polite with me – but I am. The problem is I don't know how to peg our relationship; it's quite unlike any other I've had before. She's known Scott far longer than I have. He's told me she's saved his ass on dozens of occasions over the years. They are clearly very close; I suppose I'm a little threatened by that. But then Scott has said to me that you can never be true friends with anyone you employ, and in the final analysis, he pays her a wage. He'd do anything for her but she's not quite a friend. I'm his fiancée. No buts.

I wonder how long she was listening in to my conversation with Gary. I replay it to check I didn't say anything silly or compromising.

Saadi plonks down in the seat next to mine. We've bought all the seats in the First Class cabin to guarantee Scott's privacy; she can play musical chairs if she wants to.

'Erm, thanks. I didn't know how to answer that,' I admit.

'No problem.' She sounds efficient, rather than friendly. But she did get me out of a hole, I'll give her that. 'You need media training. I'll set something up as soon as we touch down. There's a Rottweiler in LA who will be perfect for the job.' Saadi whips out her BlackBerry and makes a note. 'You'd better get used to the prying. You'll be asked that and worse. The press are going to hound you as soon as your name is released.'

'And when will that be?' I ask somewhat nervously.

Saadi checks her watch. 'About two hours ago.'

'Oh.'

'We want the press to be waiting for the plane when we arrive in LAX.'

'We *want* them there?' I don't get it. We went to such pains to avoid being spotted getting on the plane at Heathrow. Scott and I travelled to the airport separately. Scott wore a fake beard most of the day. We avoided the public like they had the bubonic plague, just in case one of them papped us on a mobile and wanted to make a tenner by sending the shot to the tabloids.

'Yes. It will be a scrum,' says Saadi.

'We *want* a scrum?'

Saadi sighs as though I'm being slow. '*Obviously*. It's his biggest story ever, this engagement. If the US media aren't interested in this, then . . .'

'Right.' Call me shallow but I'm worrying if I'll look my best emerging from an eleven-hour flight.

As if reading my mind Saadi says, 'We have Scott's beautician, Joy Lewis, and his two masseuses, Linda Di Marcello and Natalie Pennant, travelling with us. Have you heard of Linda and Natalie? They work as a team.

Their hands are wonders; all the stars use them. Those two will freshen you up. What sort of massage do you prefer? Japanese shiatsu beating? Icelandic birch whipping? Swedish pummelling?'

'Erm, not bothered.' Two masseuses at the same time? Oh. My. God. What happens, does one do the left side while the other does the right or is it split top and bottom – so to speak? This is another world.

'Then Joy will work on your hair and makeup. We want you to look wonderful but at this stage it's best if you keep comments to a minimum. At least until you do the media training. If I'd known you'd be awake on this flight, I'd have arranged for someone to work with you while we were travelling.' She looks frustrated that she's wasted eleven hours. I get the feeling Saadi is not a time-waster. 'So just smile, wave and – if pushed – say you're happy.'

'Can I say delirious?' I ask with a grin.

She eyes me for a moment with a hint of suspicion, gauging whether I'm taking the mick. I stare back and try not to blink so she can read my sincerity.

'I'd prefer chuffed. It's more street and harkens back to Scott's northern roots. Delirious has some odd connotations. Out of context that won't work. And believe me, they'll take every word you say out of context.'

'How about thrilled?'

'Bit posh. And steer well away from delighted. Just be natural.'

Right, chuffed or happy. But not delirious or delighted. Got it. 'I don't suppose anyone will care about what I have to say about anything anyway,' I mumble.

Saadi shakes her head. 'You'll be hounded like Princess Diana, doll. Get used to the idea.'

I think it's a bit of a sick and unnerving comparison to draw, considering poor Princess Di's ending, but I don't say anything as I'm distracted by Saadi's next question.

'Have you had any thoughts about what sort of ring you want?' She reaches for a slim black leather file and quickly unzips it. She pulls out a number of sketches of engagement rings. 'We've had jewellery designers work up a few ideas.'

The drawings are stunning. The stones are huge and cut in a dozen different ways. Mostly the drawings are of brilliant, dazzling clear diamonds. But one page shows more colourful designs.

'I like that ruby ring,' I comment.

'That's not a ruby, it's a red diamond.'

'I didn't know you could get red diamonds.'

'You can get diamonds in loads of different colours, including red, green, purple, blue and pink. They are called fancy diamonds,' explains Saadi. 'They're extremely rare – out of approximately eighty thousand carats of rough diamonds mined every year, only point zero, zero one per cent are regarded as fancy colours.'

'I bet they're expensive,' I mutter.

'Very,' she says, her tone making it clear that I can't overestimate just how 'very'. 'Only twenty diamonds in the world have been certified red.'

'Bloody hell. I don't want one of those, what if I lost it down the sink or something when I was washing up?'

'That's quite unlikely now, the way things have turned out, don't you think?' points out Saadi.

'Well, washing my hands then. I'll still be doing that for myself. I think I'd better go for the normal white diamond. You know, the see-through type.'

I leaf through the designs. There are rings with princess cut, round brilliant cut, baguette, bezel, opal shapes, heart shapes, oblongs, single stones and numerous stones. I can see the technical excellence and stunning beauty of every design but I don't really know what to say to Saadi. Whenever I'd imagined selecting an engagement ring I'd thought I'd be choosing it with my fiancé, not his PA. Not that Adam had a PA, obviously, and up until recently it was always him featuring in my daydreams. Saadi fills the silence with a commentary about the sketches.

'We've had three designers work something up. Two who always design for the great and the good – by which I mean the loaded – and one unknown. Some guy straight out of St Martin's. I like his stuff and it might be a good PR ploy to discover some broke, Brit, arty guy.'

I don't think the coverage in a newspaper should be a consideration when choosing my engagement ring, but for some reason I haven't got the guts to say so. I say nothing at all. It's freaky but I keep losing my voice when I'm with Saadi, like she's some sort of female Sir Alan Sugar who can silence anyone in a single glance, let alone a wag of the finger. I'm normally reasonably assured and confident but since I've been surrounded by Scott's posse I've lost my footing somewhat. It's always tricky negotiating a new relationship but I honestly don't think that's the struggle. Scott and I are fine, or at least we would be, but from the moment we became engaged he's been surrounded by a wall of *others*. I mean Princess Di went on and on about how there were three of them in that relationship; at last count there's about forty-five in mine, not including casual staff.

Saadi probably interprets my silence as some sort of stupidity. She adds, 'If you are having trouble visualizing the ring we can get mock-ups or maybe you'd like to wander around Tiffany's or Leviev and buy something off the shelf.'

'Maybe,' I mutter.

'Well, if you can make a decision by Monday that would be great.' She consults her BlackBerry list. I wasn't aware we were under a deadline. The woman is a human tornado.

'What does Scott think?' I ask.

'Oh, he's happy to leave it to us, to you. Anything that you want. Good of him, hey?'

'Yes, good of him.' I dig deep and scramble to find my voice. I try to imagine Sir Alan Sugar naked (that's meant to help with fear of confrontation); it doesn't help much actually, just churns my stomach, but still I force myself to say as firmly as I can, 'I'd like it if Scott and I chose the ring together. I'll talk to him about it when we arrive in LA.'

'OK,' says Saadi. But before I can savour my victory she starts to type something into her BlackBerry. 'I'll schedule that meeting for tomorrow morning. 9.30 a.m.'

No, no, I mustn't fall at first hurdle. Think, totally starkers. Not a stitch on him. It's Scott I'm imagining this time, not Sir Alan. The image of a naked Scott fills me with confidence and fortifies my resolution without causing any of the trauma the image of a naked Sir Alan was. I take a deep breath. 'I don't think Scott and I need a scheduled meeting to discuss my engagement ring.'

'It's just the way things work round here. Scott's a busy man,' says Saadi, as though she's teaching the ABC to an infant.

'I realize that,' I say carefully. I want to add that things might have to change now he has me, but she interrupts.

'It's not just a new man you've bagged yourself but a whole new life too. There's more to being Scottie Taylor's wife than being into him, you know.' I'm beginning to realize that too. Rather than being capable of taking on truly terrifying members of the board, I am once again the new girl at the office who hasn't got the guts to ask how the photocopier works. Saadi carries on. 'Certain things will be expected from you, one of which is a noteworthy engagement ring with a PR story attached. Is that too much to ask?' Her tone is impatient.

I think how lucky I am to be in this position. To be who I am now. Any woman would kill to be me. I'm marrying Scott Taylor. He is sexy, seductive, occasionally surly, consistently stupendous and stonking rich (sorry to be crass but it's an inescapable fact). My mind, heart and wardrobe are bursting with new and expensive, oh la la delights.

I'm kowtowed.

No, I don't suppose an engagement ring with a PR story is a lot to ask when you put it in context. Saadi suddenly adjusts her tone and digs deep to dredge up some patience. I realize she's trying to connect with me but, sadly, the new tone she adopts reminds of my dentist's assistant when she assures me that I'll only feel a tiny pinprick of pain.

Saadi continues, 'Look, I know the system, yeah? I know how things work? Why don't you just follow my advice, because I've been keeping Scott happy for quite some time now. It makes sense.' Well, yes, but isn't that my job now? 'And I know you are thinking that's your job now, which it is. But it's not yours alone. We're a team. You, me, Mark, the band, the chefs, the staff, everyone. We all want the same thing – for Scott to be OK. That's how he works. That's how it works.' I suppose. 'A team is a good thing, hey? The more the merrier?' I don't think I nod or actually offer any affirmation that I agree but Saadi doesn't wait, she just concludes, 'Fact is, you're not an ordinary couple. You didn't want to be ordinary, did you?' she reminds me.

No. No, I suppose I didn't.

36. Fern

The captain asks us all to return to our seats and fasten our seatbelts. As he says, 'Crew cross check for landing please,' a ripple of excitement creeps up my spine. Scott starts to stir for the first time since we took off. He stretches and looks around to find me. He treats me to a wide and joyful grin. He starts to undo his seatbelt so he can come to me; these first class seats are so spread out – it's wild – but a strict air steward asks him to buckle up. I have to settle for a kiss blown through the air.

I stare out of the window and catch my first glimpse of America. Los Angeles is enormous. Below me there is a perfectly ordered interlaced lattice of roads, quite unlike the organic tangle of roads I left behind in England. The order and space are instantly appealing. Although the distance means the houses look like doll's houses I can see that they are anything but small. They are all well kept; most are massive and many have pools. There are hundreds and hundreds of cars lined along the streets or parked in driveways, glittering like jewels in the sun, but there's also lots of greenery. From where the angels hang out, LA looks perfect.

As the aeroplane door swings open I am engulfed by a gush of hot air and the smell of wet palm trees; there's no sign of rain, so I can only assume the airport greenery has recently been hosed down by someone whose job it is to ensure the city of dreams is lush and green on arrival. I breathe deeply and take in my new life. How exciting is this! The ground staff hurry us through customs as fast as they can; we don't have to wait for luggage, as Saadi's second assistant is collecting it. As we stride through the electronic doors and head landside Scott scoops me into a big hug and lands a smacker on my lips.

The beautician, Joy, had long nails and was a tad unnecessarily rough but I'm glad I let her fix my makeup and Linda and Natalie massage out my shoulders as we are greeted by a barrage of cameras clicking and whirring and a hundred different voices shouting at me. 'Over here, love, look this way,' 'Give us a smile,' 'What's your name?' 'Are you Fern Dickson?' 'Show us the ring,' 'Why no ring?' 'When's the big day?' 'This way darlin', smile.'

I turn my head from left to right and back again, trying to follow the countless instructions that are being flung my way. The constant blaze of camera flashes causes me to squint. Scott squeezes my hand and slips his sunglasses over his eyes. He puts a protective arm around me and starts to speak; as he does so the dizzying glare of flashes slows down somewhat, as the reporters strain to catch his every word.

'We haven't picked out a ring yet. I want to design something personally that's really special for Fern.' He does? Wow. See, Saadi had it all wrong. I tune back in to what he's saying. 'As soon as we have a date for the wedding we'll let you know. We won't keep you waiting; I'm not a fan of long engagements. Now, I have no idea how you came to know about our arrival here today but

I hope you can understand we'd like a bit of privacy at this special time so please don't try to follow us home. That's all I have to say.'

Scott starts to lead me away and the camera flashes start up in earnest again. 'Oi, Fern, have you any comment?'

Scott stops to allow me to have my say. I'm on the verge of telling Scott that it was Saadi and Mark who tipped off the press and that's how they know our where-abouts today, but then it occurs to me that he might already know this, so instead I concentrate on what Saadi said I ought to say.

'I'm, erm, delighted,' I say. 'No, I mean, erm, chuffed.'

Scott tightens his squeeze and quickly leads me to the long, black car waiting for us by the roadside. It's so shiny that the azure blue sky is reflected in the roof and on the doors like a huge mirror. I catch sight of Saadi shaking her head.

37. Fern

Oh. My. God.

Listen to me, I really need to think up a new expression to capture my constant and escalating surprise or else I'm in danger of becoming as annoying as Janice, Chandler's ex, on *Friends*. But really, what *are* the words that can adequately sum up my astonishment? I was just getting used to the splendour of the hotel and now I'm faced with this. Scott's home.

We've driven up a winding road of high fences and tall established trees. All the houses were huge and grand but Scott's is the most enormous. It's incredibly modern, all white walls, vast windows and light decking. It seems to go on for ever; I actually have to swivel my head like some sort of cartoon character in order to take in its breadth. Our limo crawls along the gravelled drive and grinds to a halt just outside the massive wooden door. We wander into the airy hall. The floor is covered with enormous white porcelain tiles, which shine like wet ice on a rink. It's a double-height room with a glass ceiling. Sunlight streams in from above and it looks as though Scott (who is ahead of me by a step or two) is standing in a spotlight. It seems a very natural place for him to be, and I wonder whether an über-clever architect thought that through and designed the house as another place for him to be centre stage.

'Do you want a tour?' Scott asks.

I nod. Too overwhelmed to speak.

We wander through the rooms and corridors. The entire place is state of the art and rippling with the latest trends. There are acres of glossy wooden and marble floors and a rich scattering of plush rugs. There are lights hidden in the floor and recesses, throwing out interesting shadows and highlights. Some walls move. Others are made of glass and change colour depending on the mood Scott wants to achieve. Some rooms are minimalist, with white walls, white settees, white shelves and white books with round fires in the middle of a room rather than a traditional fireplace. Other rooms are decorated in deep, dark colours and opulent, lavish fabrics. There are curtains with double and triple linings and cushions that pile like mountains on the sofas. Occasionally Scott stops to point out something that means a lot to him.

'That robe was worn by Muhammad Ali, October 30th, 1974, the night he fought champion George Foreman at "The Rumble in the Jungle".'

'That is a genuine Jackson Pollock, I bought it because I thought the colours would really work well in here.'

'That caricature of Sinatra was done in 1947 by a guy called Sam Berman, it's signed by the artist and old Frankie himself. I picked it up in Christie's.'

I wonder how many rooms there are in Scott's home. Our home. I'd guess at forty or fifty in total but I don't bother asking. He'll think I care more than I do. It's not like I can be any more impressed. Besides, he's unlikely to have the answer. When I asked how many gardeners he has (his gardens are massive and as manicured as Paris

Hilton, he must need an army) he wasn't sure of the answer. He tells me the running of his home is largely Saadi's first assistant's domain. He does inform me that he owns one hundred and thirty-eight pairs of trainers. Which seems a teeny, tiny bit excessive, since he only has one pair of feet, but hey, what do I know? I already own seven pairs of designer shoes and four pairs of designer trainers and I've only been wealthy for a week. At this rate I'll out-shoe him by Christmas.

Eventually we arrive at a room in the back of the house. I can tell by Scott's body language that he's especially excited to reveal what's behind the fourteen-foot-high oak double doors. What should I expect? I've seen the cinema room, the gym, and the indoor swimming-pool.

'I could live in this one room. What am I talking about, I more or less do,' says Scott, as he flings open the doors and reveals a room that is bigger than the entire flat Adam and I have shared with Jess for four years. The walls are painted a deep aubergine purple and the floor is a rich dark oak wood. One wall is made entirely of glass but I have no clue as to what the view is because blinds are pulled down, meaning the only source of light is from the various dim lamps scattered around the place. The lamps throw off dramatic hues that are reflected off the ceiling, as it is covered in mosaic mirror tiles.

This room is, without doubt, the ultimate man's play-room. So much so, I feel the need to buy a strap-on willy just to visit.

'Let me show you around. Here are a few of my favourite things.' He sings that line in a mock Julie Andrews soprano voice. I grin at him.

One corner of the room houses a mini gym, in case Scott can't be bothered to walk to the main gym.

'My dumbbells,' he says proudly. 'They're solid granite.'

I have no idea as to the prestige or usefulness of granite dumbbells over any other kind of dumbbells; I guess it's a luxury thing.

'My "Good Versus Evil" Opus football table. It's made by the Eleven Forty Company.' Scott raises his voice at the end of the sentence showing that he's assuming I'll recognize the designer. I don't. I notice that men are always this enthusiastic about their toys. Adam would love this footie table. I shake my head a fraction. Why the hell is Adam, the loser, popping in there? It must be the effects of the flight; jet lag is making me lose focus. I push the thought of Adam out of my mind.

'Who usually wins?'

'Evil has had quite a run of luck but I'm thinking that might all change now I've met you.' Scott flashes me one of his oh-so-familiar, utterly delicious smiles and I swear my heart is beating between my legs.

A stunning grey leather corner settee divides the room. I wonder if Scott will throw me on it and ravage me until sunrise. I wouldn't mind, despite the jet lag. Because, here's the thing, as hard as this is to believe, when we left the fabulous country hotel, the sheets were barely disturbed. It was good news that I'd slept so deeply but, as I closed the door behind me, I couldn't help but sigh as I tried to exhale the dull disappointment that I had not left the sheets tangled and used. No sex. No damn sex. I'm engaged to *Scott Taylor* for goodness sake! It's accepted that he is the rudest, sexiest man on the planet. He's a man who can undress a woman in a finger click, a man who can leave a woman feeling wet and dizzy by treating her to a particularly penetrating gaze, a man who embodies all that is crazy and dangerous about lust and life. I should be having smokin' sex at least three times a day. It's not right that we haven't got naked yet.

We have been so, so busy in the last few days we haven't managed anything more than a lengthy snog and a heady fumble. We are always together (chatting, laughing, playing cards) but we are never alone (which would certainly lead to much more carnal entertainment). To be frank, I'm more than a bit frustrated with the situation. I am so pleased to be here in our home; now we'll have more privacy. Bob, the security guy, is a great bloke but his constant burly presence is a bit of a passion killer, and Saadi and her BlackBerry ought to be marketed as the western world's most effective contraceptive; talk about barrier method. But, hey, here we are . . . alone . . . in love . . . I linger by the beautiful settee and finger the wonderful cool leather. I hope Scott can read my mind.

He can't. It appears Scott isn't thinking what I'm thinking. He doesn't fling me on the cool leather and start to flick his tongue across my body. Instead he walks around the exquisite piece of furniture and excitedly points out the arcade game coffee table, the cashmere-lined hammock and the retro Champion Level 2 turntable. Now Adam would sell his mother to buy *that*. There's a sixty-inch flat screen TV dominating the room. Scott follows my gaze.

'Maybe we should watch a movie tonight. Let's make popcorn.'

Tonight? No way. Won't we be swinging from the chandeliers tonight? Surely. Watching movies is the sort of thing you do on the fifth or sixth date, after you've had loads of sex and talked yourself hoarse. Is there a way of saying this without sounding like a total hussy? I remain hushed while I think about it.

I notice that his shelves are full of amazing books about the history of art and photography. The range is incredibly broad. There are books about Neolithic, Egyptian and Grecian art. There are more on the Gothic period, Renaissance, Impressionism and Art Nouveau. (I'm reading this from the spines.) Cubism, Fauvism, Rayonism, Pop art and Kinetic art. I am *so* impressed.

'I didn't know you were so interested in art,' I say, trying not to sound too sickeningly struck. Everything he does overwhelms me. I'm worried I might pop with the intensity of the imprint.

'I haven't read any of them,' he says. His tone is a bit bored, a bit resentful and a bit apologetic.

'Oh.' I consider; am I as impressed knowing he has plans to read these books but hasn't actually read them yet?

'I don't really know much about art except that I know what I like,' he says with a shrug.

'Fair enough, I'm just the same about wine.' Should I leave it at that? I can't. 'In that case, why so many art books?' I enquire.

'Well, I had shelves that needed filling. There's nothing more depressing than an empty shelf, is there? I mean, if that doesn't scream empty life, what does? Plus I wanted a new hobby and I was at this launch party for Mario Testino. Now, his work I *do* know about. He's taken my photo. Look.'

Scott reaches for a big glossy book, *Portraits*, and starts to flick through it efficiently. Beautiful images of the beautiful people in our world jump out at me. Liz Hurley looking sexy, Kate Moss looking confrontational, Gwyneth Paltrow looking elusive. Scott pauses and says, 'Look, here I am. I love this shot.'

Testino has captured the cheeky pup Scottie. I had a postcard of this very image pinned to the cork notice-board in the back room of Ben's shop. For a mortifying moment I wonder whether Scott spotted it last week when he made me breakfast. I hope not. I'll appear scarily weird and teen-like, perhaps not an unfair appraisal but one I'd prefer to keep under wraps. I daren't ask him.

'Great shot,' I murmur. 'He has caught you. Or at least a particular bit of you.'

'Yeah, no one catches the whole of me. I'm still chasing it.' Scott snaps closed the book and turns to walk out of the room. He's forgotten he's in the middle of a conversation with me. I remind him.

'So, why so many unread books?'

'Oh yeah, the launch party was held in the National Portrait Gallery and I got all excited about art and stuff. After the party I had someone buy a copy of every book they had in their shop.'

'But you never read *any* of them?'

'No. I fell off the wagon that week. It took another eight months for me to sober up again. I'd sort of lost interest by then. But hey, it was a good day for the gallery's gift shop.' He smiles and kisses me and it's impossible not to be enchanted. 'I do read,' he says as he pulls out of the kiss.

I know this. I know that Scott is cleverer than I expected. In fact, as I am very familiar with his complex song lyrics I can't help but worry that he's almost too clever. He has the sort of mind that tires and is bored easily. The sort of mind that sees the problem of where we might all end up before he's even enjoyed the heady beginnings of where we all set off.

'What book is by your bed?' I ask.

'Mostly self-help books.'

'You should eat more fish,' I suggest.

'Why?'

'My mum says it's good for your nerves.' He grins at me as I hoped he would. 'Where do you sleep?' I ask bravely. I hold his eye and we both know what I'm suggesting. He grins at me.

'I thought you'd never ask.'

38. Fern

'Oh this is wild. I have never seen such a big bed in all my life,' I scream excitedly.

'Yeah.' Scott grins as I lunge at the bed and immediately begin bouncing up and down on the ocean of black Egyptian cotton and turquoise silk throws. He doesn't join me but starts to empty his pockets on to the bedside table; a packet of fags, a packet of orange tic-tacs and a small notebook. He jots down ideas for lyrics all the time.

'Don't you just want to bounce on this bed every single night of your life?' I ask.

'I do actually, Sweets,' he says with a slow sexy smile.

I can't help myself. I know Scott is my fiancé now, and I am in fact desperate to bounce up and down with him, so a veiled reference to sex shouldn't have me turning the colour of an overripe tomato, but hell – it's *Scott Taylor*. I still can't quite believe it.

'No. In this instance I didn't mean like that. I meant don't you just want to jump on the bed because it's enormous? For that matter, don't you want to skateboard up and down the hallways just because you can? And don't you want to run around the house just, well, laughing at the sheer bloody ludicrousness of everything being so damned big?'

Scott smiles at me. It's an odd smile, almost regretful. 'No, I've never done that.'

I stop bouncing for a moment. 'But, at first you did, hey? When you got your first huge, posh flat or I don't know . . .' I search my head for the most exciting boy toy that would likely inspire unchecked exuberance. 'Your first Ferrari.' I understand that he has three now.

Scott's smile drops off his face and sinks to I don't know where, somewhere too deep to retrieve. 'You know, Fern, I don't think I ever had your enthusiasm for it all. I mean I like it. I love being rich and having nice stuff, of course. But the actual *things*, they let me down.'

'In what way?' I sit down on the edge of the bed and he sits next to me.

'Well, take those Bang and Olufsen BeoLab5 speakers, for example, I thought owning those would make me happy. Being able to spend five grand on speakers should make you happy, right? And they did, but only for a tiny, tiny amount of time and that's not happy enough. So they sort of let me down.'

'But they work well, hey? They do something special?' I ask. Unsure exactly what they could do to justify a five grand price tag. Perhaps they make a cup of tea while pumping out music or run around with the vacuum if the place ever needs it.

'Yeah, they work. The acoustic lens technology means that music is projected around obstacles so you can place them up against a wall without distorting sound. But that's not my point. What I mean is, however much stuff I cram in my life it doesn't feel full.'

'Oh Scott, please don't give me the money doesn't buy you happiness routine. Because let me remind you, honey, being broke isn't such a giggle either.'

Scott's grin bounces back on to his face. 'You are so straight up. I love it. You're going to tell me I haven't been shopping in the right places, hey?'

'No.' I lean towards Scott, our foreheads are touching. We hold unblinking eye contact. We are so close to each other that our breathing is all muddled up and his breath out is my breath in. 'From the look of this place you have definitely been shopping in the right places, just not with the right people.'

'Are you the right person?'

'Yup, Scott. I am.'

'So this is what it's like; moving from the multiple choice to the singular?' he asks.

'Yes, in this and all matters of intimacy you'll find less is more.'

He kisses me. And I kiss him back. Tender for a moment and then ravenous. At last! We start to devour each other. His touch is desperate, swift and mind-blowing. His fingers burn me but the scalding sensation is totally pleasurable. I'm fettered to his lips just as though he'd tied me up; I never want to be anywhere other than here. Tinder in his hands, I feel I'm about to explode with wanting and desire. He starts to tug at my clothes and his own. For once, he doesn't seem in the slightest bit practised, he's clumsy with nerves or excitement. He doesn't know whose buttons or flies to loosen first and nor do I. Our fingers become tangled with one another. Never before have just days of abstinence created this intense build-up of lust in me, but as Scott pushes me back on to the black sheets, I swear I can hear the blood pounding around my body; in my heart, in my head, in my silky, frilly Agent Provocateur panties.

There's a knock at the door.

'Go away,' shouts Scott, breaking from our kisses, just for a moment.

The knock is repeated, this time louder and more forceful.

'Piss off.' He's also louder and more forceful.

The door opens and Mark, Scott's manager, walks in. So far I've had little to do with Mark. We nod at one another and pass pleasantries but nothing more. Saadi deals with me. Mark deals with Scott. I thought Scott would deal with everything: me, Mark and Saadi. I thought he'd be in charge, but I'm beginning to understand that is not the case. I think Mark is in charge. I suppose if I'm to continue Saadi's analogy that we are all a team, then Mark is the manager and Scott is the captain. Saadi's in goal. And what am I? I'm left field at the moment; I'd rather be a striker. I shake my head, this is madness; I don't even like football.

Mark has been in the music business since he dropped out of art college in the 70s. No one needs qualifications in this business. They need wits and talent, and as intrusive as I find Mark's presence (particularly at this moment!) I have to admit he comes with bags of both. He's in his fifties and has resisted the stereotype of looking, dressing or behaving like an old rocker. He does not have long hair, nor does he wear skinny jeans, from what I've seen he does not screw groupies and he's done enough drink and drugs in the past that nowadays he is happy with an orange juice and a packet of crisps. He looks like an easy-going uncle. He's bald, tubby and generally affable. He looks as though he buys his clothes in Marks & Spencer (although it's more likely to be Bond Street).

Scott told me that in the mid and late 70s Mark managed a number of rock legends. In the 80s he snorted his fortune and then spent a number of years getting clean and starting up again; first with small bands – one-hit wonders – and then he stumbled across Scott. I think Mark saw a lot of himself in Scott. Raw talent that needed channelling and controlling, otherwise income and opportunity would be blown away or rather, sniffed up. Mark has made Scott very, very rich and obviously has done quite nicely out of the arrangement too. It's clear that this time he's not going to let his fortune slip through his fingers like sand through a glass timer. He's staying sober and in charge. This is never clearer than when he sits on the bed next to Scott and me and starts to talk business, without so much as apologizing for interrupting our pash sesh.

As I mentioned, it's a big bed. I'm in no danger of actually coming into physical contact with Mark but even so I feel an irrational sense of claustrophobia; something like you expect to experience in a crowded lift. My shirt is unbuttoned and I'm flashing my bra, for goodness sake. I scrabble to the opposite side of the bed and hurry to make myself decent; I run my fingers through my hair and use the back of my hand to rub away my lipstick, which is, likely as not, smeared all around my mouth. I flash a look of resentment at Mark but he doesn't seem to notice.

Genially, he says, 'I'm not interrupting anything, am I? Plenty of time for all that. I just wanted to bring you the press so we could share the initial reactions to your engagement announcement.'

'Couldn't that have waited?' snaps Scott. I notice that he has grabbed a magazine and is holding it on his lap, obviously waiting for the evidence of our session to subside.

Mark doesn't answer directly. Instead he drops the papers on the bed. 'These are the British ones. Afternoon editions mostly. We'll see the full story tomorrow in the British press and – with a bit of luck – here in the US.'

I can't believe he's interrupted us to show us the *Evening Standard*. Scott doesn't pick up the paper. He continues to glare at Mark; he's clearly pissed off. I pick up the paper, just to be polite. The headline reads FERN DICKSON IS THE ONE. It's weird to see my name in print. I read the story. They describe me as a twenty-seven-year-old beauty, who runs her own florist's.

'But I'm thirty,' I say to Mark. 'And the flower shop is Ben's, he runs it. I work in it.' I wonder if Ben will think I told them differently.

'Yeah, yeah, love, I know all that. But thirty isn't a romantic age, is it?' says Mark.

'Well, I thought not, but then I met –'

'Look, you'll thank me when you are thirty-five and they have you down as thirty,' he continues.

'But that wouldn't add up.'

'The thing about them saying you own the florist wasn't me, though. I did give the real deal on that stuff. I thought the humble background thing would wash really well. But journos don't listen. They come to press conferences or interviews, make a big thing about recording the proceedings and asking what is on or off record and then they publish a load of crap anyway. You're lucky, they could have had you down as an ex-model.'

'No they couldn't,' I say with a laugh.

'Yeah, they could. You did that catwalk thing at school.'

How does Mark know that? I told Scott, he must have mentioned it. How sweet! He must be talking about me all the time, the way people do when they are besotted with someone. The way I would talk about him if I could get through to either Jess or Lisa.

'It was a fundraiser. I modelled the clothes I'd made in home economics. An elasticized top and a pair of pedal pushers. All the girls in my home economics class did the same, that's hardly modelling.'

'I'm just saying the press might have made that your thing.' Mark shrugs carelessly. We three sit in a loud silence until Mark gets the hint. 'Oh, got it, right. I'll let you get back to it.'

'Yeah, let's catch up tomorrow, hey?' shouts Scott as Mark closes the door. We lie back and stare at the ceiling. We're finally alone but the needy lust of earlier seems to have been dampened. Mark is a heavy cologne user, I can still smell his aftershave lingering in the room – it's almost as though he's still here with us, which is quite some passion killer.

'We'll have tonight though. I'll make it special for you,' Scott says, reading my mind and kissing my nose.

And the anticipation alone creates a feeling of creamy yumminess, much like wading into warm sea for a swim.

39. Fern

I must have fallen asleep in Scott's arms; when I wake up it is dark outside. I reach for him but his side of the bed is cool. I feel dreamy and I don't think it's jetlag. I glance at the bedside clock; six thirty LA time. I have no idea how long I've been asleep because my watch says it is early morning tomorrow in the UK. I adjust the dials. It's 6.30 p.m. in my life now. As I stretch I notice a scarlet gerbera and a note on the pillow. Gorgeous! Aesthetically, I do like a red rose but it's suffered through over-use and I think I'd have squirmed to find one on my pillow. A gerbera is much more original and startling.

Scott's note instructs me to have a deep, relaxing bath and says dinner will be served at 8 p.m. He's drawn a pic of a winking face so I know he's being a little tongue in cheek; I shouldn't expect a butler and the best silver – thank goodness. There's enough new stuff to get to grips with without having to worry about formal table manners.

After stumbling into a wardrobe and a dressing-room I finally find the en-suite. The bathroom is as fabulous as I could have imagined. Oddly, this time I don't squeal Oh. My. God. I'd have been surprised if it was anything less than stunning. It's amazing how quickly you can get used to luxury. There's a round sunken bath in the middle of the room. It's big enough for an entire football team. There are two sinks, more mirrors than ideal and state-of-the-art taps that confound me for about ten minutes. I finally discover that you turn them on by clapping (or in my case shouting frustrated abuse).

When I emerge from the bath I find that someone or many someones have been into our bedroom and freshened it up. It's like living in a hotel; the bed has been made and turned down, candles lit, curtains drawn and mellow, slow-tempo music (which I don't recognize but do like) is playing out of the stereo at a gentle volume. There are no chocolates on the pillow but I can't grumble as, instead, there's the most beautiful lilac silk, tasselled mini dress. I check the label: Bottega Veneta, I haven't even heard of the brand but its fabric sings dollar signs. I put it on. Like everything else that's been bought for me it's a perfect fit. I check my reflection. I might have benefited from bigger boobs, but hey, I look great – not much like me, but great, so who's complaining? Next, I sit at the dressing-table so I can do my makeup.

It's like walking into Harvey Nics at Christmas. I ought to be clear, Christmas is actually the only time I ever go into Harvey Nics. But when I do, I go with Jess and we spend about five hours in there, culminating in a glass of champagne at the bar after I've purchased a tin of biscuits from the fifth floor. Believe me, while I only actually emerge with one gift (and that's for my aunt, who has no appreciation of what it means to own a box of biscuits from Harvey Nics), this is time well spent. I firmly believe the spirit of Christmas is hiding somewhere in that store. I adore my five hours of wafting around being sprayed with perfumes, tasting stollen cake, oh-ing and ah-ing over striking stationery, stunning clothes and testing cosmetics that we can't afford. The times I've hungrily eyed the beautiful treasures on the MAC, Benefit, Stila, Chanel and Dior makeup concessions are countless. I've ached to dip my finger in a pot of something made by Prescriptives, Bobbi Brown or Kiehls and now here they are – jar after jar of exquisiteness on *my* dressing-table, bought especially for me. I stare at the orgy of gorgeousness and try to breathe deeply.

It's a bit intimidating actually.

It's taken me seventeen years to discover which makeup I truly suit (after many, many disasters where I ended up looking like a drag queen). I'm pretty confident with my Rimmel Kohl Kajal eye pencil, suitably smudgeable, allowing me to create sexy, smoky eyes, and Rimmel's lasting finish intense-wear lipstick; I like the pretty sugar plum colour. Having to start again with all these new posh brands and new colours is a bit of a nightmare. Suddenly, I feel the need to ring Jess. It's crazy, but other than the one call to my parents and one brief call with Ben, I haven't actually spoken to any of my friends or family since Scott proposed. I've called and left messages; we've swapped a couple of texts, of course, but no actual chat. I can sense the disapproval across the ocean. It's awkward; everyone liked Adam a great deal and Scott and I have become an item so quickly that no one has got used to the idea yet. I suppose it is quite something to digest.

If only Jess knew Scott the way I do then she'd be happy for me; I know she would. The problem is love at first sight is something you can only truly believe in if you've experienced it for yourself.

I could ring her right now and say, 'You won't believe the selection of makeup that's on my dressing table!' It's our habit to start conversations as though we've been chatting only minutes ago. Until this previous week we've enjoyed a fourteen-year-long uninterrupted dialogue. I could choose to ignore the last week. Least said soonest mended. I check my watch. Hell, it's five to eight.

Obviously, if I had more time, there's nothing I'd like more than to call Jess but I've got a pop star fiancé to shag. I grab the Dior mascara wand and quickly apply. It's good stuff, I think I can get away with that and nothing more.

40. Fern

It's just four minutes past eight when I drift into the big room that I'd call a living-room or a sitting-room although that doesn't do it justice — not glam enough; an estate agent would describe the room as the reception. I found it after fruitlessly opening door after door in order to track down Scott. Each room is utterly tasteful, peaceful and immaculate, and after a while they blur into one. I thought he might be in his 'boys-own' room but there was no sign. I was starting to panic, imagining he'd done a runner. My throat tingles with a peculiar and hideously scary mix of pleasure and panic. Trying to accurately assess that mix, I'd say that ninety-eight per cent of me is utterly, utterly out of this world, stunningly, stunningly beyond happy. The remaining two per cent is pure white terror. I wish I could shake the feeling that this is all too good to be true but I can't quite. The issue is things like this don't happen to *me*. I'm the sort of girl who is a close runner-up — at best. The sort of girl who often hears shop assistants say, 'Sorry, we don't have that left in your size, I just sold the last one.' The sort of girl who has *never* ever had a single number show up on her lottery card, despite buying them religiously for nearly a decade. What are the odds of that? But my panic subsides as soon as I enter the reception room; I know I'm in the right place.

There are about a hundred tealights scattered around

the room, giving off a fuzzy, golden glow. Even though it's a warm night there is a real log fire roaring and so the glass doors, leading out to the garden, are flung wide open. There are more lanterns and candles outside too, lined up on the decking and hanging from trees. The effect is enchanting. I spot Scott standing outside, hunched over a barbecue.

'Seared prawns. My specialty,' he calls when he notices me. 'Champagne?'

I can't believe he bothered to cook for me when he has staff falling over themselves to hold his hankie when he sneezes. It's such a massive compliment! So very thoughtful! What can I tell you? It's a night of undiluted romance. We chat non-stop and we laugh a lot too; it appears that I'm genuinely hilarious when I'm with him. Scott sings to me and lets me read over some lyrics he's working on. We slow dance to a Frank Sinatra CD and I drink champagne – all night, although Scott has to stick to apple juice. It's like something out of a movie. Right up until the fade to black moment.

As the night air cools, we move into the living-room and settle in front of the fire. Someone must have been stoking it while we were outside because it's still roaring. It's like living with a bunch of ghosts. Helpful ghosts, I'll give you that.

'So, Fern, how do you feel about an October wedding?' asks Scott as he crams a toasted marshmallow (that he's thoughtfully dipped into melted hot chocolate) into my mouth.

I chew quickly, swallow and then splutter, 'This October?'

'Yeah.'

So soon. 'But it's already late August. Don't weddings take forever to plan?'

'Well, I don't know. I've never planned one before,' says Scott with a big relaxed smile. 'But I imagine we can pull off anything we want, if we hurl enough cash at it.'

'I always imagined a summer wedding,' I say, carefully.

'It will be sunny here in LA.'

'Here in LA? I always imagined a wedding in London,' I say, somewhat shocked.

'Is LA OK? I mean, only if you want to. I want you to have exactly what you want, of course. I was just thinking the shorter the lead time the less hassle we'll get from the press and if we get married here then we'll be able to plan it ourselves – you know – so that we can make sure it's personal. If we had a wedding in the UK and we were living here in LA then we'd have to hand over to someone else. I want this wedding to be about us,' says Scott.

I think about what he's suggesting. Less than two months away. It's no time at all, not considering we only met a week ago. But then, why not? Didn't I want just this? A proposal and marriage for my thirtieth. Initially, I wanted it with a different man, admittedly, but hey, let's not get picky. Why would I want to wait a moment longer than I have to? People only ever have long engagements if they are saving up or have doubts; neither applies to me.

'I just think we should get on with it, you know, start

making babies and be a proper family as soon as we can,' Scott adds. With those words my wavering vanishes. I fling my arms around his neck.

'Brilliant! Let's do it.'

'Great! I'll have a couple of wedding planners come round asap so you can see who you are most comfortable with and then we can get the ball rolling.'

'But I thought you said you wanted us to plan it ourselves,' I say, confused.

'Yeah. With a planner. You'll need one for an event of this scale.'

'What sort of scale are we talking about?'

'I don't know. A thousand people, maybe.'

'A *thousand*? I don't know a thousand people.' Not even if I include all the Ben's B&B customers and the cabin crew who flew us over here. Nowhere near.

'You'll soon make friends. Trust me, you won't have a problem filling up the guest list.'

That wasn't what I'd meant. The hairs on my neck start to bristle and it's not through lust, as is usually the case when I'm with Scott. It's fear, or irritation, or something I can't quite pinpoint; it's tricky to do so after a bottle of champagne. I don't think I want a thousand strangers coming to my wedding.

'You see, there are certain people we have to invite. They'll be kind of expecting it,' explains Scott.

'Like grannies and great-aunts and stuff?'

'Well, yes, obviously. But also Elton John and David Furnish, David and Victoria, I've been to so many fabulous parties of theirs. Tom Cruise and –'

'You're kidding.'

'Deadly serious.'

Suddenly, the idea of a thousand strangers coming to my wedding doesn't seem so awful; not considering they'll all be A list. Call me shallow. Call me human.

'Think of the gifts,' I blurt. I blush at my own crassness but Scott just laughs. 'I can't believe I said that.' I put my hand over my mouth but it's as much use as chocolate hair straighteners. I try to recover ground. 'Maybe we should say no gifts, it's not as though we need anything. Maybe we should say charity donations only. We did that at my Uncle Terry's funeral. The announcement in the paper said no wreaths or floral tributes but donations to the lung cancer unit at St Hilda's Infirmary welcome. The hospital rang afterwards to say they'd benefited nicely. Auntie Donna got a genuine sense of satisfaction from that. It was a great comfort,' I garble. I'm working on the theory that if I talk for long enough the ground might swallow me up.

'Well, let's take advice on the etiquette, shall we?' says Scott with a good-natured smirk.

'Fair enough. Can we invite Brangelina?'

'Anyone you like.'

I'm quiet for about twenty minutes as I draw up my fantasy wedding guest list. The fantasy wedding guest list that is going to come true! Jess, Adam and I used to play a game a bit like this. As we sat eating baked beans on toast we'd often quiz one another on who would attend our perfect dinner party. Jess and I would plump for Brad Pitt, George Clooney and Matt Damon; pretty much the cast of *Oceans 11* to *13*, while Adam would swear that he'd prefer to have Christopher Wren, Dostoevsky and

Queen Victoria to his party. Liar. Although the truth was, the idea of throwing a dinner party was a fantasy for us. Adam and I never once had people round for a meal. Least not what you'd call a proper one; pizza from a box does not count.

I'm glad I didn't call Jess earlier. Now, I have even more to tell her. I check my watch. Midnight here, that makes it 8 a.m. tomorrow back home. She'll be on the tube. I don't want to get her voicemail; this is too good to leave another message. I'll call her first thing tomorrow.

'You're happy, right?' asks Scott, somewhat superfluously since I keep giggling to myself and I have stood up to dance a short but expressive jovial jig around the room.

'Never more so.'

'I have another reason for wanting to rush the wedding through,' he adds.

'Oh yeah?'

Scott holds out his hand and finds mine. He gently pulls me back on to the sofa and puts his arm around me. 'I was thinking, you know, we've both had our fair share of partners in the past.'

'I had a fair share. You've had a veritable feast, gorged yourself silly from all accounts,' I point out.

'Yep, I know and that's what got me thinking. We need to be special.'

'We *are* special.'

'Different.'

'We *are* different, we're getting married, neither of us has ever done that before.'

'I know and so I want to mark that in some way.' What, a party for a thousand isn't enough for him? I beam at him, waiting for him to explain. 'I was thinking maybe, since we haven't actually managed to have sex yet, that we shouldn't.'

'*What?*' That stops me smiling.

'I don't mean we shouldn't *ever*. I mean we shouldn't have sex until we are married,' says Scott.

'But that's two months.' The same two months that just minutes ago had seemed oh-so-brief (too brief to plan a spectacular wedding!) now seem an eternity. Two months with no sex. It's a terrible idea. Somehow no sex with Scott Taylor is a hundred times worse than all the no sex I've had in the past.

'Yes. That way we'd be like vir-er-er-er-gins.' He sings the word 'virgins' like in the Madonna song. 'I just thought it was a way of making what we have truly special. Do you see?'

I do, sort of. The sentiment is darling but the actuality is going to be dreadful, truly hell on earth. I thought that tonight – what with the candles, the champagne and the log fire that were as good as screaming *sex* – that tonight would be *the* night.

'I don't know, Scott. It's been tricky resisting thus far. Tricky and frustrating and –'

'Hot,' he adds.

'Yes, I suppose so,' I concede.

'I'm loving this delayed gratification thing. The novelty alone is mind-blowing. It's all about anticipation and control and –'

'Shouldn't it all be about love?'

'Of course it's that.' Scott's grin vanishes in a poof. He looks mortally offended.

'Oh OK, go on,' I agree, even though I really don't want to. I can't bear to see him unhappy. He looks so fragile. Like a child. I want to see his face brighten once more. 'Let's get married *early* October, though.'

Scott nods. 'Agreed. I think we'd better have separate beds until the wedding, otherwise this no sex thing is going to be really hard.'

I nod, even though hard is just what I'm after.

41. Scott

My pad here in LA is awesome. Chock-full of style and luxury. I like it out here by the pool because nothing says rock and roll as eloquently as a private pool. I have a stunning infinity pool that seemingly flows out to an endless, lush garden which is as big as a public park. The size of the garden is not an indulgence, it's a necessity. The tabloid scum have long lenses and short consciences. You can sell my discarded chewing-gum on the internet for fifty quid, so you can imagine how much a pic of me shagging a starlet fetches. Around the pool there are a number of heavy, broad wooden sun-loungers. The cream cushions lie as inviting as giant marshmallows. There are green towels, rolled into neat Swiss roll shapes. There's the occasional marble table to be found snuggled between the beds, a comfy resting place for glasses of champagne and minted water – which all my guests are furnished with within minutes of their arses hitting the seat. I have excellent pool staff. It's all very tasteful.

I like swimming and fooling about out here, although I don't like lying around on the loungers the way Gary (the bass) and Mick (drummer) are right now. Their drinks sparkle in the sun, leaving individual footprints – a wet ring of condensation – on the table. I'm unsurprised to note they are drinking Bollinger (mine) even though it's not midday. I wave to them but don't bother walking over.

As I'm not drinking at the moment, I don't much like being around people who are. As Gary takes a sip I feel a twinge of longing so I dive into the pool and start to do lengths. I swim just three confident lengths before Mark appears. He sits down with the lads and says something to them, calls over one of my excellent pool staff and the champagne vanishes. Job done.

Then I spot Fern. She's peeking out from behind my huge cacti, which are bedded in large white plant pots the size of cauldrons. My cacti are bigger than anyone else's in Hollywood, Saadi checked. I also have enormous bushes of bamboo, with stalks as thick as my arms; they stretch upwards to tickle the feet of anyone hanging about in heaven. The sun is almost directly overhead now and pounding down ferociously, throwing short, almost undetectable shadows on the dark marble floors. Fern starts to drag a sun-lounger into the shade, I make a move towards her to help her but one of my muscle-bound pool guys beats me to it. Fern looks faintly embarrassed but a bit chuffed as she watches his gentle exertion on her behalf.

Fern has a great body. Slim and toned without betraying a food phobia or gym obsession. I move towards her and am struck, the way I was the first time I met her, by her top-quality, pert, neat tits. Excellent. And that's from a man who spends a lot of time being underwhelmed.

I pull up a lounger next to hers and stand over her to let the cold drips of pool water splash on to her stomach. She jumps a foot in the air, squeals and then laughs when she opens her eyes and realizes it's me.

'Rat. I thought it was raining,' she says.

'Just blue skies for you from now on in, Petal, nothing but blue skies.' She beams at me. 'Sleep well?' I ask.

'I woke up at two in the morning and stared at the ceiling until eight.'

'Jetlag?'

'Excitement. I fell into a deep slumber at the exact moment I stopped debating huge romantic number – wide enough to shelter an entire family – versus simple shift wedding dress, just wide enough to disguise my hips. I couldn't switch off,' she says with a grin. 'Hey, look what Saadi gave me.' Fern waves about a brand new iPhone.

'She's great, Saadi. She thinks of everything.' I yawn and sit down on the lounger next to Fern's. Let's see if I can stay put for twenty minutes. That's not a ridiculous target. I should be able to do twenty minutes with Fern to keep me company. Or at least fifteen.

'It's like something Q gives James Bond just before he goes on assignment. Apparently, besides being a phone, I can use it to do my email, as a sat nav thingy, as an organizer.'

'If you want to be organized,' I chip in.

'I think the implication is that I ought to be. It has access to the internet, you can play games on it, or use it as a multi-media player or even a camera.'

'Can it tap dance?'

'Yes, and floss teeth,' replies Fern with a grin. 'Thoughtfully, Saadi has already bookmarked a number of websites that she thinks might be useful to me.'

'Like?'

'Like places I might want to visit in LA. There are so

many places to choose from. Where do you want to start?'

'I dunno, Fern. I've been everywhere.'

'Well, I've been nowhere.'

'OK, so you choose.'

'Well, the Getty Center, Grauman's Chinese Theatre and Santa Monica pier are on my list.'

'Actually, I haven't been to any of those places.'

'But you've lived here for nine months. What have you been doing?'

'Working and drinking. Not necessarily in that order.'

'Great, we can do the tourist things together.'

'Cool.' We grin at each other. Isn't it cool, this couple stuff?

'Saadi has also bookmarked websites about weddings. You know, caterers, reception venues, dress designers, etc. Plus she's made a list of the names and numbers of other people who I might find useful: a hairstylist, a clothes stylist and a personal trainer. Do you think she's trying to tell me something?' Fern looks vaguely concerned. I grin at her, reassuringly. Personally, I like her as she is, but I know that Saadi and her crew are already turning wheels and cogs in order to transform her into something, I don't know, glossier, I suppose. Mark and Saadi said to me that glossy is what's required and expected of my wife. I don't think this is something she needs to hear me say.

'She's just trying to be helpful. Justifying her obscene salary,' I say instead.

'She's arranged interviews for us to meet her favourite three wedding planners for tomorrow morning – a

Saturday. I suppose there's no time to lose but how did she get anyone to agree to a Saturday meeting at such short notice?'

'Money talks.'

'I suppose, and as you say, she thinks of *everything*.' Fern looks anxious, vexed almost. 'She told me she's going to pick up a dildo for me from some sex shop on Sunset Boulevard.'

'Hustler.'

'Yeah, that's it. She says you have an account there.'

'Guilty as charged. It's a great store, we should go shopping together.'

'OK.' Fern doesn't look too convinced but she'll look great in one of their baby dolls or maybe titty tassels. Is she vexed because I've visited sex shops? I'm a rock star, it's like a teenage girl visiting the makeup counter at Boots: essential shopping. I didn't have Fern down as a prude.

'Saadi said I'm going to need a dildo in light of our chastity vow. I hadn't realized you'd discussed our plan with her.'

Ah. So that's the cause of the vexation. I get it. 'I tell her everything,' I say smoothly, wide-eyed, innocent. It's true, I do tell Saadi everything; except all that which I keep secret. 'You don't mind, do you? Wasn't I supposed to?' I ask, showing concern. 'She thought it was really romantic,' I add with a smile.

I sense Fern does mind, because if there's one thing I know about women, it's that they are really funny about what you tell other women. I need to rush the conversation on to another subject, because it's too nice for a row or even a low-grade sulk and while I haven't seen Fern do either of these things yet, I know it's only a matter of time. Of course she has it in her to be irrationally narky; she's a woman.

I look at her hipbone and feel a twitch in my swim shorts. This no sex thing is a mind-blowing experiment. It was Mark's idea. Fern was his idea too, as a point of fact. I've had lots of sex and I mean *lots* – an amount that no normal person can even perceive (not even desperate little slappers who live in ugly small towns, who – in order to ease the tedium of their existence – drop their knickers as often as they drop cigarette stubs and usually at the same time). More sex than that. I mean lots, and lots, and lots, and lots of tits and ass and legs and holes, well, the thing about that is it gets boring, doesn't it? Hand jobs in Jacuzzis, blow jobs in bars, gang bangs in limousines, sex in yachts, sex with geisha girls, sex with starlets, sex with models, sex with aristocrats; it's all the same in the end.

An endless stream of nightclubs, alcohol, drugs and meaningless sex takes its toll. It's inevitable. I got fed up with waking up with an intolerable feeling of apprehension and fretfulness. Being on drugs and being intensely and inexplicably anxious come hand in hand after a while. I'm prone to anxiety anyway, and a feeling of uneasiness constantly shrouded me when I was using; especially when I woke up and the foul and sickening delinquency of the night before came crawling back into my mind. It didn't matter how much money I had in the bank or how many records I sold, I was riddled with the worry that I was just as desperate and pointless as everybody else. Sometimes I'd think I was insane. Other times things were easier – I knew I was.

There comes a point when you realize that no life, not even my life, is wide enough to fit in sex, drugs, rock and roll *and* responsibility. It doesn't add up. I shared this observation with Mark, just over three months ago, last time I decided to get clean. Mark was relieved; my record company were starting to get a bit nervy about the number of times I'd missed studio sessions and insulted journos because of the said endless stream of nightclubs, alcohol, drugs and meaningless sex.

I told Mark, 'Being surrounded by too much T&A is the same as being surrounded by too much luxury. You stop noticing it. It has a numbing effect.'

It's true you can be totally done-in by the absolute monotony of faultless and never-ending excellence. Who'd have thought? Maybe Mark wanted to make a sarkie comment about his heart bleeding for me but no one close to me is ever sarcastic with me nowadays; they know it hurts me and I'm mean when I'm hurt. Instead, Mark said, 'So you've done all there is to do with abundance, how about practising a bit of partiality now.'

'What do you mean?'

'Well, you know, once you've been to every fancy restaurant there is in town and you've eaten your fill of seared carpaccio, pan-seared venison and sweet duck cooked with plums and star anise, it's nice to stay in and have simple steak and salad. I'm not suggesting a burger. I mean something classy and straightforward.'

'Like?'

'Like marriage.'

'Marriage!?'

'Yeah, you could do it all properly, meet a girl, like her,

hold off shagging her and then do her in a big white frock.'

He might have been joking, but I thought about it and he was right. It would be true to say that I've never shagged a bride before; least not one married to me. I'm going to enjoy doing things properly with Fern. She's different. A hotty (although not as hot as many I've had). She's quite normal (but not so normal as to bore me, as many have). I don't quite understand it yet but she has something really special going on. Or rather, we have something really special going on between us.

Mark has all the best ideas.

42. Fern

'If you want to go anywhere let me know and I'll get Saadi to introduce you to our stateside driver, Barry. He'll take good care of you. He's a pro. You could go shopping; Saadi's arranged for you to have access to all of my accounts and I pretty much have an account anywhere you might imagine,' says Scott.

I know he's trying to change the subject. I allow him. Let's face it, offering me a chauffeur-driven trip to designer stores with unlimited credit is quite an impressive diversionary tactic. Normally, I'd have to settle for Adam suggesting we change channels.

'Yeah, Saadi already gave me a list,' I say with a big smile. 'How did she organize all of this in such a short time? It's unbelievable.'

'I know. Hats off to her – she is an *excellent* PA.'

Scott drops his sunhat over his eyes and we both fall silent. He reaches for my hand and we hold on to one another across the loungers. His touch sends shock waves ricocheting through my body. I fight the instinct to leap on him. Damn this no sex plan! I try to dampen my lust by watching the old Mexican gardener as he endlessly clears the leaves from the pool. No sooner does he scoop a net of bamboo leaves than the same amount fall back into the water. It looks a pretty thankless task but not too arduous; the repetitive action calms me. Bebop jazz pipes out of the state-of-the-art stereo that is hung on the lime green wall behind us. It's the sort of music that makes you nod your head rather than shake your hips. I can make out the clink of china and rattle of cutlery in the distance, proving that the kitchen staff are being far more industrious than we are. They're clearing breakfast or maybe setting up lunch. It's very peaceful until suddenly Scott sits bolt upright.

'What's up? Were you stung?' I look around for the offending wasp.

'No. The thing is I find it hard to relax. Sort of unnatural. Doing nothing is something I'm saving for when I'm dead.' Scott looks around for something to amuse. 'What are you thinking, Fern?'

'About the agony of not having sex with my sex god fiancé,' I reply frankly. Scott laughs but doesn't jump me, which is what I was hoping he'd do. He's very serious about this chastity thing. Couldn't we at least fool around? I suppose neither of us would be able to stop if we started; still, would that be so awful? My throat becomes parched and scratchy and my hands become damp as I indulge the idea of us flinging ourselves in among the bamboo in order to pull off each other's clothes. We'd speedily slip out of our swimwear and slowly, oh so slowly, his tongue would venture over my body. His tongue, lips, hands would uncover zones of delight; I'd burble and flood. He'd caress my shoulders, kiss the back of my neck, nibble at my jawline, lick between my breasts. But this time we'd finally get past the delicate discovery. He'd thrust suddenly, deeply, certainly. He'd fill me, pushing, burning, grabbing, pulling, taking until I moaned and screamed with a smarting, scalding desire.

I realize I'm making odd mewing sounds when the pool guy asks if I've swallowed a fly? Am I choking? Do I need a drink? I do. I need him to throw it over me. I'd better think about something else.

'I have to keep giving myself a mental pinch,' I tell Scott. 'I need to keep reminding myself this is real, these are the sights and sounds of my home now. It's a leap. I never, even in my wildest dreams, imagined that my home would have a view like this.' I sweep my arm out towards the blue skies and tall trees. 'Or that I'd listen to the sounds of staff preparing lunch. Kids yelling, a dog barking, TV blaring was as much as I dared hope for. It's surreal.'

'Bit much to take in, hey?'

'Yeah.'

'What do your friends make of everything that's happened to you?'

'Not sure. Haven't talked to any of them.' I try to keep my smile attached to my face. One moment's lack of concentration and I fear my face will crumple and I'll look like a discarded crisp bag. Not a great look and very ungrateful. 'I thought they would be really thrilled for me. You know. Especially Jess, she's my best friend. I thought she'd be wowed about my meeting you and getting engaged and everything. But I get the feeling she's avoiding me.'

Scott takes off his hat and looks at me with painful sincerity. Am I actually dribbling? It's possible – he's gorgeous. I'm pretty sure he could make me worry less about Jess *et al* if he just took me now and said sod the chastity vow. I know, I'm being shallow.

'The thing I've found hardest to appreciate is that success can fuck stuff up more than failure,' says Scott, understanding everything without me having to say too much. 'Why don't you call her now? Try again. Use your new phone, put it on speaker, then I can say hello too,' he says, helpfully.

As soon as Jess picks up, I elatedly yell, 'Hi, it's me!'

'Fern!' Jess shrieks. 'Finally we talk!'

'Didn't you get my messages? I've called loads.'

'I've tried to call you back but your mobile is dead and you didn't leave another number – you silly sod.'

The relief. Of course, a simple explanation. 'God, how stupid of me. So sorry. I'm all over the place. I've been living in a dream world.'

'I see that from the papers. They say you're in LA!'

'Yes!'

'I can't believe it!'

'Nor can I!'

'You're marrying Scottie Taylor!'

'Yes!'

'I can't believe it!'

'Nor can I!'

'So you've gone. I really can't believe it. You didn't say goodbye.' This time I can't hear an exclamation mark.

'There wasn't time, I –' I falter and then try again. 'It's not like it's goodbye, *goodbye*.'

'How can you have gone? You haven't picked up any of your clothes.'

'I had someone come by to pick up my passport and

photo albums while you were at work. I don't need my old clothes,' I explain.

'Oh. I see. You didn't take the makeup brushes that I got you for your birthday.'

'Hell. That was a mistake. I meant to.'

'I suppose you can buy more.'

Suddenly, I don't want to tell her about the plethora of goodies on my dressing-table or the size of the house, the infinity pool, my new wardrobe. I don't know how to. All at once the root of Jess's silent censure is clear to me. 'Oh shit, Jess, I'm so sorry. You're concerned about the rent. Don't worry about what I owe you, I'll keep paying until you find someone to take my place.'

'Very good of you.' She doesn't sound at all grateful.

'How about we say I give you six months of rent on the old place upfront, you'll find someone to replace me by then.'

'You think it will take six months to find a new flatmate but you found a new fiancé in three days,' says Jess.

Ouch. I look up at Scott, startled and wary of his reaction. 'Adam was never my fiancé,' I say pointedly.

There's a silence. It lasts for about a week and I'm beginning to think Jess has hung up; eventually she sighs and says, 'So what's he like then? Scott?'

'Brilliant, amazing, beyond words,' I garble; instantly grinning broadly.

'And you're sure of that, already?'

'Everyone knows that much,' I answer simply. I try to turn the conversation. 'We've set a date.'

'For the wedding?'

'Yes. October second. It's a Friday. And of course, it

goes without saying that I want you to be my chief bridesmaid. Lisa can be maid of honour. You can have both, can't you? They are different but sort of the same.'

'*This* October? Jesus, Fern, what's the rush?'

Jess's tone suggests that marrying Scott in a hurry might not be a brilliant idea; which is awkward considering he's listening. Maybe I should tell her that she's on speaker-phone.

'I'm marrying *Scott Taylor*. Explanation enough, surely,' I say confidently and then I blow Scott a kiss. There's another silence; stupidly, I try to fill it. 'I feel really rough today. We had such a big night last night. I think I peed pure champagne this morning.' For lack of anything better to say – after all, I daren't broach the subject of my new home and my chat about my new fiancé was stonewalled – I add, 'Just think, Jess, I can pee champagne every day of my life from now on, if I want to!'

'Nice thought,' she mumbles.

'You should come here before the wedding. Have a holiday. Why don't you?'

'It isn't a good time for me to do that.'

'Is it the money? You needn't worry about the money. Scott will buy you a ticket if I ask him to. He's really ridiculously generous.' I flash Scott a beam. I'm a little self-conscious about singing his praises in front of him, although he seems happy enough to listen. He nods encouragingly.

'You do love the man don't you, not just the money?' Bloody hell. I really should have mentioned the speaker-phone.

'Yes, Jess, I do,' I reply hotly and firmly. However understandable Jess's question is, Scott must find it offensive. It's offensive to me actually! I'm not a gold-digger or a star-fucker, Jess knows that. Doesn't she? She's known me for ever. I look at him while I speak to Jess. 'He's sensational. And he wants to marry me and have babies with me. It doesn't get any better than this.'

'If the papers are anything to go by, he's quite a handful. He has so many demons and is constantly fighting his addictions. It's not your scene at all.' Jess sounds quite breathless, as though she's rushing through a prepared speech. I'm beginning to think she might have been working on it all week. She carries on, 'People in bands, they have breakdowns, do drug overdoses and do weird things during sex with oranges. It's not for you, Fern.'

I struggle to simultaneously control my temper and hide my embarrassment. Behind his back, people probably say this sort of stuff about him all the time but that doesn't mean he wants to listen to it. I take a deep breath. 'He's really special and special people are always complicated. I want to help Scott deal with the whole enormous adulation thing. Maybe he can be the pop exception and just come through as a normal human being. He's clean, now,' I insist.

I stare right at Scott as I deliver this speech defending his honour. I really want him to see that I'm innocent and hopeful and loyal. My views are different from Jess's. I'm different.

'He's clean *right now*, maybe,' says Jess.

Abruptly Scott gets up and walks away; he's heard enough. Neither my best smile nor my pleading eyes can persuade him to stay. It's probably a good thing. While I want to demonstrate that I can be totally honest in front of him I also know that Jess wants to say her piece and it will be very awkward when they meet if he's sat and listened to what she thinks.

Once he's safely out of earshot I round on her. 'Jess, despite the fact that he's a ludicrously wealthy pop star, who has travelled the world, met interesting people and slept with them, and I'm a painfully skint florist, who has travelled Zone 1 and 2 by tube, met the same people again and again and slept with a few of them – we are a lot alike. I've never been happier. Why can't you be happy for me?'

'I don't believe in fairy tales.'

'I thought you did.'

'No. I believe in dreams coming true. It's a different thing.'

'Being with Scott has reminded me that life is supposed to be utterly splendid. We're meant to enjoy as much of life as we can.'

'Yeah, without hurting anyone.'

'Goes without saying.'

'But as you've run off with Scott you've hurt Adam.'

'Are you suggesting that I should have stayed with Adam to save his feelings? What sort of relationship is that? Adam had his chance. *I* wanted to marry Adam. *I* wanted to move things on to a more serious and committed level. *I* wanted him to propose. But *he* didn't.'

'What if he had? Would you still have left him for Scott Taylor then?' demands Jess.

'He didn't,' I reply firmly.

Suddenly my mouth tastes metallic; a taste I normally associate with waiting to see if my card will be rejected at the till point or going to the dentist – fear generally. That Buck's Fizz I had earlier must have been off. What have I got to be afraid of? A third long silence stretches between me and my best hate – sorry, I mean best mate. But honestly! Couldn't she have pretended to be happier for me? What would that have cost her? I can feel every one of the 5,456 miles that separates us. I want Scott to come back. I want him to put his arms around me; maybe then I'd have the guts to hang up on my old life, although there probably isn't any need. If Jess's reaction is anything to go by then I think my old life will hang up on me pretty damn soon. Why does it have to be like this?

'You need to call Adam. You see it as a done deal.'

'I told him it was a done deal.'

'You were both drunk, he didn't take you seriously. He thought it was a fight you'd get over by the next evening.'

'Well, I'm sure he sees things differently now,' I say with a frustrated sigh. 'He does read the papers.'

'You owe him a proper explanation, at least that much after four years. He's a good guy. You know that.'

'OK, OK, if I agree to call him will you agree to talk about something different? Like bridesmaids' dresses for instance,' I bargain.

'I am not wearing pink.'

'Fine, how about mauve?'

For a moment I think she might show an interest but my hopes are dashed when she says, 'He'll be back in a few minutes, you can talk to him then. He's just nipped out for a takeaway.'

He's eating then. Not so heartbroken. I've had enough of this nonsense from Jess. She's supposed to be *my* friend. Snippily I say, 'He won't want to have a big emotional talk and risk his pork chow mein going cold. Anyway, I've got to go now; I'm supposed to be some-where else.'

I hang up. I don't bother to explain to my naggy mate that my pressing engagement is dragging my sun-bed out of the shade (or watching someone else drag it, to be precise). Rolling on to my stomach, so that my back gets tanned, would probably seem like a flimsy excuse for not talking to my ex.

43. Scott

Straight after lunch Fern and I jump in my yellow Lamborghini Murciélago and speed off to Santa Monica pier. Fern's really chuffed because we are alone; which – apart from Bob, who follows us in the Audi – we are. We don't talk about her phone call with her mate. It's a downer and I don't want to do 'down' this afternoon; I want to do 'tourist'.

The sun guarantees smiles as well as flip-flops and we wander hand in hand and on air. We cross a bridge above a busy, multi-lane road. The air smells of gasoline and hot tarmac but when I breathe deeply there is a hint of sea breeze, accentuated and made more convincing by the sound of seagulls. Fern reads a little plaque and tells me that the wooden pier dates back to 1909; the wood is worn to a shine with the feet of thousands, if not millions, of souls who have also sought a bit of easy fun in the amusement park.

It's a beautiful day. We ride the rollercoaster and the carousel, we eat candyfloss and drink Diet Coke, then we wander down to the beach and walk along the waves. We kick off our footwear and I keep dashing us both in and out of the sea, trying to race the surf. We get soaked but we'll look pretty cool if we happen to get caught on camera. I don't think any photographers are trailing us but I'm just saying – if they are – they'll get some great shots. It's fun anyway, even if no one is watching us. We lark around and I make her lose her footing. We both fall to the ground in hysterics.

'I feel as carefree as a child and yet I'm an engaged woman with a home and a future. It's marvellous. How come when I was with Adam I owned nothing and had no plans and yet I felt weighed down?' asks Fern. She's panting and she has sand stuck to the side of her face. She's lovely.

I don't answer her because I don't have the answer. I have very few answers, actually, but I am listening to her. I'm finding that nearly everything she says is interesting. Unlike most men I love to talk about moods, and beliefs, and life's incidents that we call experience. I find it helps my work. For instance, there's a lyric somewhere in what she's just said. Something about the weight of freedom or the lightness of commitment. Not sure; I jot it down anyway.

I've been working on the new album for some months now. All my albums to date have had songs about being, well . . . me – angry, cheeky, humble beginnings, rich and famous now, misunderstood, too well understood. I use my song writing to replace the confessional box which I gave up when I was about thirteen (roughly the same time as I really started to sin, actually). I offer my fans brief glimpses into my infamous life. I lay out my sordid and soiled self. I flaunt my fame-induced neuroses and I dazzle them with my humongous success. It's complex. But people are. And me, I am especially because I'm like other people but more so. The Europeans love all that stuff, always have done. They love hearing about my sex life; my vice and my victories. They sort of kid themselves they are my friends. Sad buggers.

But not the Americans. The albums haven't worked in America. How come even when I'm having the best times that thought punches me? Floors me.

Thinking about it (and I do think about it, endlessly), it's not a surprise my albums aren't doing it for the guys of the stars and stripes. For one thing they don't like messy famous people. They like their famous people to be happy and uncomplicated (because otherwise what are they all working for?). And for another thing, they don't really accept I'm famous at all because I'm not famous here. It's a fucker.

So I have two jobs to do out here in the States. One, I have to show them just how big a dick I swing and two, I have to produce an album they will like – which probably means I have to stop talking about swinging my dick. I need to do less of the fame stuff, they're not buying it – literally. And I need to talk about love. The happy sort. The celebratory, blissful, ecstatic sort. Enter Fern.

Fern is so clear-cut and straightforward. Her dilemmas are few and far between and so ordinary. The Americans are really going to relate.

'The stuff you talk about, Fern, is so fresh and frank and authentic. I love it. You're helping me think new thoughts. I've written so much in the last week. I'm working on this new album, called *Wedding Album*, it's a bunch of love ballads. Something very different for me. It's all about you.'

'Really?' Fern flashes one of her astonishing smiles.

No, not really if she means really in the absolutely, one

hundred per cent truthful sense. But yes, really, the album is all about her, *now*. I've dropped her name into two or three of the songs, which only required the smallest of changes in the lyrics. It's pedantic to insist on believing that just because I wrote the vast majority of the album before I met her, it's any less about her than it would have been if I'd written it after I'd met her. I'm like dedicating it to her. The press will think it's about her. My fans will think it's about her. And in my experience if enough people think a thing, it makes it true. True enough. The thing is, more people will buy it if they think it's about her.

I start to tell Fern more stories about myself. This isn't just because I like talking about me, I'm wondering how she will react to it all. She's appropriately (and understandably) enthralled, but more than that, her responses to my experiences are really fascinating. Fern understands my ordinary roots and extraordinary flowering. That's special. I offer up fragile, immersed memories and she appreciates what I'm on about; I can elaborate on them, giving them warmth and texture and a meaning they sure as hell didn't have when I was living them. Story after story pours forth. Some are blazingly bizarre; she's surprised to hear I've had coffee with Nelson Mandela. Others are painfully predictable; everyone expects me to have snorted cocaine off the arses of women whose names I never knew.

'I think it's brilliant that I can tell you all this stuff,' I mutter as I kiss her. I slip my tongue in her mouth and my hand up her skirt. I feel her warm wetness in both places. We're lying side by side on the sand. It's fun to push a fraction further, go a bit deeper, play a little harder.

I allow this kiss to linger before I pull away, fall flat on my back and look at the sky. 'I wonder if we're going to manage this pre-wedding chastity thing?'

'Not if you insist on giving me filthy looks and probing kisses in the sunshine,' she laughs. We both know she wants it.

I love it that she's so horny for me but I love controlling myself (and her) more, so I keep talking. There's loads more stuff to tell her about me yet and she, like everyone else, can't get enough. The difference between her and everyone else is that I don't edit. If she's shocked she doesn't show it. The thing is, for a long time I believed that as a rock star I sort of had a duty to enjoy myself to the absolute limit. That's what's supposed to happen; it's part of the natural order of things and rock stars don't enjoy themselves line-dancing or whipping up a really tasty meal for two with only four ingredients. Decadence and depravity are the birthright of the rock star. It's my job to be reckless and extreme. People expect it, because if I'm not shagging and snorting to excess then who the hell is? It would be an ungrateful waste of opportunity to be a rock star and to just turn up at a gig or the studio, play some songs and leave quietly by the back door. No one wants that. I'm in a unique position, not even models or princes get the same opportunities. I answer to no one. The stuff I've done isn't evil; it's just dirty. Really, very much so.

I tell her about parties where people left their clothes and sense at the door, where joints and women were rolled on glass-top tables and champagne and bullshit flowed and was lapped up with ravenous greed.

However sensationally beautiful and cool the party

venues were (and they always were), it surprised me to learn that by the early hours of the morning these places had always become menacingly sinister and balefully sordid. Penthouses – with minimalist wood-burning fire-places, enormous glass chandeliers and custom Starck-designed furnishings – were hell. Luxury yachts, with polished decks and sharp white sails, docked in Monaco marinas, became prisons. Hotel suites with Jacuzzis, flat-panel HD TVs, Dean & Deluca gourmet mini-bars seemed like pokey brothels. It turns out that the lushly landscaped terraces with panoramic city views are forget-table – despite what the host might promise. But the memory of emaciated models, eyes blackened with smudged makeup and lives, sliding on the floor, gamine legs splayed as they slip in their own spilt spirits (both literal and metaphysical), is an enduring one. Sadly.

'I guess we won't be going to many parties,' comments Fern.

'No, not at the moment. I don't feel like it. Does that bother you?'

'No.' She hesitates and then adds, 'But maybe parties would be more fun together than they ever were when you were alone.'

'Yeah, maybe. That's what I'm hoping.'

We kiss again and I don't tell her that my hope has a way of vanishing; I spend it like liquid gold. That sort of thought won't help *Wedding Album*; it's not the right chi. Instead I say, 'It's great that I can tell you the most sensational and sinister things about myself and you seem equally interested in both.' I shake my head with a mix of disbelief and delight.

'That's what love is, accepting the person faults and mistakes and all,' says Fern in a matter-of-fact way.

'So it appears.'

We stare peacefully out to sea for a few moments, then Fern asks, 'Do you think I'll get a signal here? I'd really like to call another one of my mates, Lisa.'

And we were having such a nice time; she must be a glutton for punishment. I smile and try to appear supportive. As it happens it pans out better than I hoped as this Lisa practically wets herself when I grab Fern's phone and talk to her.

'Hello, Scottie Taylor here,' I say. 'How's tricks?' This is the routine I use at my gigs. I grab the phone off someone in the crowd who is taking a photo and then I call their mum. It's hilarious. The effect is just as awesome with Fern's friend as it is with the people in the crowds. Of course, Lisa squeals with laughter.

I like this Lisa better than the other mate. At least she doesn't give Fern a hard time about leaving her old boyfriend in the lurch. In fact, she doesn't say much at all beyond, 'Fern is a lucky, lucky cow.' Which she says about ninety times, but sort of nicely.

Fern takes the phone off me and asks Lisa to be bridesmaid so I hope she's fit. Lisa says yes and gushes that she'll do anything to help out, that she'll come to LA at the drop of a hat. But when Fern offers to fly her out and to hire a nanny for her sprogs Lisa says she is meant to be running the NCT nearly new sale in the town hall next Saturday, so it's tricky. I'm not sure what that is but it must be pretty important, sort of on a par with a global summit about climate change, I guess. Fern looks crushed. I point to my watch and to my stomach and so she says goodbye to her lacklustre mate and we head off to find a burger and fries.

Poor Fern, I think she's beginning to realize that the tiresome thing about getting what you want is that you always have to lose what you had.

44. Fern

America is built with giants in mind. Everything is on a galactic scale. Skyscrapers actually do scrape the sky, there are ten- and twelve-lane road systems and flyovers that look big enough for spaceships to land. The plates of food are vast, the cartons of yogurt are enormous and you can swim in the beakers of coffee. And as far as I'm concerned, the best thing of all, the stores stretch on and on and on and never seem to meet the horizon. The size of the US is probably one of the reasons Scott fits in here – as he's gargantuan too.

Scott is being such a sweetheart. He must be really busy with his album and yet he's making a huge effort to help settle me in. He carves out time to show me all the sights. I don't just mean the tourist stuff I've circled in the guidebook; he's keen to show me his LA too.

We visit Disneyland, we go and watch the whales swimming, we visit the zoo and we go to the predictable (unmissable), if not slightly crude and tasteless, Hollywood Boulevard. There's a shockingly bad waxwork museum there. The models are all slightly out of focus, off-scale versions of American actors. It's not a patch on Madame Tussaud's. I once had my photo taken with Scott's model in Madame Tussaud's in London but I don't confess to it. He knows I was a fan before I met him, not a crazy fan but enough of a fan. Yet confessing to the fact that

I was sad enough to pose with a glorified candle would seem weird now. I'll have to find that photo and get rid of it. Knowing it exists sort of says I was half in love with Scott before I met him, which is bothersome.

We also visit the Guinness Book of Records Museum, where being a freak is celebrated; God Bless America. I insist that we go to Grauman's Chinese Theatre and take pictures. I'm desperate to put my hands and feet in the prints of Sophia Loren and Susan Sarandon. Scott is reluctant.

'I'm not mad about actors,' he says.

'Why's that then?'

'The people who make it their business to be vicious about me say that's because I've never been offered a role on the silver screen and I'm consumed with vulgar jealousy. It's nothing as crass. I just don't think they should be paid such obscene amounts for doing what the rest of us do all the time for free.'

He says this so casually that I almost miss the importance of what he's saying. Poor Scott, he certainly has come across more than his fair share of fakers and I suppose he does have to perform for strangers a lot of the time. 'Everyone isn't acting *all* the time,' I point out encouragingly. 'I'm not acting. You're not acting.'

Scott grins, 'OK, let's go to Grauman's then. You know I can't deny you anything.'

We spend a lot of time on Sunset Boulevard. The road is massive. In fact all roads are unfeasibly long in the US; when I was first given someone's business card I thought the house number was a telephone number. Other than length, it is a surprisingly mundane road to look at. Despite this, the illustrious and celebrated regularly come here, not just to score drugs; it has history. Scott tells me that a part of Sunset is known as 'Guitar Row', due to the large number of guitar stores and music-industry-related business dotted about. He points out the legendary recording studios – Sunset Sound and United Western Recorders – and he takes me to the Whiskey, a club renowned for launching the Doors and where Elton John made his US debut.

We visit Johnny Depp's old nightclub, the Viper Room, but we don't stay long; nightclubs and addicts are an explosive brew. We move on to the Standard to eat chips at the twenty-four-hour restaurant; Leonardo Di Caprio and Cameron Diaz reportedly have shares in that establishment. We sit in a cosy booth and chat over the sound of ice being crushed as pomegranate margaritas are being prepared for other people. When I'm in the mood for champagne we pop to Chateau Marmont, a plush, fantastical hideaway, or we float in the clouds at the Sky Bar. All these celebrated hotels, with legendary bars, boast famous patrons. We (and a lot of other recognizable people) do our shopping at Ralph's supermarket, also on Sunset. The bread's good but the thrill for me is that I stood behind Drew Barrymore in the checkout queue. I'm secretly keeping a list detailing the famous people I've met or spotted. Besides Drew, I spotted Jennifer Aniston while dining at the Mondrian and I stood in the loo queue with Emily Blunt at Mel's (it's a diner that's celebrated for its customers – strike that, I meant to say its waffles, strike that, I did mean the customers). I sat at a sushi bar next to Anne Marie Duff. It all leaves me gasping with excitement.

Scott keeps the best until last. Just when I start to insist that I simply can't be any more impressed with the razzmatazz, glitz and notoriety, he takes me to Rodeo Drive.

I stand, mouth wide open, gaping in absolute awe. Rodeo Drive is truly dazzling. Everything shines; the expansive windows displaying breathtaking clothes and jewels, the dark, sleek cars, the blonde glossy women and even the older plump men who accompany them, shine. These men wear a uniform of the confident wealthy: pale blue shirts, red ties and navy blazers with buffed buttons and cufflinks and enormous watches that . . . yes, you've guessed it . . . shine. The street is clean enough to eat your dinner off and every street lamp is decorated with hanging baskets full of pretty bougainvillea that gently sway in the breeze. I turn around and around in circles.

'Where should we start?' I gasp, craning my neck to take in the enormous, shiny buildings. 'I know, I know.' I scrabble in my bag and find my all-singing all-dancing iPhone. 'I have to call Ben,' I say excitedly. He is the perfect person to appreciate this perfection.

'Ben?' asks Scott.

'My old boss, remember?'

'Oh yeah.'

'Darling, how utterly fabulous to hear from you,' shrieks Ben. 'My most famous, famous, famous friend.' I'm pretty sure Scott will have overheard him.

'Well, *I'm* not really famous,' I point out, blushing a little.

'Clearly you haven't been keeping up with the press, darling. You are a *face*,' he yelps excitedly. 'Every glossy has you plastered across the front page. Headline: "She's delighted, er, make that chuffed." Too funny.'

'Which paper wrote that?' I ask, distraught (Saadi had been too; Scott thought it was hilarious). 'I sound like a trying-too-hard idiot.'

'Most of them ran with that, since it's the only comment you've made so far. And I noticed that you are taking all the credit for B&B. Most papers say you *own* it.'

'I'm sorry about that,' I mutter. 'The papers aren't always that accurate.'

'No kidding. Don't sweat it. Your engagement has been marvellous for business. I've had to take on three new fulltime staff.'

'Three!'

'One permanent and two on contract. When the fuss dies down I won't need the contractors but I might as well milk it while I can,' says business savvy Ben.

'So the permanent girl, she's –'

'To replace you, that's right. Well, you aren't coming back here, are you?'

'No, I suppose not. Although it seems weird to think of someone doing my job. I love my job. I suppose I should say *loved* now. I miss it.'

'What's to miss? You hated the fact that you had to work Saturdays and you moaned that your hands were always scratched by rose thorns or chapped due to the constant dipping in and out of water,' points out Ben.

'True, and some of the customers were irritatingly indecisive.'

'I know if I was in your position I wouldn't look back and I *do* own the place.' The florist is a business to Ben, flowers are a religion to me. He'd be just as happy selling chocolate or shoes as long as the chocolate and shoes were truly beautiful and his profit margin was reasonable. He could turn his hand to anything. I'm all about flowers so despite the drawbacks I still insist, 'I loved my job.'

'You must be loving your new life,' says Ben more seriously.

'Oh I am! You'll never guess where I am right now.'

'Rodeo Drive,' he says drily.

'How did you know?'

'Because if I was in Rodeo Drive I'd be doing exactly the same thing in your shoes. I'd be calling all my friends to brag; who wouldn't? Crazy world you've landed in though, isn't it? I've been approached by half a dozen papers all desperate for an exclusive story. You know the sort of thing; they want details of your past loves, hopes, dreams, etc. etc.'

'You're not doing any interviews though, are you?' I ask.

'Of course I am. Adam, Jess and Lisa are being very tight-lipped, which is marvellous because that's driving up the price the papers are prepared to pay me.'

'But you won't say anything too stupid, will you?' I ask hopelessly.

'Of course I will,' says Ben cheerily.

I sigh. 'What did I expect? Discretion has never been your thing. Please, please, *please* don't show the press any photos of me dressed in my Moulin Rouge fancy-dress costume.'

'New Year's Eve 2007, when you got so drunk you ended up wearing your basque around your waist. And your modesty was only just saved because Adam strategically placed a feather boa over your –'

'Yes,' I say quickly, desperate to shut him up. I'm grateful that my past life was so ordinary that I have no more dramatic skeletons in the cupboard. If I did I'm pretty sure Ben would have inadvertently flung them all into the daylight by now.

'OK, I won't show them those photos. But don't be greedy with this, pleeease. And don't be a "no comment" bore. Where's the fun in that?' says Ben. 'Odd to think I'm going to be famous because we shared face masks and pizza.'

'And four years' hard graft. Would it kill you to mention I was actually very good at my job?' I ask.

'OK. Will do. You don't really object to me riding on your coat-tails, do you? I mean *you* couldn't.' His implication is painfully clear.

'I wasn't looking for fame, I'm in love,' I point out.

'Brucie bonus, darling. Now you are showing off. Your persistent belief that people care about the distinction is endearing, darling, but haven't you noticed that they don't? Never mind, Cinderella has got her fella. Could your life get any more perfect?'

'Only if you came to stay with me for a few weeks,' I suggest, impulsively.

'You're kidding.' I think Ben might have stopped breathing with the excitement.

'Not at all. I need help with –'

'Styling. You do, don't you? I thought you were very slouchy in this pic in *Heat*. I was going to say something but I didn't want to hurt your feelings. Look around you.

The women in LA have a rich walk, a swagger, almost. I've seen it on *Ugly Betty*. You should try to imitate that.' I glance up and down Rodeo Drive. Ben is right. These women know how to strut. 'Plus I have a million ideas for the wedding.'

'There are loads of people who can help me here but I'd like a friend. I know it's a lot to ask, especially when you are so busy in the shop.'

'Give me an hour to pack. No, realistically give me a week.'

'To pack?'

'No, to brief the new staff in the shop, silly. Then I'll be all yours.'

'Really?' I'm delighted. 'What about your interviews?'

'They'll wait.'

'Jess and Lisa both had their reasons for not coming. I'm so touched that you're going to drop everything for me,' I say, beaming from ear to ear. I was beginning to fear I didn't have any old friends left.

'I'll try to pretend I'm not hurt that I was your third choice. You'll get me Club Class though, won't you? I've always wanted to fly Club.'

'I'll fly you First. With a bit of luck you might bump into my pal Gary. He was a steward on our flight. He's just your type.'

I'm ecstatic that Ben is coming to visit. All aglow I hang up and turn to Scott. 'You'll love Ben. He's great fun. He just wants everyone to be happy all the time.'

'Not a bad philosophy,' says Scott with a huge grin. 'Now, shall we shop?'

45. Fern

Surreptitiously I finger the cool, calm, creamy cardboard bag that is sitting at my feet. Inside it (beyond the yards of thick black velvet ribbon and the endless sheets of dainty, floaty tissue paper) lies a dress that cost two months' salary. At least, two months of *my* salary, that is – if I still earned a salary, which I don't of course. In the boot of the car (or the trunk as they say over here) there lie a further dozen or so similar stiff cardboard bags, inside which there are Moschino sunglasses, a Bally bag, a pair of Jean Paul Gaultier jeans, two Matthew Williamson maxi dresses (we couldn't decide which colour suited me!), a Tommy Hilfiger day dress, a Gucci purse and a Prada jacket. Oh. My. God.

'Happy?' asks Scott.

'Very, very, very,' I confirm.

'What are you thinking?'

This is why Scott is more of a deity than a man. He cares what I'm thinking! 'I was just wondering when I'll wear the Fendi dress.' It's a scarlet silk dress with cap sleeves and beautiful beaded detail around the collar. It's elegant and stylish. I can't float around the pool in it, even an infinity pool, even if my boyfriend is a rock star. 'It's a going out dress. A special occasion dress.'

'We could go to a movie premiere or a charity gala or something,' says Scott with a yawn.

'We could?' I splutter on my excitement and almost choke.

'Yeah, we could.'

'Have we been invited to any?'

'We're always being asked to them, we get two or three invites a night. But Mark usually says no.'

'He does? Why?' Why would anyone turn down an invite to a movie premiere?

'Worried I'll get pissed or . . . I don't know, distracted,' murmurs Scott; he is staring out of the window now and doesn't seem to be totally focused on our conversation. He hates travelling at this time of day, traffic jams irritate him. As do queues (which, to be fair, he rarely encounters because he can always sweep to the front of any queue).

'Distracted? From what?' I ask, drawing him back to the conversation. 'From me?' I pursue, concerned. A tiny, tiny bit of me is still terrified it might all disappear; Scott might stop thinking I'm special, just as suddenly as he decided I was. Following a secret signal Barry might skid to a violent halt; they might fling open the car door and drag me from the plush leather seats and shiny coolness of the Bentley. I might be cast on to the street and have to fend for myself by burrowing through litterbins in a desperate effort to hunt out returnable bottles and cans. I'd explode with grief. I cast a quick panicked glance at Scott. He beams at me. It's the slow, sexy smile that sends deep crinkles around his face. Crinkles that I'm beginning to be oh-so-familiar with; crinkles I can trust.

'No, Sweets. Of course not. From my work.'

'Oh, I see.' I feel a bit foolish. I have to try harder at

submerging my occasional insecurity; it's not the impression I want to give. It's not a good look on a rock star's chick – although let's face it, it's a familiar one. Whenever there's a beautiful man, there's usually an insecure woman following behind, just as certainly as there's a clever and knackered woman behind every great man. Honestly, sometimes I do think it would have been easier to be born with a penis.

'Shall I see where we've been invited to tonight?' asks Scott.

'Tonight?'

'Why not?'

I decide there is no reason why not. Scott is a man who likes to strike while the iron is hot. Tonight he thinks it might be fun to go out and give my dress an airing; there is a possibility that by tomorrow this idea will have lost its allure. I'd be wise to grab the opportunity with both hands.

He calls Saadi. I try to follow the series of grunts, in an effort to decipher whether there is anything noteworthy on offer this evening. Scott looks nonplussed, teetering on the bored rigid, so I assume it's not a happening night.

'There's a movie premiere at Mann's,' he says with a careless shrug.

'A movie premiere! With a red carpet?'

'Yes.'

I let out an involuntary yelp of excitement. It's quite an embarrassing sound, not unlike a sound you might make in bed just before you totally give in to the big O. Still, he won't recognize it – more is the pity. 'And stars?'

'Yes.'

Another ridiculous squeak escapes from my lips. I barely waste time being embarrassed as I rush to ask my question, 'What movie?'

Scott stares at me with his huge, green unfair advantages. 'A political thriller with George Clooney and James McAvoy –'

I start to screech and scream; a full-throttle orgasm now. Scott grins at my excitement. His vaguely jaded expression dissolves into something much more expectant. 'Think that will be good?'

'Immense!' I yell, sounding not unlike my young nephew. 'Utterly, totally and properly immense!'

46. Fern

Scott makes a few more calls to put Saadi and her team on red alert, and so the moment Barry pulls up outside Scott's mansion I am pounced upon by a gang of hysterical women. I know the beautician, Joy, I see her almost daily now. Although I tell you Joy's mum was being ironic when she named her; the face on that girl – she is always tripping up on it. She sighs and huffs and puffs with exasperation as she pulls me up the stairs. Linda Di Marcello and Natalie Pennant, the women with healing hands, are there too, as are a hair stylist and a fashion stylist, Saadi and two of her assistants.

'There's so much to be done and so little time,' says Joy in despair. I start to giggle. Honestly, modesty aside, I've never looked better. As luck would have it, I had a spray-on tan applied yesterday and my hair is professionally blow-dried every morning. OK, maybe I'm not red-carpet perfection right this moment. After six hours of aggressive shopping my hair is no longer coiffed to be camera-ready – there are countless dangly stray bits and a few sticky-up stray bits too – but they ought to have seen the state of me on some of my dates with Adam. He knew I'd made an effort if I changed my T-shirt.

For the next hour I'm cast adrift in an ocean of novelties such as industrial-strength girdles, fake hair and emergency skin treatments – one for the 'blemishes' on my chin (kissing rash) and another for my sore feet (shopping rash). While Linda and Natalie soothe and Joy tuts I find it impossible to regret either physical imperfection – even if I am going to meet George Clooney and James McAvoy tonight – it was such fun acquiring them.

Saadi's assistants continually mutter the words 'seamless and bumpless' as though it were a catechism. They wrestle me into Spanx bodyshaper underwear that starts under my boobs and stretches all the way past my knees. I have to wonder. While these garments do dissolve love handles, muffin tops and even hide cellulite, as promised, what is the point? Even if the results do drive a girl's *amour* wild with desire, no woman would ever want to be *seen* in them. It takes a team of dedicated experts fifteen minutes to hoist me into these anti-briefs, so how could I slip out of them at the correct moment? For the first time since I met Scott I'm actually pleased there will be no sugges-tion of sex tonight.

The stylist (a new addition to my entourage, and I'm sorry to say I didn't catch her name in all the haste) informs me that 'Breasts have their own set of needs.'

I'm very aware of this. Plus I'm aware that my little babies aren't seeing as much action as they'd like, but before I can discuss the matter at length the stylist starts to chatter about Flex Body Bras, which are made of adhesive-backed silicone cups that fit separately over each boob, sort of self-sticking bras. I can only imagine the agony of taking those off, I feel squeamish with pain when peeling off elastoplasts.

'Designed for busty beauties who want to wear a back-less gown,' she explains. She stares (almost pityingly) at my

A cups and mutters, 'Well, at least that's one problem we don't have.' The stylist hands me a couple of large smooth tiddlywinks. I assume they are some sort of eye patch (a modern-day slice of cucumber, perhaps) and I tentatively place them over my eyes. She tuts, snatches them back out of my hands, and then whips open my robe and before you know it has stuck the tiddlywinks on my nipples. In horror, I stare at this woman (who I'm not even on first-name terms with but has just touched my nips).

'It's a backless dress,' she points out. 'Be grateful for the silicone versions, they are undetectable under dresses. We weren't always so fortunate. It wasn't long ago that we had to put cotton balls on clients and fasten with Scotch tape.' It sounds like something out of a Blue Peter creative project. I nod, trying to meet her level of gravity and demonstrate my respect for her craft rather than hoot and express my astonishment. 'Although you should never underestimate the importance of Scotch tape, especially the double-sided stuff. It can be wrapped beneath the breasts, squashing them together to create cleavage, used to hold spaghetti straps in place, or to keep loose dresses close to the skin and, importantly, prevent plunging neck-lines from becoming pornographic.'

'Thank God for sticky tape,' I mutter, just a little cheekily. She doesn't seem to notice.

'Amen,' she says seriously. 'Do you sweat much?' Not unusually so but recently my palms seem to be constantly clammy; I'm not sure if this is something I want to share. Before I stutter any reply the stylist says, 'It's too late for paralysing the glands with Botox. We could try Drysol, a prescription treatment that dries up the sweat glands.'

Lovely.

I want to ask them all to leave. I can zip up my own dress and daub a bit of Rimmel Lash Maxxx. I've always managed to dress myself in the past and no one has actually thrown stones when I emerged in public. But I don't ask them to go. For a start there are eight of them and one of me and I feel feeble. I'm pretty sure Saadi will just remind me that this is part of my job now. My first big, glam night out with Scott is bound to draw press attention; it's my duty to look the part. And besides, I know the results they'll achieve will be . . . well . . . better. I'm unlikely to be recognizable.

The hair stylist clips on a mane of sleek blonde hair to my head; this finally makes me find my voice and I insist that she takes it off again. I once read this article about poor little girls in underdeveloped countries having to sell their hair to feed their family – I wouldn't have a nice night knowing that some eight-year-old is running around looking like Kojak so that I can look like the woman from the Timotei advert. Saadi's first assistant argues that the kid would not eat at all if people like me didn't buy her hair. I firmly tell her to send the five hundred dollars that she spent on the hair to some charity committed to providing kids with an education. I'm quite chuffed with that. I'll have to think of a more regular and sustained way I can 'do more'. In the meantime we settle on an up-do and Joy says that maybe I'll bump into Angelina Jolie tonight and get some charity tips. The way she pronounces *char-idie* makes me think that she's being sarcastic but I can't be offended because I'm bursting with excitement at the very possibility. Where there's

Angelina Jolie, there's Brad Pitt; does life get any better?

Despite the constant stream of gloom and despondency at the prospect of making me red-carpet-worthy, we do manage to get me ready in time and I look, let's face it, fabulous. I glide down the stairs into the atrium where Scott is waiting for me, the very picture of gallantry and perfection in a midnight blue jacket with mandarin collar and skinny jeans. Obviously he resisted wearing a tux, social death for a rock star. I'm a little envious because I bet it took him ten minutes to get dressed and I doubt anyone stuck silicone to his bits.

'You are breathtaking,' he mutters, his eyes wide with desire and appreciation.

My nipples push against the tiddlywinks and my groin aches with lust and longing. Suddenly I'm certain all the effort, all the teasing, spraying, brushing, pummelling, poking, prodding, pruning, was worth it. To get that response from Scott Taylor I'd walk on hot coals.

47. Fern

The grand opening of Grauman's Chinese Theatre, in Hollywood Boulevard, took place on 18 May 1927. It was the most spectacular theatre opening in motion picture history. Thousands of people lined the streets and a riot broke out as fans tried to catch a glimpse of the movie stars and other celebs as they arrived for the opening. Authorization had to be obtained from the US government to import temple bells, pagodas, stone heaven dogs and other artefacts from China to construct the ornate and opulent theatre. Film director Moon Quon supervised Chinese artisans as they created elaborate pieces of statuary that still decorate the flamboyant and lavish interior of the theatre today. Protected by its forty-foot-high curved walls and copper-topped turrets, the theatre's legendary forecourt serves as an oasis to the stars of yesterday and today. Ten-foot-tall lotus-shaped fountains and intricate artistry flank the footprints of some of Hollywood's most elite and welcome its visitors into the magical world of fantasy and whim known as Hollywood.

All of this I knew before I arrived at the premiere – I'd read it in my guidebook when Scott and I visited last week – and yet nothing could have prepared me for this spectacle.

New movies open every week in Hollywood, of course,

but when the big studios decide to pull out all the stops and throw an old-fashioned, full-blown Hollywood premiere, Grauman's Chinese Theatre is *the* most sought-after venue. I'm told they always, always, always put on a good show. Crazed fans flock religiously to premieres, in the desperate hope of snatching the briefest peek at the brightest stars. Today's movie is especially big and has drawn unprecedented flocks of thousands.

George Clooney and James McAvoy, undisputed sex gods, are clearly worth queueing for (even in a snowstorm – it's sunny but you get my point), and the actress providing the love interest, Amanda Amberd, is a delicate and fragile British beauty, currently linked with no fewer than three Hollywood heart-throbs – all of whom are married. The press are desperate to inspect this precocious seducer, the fashionable need to know which designer she's wearing, and the wives of her (alleged) lovers want to know if her boobs are fake.

Scott and I don't talk in the car; he hums a tune (one of his own) and drums his fingers on the creamy leather. I pray I won't sweat, or step on the hem of my dress or flash an inelegant amount of leg as I get out of the car (by which I mean show my Spanx bodyshaper). Saadi's first assistant has drilled me on exactly how to glide gracefully in and out of a car. She repeatedly reinforced the fact that if I forget her instructions it *is* the end of the world as we know it; instant social death, as my knickers are not Agent Provocateur, La Perla or similar. If they were then it wouldn't matter if a speedy photographer got a flash of my gusset.

Saadi breaks the silence in the car when she says to

me, 'Don't be drawn into *any* comment about Amanda Amberd.'

I stare at Saadi, puzzled. 'What sort of comment could I make? Who would want to know what I think of her frock?'

'You don't know?' Saadi looks both dispirited and resigned. 'I thought you were up on celeb goss, at least.' It's become transparent that I fail to fulfil many of Saadi's expectations as to how a future Mrs Taylor should manage herself. I can't get the hang of the remote controls for the TVs, stereos, walls, or cinema, I am forever forgetting to re-apply lipstick before I nip out of the house and I thank shop assistants – profusely. She glowers at me, silently communicating her irritation at this new disappointment.

I do read many of the gossipy glossies but not as regularly as I'd like (I've heard other women say the same thing about the *FT* but I don't believe them, no one can regret the lack of broadsheet gloomy statistics in their life). I usually only get the chance to fully devour these orgies of guesswork and hearsay when the shop is quiet and Ben and I need something new to bitch about; during busy periods I can go for weeks completely oblivious about which star is avoiding which food group.

'Why? What's the story with Amanda Amberd?' I ask.

'Last February . . . a few months after Scott arrived in LA, he went to one of Amanda's premieres . . .' Saadi trails off and looks at Scott. He stares out of the window, watching the crowds that line the street. The crowds can't see him. The windows of the limo are blacked out and yet still they yell and scream their excitement as we crawl past. Some lean so close their breasts are pressed right up against the window, misshapen like the water-filled condoms lads throw off balconies. It looks like a pair of generous D cups are growing out of Scott's head right this moment.

'February is Valentine's. It's hectic in the shop. I don't get a chance to read magazines.' I start to justify and excuse my ignorance and then something flickers in the back of my head as though a light has been switched on in a room down a very, very far-off corridor. Amanda Amberd was linked to Scott. Romantically.

'Just a fling,' mutters Scott. He snatches up my hand and holds it to his lips, staring very keenly into my eyes. 'Nothing, nothing like this. Like us,' he says intently.

I believe him. It's true. I know it. It feels as though I've dived right into his two huge green lakes and am swimming around his brain. I might float away on this amazing, certain, flattering, overpowering exquisiteness. We kiss. The intensity lights up my entire body. Whoosh, I'm scalding, burning, blazing with desire. I feel it in my toenails and in the tips of my ears, all my extremities are buzzing with lust. I'm wet with longing.

'Whatever,' sighs Saadi. Coughing, no doubt slightly embarrassed by our palpable passion. You can taste sex in the air or at least, I can. 'Just don't be drawn. Amanda had to go into rehab after Scott dumped her, the scheduling of the film slipped, it cost the studio loads of money. Questions will be asked.'

I pull out of the kiss. 'She had to go into rehab after a fling?' I'm confused; I thought these starlets knew the score. I thought famous people only ever got involved with one another for publicity purposes. I didn't think anyone ever got hurt.

'Broke the cardinal rule,' says Scott with a regretful sigh. 'Poor girl. I had no idea.'

'She fell in love with him for real,' says Saadi with a shrug. 'Very inconvenient. Tricky to handle. She's popular. Scott was in danger of looking like a total louse.'

'I really had no idea,' repeats Scott. He looks genuinely aghast. I pity him. With so much fabulousness comes great power. He doesn't get it.

'Poor girl,' I mutter.

'Worked out OK in the end,' says Saadi confidently. 'She lost eighteen pounds thanks to stress. The movie got tonnes of pre-release PR. No harm done.'

'Maybe we shouldn't be here tonight,' I suggest, carefully. It seems really insensitive. Cruel almost. It is Amanda Amberd's big night and I just can't accept any woman, even an actress, would believe that losing eighteen pounds compensated for the loss of Scott. She *must* still be gutted. The last thing she needs tonight, or probably ever, is to see Scott again – especially with his new fiancée. Me. We can't rub her nose in it. 'We should turn round, go home,' I say.

'But you wanted to show off your new dress,' says Scott.

'It doesn't matter.'

'I've worked all afternoon talking to the studio to get this cleared,' says Saadi irritably. 'Amanda is expecting Scott now, the press are expecting Scott now; we can't go home. That would be a bigger snub and scandal.'

I'm doubtful, but this isn't my world. Or rather it is, but it hasn't been for long. It's much more Saadi's world. She knows what she's doing, I have to trust her. Scott squeezes my hand. 'She's linked to other names now,' he reminds me.

Yes. Three of them. All married men. If that isn't the sign of a lost, confidence-sapped individual I don't know what is. Why would a woman as talented, beautiful and desired as Amanda Amberd dally with married men unless her self-esteem was in ribbons?

Then I think of the poor wives of Amanda's lovers and all my sympathy is brushed away. Amanda Amberd should not be spreading the hurt. Single people date and then split up, that's normal. Sad but true. She must be a selfish, uppity little madam to choose the route of dating married men. She doesn't have to, she must have potential suitors tripping over themselves to impress her; it's spiteful and irresponsible. Sod her, she doesn't deserve my sympathy, pity or consideration; she's not showing any to those wives.

'I don't care either way,' says Scott with a filthy, distracting, utterly fabulous smile. 'I'm just going to look at you all night anyhow. It doesn't matter to me whether we do that in Grauman's or at home.'

More kissing. 'Let's go,' I say.

Saadi looks relieved.

Apparently there is etiquette or at least an unwritten rule about the correct time to arrive at functions such as these. Of course there is. There's an unwritten rule about everything. I wish someone would just write down all the blinking rules and I could learn them off by heart and not have to be subjected to the continuous eye-rolling that seems to accompany me everywhere. Not that Scott ever rolls his eyes when I ask him a specific about how something works or how I should act; he's patience personified. He repeatedly tells me that he likes it that I'm not sullied, or jaded or in anyway tired of all the stardom stuff. He says I'm refreshing. Good-naturedly he explains that the C-and B-listers arrive first, to warm up the crowd, and only when the onlookers are practically hoarse with shouting can the A-listers start to arrive.

Saadi is given a signal and our moment has arrived. I step out and am hit by a blast of warm air and manic noise from screaming crowds. The intensity nearly knocks me over; I thought I had a clear concept of just how loud human beings could get (after all, I do faithfully attend my nieces' and nephews' birthday parties; I've been in a room with twenty little four-year-olds jacked up on Smarties), but still I'm astonished.

I (elegantly and successfully – hurrah) emerge, Scott glued to me. The warmth of him incites the giddiest feelings of pure, undiluted bliss and suddenly I'm not nervous, or tense or panicky; I am amazing.

A lot of the press are European. Because Amanda Amberd and James McAvoy are British there's a lot of interest in this film back home. This works well for Scott, as the British press love him. Or hate him. Or whatever. It's fair to say they want to photograph him and talk to him. I know Scott moved to the States to get away from the constant press intrusion and carve out some sort of private life, but it would be awful to turn up to a public event like this and not be recognized. The calls come thick and fast. I hardly know which way to turn.

'Over here, love!'

'Look this way!'

'Fern, are you excited? Is this your first premiere?'

'Give me a beam, darlin'!'

The Americans are impossibly positive and vibrant; even though I get the sense that they don't recognize Scott immediately they take their lead from the UK press and tourists and they give out wild, relentless cheers. I've seen for myself, when watching similar events at Leicester Square on the local news at home in London, that generally rock stars don't smile for their fans or the press. They are pretty much duty-bound to be eternally grumpy and dour. Indeed, I've seen photos of Scott papped with a face like thunder, but not tonight. Tonight, Scott is instantly and unapologetically the very best Scottie Taylor can be. He beams, holds my hand in the air and then twirls me around. Utterly, utterly delighted in me, as I am with him, as we are with each other; we exist in an endless circle of delight.

I'm dizzy.

Through the blur of handbags and gladrags I spot Rachel Weisz in a stunning silver Vera Wang gown (I can't believe I recognize the designer! I probably wouldn't have but I saw the very same dress today on Rodeo Drive). I am a big fan of Rachel Weisz's work and I want to tell her how talented I think she is. I want to say it in a way that is profound, or at least funny or original. After an age I come up with, 'Nice dress,' and beam at her. Gracefully, she ignores the fact that my smile is so desperate I resemble the village idiot; she nods and smiles back warmly. It's not the first impression I hoped for, but before I have time to kick myself Ewan McGregor shakes hands with Scott and kisses me on the cheek. He congratulates us both, poses for a quick photo and then asks me whether I'm a fan of James McAvoy. I am. But somehow I don't manage to articulate my considered appraisal of Mr McAvoy's work from *The Near Room* to *The Last Station*. I just say, 'He's Scottish too, isn't he? Do you know him?' No one need point out just how lame I'm being, I know. Funny thing is I'm too excited to care.

We seem to be lingering on the red carpet longer than other stars. Scott is conscientiously signing autographs and I stand grinning until my jaws ache. I swish my dress around my legs and the material shimmies and glides across my thighs. I'm buzzing. Despite challenging my facial muscles I can't stop smiling, and not just because those were Saadi's instructions but because I am completely, unequivocally, utterly exultant.

Kate Hudson is looking fabulous in a gorgeous polkadot sleeveless blouse, a satin high-waisted pencil skirt with a bright red belt and shoes (that could double as stilts). She throws me a kind smile and a big wave as she glides past, causing the camera bulbs to become frenzied once again. I consider having a word. I could tell her that I think she's courageous, funny, talented, complex and interesting, but evidence suggests the best I'm likely to come up with is, 'You're *gorgeous*!' Which doesn't really lead anywhere, so I stay silent. When Cameron Diaz sashays past I'm realistic; I just concentrate, very hard, on not exploding with admiration. No one wants to see blood and guts and innards and stuff on the red carpet.

Scott lingers talking with the crowds as star after star

files past. I cannot believe these people have stepped off the pages of my *Heat* magazine and are now, larger than life, stood in front of me; actually most of them are smaller than life, wisps and slips of women, delicate and fragile. When Scott has signed dozens and dozens of the bits of paper, books, photos and knickers (clean I hope!) that are thrust under his nose, he returns to me and takes my hand once again. We start to walk towards the movie theatre, which means we have to pass a wall of photographers. I expect Scott to move us quite swiftly past the flashbulbs but in fact he stops right in front of them. Microphones pop up like acne on a teenager's skin, obstinate and relentless. The professionals sense that Scott is going to sprinkle a few words their way and so quieten down a fraction in order not to miss a single morsel he throws out.

'I've something to show you,' he says with a big, cheeky grin. He reaches into his trouser pocket and pulls out a small box. A ring box. The flashing begins once again in earnest. The press understand what's happening a moment before I do.

A ring box.

My ring.

My *engagement* ring!

Scott opens the box and turns to me. It's a huge, *huge* oval-shaped diamond on a plain, contemporary platinum band. It's simple, it's elegant, it's perfect! Scott slips the ring on to my finger, carelessly dropping the box on the floor, and I squeal. Really very loudly. I'm not aware that I'm screaming or just how loud said scream is, until Scott clamps his lips over mine and the high-pitched noise stops. The photographers become crazed; their flashes light up the night, competing with the high-intensity searchlights that criss-cross the indigo sky. I bet we can be seen from space.

48. Fern

I float inside the theatre, vaguely aware of Saadi handing out press packs to the rabble of journos. I hear her gabble, 'Three point five carat. We took into account her slim fingers, didn't want anything *too* flashy, catch on clothes. Have to consider lifestyle when choosing a ring.'

The ring weighs delightfully heavily on my hand. I can't take my eyes off it. Not even to look at Scott; partly because it's out-of-this-world beautiful and partly because I'm utterly terrified that it will slip off and I'll lose it. We are shown to our seats (we're sat between Jonathan Rhys Meyers and Sienna Miller) but I can't be dazzled further; if I am, I'll die. Fact.

The lights dim and I drag my eyes from my ring to the screen; it would be rude not to but with my thumb I endlessly caress the beautiful, breathtaking ring. Occasionally the diamond catches the light bouncing from the movie and winks at me.

Everyone seems to enjoy the movie; when it's over, people leap to their feet and clap and cheer enthusiastically. Scott stands and slowly (coolly) claps and I join him, although I have little idea whether it's good or not as I was unable to concentrate at all. I have no need for the movies any more. I no longer need to be drip-fed other people's romances, dramas or thrills; I am living an extraordinary life, a one hundred per cent, sensationally dream-like life. It's all too much to fully comprehend. I feel as though I'm floating above my true self. I am just an astonished onlooker; not that dissimilar to the boisterous, buoyant crowd of fans outside. I can't believe I'm this lucky. I can't believe *anyone* gets to be this lucky.

After the movie there is a party.

'Do you really want to go to the party?' asks Scott.

I sense he doesn't but I gently push. I don't want to go home now. I would, if shagging were on the cards. Honestly, there is nothing – absolutely nothing – I'd like to do more than get butt naked (other than my ring!) and bang my increasingly insistent needs out with Scott. We could kiss, lick, touch, poke, caress, squeeze, sex the life out of each other. Twice, and then again in the morning. But that's not on the cards. Damned chastity vow. So, second to that, I'd like to rub shoulders with the world's most glamorous and dazzling people (while showing off my ring; did I mention my ring?).

'Yes please, I really would.'

'OK, your wish is my command,' says Scott, giving in gracefully and quickly. He kisses me flat on the lips, which causes my knickers to cartwheel. Even through closed eyes I'm aware that someone takes a photo of us laying the lips; I don't much care. I feel as though we are alone – despite the crowds and despite the popping camera flashes. I'm loving every moment of tonight.

'I have to go and touch up my lipstick,' I say, reluctantly pulling away from him.

'I'll wait for you.'

'I won't be long.'

'Take your time, I'd wait for ever,' he says with a wide, sincere grin.

I skip into the loos and bang straight into several dozen other women all fighting for mirror space. It seems that these women have been put together by the angels themselves. They are groomed and glammed-up beyond lovely. I'd have sex with any one of them (assuming I was a guy or at least had lesbian tendencies and assuming I wasn't committed to a highly inconvenient chastity vow). In fact I'd *marry* any one of them, they're all that gorgeous. No one's forehead moves, true, but an animated forehead has never been a deal-breaker for me. As the clouds of perfume and hair spray dissolve I recognize two or three faces; newscasters and soap actresses, mainly. As I rummage in my handbag to locate my gloss I become aware that everyone is staring at me. Most are looking at me through the mirror while keeping up the pretence that they are still involved in fixing their shiny chins or re-applying another layer of mascara; some are slyly taking side-glances, the cheekier types are plainly ogling. I feel like a small grub under a microscope.

For a moment I think I'm twenty pounds overweight. I mourn the fact that I have a snogging rash on my chin. And I'm deeply ashamed that my forehead moves.

But then I remember I'm marrying Scottie Taylor. I'm light as a feather. He's to blame for my snogging rash. And my boobs are pretty steady.

I must grow a fraction taller or in some other way subliminally communicate my contentment because, as though in a choreographed dance, the bony (but silky) elbows instantly move to make way for me; a path to the mirror opens up.

'Beautiful ring,' says one girl.

'Thank you.'

'I love your hair. Is it all yours?' asks a second.

'Yes. Thank you.'

'The dress, is it Fendi? It's to die for.'

'Yes, it is. Thank you.'

Suddenly I am surrounded by a collision of smooth, moisturized, silky limbs. Women and girls are reaching out to me, touching me lightly on the arm, gently brushing their fingertips across the skirt of my dress, carefully caressing the beads of my bag. I get it. They all want a piece of me because I have him. Even if Scott is still relatively unknown to the masses in America, these women are the in-the-know elite and they understand his worth. They all want to be me, because I have him. The attention from these women is quite unlike the (almost brutal) preparation I endured from the army of stylists who work under Joy's supervision. These women wrap me up in countless beatific smiles, their butterfly touches are like a lover's caress, their smiles are pure and reverential. They pull cards from their adorable, glittery handbags and press them on me, inviting me to coffee, to shop, to cocktails. They battle to out-do one another in the extravagant compliments that cascade my way. My skin is perfect English rose, no – it's creamy, no – it's pearlescent. My hair is glossy, no – it's glistening, no – it's simply divine. And my dress? What adjectives can they pour on my dress? Before I get to find out, a cubicle door swings open and Amanda Amberd emerges, abruptly silencing my admirers.

Amanda Amberd slices through the throng and starts to wash her hands. I notice that she carefully soaps the palms and the backs of her hands and gives individual attention to each finger. The fastidious ritual takes a couple of minutes but feels like a lifetime and definitely suggests that either she has a cleanliness compulsion (very fashionable) or that she's stalling for time. The beautiful women, who had been fawning and flattering me, abruptly turn to Amanda and proceed to shower her with compliments; many of which are identical to those that washed up my way.

The difference is, I don't doubt for a moment that Amanda deserves these generous words. She is intensely, almost excruciatingly, superb to look at. She's about five foot eight but is wearing heels that push her towards the six-foot mark; yet she's the epitome of the word delicate. She reminds me of an unfurled, blush-pink rose early on a summer morning; one that is dappled with dew and sunlight. I'm not saying she's sweaty – she's not. I doubt this woman ever sweats, or pees or even hiccups; she seems to transcend all that is human. She has long, pale blonde hair that tumbles in fat, healthy curls around her (toned) shoulders and (pleasantly muscular) back. She's a unique blend of ethereal and strong. Her jaunty bone structure suggests a vigour that is potently seductive. She's wearing a plum, empire line maxi dress (without giving the impression that she is in her third trimester). She's adorned with an antique amethyst bracelet and butterfly clip in her hair. She steals my breath.

Some of the women seem to dissolve. A few cast shy or sly glances at Amanda and then scuttle away. Two girls come into the loo, clock Amanda and me sharing a mirror and freeze. What I want to do right now is make a polite comment on the film. I know I wasn't concentrating on the plot quite as closely as I should have been (the ring, the ring!) but I've seen Amanda in other movies, she's a good actor, brilliant in fact. My tongue stays clamped firmly to the roof of my mouth. I'm aware anything I say right now might sound patronizing or gloating. This woman, this vision of loveliness, was rejected by my fiancé. I'm aware of the crowd around us; whatever I say will be quoted and misquoted and Saadi told me not to be drawn into comment. I stay resolutely silent.

Amanda carefully dries her hands on one of the individual linen cloths provided and then massages moisturizer into her palms. I've always wondered what sort of girl actually remembers to re-apply cream every time they wash their mitts; now I know – beautiful ones with soft hands. This ritual takes a Jurassic age. Then she turns to me.

'May I see the ring?' Her voice still has a soft trace of her West Country origins. It's a pleasant lilting that oozes sweetness. I can't very well refuse, although now I wish I hadn't ever come in here to touch up my lippy. I hold out my hand for her inspection. She clasps my finger ends and I notice that we are both trembling.

'It's a very beautiful ring,' she pronounces. 'You are very lucky. Very.'

'I know.' My reply comes out in a scratchy whisper. We don't look at one another. We can't. She suddenly drops my hand and then leaves the bathroom. Her hasty exit reaffirms the impression that she's some sort of mythical creature; like a sprite, fairy or angel she simply vanishes.

I turn back to the mirror and with a trembling hand I re-apply my gloss; luckily it's not a deep colour, as I might end up looking like Batman's joker. The bathroom is silent. I can't help thinking that every single woman is wondering why oh why Scott chose someone like me when he could have had Amanda Amberd as his lifelong companion. I could tell them that Scott appreciates my normality or that he's stoked by the way I influence his song writing but I have the feeling they wouldn't get it. I hardly do. Instead I say, 'My pelvic floor muscles are like clamps,' and I dash for the door.

I hope to God no one here knows about the chastity vow.

49. Scott

'Fuck me, being someone's fiancé is hard work.' I throw myself on the sofa and wait for Mark to sympathize.

'Fern can't be as much work as the actresses and models and whatever who you've dated in the past,' he reasons as he offers me a fag.

'They came with their fair share of aggro, no doubt about it. But I'd sort of got the hang of that type of relationship.'

Providing you guarantee them enough column inches (by which I mean space in the newspapers – column inches is not a reference to my manhood), they were, often as not, more or less happy. And there are loads of ways to get the coverage. Get pissed, stay sober, go speeding, go horse riding, go to the Ivy for lunch, go to the Priory to dry out. My relationship with Fern is on a whole different level. She's not bothered by press coverage. She wants my time.

'Fern's demanding in a totally different way. She always wants to be doing stuff together,' I explain.

Mark nods. 'That's to be expected. Fern wanted extraordinary, you needed something a bit down to earth. The hope is you'll meet in the middle.'

'Yeah, yeah, I know, and mostly, it's cool this couple stuff. She's lovely. I like being with her. But she seems to want my *exclusive* time. And that, my friend, I no can do.

I have commitments you know. People depend on me. People expect things from me.'

'I know, lad, people all want a bit of you.' I can hear the sympathy in Mark's voice and I feel better because he gets it.

'To be frank, I'm tiring of sight-seeing with Fern. Going out is OK but now I'm in a mood to stay in.' I inhale deeply and scowl at Mark. I'm behaving like a kid but Mark doesn't mind that. He knows I want him to make it better. The good news is, he can and he will. It's Mark's job to fight my battles. He fights the battles I don't understand (with lawyers, accountants and the record company) and the battles I don't want to fight (with the press and disappointed women, mostly). That's what managers do, and because he fights my battles I get more time to do the things a rock star needs to do. Like write songs and, in the old days, get drunk and shag women. He's a great manager; he's so good he sometimes spots battles that I didn't even identify to be skirmishes.

'That's fine,' he says soothingly. 'The press have plenty of shots of the two of you feeding monkeys, riding rollercoasters and eating burgers.' He glances across at the file of recent press cuttings. I know he's delighted with the attention Fern and I are attracting. Everything is on plan.

'Presenting the ring was a coup,' I say with a grin, immediately cheered when I think about how well I handled that whole show.

'Amanda's premiere was the perfect opportunity. We scooped the undivided attention of the world's press,' agrees Mark. He's also wearing a massive self-satisfied smile. 'And that means you don't have to do any more sight-seeing if you don't want to.'

'I don't want to.'

'OK then.'

'I need to be in the studio more,' I point out.

'I'm never going to argue with that,' says Mark. We fall silent for a moment as we both suck on our fags. Then Mark adds, 'I have to say, you've done well, son.' He stands up and walks towards me and gives me a hearty pat on the shoulder. I like it when he calls me son, which he does from time to time. In so many ways he is the dad I never had. And I am *definitely* the son he never had (the son he *did* have is a civil servant and no trouble at all but probably not much fun either). 'I was worried about sending you out to all those watering holes. I thought it was too early. I thought you might fling yourself off the wagon.'

'Ninety-eight dry days and counting.'

'Well done, lad.' He slaps my shoulder again but we don't look at each other. We both know that in the past I once went 614 days and then woke up in my own puddle of vodka and urine. They say a day at a time because if they said what they mean – 'for ever' – no one would ever go to an AA meeting.

'And you are still OK with the no sex thing?' he asks. I detect concern in his voice.

'Yeah. Cool.' Actually, not having sex with Fern is hard work. The novelty is beginning to wear a bit thin; that's the thing about novelty. But I'm too stubborn to concede a challenge.

'Do you know what, son, if you want my advice, I'd shag her, asap.'

'Nicely put.'

'You've made your point now, you've known the girl three weeks and you haven't shagged her. You not shagging someone after you've known them a few weeks is a bit like anyone else taking permanent Holy Orders.'

'I made myself a promise,' I point out.

'But Fern is gagging for it.'

'I know, I am too. But I hate giving up on stuff. I'll make it worth her wait.'

Mark sighs and looks weary. His flat bulldog face constricts with concern. 'Thing is, Scott, as you are currently off drugs and booze I'm worried you're overdoing the abstaining thing.'

'You're scared I'll break,' I say flatly.

He won't answer me directly. 'Having sex with your fiancée will not damage the record label, getting high or pissed will.'

'I'm OK.'

'Is this your latest addiction? Are you now addicted to not having sex? God, things have really changed since my day.' He shakes his head wearily. I stay silent and he knows better than to try to argue with me. 'All right then, we'll have to make sure you are *very* busy in the studio. Keep you out of trouble.'

'Yeah, and I'll exercise more.'

'Fine.'

'What about Fern?'

'Oh, she'll be easy to distract. There's the wedding to plan, and besides, she'll soon have her mate to keep her amused.'

'Ben.'

'Yup. He's the perfect best mate for her to have. Women are jealous, heterosexual men always try their luck with pop stars' girls, we don't need the hassle. Homosexual best friends are a manager's godsend,' says Mark.

'OK, so sounds like a plan. Studio and gym for me. Dresses and wedding cake and things for her.'

'Sure you wouldn't rather just fuck her?'

'Thanks for your concern but I think I've got it under control.'

'OK. Sure?'

'Sure.'

'OK. Great.'

'Great.'

50. Fern

'First Class and a chauffeur! Pinch me!' cries Ben as he flings himself into the back of the Bentley. I do. 'Ooch!' He playfully swats me away but then immediately pulls me back towards him, enveloping me in another enormous, effervescent hug. About the tenth he's given me since he came through customs. I feel the slight scratch of his sandpaper stubble on my forehead and can smell the aeroplane on his clothes; even so his hug is delicious. It's so fantastic to have him share all this with me!

'Wow, look at you! You're glowing. Posh clothes suit you. And I love what you've done with your hair,' gushes Ben.

'Thank you. Scott's staff are engineering a re-vamp.'

'What fun!'

'Can be. Or can be a bit intimidating,' I admit.

'The knack with these people is to appear appreciative and show respect for their professional experience but don't allow anyone to bully you.'

'How do you know this stuff? Will you help me?'

'Of course.'

'Today I have an appointment with my clothes stylist. Will you come?'

'You have a lovely little waist, we ought to make more of that.'

'And my nutritionalist.'

'You look so skinny. How much have you lost?'

'I'm not sure. The scales in my old flat were always dodgy because the floor sloped and so I couldn't get a proper reading. However much I've lost Joy keeps saying I need to lose more.'

'Who's Joy?'

'Scott's beautician. She seems to hate me. She lives her life as though she's eternally auditioning for the part of wicked stepmother in the Christmas panto.'

'She probably had a thing for Scott.'

'Probably.'

'Have they slept together?'

'I don't know. There's no reason for me to think they have,' I reply, taken aback by the suggestion.

'There's no reason for you to think they haven't. It's Scottie Taylor we're talking about here,' says Ben calmly.

Ben fusses about the car's air-con; he insists that it's icy and has it blasting on our calves. He comments on the towering palm trees lining the streets and then asks, 'So how is the sex?'

'Ben!' I try to sound shocked.

'I promise I won't tell a soul, Scout's honour, or should that be Scott's honour,' he grins, tickled by his own pun. 'Tell! I want to know, I'm only human.'

'I don't know yet,' I admit.

'What?' Ben looks as though I've slapped him.

'We're saving ourselves until our wedding day,' I explain simply.

'You're kidding.' He's aghast.

'Deadly serious.'

341

'But why?'

'Scott and I want to do things properly. It's important our relationship is completely different from anything else Scott has ever known.'

'How very romantic,' he mutters, not really bothering to hide his dismay.

'Not my idea. It's a nightmare, actually. I think I'm going to explode with lust,' I confide.

Ben looks sympathetic; touched by my frankness, he tries to comfort me. 'Well, only about a month to go and it's not like you are stuck for things to do. We'll just have to keep you very, very busy. How's the wedding planning going?'

I'm happy to move on to a less frustrating topic. 'It's in good hands. The wedding planner, Ms Colleen Lafontaine, born in New York and bred in LA, seems perfect for the job. She came very highly recommended, as she's planned a number of high-profile Hollywood weddings; she understands the security requirements and the complications of working with slash keeping at bay the paparazzi.'

'Marvellous, I can't wait to make friends with her. I am here to encourage your inner Bridezilla, not that it needs much encouragement. We are going to have endless conversations showered with words such as sparkle, vintage, memorable, expressive and wow factor.' I laugh at Ben's excitement. 'This wedding can be so much bigger than anything you could possibly have perceived of when you were with Adam,' says Ben as a matter of fact. I shift uncomfortably on the seat. I haven't allowed myself to say Adam's name in my head let alone out loud for some time now. I feel Ben's eyes on me but I don't meet them.

'Have you seen Jess or anyone?' I ask casually.

'Not for a few days now.'

'Does she know you are coming here?'

'Yes.'

'Any messages?'

'No messages.'

'Oh.' I wasn't expecting any. It's proving really difficult to stay in touch with Jess. I've called her a few times but I keep catching her at awkward moments. Once, she was just about to get something to eat (and just had time to remind me to call Adam), another time she was busy at work (but just had time to remind me to call Adam) and on the third occasion she was on her way out of the door (she must have been in a genuine rush because she never mentioned that I ought to call Adam). She did listen to my account of my heady night at the movie premiere but she wasn't as thrilled about it as I'd hoped. I poured out my excitement but she seemed unable or unwilling to engage. She barely asked any questions other than whether so and so had had surgery, she always sounded vindicated when I admitted that yes, so and so had. She sniffed out words like 'fake', delusional' and 'unrealistic'. When I got to the part about my witty one-liner explaining Scott's devotion, she didn't even laugh. She just said, 'It *is* a mystery, isn't it?' Which is hardly a polite thing for your best friend to say.

'The press and magazines are fascinated by your nuptials, so who's got the exclusive?' asks Ben.

I'm grateful that Ben isn't wasting his breath or our

time on berating me with how I left Adam in the lurch or how quickly I'm moving on. It's so much more pleasurable that all he wants to think about is my future. We spend the hour's journey home excitedly chattering about all things bridal: the dress, the venue, the wine, the chairbacks, glasswear, ribbons, sweets, lanterns and everything in between. It's going to be such fun having Ben here.

51. Fern

I am the prodigal daughter. Following the initial rather lacklustre response to my engagement announcement my mum (which means my mum *and* dad because they think as one – she's always telling him this is the case) are now extremely excited by the idea of me marrying Scott. Mum calls me every day. She says, 'Thisiscostingafortunecallme-backstraightaway,' and then she hangs up. I do call her back because if ever a mother and daughter are going to bond it's going to be over a roll of tulle destined to be said daughter's wedding dress.

On a rare occasion when I actually get to talk to my dad, I ask him what was the cause of my mother's Damascene conversion.

'The papers are very nice about you. Most of them say that you come from a nice home and that you are just very ordinary. She likes that,' he says.

I'm not sure I do but as I am no longer ordinary – I am now far from it – I can ignore the former accuracy of accusation.

'And it was part fuelled by the fact that Mrs Cooper, from up the road, her that goes on them world cruises. Can you imagine? A singles holiday at her age? Well, she turns out to be a fan,' adds Dad. Scott would probably be horrified to hear how seriously he commands the grey pound. 'Mrs Cooper has apparently always thought that

Scottie is not a bad lad. You know, despite the drugs and the drink and everything.'

Dad pauses. There's a catch in his breath which suggests to me that his fears are not completely put aside on account of Mrs Cooper's endorsement. But after so many years of wholeheartedly agreeing with my mother he's not foolish enough to start publicly disagreeing now.

'She reckons he just needed the love of a good woman. Your mother seemed somewhat reassured by that but I think the deal was clinched when Mrs Cooper shook her head, in obvious bewilderment, and added, fancy that woman being *your Fern*. Naturally your mother was then shoved headlong into defensive outrage. What do you mean? she demanded. Well, she's never really shown any ambition that way, says Mrs Cooper.' Dad is clearly enjoying the drama of relaying this little exchange. He mimics both women with accuracy. 'Any ambition what way? asked your mother.'

Mum can be very touchy about veiled criticism of her children – we have Jake's stretch in the clink to thank for honing that particular skill.

'And Mrs Cooper says well, she's never shown any ambition to marry money. Plus, I never believed she really liked pop music. I thought that was the stumbling block with that other beau of hers. The last one.'

Dad and I know Mum would, if she could, rewrite history in a way that Stalin could be proud of. Given half a chance, Adam would vanish, my hymen would magically be restored to its former intact glory and she'd have the complete fairy tale. Mrs Cooper's insistence on reminding her that this is not the case will be testing their thirty-five-year friendship.

'So what did Mum say to that?' I ask Dad.

'Oh, she told Mrs Cooper good and proper. She says our Fern is passionate about music. Pop and stuff. She said that you dumping Adam was nothing to do with him being in the music industry. Obviously, it was because he was poor.'

'Oh, marvellous.' I roll my eyes at my mum's misguided attempt at defending my honour. I can't believe she thinks it is better for people to think I'm a gold-digger than that my CD collection is limited. 'It's not true,' I moan.

'I know, love, but she couldn't admit to the neighbours that he was tardy about making an honest woman out of you, could she?'

I suppose not.

Lisa calls regularly, as do my siblings Bill, Fiona and Rick. As Lisa, Bill and Fiona's kids are bridesmaids and pageboys, they all have very clear views about exactly what the little darlings ought to wear. How I'm supposed to combine 'pretty and romantic but understated' with 'chic and simple yet dramatic' and 'pink and flouncy, very, very flouncy' is a conundrum I'm just not up to. I simply pass all comments on to Colleen and Ben; between them they are more than capable of dealing with it. Rick calls because he likes to give me updates about just how pissed he got at whichever party or gig he most recently blagged his way into. He's suddenly garrulous, gregarious and popular as the future brother-in-law of Scottie Taylor. I'm glad he's having so much fun. Even Jake sent a letter from prison. It was written in his messy, barely legible scribble that has remained unchanged since he was about seven.

Dear Sis,
Can your bloke pull any strings in here? I'm up for parole in a fortnight. Would be good to be out of this place by the time you tie the knot. Always wanted to visit LA. If no can do, can he come and visit me? Would make me look cool. You don't need to come, just him. If that's not happening, then send smokes.
Jake.

The combination of his naive print and upfront request affected me more than I expected. I know I can't do anything to help his situation but it was somehow touching that he believed I could. I send the fags and loads of signed CDs.

Most people think I can help them now. I've received hundreds and hundreds of letters from various charities and individuals begging for my help. To start with I read them all and asked Scott for cash, signed photos, signed guitars and old clothes for raffles and auctions, then Saadi suggested I pass them straight to her second assistant to deal with. It was agreed that after the wedding I could choose a couple of charities to support but that reading fifty begging letters a day (all of which made me sob like Veruca Salt when Willy Wonka denies her an Oompa-Loompa) wasn't doing much for my complexion. I suppose I am prone to being a bit weepy at the moment – well, it's natural to be emotional, I'm getting married. But I never seriously considered funding a party where all the guests were supermodels – something the Institute of Caligynephobia (fear of beautiful women) assured me was vital as part of their recovery programme. I could see that Scott was right, there was something fake-looking about their stationery, and the fact that it was signed by 'All the lads who drink in the Black Bull' cleared up the issue once and for all.

But it's not just my nearest and dearest and complete strangers who think I can do something for them, it's everyone in between too. The other day I checked my e-mails and I had one from the Friends Reunited website; it said I had 742 new messages. I joined Friends Reunited six years ago when my love life was going through a dry patch and I thought I might look up a few old boyfriends to see if any of them were worth another onceover. Most had filed the obligatory two or three lines. 'I'm married with two beautiful kids,' or, 'I still live with my mum and dad – it saves on rent.' Nothing of interest. I sent a few e-mails to old girlfriends, girls I'd gossiped to when I should have been listening to exactly how (or why!) you might calculate quadratic equations. I got just one response. It was from Helen Davis, who wanted to know if I still had her copy of *Mansfield Park* because she was sure she'd lent it to me just before our GCSE and I hadn't ever returned it; she'd had to buy another copy, apparently. I e-mailed back denying all knowledge and that was the end of our correspondence. I've stayed registered for the last six years (because I signed up by direct debit and don't know where people find the energy to cancel direct debits) and in those six years I've had a grand total of three messages, until last month.

Each and every one of the messages I opened was

lovely. Everyone wished me well, congratulated me on my engagement. Surprisingly, most agreed that they'd always known I'd do something extraordinary, many said they were delighted to see my name in the newspaper because they thought of me often and had long looked for an excuse to get back in touch because we'd been so close once. Strangely, about two out of every three had an ambition to travel to LA; I hadn't realized it was such a popular destination of choice. Helen Davis wrote again reminding me how we always liked to share books.

'Delete the lot,' said Scott, when I told him about the sudden influx of messages.

'I haven't finished reading them.'

'Waste of time. They all want the same thing. Association. This happened to me when I got the record deal with X-treme. A zillion liggers wrote to remind me how we'd once been best mates, even my old German teacher, which was odd because I distinctly remember him saying that he hated the very sight of me and dreaded Tuesdays when he'd have to be in the same room as me.'

I deleted the messages.

There have been no messages from Jess. I miss her. It's weird. I'm constantly surrounded by an endless trail of people. There are people to brush my hair, draw my bath, warm my towels, fix my makeup, drive me places, dress me, cook for me, do crosswords with me, whatever – but this crowd doesn't stop me feeling . . . what? Lonely? Not quite lonely. That word is too strong. It's just that while I'm vital to these people (their jobs are dependent on me) I sometimes get the strangest feeling – I feel they don't see me. I'm invisible, and no amount of designer clothes can get me noticed the way Jess used to notice me. How odd. Of course, it's great having Ben here and I'm sure I will make proper friends here in time; I just don't know how much time it will take. I've known Jess fourteen years.

I grab my phone and call Jess again before I think of a reason not to. The weeks of not speaking properly to one another have opened up a chasm, and I wonder if I can leap over it. I want to.

Amazingly she picks up. 'Hey Jess.' I gush excitedly. 'Is this a good time to call? Or am I interrupting anything?' My opener is pretty much an apology.

'I'm in the supermarket.'

'Oh. How are you?'

'Good, the same. You know.'

She sounds a bit odd. Distracted. I tell myself she's busy but I'm pretty sure she's miffed. The odd thing is I'm not sure what I've done wrong besides become rich and famous, but how can that be wrong? I don't know what to say next. She hasn't asked how I am. If I volunteer the information I'll risk sounding unbearable. What can I say? Oh your life's 'the same,' is it? Well, mine has completely turned round and is so unbelievably fantastic I think I might explode with joy. Er, no, not right.

'Did you get your invite?' I ask.

'Yeah, and the plane ticket. Thanks, very generous of you.' Her tone is grudging. I hoped she'd be thrilled.

'No, not at all. It's the least I can do. I'm the one getting married bloody miles away, I can't expect everyone to fork out for a flight.' I try to down-play the three grand, Club Class ticket. It's odd. I always imagined that one of the perks of being silly rich was that you'd get to be seriously generous with your nearest and dearest. I imagined that splashing the cash would be a wonderful and rewarding thing to do. But it's not especially. Now I have so much more money than any of my friends – well, I have so much more money than everyone really – and I don't know how to behave. When I make big gestures I seem flash and showy but if I don't cough up, I seem tight. I can't win.

'How's Adam?' I hadn't planned to say that next. Or indeed ever. I just did it to fill in a conversational gap. I think Jess is as surprised as I am.

'You said you'd call him.'

To say what? 'I've been meaning to but things have been so hectic, you know.'

'Well, you can talk to him now, if you like.'

'He's with you?' I'd deliberately called Jess on her mobile and not at the flat to avoid this happening. What are they doing in the supermarket together?

'He's in the tinned food section, I'm in the pasta aisle. We take it in turns to cook for one another now and so it makes sense to shop together. It makes a dreary job more fun.'

Very cosy. 'You take turns to cook for each other?'

'Adam wasn't eating. He needed looking after.' She then whispers, 'He's been really floored by you leaving like this, Fern. You really should talk to him.'

'OK, OK, put him on.' I know I have to face him eventually. I was just hoping that eventually meant on my deathbed.

I imagine Jess hunting Adam down among the baked

beans or tinned sweetcorn. If she can't find him there, he's probably drifted over to the DVD and CD section. On the few occasions we did shop together he'd invariably drift that way and then linger while I filled the trolley, queued at the checkout, paid and packed the groceries. He was never much help shopping, although he did carry the heavy bags to the car. My God, supermarket shopping belongs to a different world. I can barely remember the pain. Scott and I have been grocery shopping but just the once, and it was a completely different experience because really we went to Ralph's Store to star-spot and be seen rather than to actually buy stuff to eat. At Ralph's we pointed to things we might like to try, someone else picked them up, packed them and carried them to the car – I don't even know who, I can't remember. We have a nutritionist and a chef, so food seems to appear magically on my plate nowadays.

After a moment Adam comes on to the phone.

'Fern,' he says gruffly and formally.

The formality, although probably appropriate, is strange and uncomfortable. My mouth feels dry; I could do with a drink. A large G&T might help. 'How are you, Adam?' I ask, stepping into the boxing ring.

'Great.'

Not what I've heard, but what can I say? I try to sound bright and casual to counter his dark and serious tone. 'So you're cooking dinner for Jess tonight.'

'So you are marrying Scottie Taylor next month.'

Whack. Blow straight between the eyes. 'That's not what I meant.'

'You have no right to imply that I shouldn't be cooking for Jess.'

'I wasn't implying that.' Was I? No, I wasn't because it doesn't mean anything that they are shopping and cooking together. They're just buddies, and besides even if it did mean something, it's none of my business.

'It doesn't mean anything that we are shopping and cooking together. We're just buddies, and besides even if it did mean something it's none of your business,' says Adam. When did he develop the ability to read my mind?

'I know that, I'm just trying to be polite to take an interest in what you are doing with your free time.'

'The implication being that I've had plenty of that recently,' he says sarcastically.

'Adam, don't,' I plead quietly.

He cuts straight to the chase. 'You shouldn't marry him, Fern. He's a mistake.'

Ah, round two already, I didn't even hear the bell. I take a deep breath and try for a measured reaction; I must not let Adam rile me.

'You're wrong, Adam. He's the biggest thing that ever happened to me.'

'Yeah, the biggest mistake you'll ever make. I worked with him. I know what he's like.'

'You worked with him for a few days, you don't *know* him.'

'He has a reputation. He's an addict. He's a man trampled by regret and torn with choices. He's angry and unreliable. You should keep away from him.'

This is why I didn't want to ring Adam. Of course he's not completely incorrect. I'd be a fool to try to pretend to Adam that I think a relationship with Scott is going to be all plain sailing; it would be easier fooling myself. Scott does have some problems, he's the first to admit it, but we love each other and that will be enough to get us through anything, won't it? Yes it will. I'm shocked that a flicker of doubt entered my mind even for a split second. Where did that come from? I snuff out the doubt as quickly as I can. Of course our love is strong enough to get us through. We've had a blast so far. Really good fun, nothing but laughs. We're amazing. We're different. Sod Adam for rocking my boat.

'I'll be able to sort it all out, smooth it all over,' I insist.

'You'd need to be his mother, wife, counsellor, doctor, best mate. There isn't enough of you to go round to patch him up.' Adam pauses; I think his attack is over. Hurrah, I can run back to the corner of the ring, relatively unscathed, but then he relaunches. 'Look, I don't want to shock you but he's awash with rumours. He sleeps with everyone that moves.'

In a way it's quite sweet that Adam, my lover of four years, thinks I might be somehow shocked to hear that my pop star fiancé is not a virgin. If Adam had any idea of the level of detail Scott has gone into when revealing his past, his hair would curl. Sometimes, I do wish Scott would keep a tiny bit back. It might have been nice if he'd been as delicate as Adam is trying to be. It's hard not to have nightmares about the endless breasts Scott's caressed, the legs that have wrapped around him, the lips he's known, the sound of their moans as they've come. Especially since I've yet to have that pleasure. Adam interrupts my horrid thoughts, or rather, in some ghoulish telepathic way, he elaborates on my horrid thoughts.

'Scott just goes from one conquest to the next. He's incapable of commitment.'

And yet Scott's the one who proposed. A timely reminder.

'Well, it takes one to know one,' I say sharply.

I wonder if this is the moment to remind Adam that I'm with Scott because Adam couldn't commit. Wouldn't commit. He had his chance and he didn't want to grab it. What is he doing now? Has he turned into one of those men who doesn't want me for himself but doesn't want me to be happy with anyone else either? How mean! How dare he talk about my fiancé like this? What right does he have? I've had enough. I know Jess wants me to go easy on Adam but why the hell should I? He's not being easy on me. I summon my dignity.

Calmly I say, 'Adam, Scott's told me all about his past. He's been really honest. He told me everything. You can't shock me. You can't ruin this. Scott's already dished his own dirt. But he's clean now.'

'And what are you? Part of his recovery plan?'

'I would be if he needed me to be,' I say firmly.

Adam sighs. I can hear his despair across the ocean. He must know I'm not going to listen to him and yet he carries on. I wonder why he's bothering.

'He's unstable and he's an actor. You'll never know when he's for real. Like, when he does that overwhelmed shrug thing to the audience, like he's just amazed. He did that on all three nights of the concert.'

'He *was* overwhelmed.' I'm fed up with this now.

'I've been watching the DVD of his Wembley gig, Fern, over and over again. The man can't be trusted.' It's official, Adam has turned into a psycho. What is he doing watching Scott's DVD over and over? 'Do you remember he'd act all nervous and he'd beg the audience not to believe the stuff that was written in the tabloids? He'd be practically crying and then in an instant he'd be as hard as nails again. It's an act and you don't want to be part of that.'

'How do you know what I want to be part of?'

'I know you,' he says confidently.

I swallow an elephant. That's the first thing Adam has said that I can agree with. He does know me. Or at least did. I'm different now. Or at least things are different now. Suddenly I feel tense and anxious. I had a massage only this morning, there's no reason for me to feel uptight. I was dreading this conversation but I didn't expect it to be this upsetting.

'Look, thanks for your concern, can you give the phone back to Jess now,' I say wearily.

'How did it go?' asks Jess. 'I didn't listen in, I wanted to give you some privacy so I skulked around the yogurt section for a bit. Have you two cleared the air?'

'You could say that.' Or you could say that my ex is a lunatic. A vengeful, cruel lunatic. I don't think there's any point in saying this to Jess. It's clear her sympathies lie with Adam and she's not in the frame of mind to hear it from my point of view. Instead I just add, 'Yeah, we're all sorted now.'

'Good, you'll both feel better for it. Now you can both move on.' Jess's tone is considerably brighter than I've heard from her in a long time.

'I've already moved on,' I tell her haughtily. Adam's

words, inaccurate and spiteful, have had a much bigger effect than they deserve; I feel irrationally narky. '*I* moved on weeks ago.'

'Yes. Yes, you did and that's why I hope you'll have a think about what I want to ask you.'

'What?'

'Well, you know the invite to your wedding said plus one.'

'Yeah.' Please God, don't let her ask that. Let me be wrong about what I'm sure is coming next.

'Do you mind if I bring Adam?' God, are you listening?

'Bring Adam as your date?' I ask, stunned.

'No, no, no nothing like that. Adam isn't ready to date, but bring him to help him get closure.'

If Adam were ready to date, is that what she's hoping for? Jess wants to date Adam? I remember the first gig at Wembley, Jess turned up done up to the eyeballs. Lisa said Jess was hoping for a brief encounter with Scott, seems like we had that all wrong. Could she have been interested in Adam all along? How long? When we were all living together? Is that possible? I mull it over. It would explain why Jess has so suddenly and decisively distanced herself from me and why she's been so keen for him to have closure. I distinctly remember her saying she wasn't averse to sloppy seconds.

I feel terrible. Sick to the pit of my stomach. I don't understand why. It's not like *I'm* one of those people who doesn't want someone but doesn't want anyone else to have them either. It's mean. It's not possible that I still want him for myself. Why would I want that? I have Scott.

Scottie Taylor. I have all of this. I cast my eyes around the manicured gardens; all's quiet right now except for the sound of birds singing and the gentle whiz as the sprinklers discreetly do their job. The grass is lush and green, the sky is a vivid, vital blue; pretty soon I'll see Scott drop from the sky in a helicopter – he's just popped over to Mexico, as he's buying a racehorse. While he's there he will no doubt pick up shoes, bags and other treats for me. But. But I feel terrible.

I know why. For one thing I'd lose Jess's friendship if she and Adam dated. Irretrievably. And for a second, well, it would be weird! Adam kissing Jess's body. Adam meeting Jess from work. Adam patiently sitting outside the changing-room while Jess tried on dozens of tops in H&M. Adam and Jess doing all that everyday stuff that Adam and I used to do. That would be so weird.

'I thought the phone call was for closure,' I stutter.

'Well, let's hope it is.'

'I'm not sure Scott would like Adam coming to the wedding,' I stall.

'But the church will be half full of his exes. How could he possibly mind?'

How indeed? And how could I? I take a deep breath, one from far down in my flip-flops. 'Great, yes, invite Adam.' He won't come anyway. Will he? Why would he want to come? Other than for a free holiday in LA, with Jess.

Oh. My. God.

52. Scott

In absence of actual sex Fern and I turn each other on with our thoughts and words. We often talk through the night until the sun comes up. Ben joins us more often than not but that's OK, he's a great chaperone, and happily his presence doesn't take anything away from the intimacy. We're busy all day, doing our separate thing, but we come together at dusk like tired snow cranes flocking to watch the sunset. We three lie next to one another, outside in the hammocks or on the sun-beds, Fern and I holding hands across the gap. We listen to the sounds of Beverly Hills and watch the black sky turn purple, then red, then orange and finally a bright morning blue. I love studying the colours as they unfold. Ben says it's like watching a bunch of flowers uncurl and bloom; Fern got that – they have this flower thing going on between them. I need to get into flowers more, maybe.

I sometimes read them the lyrics from *Wedding Album*. They both love everything I've written and Ben keeps begging me to let him come to the studio to listen to the recording. He's so full of enthusiasm, Ben is. When I read to them he sits up, mind wide open and legs swinging, leaning towards me. If he likes something particularly, he can't stop his hands gesticulating wildly to make a point; he's like some jacked-up windmill. When Fern likes something she's very still, she treats me to a slow, wide, face-splitting smile. I'm beginning to appreciate stillness a bit more. It's not something I have hope to be but it's restful to be around. Very pleasant.

There's always a stage in the night, sometimes two or three occasions, when the atmosphere, already thick with cigarette smoke, becomes denser still with palpable longing. As I open and shut my mouth I gulp in oxygen and want, and soon I don't know which I need the most. I expel ideas and yearning; both are lapped up.

Inevitably we begin to fidget and struggle in our hammocks; uptight and edgy as we imagine banging out our need on each other's bodies. I ache to pull at her clothes hungrily, to repeatedly and insistently grab, bite, lick, kiss and consume her. I'd like it deep and fast in illicit places, long and slow on one of the many beds.

I'd have it any old way. Then I think, screw stillness.

Why do I make these things so hard for myself? Mark is right, I should probably just fuck her and get it over with.

I can hear Fern and Ben heading my way; they're in the corridor debating which champagnes they prefer.

'I think I'm a Taittinger man, on reflection, it has a crispness to it that I appreciate. Bollinger and Moët are more yeasty,' says Ben seriously.

'Can you really tell the difference between all these champagnes?' Fern asks. She sounds impressed.

'Yes. Can't you?'

'Not really.'

'Then don't touch the Cristal, leave that for me,' says Ben. The man has taste. Cristal costs upward of a hundred quid per bottle. I have stuff in my cellar that cost three thousand.

I'm so glad Fern has Ben to play with while I'm busy. He's good to have around. I liked him on first impression when he helped me fit out his shop with those flowers Fern likes. Frankly, I couldn't have done it without him. He sourced the flowers, arranged delivery, sourced the vases and buckets and arranged the flowers. I paid. It was clear to me from the moment I first set eyes on him that he would do anything for her, and me, of course; but then everyone will do anything for me. It's turned out that he's a natural Los Angel. He is polite, polished, upfront and unapologetic. He's becoming more camp by the second and when he's not playing Professor Higgins to Fern's Eliza Doolittle he's at the gym or the tanning shop or the beauty parlour. Somehow he still manages to squeeze in almost daily calls to his florist shop back in the UK to check that his business is thriving.

They come into the den. 'What have you two been up to today?' I ask.

'I've just picked up some zero fat frozen yogurts and a re-supply of E-boost dietary supplement from the bagel café,' says Ben. Gone are the days when any of us would buy curry or a pickled egg at the chippie.

'And now we're meeting Colleen to talk about the wedding,' says Fern. Of course they are.

I've been so busy in the studio that I haven't been involved in the planning at all. Too many cooks spoil the broth and all that. But Mark says I have to show I'm supportive and interested. 'How's it all coming together?'

Fern looks delighted I've asked. She flips open her Smythson leather-bound wedding planning notebook. 'Colleen gave me an updated status list this morning. Should I take it from the top?'

'Go for it.'

'Well, we've chosen the diamonds for my jewellery and for the bridesmaids' presents.'

'All very sparkly,' chips in Ben.

'We've confirmed the venue, menu, wines and champagne,' Fern adds.

'All very yummy,' encourages Ben.

'The booklets for the service are at the printers.'

'We've ordered three thousand candles.'

'Four hundred ornate birdcages.'

'Packed with silk butterflies.'

I raise my eyebrows 'For?'

'For the tables.'

'Right,' I nod.

'Yesterday we earnestly discussed feathers, tea-light holders, baubles and the exact shade of icing for heart-shaped biscuits for ten consecutive hours. We all agreed it was a great Hollywood moment and Colleen opened the champagne,' says Fern with a full-on laugh.

Ben puts his hand on Fern's shoulders and starts to lead her out of the door. 'Speaking of Colleen, we're supposed to be meeting her right about now and Mark sent us to find you, Scott. He wants you to come too.'

Mark has an A-list quota he's keen to meet and is fanatically monitoring the replies as they come in.

'But you can't see the dress designs,' says Fern, looking concerned. 'It's unlucky.'

'It's unlucky for the groom to see the bride *in* the actual dress,' I correct.

'Just stay by the door,' insists Ben.

53. Fern

Jenny Packham is designing my dress. It was almost impossible to choose who should, as Vera Wang and Amanda Wakeley also showed me their sketches. My dilemma was that all the designs were heart-bleedingly beautiful. Saadi's dilemma was which designer would cause the biggest sensation. In the end we plumped for Jenny because when one of Saadi's assistants did the initial scouting to each designer's studio she noticed that Jenny had Scott's official calendar hanging in her office. Mark loved that and fed the story as a titbit to the gossip columns.

Ben, Colleen, Saadi and I sit at the dining-room table looking at sketches of my wedding dress while Joy and a couple of pretty, nameless assistants mill around. The sketches are breathtaking. Jenny specializes in luxurious bias-cut dresses with delicate, intricate beading. Her creations are drenched with a dazzling glamour and beauty that harks back to gentler, more romantic days; they are elegant and feminine. I absolutely can't wait for my first fitting.

Mark drifts over to where we are sitting; I wondered how long he'd be able to resist interfering. He picks up a sketch of the dress.

'Don't go too flouncy, she needs to be rock chic,' he says to Colleen.

Hello! I'm here! I can't get used to people talking over

my head, as though I'm not even in the room; they do it to Scott all the time. When they do it to me I always want to wave a big red flag or throw a big red strop.

Mark goes on. 'Don't over-style. Loose hair. Almost dirty-looking. Was it Sting's Trudy who arrived at the church on a horse or was that Paula Yates? That's what we need. Something different and eye-catching.'

Ben, Colleen, the entourage and I all glare at Mark in unison. He takes a hint and goes to sit down with Scott. The rest of us turn back to the matter in hand.

'Mark's right about one thing. We do need a unifying USP,' says Colleen.

'A what?' I ask.

'A unique selling point,' clarifies Ben.

'For my wedding?'

'If not then, when?' says Saadi, rolling her eyes.

'Bollywood?' suggests Ben. 'Bangles, spicy food, girls in saris serving lychees.'

'French boudoir? Wide skirts, bosoms on show, garters,' suggests Joy.

'Oriental? Fern could arrive on a dragon,' says Saadi's first assistant.

'I don't think there are any dragons left,' sneers Saadi's second assistant (clearly on the look-out for a promotion).

'What, not even in China? We could ship in.'

'Silver ice,' offers someone else. 'We'd need snow machines and ice sculptures. Fern could arrive in a sleigh pulled by huskies.'

'Flowers,' I say firmly. My voice slices through the madness.

'That's your theme?' asks Joy, raising a perfectly arched (threaded rather than plucked) eyebrow.

'Yes, flowers and romance. I want beads and flowers, and glitter and flowers, and satin and flowers,' I gush. 'Mostly just lots of flowers. Romantic flowers.'

There's a silence. After a while Colleen says, 'Don't you think romance has been done to death at weddings?'

I ignore her and continue to describe my vision. 'I want inches of petals for the guests to stride through and the smell of flowers floating through the air for miles around.'

'Or maybe fur but I'm not talking white fur, I'm thinking leopard skin,' says another complete stranger. I glare at her.

'And flowers threaded through my hair.'

'I'm not suggesting real leopard skin. The animal rights activists would be all over us, mobbing the reception. I just meant –'

'Give the lady her flowers,' Scott shouts from the corner of the room where we banished him.

There's a hiatus in the conversation. We'd almost forgotten he was there; a rare occurrence but his imperial power has now been reinstated.

'Fine,' says Colleen with a heavy sigh. 'I suppose we can do *something* with flowers.'

Then there's complete silence. I turn to him and send out a look of pure, undiluted love and mouth, 'Thank you'. He is so unselfish with me. He is one hundred per cent behind me. For me. My happiness is his everything. He's wonderful. Adam was so wrong about him.

54. Scott

'Son, you're a pro,' says Mark, his delight and admiration oozing from every pore as we leave the room.

'Agreed but what are you talking about in particular?' I ask, giving in to a wide yawn. I love yawning. And stretching's good too. Not the sort of stretching you do in yoga – can't be doing with that. Well, I did go through a phase where I practised ashtanga yoga but that phase didn't last long; it gets dead fucking boring, really quickly, and hideously uncomfortable too. But a normal stretch, first thing in the morning, or an I've-been-sat-still-too-long stretch – well, nothing beats that.

Mark continues, 'Stroke of genius, you intervening when the wild cats were backing Fern into a corner about the wedding theme. Now she's feeling all gaga about you.'

'Default setting.'

'Yeah, but now *even* more so.'

'Flowers mean a lot to her. It's sweet.'

'Now would be a good time to talk about the pre-nup.'

'Do we have to?'

'Yes.'

'I think she might get upset about it.'

'I think she's bright enough to understand exactly what we are trying to achieve,' says Mark confidently.

'Yeah, that's what I mean.' I don't want to upset Fern. I've enjoyed the peaceful, no drama, no tantrum existence we've had up until now. Of course I know it's got to end, everything does.

'Let me handle it. I'll call the lawyers, they can be here in fifteen. At least they'd bloody better be, considering the retainer we pay them. You go and find the little lady.'

He flicks out his phone – I think he keeps it permanently up his sleeve, like some sort of magician.

I wonder what approach Mark will use to introduce the subject of the pre-nup to Fern: subtle, humorous or sympathetic? He goes for direct. He clamps his chubby hand on the base of her back the moment she comes through the door and he steers her towards the gang of crows, suited and booted, huddled in the corner. I sit behind the pianoforte. I always play chopsticks at tricky moments. Everyone loves chopsticks.

'These are the lawyers that are dealing with the pre-nup,' says Mark starkly. 'I wanted you to meet them, Fern.'

'The pre-nup?' Fern looks like a rabbit caught not just in headlights but in the actual pie.

'A pre-nuptial is a contract that clarifies your shared responsibilities and gives you and your partner peace of mind, security and more time to concentrate on enjoying your relationship,' says one of the Blues Brothers look-alikes.

Fern looks around the room. I think she's searching for the autocue because that sure sounded rehearsed. 'I know what a pre-nup is,' she snaps. 'Although not necessarily from that description. I'm wondering why Scott and I need one.' I feel her glance bounce my way but I keep my eyes firmly on the ivories.

'To predict the outcome of any divorce settlement before the marriage even takes place,' says another one of the gang with a studied grimace.

'To prevent speculative claims following a short marriage,' adds a third with a slight shrug.

'To save thousands in legal costs in the event of a divorce,' adds a fourth man gravely.

Fern doesn't say anything and the lawyers take this as encouragement enough. The lawyer who spoke first picks up the baton. He sends a thin smile in Fern's direction but it's too weak to make it across the room. 'Both parties should have lawyers to represent them to ensure the agreement is enforceable. You'll need to hire a firm. You have to have the contract for a week before you can sign it. So we'll meet again, Ms Dickson, with your attorney, next Wednesday. Shall we say 2 p.m.?'

He puts down the fat document and with that the suits vanish in a puff of smoke leaving Mark, Fern and me alone. I tinkle with the ivories again and wait for someone to speak. Fern is focusing on a small box of beads that Colleen has inadvertently left behind. I understand that these beads are going to be liberally scattered across the tables at the wedding, so the whole place gleams. I get the feeling Fern thinks their glistening promise is a tad tarnished in light of the lawyers' visit. It takes a while before she finds her voice.

'Did you want this, Scott?' she asks.

'Oh no. Scott rarely initiates discussions around money matters,' says Mark jovially, saving me the effort of replying.

'But you want me to sign?' Again she launches the

question in my direction but again Mark intercepts it, like the skilled ninja he is.

'It's for the best. Look, Fern, these things aren't watertight if that's what you're fretting about. Pre-nups are, at best, a partial solution to minimizing the risks of marital property disputes in times of divorce.'

'We won't be getting divorced,' says Fern firmly.

'No one ever thinks they will, but forty per cent of the blighters who walk down the aisle are wrong, aren't they? You can see my concern,' says Mark.

Finally Fern drags her eyes from me and glares at Mark. 'No, I can't actually. Do you think I'm just marrying Scott for his money?'

'Love, no one would blame you,' says Mark, treating Fern to some rare truth.

'I would blame me! I'm not marrying him for his money.' Glancing back at me she yells, 'I'm not marrying you for your money.' It's really uncomfortable.

'Then there won't be any problem with you signing it, will there?' says Mark reasonably.

'Yes, there's a problem. The problem is, this means Scott does not believe that we're for ever. Or at least he's considering the possibility that we might not be and he's already protecting himself against that possibility.'

It's the first time she's done that – talked about me as though I'm not in the room. I don't care, as such. Everyone does it sooner or later and I've just blanked her direct questions. I'm just saying it's a first for us. Fuck, I wish I *wasn't* in the room. I really don't think it was necessary for me to get involved in this.

'Look, Fern, read it. Take some legal advice. It's a very

generous agreement. It's to protect you as much as him. It really is. Now, if you'll excuse us, I need Scott to come and look at some artwork. We'll see you at dinner, hey love?' Mark beckons me and I get up and follow him.

I leave her alone with her shiny beads.

55. Fern

I call Lisa.

'Ouch,' she says when I tell her about the pre-nup. It's nearly midnight her time, but she doesn't appear to mind. She's very nice about the fact that I keep crying. The children are in bed and Charlie is away on business – situation normal. She's alone with a glass of wine and the latest novel she's reading for her book club. I can imagine it all. Her house will be calm and immaculate; she and everything in it will give off an aura of order and self-satisfaction. Often, over the last couple of years, when my old flat became grubby beyond repair (a single dirty sock breaking the camel's back), I'd run to Lisa's home and take sanctuary. I love it there and not just because of the pristine and expensive fixtures and fittings or the air of almost religious serenity but because of the tangible sense of contentment; Lisa has caught it and bagged it, that most precious of commodities. I hang on her every word as though she is the Dalai Lama. She's cracked this relationship thing. I want to get it right too.

'So what do you think? It's outrageous, isn't it?' I demand.

'Are the terms as generous as Mark says?' she asks.

'I don't know. I haven't read it, but that's not the point.'

'Isn't it?'

'No!'

'I'd say it is. I don't think a pre-nup is a surprise or unreasonable, considering Scott's wealth. You just have to make sure you've got a good deal. Rich people do things differently. You knew that. You wanted different,' she says calmly.

Suddenly, I find her calm very annoying – almost sanctimonious. Doesn't she understand I want Scott for ever, not on loan? A pre-nup says that this is a flimsy little effort at a marriage. I want a solid commitment. It's no surprise that Lisa assumes this is all about the cash, that's her take on things.

I think about calling Jess but can't bring myself to do it. If she's in, I'm pretty sure she won't pour on tender words of consolation and encouragement; that hasn't been her bag of late and if she's out I'll be left wondering who she's out with. Adam? The thought does nothing to calm me. She wouldn't, would she? He wouldn't, would he? I can't think about that now.

So next, I call Rick. After giving him a lengthy blow-by-blow account of what the lawyers said to me, and what Mark said to me, and what I said to him, and what I wished I'd said to him, and what I'm going to say to Scott and what I expect Scott to say to Mark, I pause for breath.

'Bummer,' says my younger brother.

Then, I call my big sister Fiona. Her response is at least more in-depth, although not totally comforting.

'I can't see that you have any choice but to sign.'

Again I try to explain. 'I'm not objecting to signing, I'm objecting to the very existence of a pre-nup and what its existence says about me and Scott. We aren't entering this marriage with the same expectations –'

I don't get to finish. Fiona interrupts, 'Oh, get over yourself, Fern. You're the luckiest woman in the world. Don't you dare muck this up. The kids are really looking forward to being bridesmaids. They've told everyone in school that their aunt is marrying Scottie Taylor. They've never been so happy. Get a lawyer, get the best deal you can and sign.'

I've nobody left to call.

I pick up the blasted pre-nup and I read the first paragraph; it's a hefty and confusing document. I remember my history teacher explaining that contracts used to be written in Latin, now it appears they are written in gobble-dygook. I need a lawyer to explain it. I don't know any, so I call Mark and ask him to find me one.

'That's hardly independent, is it, Fern?' he says, but he sounds relieved that I'm asking for a lawyer at all.

'My other choice is sticking a pin in the yellow pages,' I point out wearily. I'm not even sure if there is such a thing as the yellow pages in LA; it's scary that there's so much I don't know about my new life.

'I'll ask Colleen. She's a wedding planner, she knows all the best divorce lawyers,' says Mark, without apparent irony. 'I'll get her to set something up asap.'

'Yeah, Mark, you do that.' I put the phone down and curl up into a tight little ball on my bed.

56. Scott

We don't see Fern at supper after all. There's a whole gang of people hanging around, and she's sent word to say she just wants a quiet one in her room. Her nutritionist sends up a bowl of snow-pea shoots, apparently rich in vitamins A, B, C and E but – let's face it – not as tasty as chips. After supper most of the guys go to the movie room to watch a DVD and a few go to my den to play on the footie table. Ben and I wander outside to the hammocks, so we can lie on our backs and watch the stars as usual. I find this ritual the three of us have developed really relaxing; it's a shame Fern's not up to it tonight.

'Have you checked in on Fern?' I ask Ben.

He sighs, flops back into the hammock and folds his long limbs in after him, in that elegant way he has.

'Yeah, I did.'

'She OK?'

'Yeah, OK.'

From his tone I guess that Fern isn't buzzing but I don't particularly want to get into it. Luckily, nor does Ben. He doesn't mention the pre-nup but says instead, 'The wedding plans are exhausting her. I've told her she ought to have a day off from it tomorrow, before she becomes unbearably stressy.'

Fern does not plough fields or chop trees, she doesn't even have to put a full day's graft in at the flower shop any more, but Ben understands that they are now in a world where exhaustion is something someone suffers from after a gruelling day at the spa, a nightmare is a nail breaking and a global calamity is turning up to a party in a dress someone has seen you in before. Ben once again demonstrates that he gets this, all so perfectly, when he tells me that he has to go shopping for new T-shirts tomorrow because today he spotted Zac Efron in one like one of his (in a magazine, but when he tells the story you'd think they were having supper together). Ben's funny.

We both stare at the blue-black sky. I can't do that pointing out the Great Bear and the Hunting Dogs and what the fuck. I think it's all ludicrous. Honestly, you can join the stars up to draw anything you want. But I do like counting them. Tonight there are loads and I keep losing count. Ben starts to chat about whether he should take up surfing; motivation being that there are loads of fit blokes out on the surf. And he asks me about my tattoos and whether I think he should get one. Is he too old at thirty-three, he asks. I know for a fact that he's thirty-five but I don't call him on it.

Then Ben starts to talk about *Wedding Album*. He's been to the studio once or twice now and he thinks the album is amazing; I never tire of hearing him (or anyone, for that matter) say so.

'I take in the words and it's like taking air into my lungs, their meaning swills about, nurturing my every organ, giving life to my body,' he says with a big, giddy grin.

'Wow,' I smirk back. 'You are so gay,' I tease.

'That *is* a point of fact. But you know what I mean,

don't you?' He looks earnest and clearly wants me to get the intensity of his deep approval of my latest album. I've seen that solemn, desperate longing for a connection before. Often. I smile indulgently as he continues. 'And then I breathe out and the meaning returns to where it came from, everywhere around me. These new songs chronicle the *ultimate* experience of life. This album is going to be huge. It's like this album is saying Scottie Taylor has *all* the answers.'

'Which is somewhat ironic, don't you think? I know nothing.' I say the last sentence in a jokey quasi-Mafia voice to dispel the intensity of the confession.

'Oh, I don't know, you're not so ignorant,' says Ben. 'I think you've got this living stuff sussed more than the rest of us. More than you know.'

'What's the point of being sussed beyond your own understanding?' I challenge. 'That doesn't make sense.'

It is great being sober; you can at least spot it when someone starts talking bollocks. The problem I used to have when I got drunk so often was that I started to confuse being insensible with being invincible. Maybe that's what I liked about it at first. At least now I'm clear that I'm not invincible; even if knowing this makes me sad.

Ben sits up in the hammock. To do this well, a certain amount of grace and skill is required. Few have this but he does. The hammock sways gently as he leans back on his elbows.

'Look around you, Scott. You've said yourself that no one stumbles upon success, you have to earn it, and from where I'm sitting, it appears you are up to your neck in success. You must have *some* of the answers.'

His confidence is touching. He reminds me of Fern, enthusiastic and optimistic – I can see why they are such good mates.

'Should I tell you something I've worked out?' I ask him. 'It's a secret.'

Ben looks excited. I think he's expecting me to tell him how to achieve eternal life. I lean closer to him and whisper in his ear.

'The truth is success doesn't exist. At least, not for me. Anticipation of success is the best thing there is. It's not finite, you see. It's not complete or done with.' Ben looks disappointed. He draws away from me sharply, as though I've just infected him with more than bad news. I go on. 'Success never *is* actually. Which should be an exciting thing but turns out to be hugely frustrating. Whereas failure, failure is blocking and choking and everywhere, so that's no good either.'

We stay silent for some moments. Ben pours himself another glass of champagne. It's his fourth or fifth this evening, I think. He swallows it down in two gulps.

'Can I ask you something?' he says.

'Ask away.'

'Why are you marrying Fern?'

I thought it'd be that. 'She's lovely,' I say plainly.

'True, but you've met a lot of lovely women. Why her? I only ask because she's my friend and as you said yourself, she's lovely. I don't want to see her –'

'Hurt.'

'I was going to say crucified. I'm expecting a fatal wounding.'

I don't even pause. 'I'm marrying her to capture the

US market and because when I'm not doing drugs nothing amazing happens and I'm bored.'

The truth sits between us like a massive shard of glass; dangerous, brittle, beautiful.

'I see,' says Ben with a deep sigh.

This is an interesting moment. I like to fill my life with as many interesting moments as I can and this is definitely one. It's dangerous and it's faulty but it's also honest.

'Both those things ought to reassure you,' I point out. 'If I am to capture the US market I will have to be faithful and fair for a substantial period of time and I don't plan to do drugs ever again.' I flash him my cheeky, winning smile. It never fails. I know he'll be flattered that we are talking so frankly. He'll hand me his loyalty on a silver plate. In case he thinks I'm callous, I add, 'I plan to do my best by her.'

'How good is your best, Scott?'

'In my career, my best is excellent. In my love life, it's piss poor.'

'And which is Fern part of?' I can't answer that. I'm undecided and that lack of clarity is not something either of us can celebrate. 'Do you think you are ready to settle down?' he probes.

'Settle down is such a depressing term. I don't want to settle for anything,' I say awkwardly. I still want to reassure him. 'She's going to be OK, Ben. I'm going to give her what she wants.'

'Which is?'

'Marriage, babies, a home. A crack at being extraordinary. I can give her more than she could ever have imagined, even in her wildest dreams. And I don't just mean clothes and shoes and stuff. I mean the people she'll meet, the places we'll travel to. It will blow her mind. I can give her a fuck of a lot more than she'd ever have got out of Adam, the loser. I'm saving her from a man whose response to an ultimatum, asking for lifelong commitment, was producing a couple of blagged tickets for a gig.'

'How do you know about the ultimatum? Did she tell you?'

'No, she doesn't know I know. She's never talked to me about it. I guess she doesn't consider it her finest hour.'

'It wasn't.'

'Saadi told me. After Fern delivered her deadline Adam was forever procrastinating with his crew. Everyone working at the Wembley gig knew all about the fact that his girl wanted to get engaged on her birthday. He didn't deserve her. He's a loser.'

'You know, he isn't such a loser,' says Ben carefully.

'He let her go,' I reply firmly.

'How could he have fought you?'

'He could have acted before she'd even met me.'

Ben pauses, then sighs and says, 'He had. He'd bought a house.'

'What?' That's news.

Ben looks agitated, torn. 'She doesn't know. I never told her. I've often wondered whether I should have but what would the point be now? I only know because Adam let it slip the day before her birthday. He wanted it to be a big surprise. His plan was to take her there after the Friday night gig. He had the keys; he was going to do the whole carrying her over the threshold thing. Get down on one knee in the kitchen. But instead, he stayed late to work on the light sequence and when he got home they argued about you singing "Happy Birthday". It was all such lousy timing. He'd bought the house before her ultimatum. He was just arsing about when he said he didn't know how or whether to commit. He was trying to keep the surprise. Poor bugger.'

'Fuck.'

'Yeah. That's what he thought.'

57. Fern

The lawyer spends hours trying to explain to me the ins and outs of the weighty tome. It's very dull but she reassures me that I am getting a generous deal. After only two years' marriage or the production of a baby, whichever is sooner, I have a good chance of walking away with half Scott's enormous fortune. The lawyer seems really happy with the arrangement. I mumble that if she's so happy with it then perhaps she should sign it.

'Oh, don't be silly, Ms Dickson. This is a marvellous contract. Drawn up by the industry's finest but very fair. No need to be petulant. You're marrying a very generous man.'

'And he can prove his generosity when he divorces me,' I mutter sulkily.

'Providing you're faithful,' she cautions.

I haven't asked a single question but suddenly one drops from the sky. 'What about his fidelity?'

'If you look at page 92, clause 13.4, subsection 6, item 2, addendum 3, you'll note that his infidelity is covered.'

'Covered? In what way?'

'In so much as his infidelity is recognized as grounds for divorce but you would not receive any extra recompense, over and above that stated on pages 45 to 71, with particular reference to clauses 17 to 17.9, subsections 4.2 to 4.7.'

'In English?'

'I think your fiancé's lawyers are anticipating infidelity.'

'*Anticipating* it?' I can't keep the shock out of my voice.

'At least acknowledging that it's a very real possibility and therefore they're not prepared to offer you extra compensation if that were indeed the case. But, as I say, the divorce terms are particularly generous anyway so you have little to worry about.'

Right.

'The important thing to remember is that you don't get a penny if you ever talk about any aspect of your relationship to the press. That's covered in multiple clauses. That's watertight.'

As if I would. How can Scott think that of me? I pick up the hefty contract and as much of my dignity as I can scrape off the floor and go to find Mark.

He's in the second reception room. It's one of my favourite rooms; south-facing, it's always warm and bright. It's definitely sunnier than my mood. Exasperated, I demand, 'Can you explain page 92, clause 13.4, subsection 6, item – oh, you know what I'm talking about.'

Mark, Saadi and Joy look up from their work. They're pawing over press cuttings. Every magazine and paper in the western world finds the wedding plans fascinating. There are bets running on the number of bridesmaids I'm having (ten; including three of Scott's celeb friends I haven't yet met), the colour they'll be wearing (pink, although I haven't told Jess that yet). Tabloids are battling to discover where the wedding is going to take place but the venue is top secret. Everyone who knows anything is under contract embargoing any discussion with the press; even revealing a detail as small as what we'll be pouring is a sackable offence. Mark predicted that the secrecy would guarantee the most lucrative media deal and the most hype. He's right on both counts but I'm still struggling to understand why either thing matters to our wedding.

Mark stares at me and then turns to Saadi.

'The infidelity clause,' she prompts. Why am I not surprised she'd know the finer details of the pre-nup by heart?

'Oh, yeah. Well, that had to be included for obvious reasons.'

'Obvious reasons?' I ask. I hope my voice isn't as shaky as my legs; I'm practically dancing a jig.

'Don't get us wrong. We adore Scott and want him to be happy. We'd like to believe that the pair of you will last for ever. But . . .'

He leaves the 'but' hanging in the air. It's damning enough to have sucked all the pleasure out of the day. I'm unsure who he means by 'us'. The record company, the band members, Scott's mum? I have no idea, but I suddenly feel weighed down by the sense that there is a silent army behind Scott and no one in my corner. It shouldn't matter. We're not at war. But it does matter. I stay silent and Mark is forced to fill in the gap.

'Well, you know how it is. Scott gets infatuated with things. With people. Spellbound almost. We've seen it before. And then there's the danger he might act on that infatuation. We're just protecting him against any possible indiscretions he might succumb to.'

Mark, to his credit, sounds embarrassed that he has to tell me this. I've never seen Mark stirred before. It depresses me that he gives this subject so much weight.

'It's nothing to be worried about. Even when he does act –' Mark struggles to find the right word '– imprudently, then the interest dries up quickly enough. On average his obsessions last twenty-four hours.'

'We're all stunned that you've lasted a month,' says Joy bitchily.

I shoot her a filthy look and turn back to Mark. His gaze bounces around the room, resting on the drapes, the rug, the smooth obelisk ornaments; anywhere other than me. To date, I've been overwhelmed by the tasteful-ness of all that I am surrounded by. Now the room looks vulgar. It is quiet and the sun beats through the windows; I feel suffocated.

'Even if I accept that Scott has fallen prey to these fleeting obsessions in the past, what we have is quite different. What we have is called love,' I say firmly.

Mark stands up and walks towards me. Awkwardly he puts both his hands on my shoulders and faces me. It's the first time I can remember him deliberately touching me. It ought to be a comfort but it's not.

'I'm not saying he wants to have sex with anyone else, right now.' Well, that's a relief since he isn't even having sex with me yet. 'I'm saying somewhere along the line he might want to. Sex is just another compulsion for him. He can't really help himself.'

'I think you're wrong,' I say, struggling to sound calm.

Mark shrugs. I get the feeling he doesn't much care

what I think. 'But if I am right and he does stray and you get fed up, well, he's my boy. I have to look out for him.'

Where is Scott? It never crossed my mind to go and discuss my worries about this contract with *him*. That's odd. That's not right. I think it's because he stayed absolutely silent when the lawyers presented the pre-nup. No matter what I asked him, he played dumb. So now I've come to Mark, hoping he can sort it out, explain it, tidy it away. After all, that's what Mark does.

I was quickly made aware that there are a number of people who put themselves between Scott and me and I've co-operated when necessary, but I'd always assumed – hoped – they'd fade away as I settled into my life in LA. I realize the opposite has happened; their influence seems to have spread and stained – like billows of blood after a shark's bite. It's wrong. It's all wrong.

'And if I don't agree to sign this?' I ask.

'Well, that's your right,' replies Mark. 'You can say that you don't want a pre-nup and that you want to go into this marriage with as much hope and as little chance as every other bride does.' I nod, ferociously confirming this is indeed my wish. Mark shrugs, pauses and then adds, 'But he might not go ahead. He might not want to marry you if he knows you can embarrass him in public, perhaps ruin him. He's been damaged enough by the media. He might not want to take that risk.'

I feel as though I've just been dropped into a bag of spiders as every hair on my body stands up tall. I *can't* lose him. I *can't*. Scott has become my everything. His world is my world. I love it. I love him; everyone does. I am the luckiest girl on the planet. Everyone from Ben to Amanda Amberd says so. Lisa thinks I should sign. Fiona thinks I should sign. Even Rick thinks I should.

I look at Mark and try to weigh up whether he is a dependable conduit of communication or whether he's as much good as the 'telephones' Fiona and I used to make as kids. We would tie a couple of paper cups together with a piece of string, run in opposite directions until the string was taut and then bellow to one another. The message never carried around corners and all subtleties were lost.

Mark smiles at me. I don't respond. He shrugs at me; it seems a more truthful gesture.

'OK, I'll sign it,' I say wearily.

What choice do I have? I just want to get out of the room.

58. Scott

Fern and I haven't rowed but I've been on the receiving end of an inevitable low-grade sulk since Mark first introduced her to the lawyers. It's to be expected, all very normal, all very predictable, but somehow, the fact that she is behaving as expected is disappointing to me. She's not extraordinary then. She's like all the other hundreds of women I've met. When I say this to Mark he sighs, 'I hope to God you are right, son.'

'What do you mean?'

'I'm counting on the fact that she's as weak and malleable as every other bugger. The last thing we need now is an autonomous philosophy emerging; that could only lead to trouble. In fact, I think you need to go and apply a band-aid. Do a bit of fussing and soothing, make her feel better about everything. Loved up. The most important thing here is that she remains head over heels about you.'

'I hope you're not suggesting that's in any doubt,' I say huffily.

'No lad, I'm not. She was half in love with you before she met you. You saw the postcard pinned to her staff-room wall. I spotted the photo of her with your waxwork when I was scouring her albums.'

Mark isn't going to say what we both know; being half in love with the *image* of me is quite different from being totally and absolutely in love with the *real* me. Pretty much everyone on the planet is the first; my mum is the only absolute definite in the second camp.

'We don't want to fuck this up, Scott, not when we're so close and we've all worked so hard,' adds Mark, warily.

'OK, OK, I'll go and sweet-talk her.'

I find her outside, stood near the pool. It's getting dark but it's still warm. I put my arms around her waist and kiss her neck. I feel the hairs on her body respond, confirming what we all need to know – I'm irresistible.

'Hey, my beautiful wifie-to-be, what are you doing out here all on your own?'

'Just thinking,' says Fern. She doesn't turn towards me but she does lean her head back to rest on my chest; she melts into me and we both silently watch the sunset. For about three and a half minutes. I can't stay still for longer than that.

'Did you have a chat with Ben today?' I asked Ben to talk to Fern about the pre-nup stuff. To point out that he thinks it's perfectly reasonable (which he does) and that she's done the right thing by signing (which she has).

'Yes.'

Well, that's good, although her staunch silence suggests that I still have to put a bit more effort in. I don't want to talk directly about the pre-nup; it's a can of worms, so instead, I go tactical.

'What is it you want, Fern?' I ask with a sigh.

Clever this, for two reasons. One, by calling her Fern, instead of 'Sweets' or 'Petal' – my usual endearments – I'll make her realize I'm being very serious, taking her very seriously, etc. etc. Women love that, and, importantly, I'll make her feel ever so slightly insecure because 'Fern' is a bit cold in comparison to the other forms of address. Plus, the sigh is genius because that will make her feel sorry for me; she'll think I'm weary with trying to please her. It's amazing how much subtext there can be in a single sentence if it's delivered with the correct nuance. It's always worth remembering that you can never under-estimate the level of meaning women'll load into just one question. Always better to be a step ahead.

'I wanted the fairy tale,' she murmurs. Her answer surprises me. It's very honest.

'That's what you've got, Sweets,' I say, tightening my hold around her, drawing her closer to my body. I start to think about having sex with her because then my cock will stiffen and women love that too. They all love to think I can't restrain myself around them; that they're irresistible to me. Nothing doing, so I start to think of having sex with her and Scarlett Johansson. That does it. Fern doesn't say anything, so I'm forced to go where I wanted never to tread. 'This stuff with the lawyers doesn't mean you have any less of a fairy tale, you know.' Of course, this isn't strictly true. Let's face it, when reading Cinderella no one has ever seen the page where a bunch of overpaid, over-educated arseholes divide up Prince Charming's property, have they?

'In a way I think it does,' says Fern, insisting on remaining committed to telling me stuff as she sees it. 'But, actually, that's not what I'm thinking about.'

Really? I know curiosity killed the cat. Thing is, there are times when I can be really strong and other times I'm just dead weak. Now's one of the weak times. I don't want to, but I find myself asking, 'So what are you thinking about?'

'Oh, Jess and stuff.'

'Is she still acting all jealous and grumpy?'

'Something like that.'

Problem is, Fern is so wrapped up in her new life she has no idea what the people left behind are feeling. This mate – all her mates – no doubt feel jealous, abandoned, resentful or just plain old-fashioned shy – I've seen it all in the people I left behind. And even if I'm wrong and this mate of hers is exceptional and is genuinely blissed-out by Fern's good fortune, she still won't know how to handle herself; she won't want to appear sycophantic or on the make so she'll probably go too much the other way and be chilly. I'd have thought Fern would have a grip on this by now.

'Still ignoring your calls?'

'She seems to have a very active social life at the moment,' says Fern with a sigh. 'She still hasn't given me her measurements. I've had her dress made up in a size eight and a ten. It seems extravagant to make two, as the dresses are costing over a grand each, but –'

'Well, we can afford it so don't worry about it,' I say, turning her round and leaning her face into my chest. I kiss the top of her head; her hair smells great. 'She can try them on when she gets here.'

'Mmmm, I suppose,' mumbles Fern. She still seems distracted.

'So there's nothing else you are worrying about, right? Everything is super cool.'

Fern tilts her head up to look at me. I see something play in her eyes and almost make it to her lips. I swoop down and kiss her. Silence her. To be honest, I've done my share of sensitive guy stuff for tonight. Above and beyond the line of duty, I'd say.

We stand there for ages just holding each other. Content just to do that. After a bit Ben comes to find us.

'Darlings, I've brought refreshments! Champagne supernova for me and Fern, and non-alkie drinkies for you, Scott.'

Perfect.

59. Fern

'Come on, time to get up.'

Ben draws back the bedroom curtains, allowing a ferocious shaft of sunlight to flood into the bedroom. He swiftly tugs my duvet off too. Luckily for us both I'm wearing pyjamas. I always do now. It's not like I sleep with anyone who might appreciate the feel of my naked skin pressed up against theirs, plus living here is a bit like living in a hotel; you never quite know when someone is going to bring flowers into the room or adjust the air-con or something. Birthday suits are not an option; I'd rather save everyone's blushes.

'What is it today?' I ask as I swing my legs out of bed. I manage to make it into the bathroom without actually opening my eyes; quite a feat. I'm so tired. Who would have known that the quest for perfection could be so exhausting?

'Forty minutes in the gym, then sauna, swim, shower, blow-dry and then we need to meet Colleen and the photographer to footprint the wedding.'

'Footprint the wedding?'

'Walk through the event to decide on the best photo opportunities.'

'I thought we agreed that the photographer was going to be discreet and unobtrusive. I wanted natural reportage shots,' I yell over the sound of my electric toothbrush.

'Of course you do, darling. They are by far the loveliest. We just want to know where *exactly* those reportage shots ought to be taken so that we get everybody's best side,' says Ben, seemingly unaware of the crazy contradiction.

My mouth is full of toothpaste so I can't argue, and by the time I've done a full two minutes for both upper and lower set (as instructed by the hygienist), the conversation has moved on and I can't be bothered to pick it up again. I'm finding it's often easiest to go with the flow.

After visiting the gym, the stylist and the wedding venue, I insist that Ben and I go for lunch and I also insist that we have pizza, chips and full fat Coke. Ben appears scandalized and says he's going to tell on me. My nutritionist and Colleen will have kittens; they've decided I still need to lose more weight before the wedding; perhaps I could cut my toenails and have my hair trimmed again. I ensure Ben's silence by offering to pay for lunch *and* buy him the set of matching luggage from Louis Vuitton he's been coveting.

We make a brief stop at Rodeo and then go to eat. After just one bite I decide that I don't care I've had to spend thousands of dollars to be allowed carbs. The pizza is sublime; it seems like good value to me.

Ben squeezes my hand. 'You know, you didn't really have to buy the very stunning luggage – although thank you, thank you, thank you – I'm just delighted that we are out together. I would have let you cheat the diet without telling.'

'You say that now!' I laugh.

'It's been such a long time since we've had a good old scandalous natter.'

'And even longer since we talked about anything other than the wedding,' I add.

'It *is* becoming all-absorbing.'

'Can I tell you something?' I lean closer to whisper in Ben's ear although I seriously doubt there's any press about as we've picked a grimy, low-key pizzeria – much to Ben's disgust. But I thought a change is as good as a rest and, somehow, I was hankering after a place with plastic table-cloths and hopeless waiters. At least this way we won't be continually disturbed by someone refolding our napkins or pouring gallons of water every two seconds; that level of attention is distracting and detrimental to a good old gossip. Still, I take the precaution of whispering; I've learnt that I have to be careful about everything I say in public now.

'Tell,' urges Ben.

'I'm using the wedding to suppress my sexual desires.'

'What?' Ben looks surprised, confused and amused.

'I once read, somewhere, that in the old days – when soldiers were serving long stretches away from their wives or even a convenient lady of negotiable affection with loose lips and knicker elastic – their superiors used to put bromide in their tea to suppress sexual urges. My equiv-alent is planning the wedding.'

'You're insane,' shrieks Ben.

'Not really, not when you think about it. Weddings are all about romance, the lace and flowers and white dress sort of romance. They have nothing to do with lust and shagging and lewdness. Perhaps they are supposed to be, that's what relationship experts would have us believe, but it's not actually the case.'

Ben is laughing out loud now. 'Women, you're a funny lot. I'll never understand you. It's such a relief I have no ambitions that way.'

'If they were honest, I'm sure most brides would agree that being taken roughly, behind the rose bushes on their wedding day, is the very last thing on their mind. The dress will get creased, perhaps muddy – oh, hell on earth – maybe even torn.'

Ben chuckles some more. 'And here's me thinking that was the exact reason you asked Colleen about the thickness of the foliage in the hotel today.'

'The purpose of the rose bushes is to make a nice backdrop for the photos. The copious champagne consumed is not to make the bride feel frisky, it's to make her feel pretty and chatty and expensive. Wedding days are refined, exquisite, look-don't-touch days and every bride knows it,' I say firmly. 'I think that's why I've recently found I'm handling Scott's sexual embargo better than I expected.' I cram a really fat slice of pizza into my mouth and chew. The cheese sticks to my teeth.

Something like surprise or concern, certainly extreme interest, flickers across Ben's face. 'You mean you aren't desperate to do Scott.'

The funny thing is, no, I'm not. Or at least, I'm not as desperate as I was a month ago. I know this is back to front. I know my desire should be increasing, but no, no, I'm not. The shock on Ben's face stops me from saying quite this much. He's looking at me as though I'm a circus freak.

'Of course I am. I'm just saying that I find if I concentrate on the wedding plans, the impulse to hijack Scott at *every* given opportunity slowly subsides. He's the same. He channels his energies into *Wedding Album*. We've both had to find distractions or else we'd go insane. As it is, I eat, sleep, breathe wedding plans.'

'Yeah, well, that's understandable. You've wanted this day for such a long time – longer than you've been engaged, actually.'

'Thanks, Ben, I'm pretty sure that's the sort of thing a friend is supposed to conveniently forget,' I say as I reach for my Coke.

'Although all the hours you put into planning a wedding to Adam were wasted, weren't they? You could have used your time more wisely, perhaps tried to find a cure for the common cold. I mean, besides the fact you were never actually engaged to Adam, it's not like any of that learning can be recycled. The plans you made then just don't compare to the wedding you're actually going to have.'

True. When I imagined my wedding to Adam I took into account that there would be budget constraints. I imagined that a fair amount of time would be spent walking from one shop to the next, comparing prices and hunting for sales stuff and cheap deals. I also expected to have to cut corners by perhaps making the invites myself: I'd have arranged the flowers, my mum would have made the cake and perhaps we'd have bought the bridesmaids' dresses off eBay. Funny to think I got so much pleasure planning that simple wedding. Naturally, planning my wedding to Scott is quite unlike anything I could have imagined. For a start I don't take a step out of doors; everyone comes to me with their wares. I never look at a price tag; well, there aren't any – and it's clear that I'm being shown the sort of things that if you have to ask how much they cost you can't afford them. I can afford anything. However, I find I'd still prefer to know prices. I like to make choices based on the best value for money – it's what I'm used to.

'You're right. This wedding is nothing like the wedding I imagined.' I push the final slice of pizza into my mouth. Ben hasn't eaten half of his. He's trying to shift a few pounds for the wedding too. He's likely to be more successful, as he enjoys being a gym bunny. I nibble a chip and add, 'In fact, no matter how many lists Colleen and Saadi provide me with, I'm not sure *exactly* what this wedding *is* like. Obviously, it will be beautiful, exquisite and gorgeous, that much is clear from the mood boards, samples and books that litter the many, many rooms of Scott's house. It's just that it has become hard to keep track of all the detail.'

'Well, it is a twenty-four-hour event with one thousand guests,' points out Ben.

'Many of whom I've never met in my life, a few of whom Scott hasn't met.'

'All the more reason to impress them,' says Ben as he carefully puts his knife and fork together and pushes his plate away. He flings his paper napkin over the chips to put temptation out of sight.

'For example, I'm not sure what we decided to have for a starter. In the end, did we settle on the ballotine of foie gras marinated in white port, served on toasted brioche, or did we choose the ravioli of blue lobster and salmon, with a basil dressing?'

'We chose the ballotine of foie gras.'

'Really? And what is ballotine anyway?'

Ben laughs. 'Oh, don't worry. Put these details out of your head. That's why you've employed Colleen. Anything you aren't sure about will just be a lovely surprise on the day. It's almost like being a guest. A guest and the centre of attention at once. What could be finer?'

What indeed?

Ben passes on dessert but I order banoffee pie. Just as I'm spooning the first delicious bite into my mouth, Ben asks, 'Have you heard from Adam?' Suddenly Coke and banoffee pie no longer seem enough; I could really do with a glass of wine.

'No, why would I hear from him? We've said all we have to say to one another.'

This isn't actually as true as I'd like it to be. I can't count the number of times I find myself going over an imaginary conversation I want to have with Adam. Mostly these consist of me saying, 'And another thing . . .' How dare he warn me about Scott's behaviour? How dare he imply that I'm rushing into this marriage? Oddly, these imaginary conversations bother me less than the other types of conversation that run through my head; the ones full of sweet memories rather than angry reprisals are much more distressing.

Plus there's something I daren't confess even to Ben.

I've been having a lot of sexy dreams recently. No doubt it's my subconscious dealing with the lack of any conscious sex with Scott, and the other night I had the most sexy dream *ever*. This dream was full of deep back-of-throat groans as his hand worked his way over my body, his kisses trailing along behind. Starting at my neck, over my breasts, slipping down, down, sliding from my waist, to my stomach, to my thigh. The kisses scampered over my body and then his head was between my legs. He looked up, asking for acceptance, receiving my gratitude. His face was in the shadow. His arms were scooped under my legs; my knees were bent. His breath was hot on my skin. He started to kiss me there; he licked and lapped and I bucked my delight as I spilt for him. Grabbing his hair I pulled his face towards mine. I wanted to taste me on his lips, his lips on me. Adam.

The eyes were chocolate brown, not sparkling green. Adam!

The shock woke me from the dream instantly. Remembering it now causes me to blush again. It's wrong. Wrong. I shouldn't be dreaming of Adam! My heart was beating so fast with shame and panic it took me a good hour to fall asleep again. Of course this dream doesn't *mean* anything. It's just because Scott and I haven't actually had sex that somehow my memories got muddled up in my fantasies. But still.

'Is he coming to the wedding?' asks Ben.

'I'm not sure. As you know, Jess has invited him. I don't know whether he'll come. I don't even know if she will.'

'Why do you say that?'

'She's never threatened a no-show but clearly things between us are strained, which is horribly sad. Initially I thought she was a little bit jealous, but since my phone call with her, when she asked if she could bring Adam, I've been inclined to think the awkwardness between us is something altogether more complicated.'

This is the first time I've hinted to Ben that Jess and Adam may possibly be getting together. I'm not sure why I've found it difficult to broach the subject; maybe because we are always with other people or maybe because I don't want to hear Ben say Adam and Jess were always destined for one another, that they make a perfect couple, and it's none of my business who Adam dates now.

'They'll come,' Ben says confidently, giving me a big reassuring smile.

The thing is I'm not sure if their attendance is something to smile about or not.

60. Fern

It takes a great deal of courage but I drag it from the depths of my toes and call Jess to ask her whether she is bringing Adam to the wedding. I try to kid myself that I need to confirm numbers, but this is a lie. So far, we have seven hundred and thirty-eight confirmed 'yeses' and one hundred and nine 'regrets', which leaves over one hundred and fifty people who have yet to reply. I can't pretend that Adam's attendance or absence will have a profound effect on the catering. No, not the catering. But I do need to know.

I call the flat. There's no reply so I leave a short message.

'Hi, it's me. Erm, Fern. Just wondered how you guys are and if, erm, you've made a decision about, erm, LA and things. Who's coming? I mean, have you decided, Jess, who you are bringing?' I pause and then as an after-thought I add, 'As your non-date.'

Bugger. I hang up. That wasn't too clever a message. I wish I could delete it. I wanted to avoid sounding as though I was pairing them up but, at the same time, I was trying to sound cool in case they're already paired. I think I failed on both counts. I hope to God Jess listens to that message before Adam does and that she deletes it. Surely fourteen years' friendship has earned me that small mercy.

My phone rings back almost immediately. It's the flat. Hurrah, Jess has listened to the message and is calling me straight back. Hopefully to confirm she is not bringing Adam.

'Hello, Adam here.'

Those three words wound me on so many levels. One, he's obviously heard the stupid message I left (how humiliating). Two, he thinks he has to introduce himself when he's talking to me because he sees a certain distance and formality between us is required (however predictable this is, it's sad). And three – three I don't understand at all – I feel a weird physical blow low in my gut; his voice turns my belly to liquid. Damn, why did I leave such a pathetic message?

'Hi Adam,' I say as calmly as I can.

'I picked up your message.'

'It was intended for Jess, really.'

'I know, but I figured you'd be doing numbers for the wedding and things and that you might need a quick response,' says Adam.

This is unusually thoughtful of him. I had no idea he had any concept that RSVPs had a purpose at all. I'm so surprised by his consideration, I almost forget to lie. Almost.

'Yes, that's it. I need to confirm the numbers to the caterers.' I cross my fingers on my left hand.

'Jess said you're OK with me coming to the wedding.' There's some hesitancy in his voice.

'Of course, delighted.' I nearly drop the phone as I cross my fingers on the other hand too.

'Really, you don't think it's weird or anything?'

'No, no, not at all. We're all grown-ups.' I kick off my flip-flops and try to cross my toes too. Yes, yes, it's completely weird. He can't be serious! He's not really thinking of coming, is he? Surely he'd find it uncomfortable? Who wants to see their ex get spliced? Who wants to get married in front of an ex? It's so civilized. It's so passionless. It's wrong. If he comes it shows he does well and truly have closure. If he comes it shows he really wants to please Jess.

'OK, well, I'm a yes then. Count me in.'

Bugger. Bugger. Bugger.

'Great, great, great. Any special diet requirements?' I blather, in a pathetic attempt to hide my embarrassment and annoyance.

'Er, no, Fern, we went out for four years and lived together for three of those, I think you'd have noticed if I was a vegetarian or lactose intolerant.'

'Well, yes, but things change,' I twitter mindlessly.

'Don't they,' he says.

There's a long pause. I should probably hang up.

'Well, I'll see you in two weeks then,' I mutter.

'Yeah, looking forward to it. Jess showed me those photos you e-mailed over. His gaff is like a set from a James Bond movie.' That should be a compliment but somehow I know it isn't.

I decide the way forward with Adam is to be determinedly upbeat. It can't be so hard after all. Not under the circumstances – I'm marrying Scott Taylor in a fortnight. 'Well, doesn't every man secretly harbour a desire to be James Bond?' I ask pleasantly.

'Not me. You know, I've always been happy with simply

watching the movies. I've always known he's a fictional character. Must be fun though, having all that.' He pauses, to be sure he's got my attention, and then adds, 'All that *stuff*. It makes a man pretty damned attractive. Pretty damned *likeable*.'

This is not the first time I've been forced into defending my relationship with Scott, and I doubt it will be the last; but it's not a position I wanted to be in with Adam. I really don't want to be drawn into these dangerous waters. Doesn't he realize that the decent thing for an ex to do is stick to polite small talk about the weather? What makes him think he can be this direct?

Four years' intimacy?

Polite small talk is not an option. 'I'm not in it for the stuff. There's much more to Scott than his stuff,' I argue.

'Like?'

'He's luminously, intensely creative but exposed. He's stunningly desirable and modish yet quite charmingly open,' I say.

'Have you been practising that?' asks Adam.

Well, yes, I have. I've started to write my wedding speech and I'd thought that was a pretty good opener but I'm not going to admit as much to Adam. I hoped my declaration would sound spontaneous.

Adam sighs, 'You sound like a fan, not a wife. But maybe that's no bad thing. I mean, you need to be a big fan to stomach hearing him go on about himself all the time, in that way he does.'

I don't bother pretending that Scott doesn't talk about himself; the truth is, he is rather self-focused but that's natural under the circumstances and not in the least bit annoying, as Adam is hinting.

'It's not like he goes on about himself all the time out of vanity. It's just he's never met anyone more interesting than he is,' I say. I'm disappointed that my tone is more defensive than upbeat.

'The man met Nelson Mandela!' points out Adam, snappily. 'I can imagine that conversation, can't you? Er, Nel, mate, did I tell you about the time when I shagged a couple of Scandi twins?' Adam does an impressive impression of Scott's northern accent; in other circumstances I'd be tempted to laugh. 'I've just read this interview in *Dazed and Confused*; all he talked about was sex – all he joked about was sex,' says Adam.

'Well, sex is funny if you think about it for long enough,' I defend. And I should know, as sex has been all theory to me for weeks now. Obviously, I'd rather strap raw steak to my body and stroll into the lions' den at London Zoo than admit as much to Adam. Instead I concentrate on shielding Scott. 'That interview took place before we got engaged.'

'Oh yeah, *ages* ago,' says Adam mockingly.

I'm sorely tempted to point out that not everybody needs four years to decide precisely nothing at all. There is such a thing as love at first sight and whirlwind romance but I sense that Adam would only scoff more, so instead I try to explain why the *Dazed and Confused* interview was so graphic. Truthfully, when I read it, I had been a little surprised that Scott mentioned the nun he deflowered and defrocked.

'It's not like he goes on about sex all the time out of

choice either. People who interview him never ask him anything else. He's got into the habit of talking about the stuff the rest of us keep private.'

'Whatever you say. You're the one who knows him.'

'I am,' I say hotly.

'You're the one who's marrying him.'

'That's right.' I *need* to draw this conversation to a halt. I hate it that Adam can rile me. I wish I was in a place where I was impervious to his digs. I should be. Why does he care so much anyhow? He has Jess now. And I have Scott. We're not an 'us' any more. It's none of his business.

'Look, I've got to go. I'll see you here.'

'You will. Jess and I will be there supporting you every step of the way.' His sarcasm is loud and clear, which is irritating, and more irritating still, he manages to hang up first, leaving me with nothing but the buzz of a dead line.

61. Fern

Suddenly, with the wedding now just ten days away I find myself with a free afternoon. Following a call from Colleen, who confirms her final decision with regard to which toiletries we ought to have in the portaloos (Huiles & Baumes, 'being organic and eco aware is *so* important'), I decide to hop in the car and surprise Scott at the studio.

I visited the studio once when I first arrived in LA so I recognize the producer, the engineer and the assistant, plus there's a delightful, unexpected bonus – Ben.

'What are you doing here?' I ask, giving him a big smacker of a kiss on his cheek.

'I come here when I'm not playing with you.'

Really, since when? He's never mentioned it. I feel a little guilty that I've been so caught up in wedding preparations that I haven't made more time to come down to the studio to listen to Scott's new work.

Scott is thrilled to see me now. He rips off his bulky earphones and rushes out from behind the glass wall to meet me. 'Sweets, perfect timing. We are just wrapping this up. You can tell me what you think of it. Ben loves it, don't you Ben?'

'Wait until you hear this album. The man is a genius,' says Ben excitedly. 'There are *at least* half a dozen number ones. This album is going to grab America by the throat!

It's got everything they'd want and even some stuff they don't *know* they want yet.'

Scott signals to the producer and suddenly the room is bursting with his growly, irresistible voice.

Ben's right; this is an amazing album. In the past all Scott's lyrics have read like a tabloid story; raw, open, apologetic and angry. To understand his songs is to know what it feels like to have nothing and feel everything. The lyrics in *Wedding Album* hold on to his trademark honesty but they are much more idealistic and celebratory. The album perfectly encapsulates just how dazzlingly astonishing it is to fall in love.

I listen carefully and know with an absolute certainty that these songs will be the songs a generation falls in love to: men and women will choose them for their first husband and wife dance; these tracks are the sort of tracks that will play in the background as teenagers lose their virginity and disappointed women throw their drinks over betraying lovers. They are seminal, decisive and romantic.

The songs are buffed to perfection. On each and every track, before the chorus even runs for a second time, everyone in the room is humming along; that sort of reaction guarantees this is going to be an album that enjoys buckets full of air time.

'Oh my God, did that lyric just say, *Fern, you make me burn*?' I ask excitedly.

Scott grins at me. I dash to him and plant an enormous kiss on his mouth. If we were alone I might have tried to persuade him to forget the chastity vow.

'I can't believe you wrote a song about me!'

'Three,' he says with obvious pride. 'You're named in three.'

I listen to the rest of the album even more carefully. Sure enough my name pops up in two more songs; one about making his head turn and another all about how he yearns. Out of context these lines sound pretty corny, but believe me, when he sings them accompanied by the irresistible beat as part of a love ballad, they work. I'm overwhelmed. I beam at Scott, thrilled to be the inspiration behind this immense work. The album is the utterly perfect tribute to our love affair.

'The Americans are going to adore this!' says Ben again. He actually can't resist jumping up and down on the spot.

'Not just the Americans, everyone will love this,' I enthuse.

'Yes, but it's the Americans who are important,' says Scott seriously.

'*Wedding Album* is a flawless record compiled by a man shot through with flaws,' says Mark with a grin.

'He's not so bad,' I reply indignantly. I haven't quite forgiven Mark for the pre-nup and can't look at him without thinking about it. I don't like thinking about it, so the easiest thing is not to have too much to do with Mark.

'Fern, darlin', he's pure gold and you know it and I know it and soon the American public are going to know it too. Now he's in luuurve he'll be irresistible.' Mark grins and lights a big cigar. I turn away from him and drape my arms around Scott.

'It's brilliant,' I gush. 'This album is the embodiment

of everything everyone ever believes love can be. Everything you ever believed life could be!'

Scott pulls me close to him. We stand foreheads touching, my arms around his waist, his arms hung around my neck. I can feel his breath mingling with mine. He kisses my nose and beams back at me.

'You're great,' he says simply as we reluctantly break apart.

'When's it going to be released?' I ask.

'Tomorrow. Which gives us eight days for it to climb the charts before the wedding.'

'Tomorrow?' How's that possible? I don't know much about the music business (far less than I should) but I thought that it took months to bring out an album. It's clear that we've been listening to the edited version and that the sound has been mastered by an engineer – but what about the packaging, won't that take weeks to develop? I must have missed the bit where Scott gets to have his photo taken in loads of different outfits, hanging out with lots of different kinds of people – like leggy blondes, or footballers, or scuba divers or something eye-catching.

'When's the press conference announcing the release?' I ask.

'Yesterday,' says Scott with a beam.

'Yesterday! And the promotional tour?'

'Just after the wedding. Things haven't been standing still while you've been planning this wedding, you know,' chips in Mark.

Clearly. Something occurs to me like a brick flying out of the horizon. 'When you say just after the wedding you mean after the honeymoon, right?'

'Not exactly. We thought we'd make the tour into your honeymoon. We'll be travelling all across America; New York, Chicago, Boston, Las Vegas,' says Mark, with a self-satisfied grin.

'You said you always wanted to go to New York,' adds Scott.

'And you said you hated being on the road,' I point out. He'd said that being on the road was soulless, that the cities, hotels and crowds always blurred and merged into one, and the long highways – that led to out-of-town fast food joints – inevitably drove him to drink. 'The last two times you fell off the wagon was when you were on tour,' I add. It seems like a big risk to me. Is he ready for it? 'Shouldn't we have discussed this?'

Scott smiles at me, kisses my nose again and then wanders back behind the glass and picks up his headset without answering my question. He doesn't need to. In my heart of hearts I know the answer. Yes, we should have discussed this, the way we should have discussed the pre-nup and the three celebrity bridesmaids I've never met and the sleeping arrangements in the country hotel. Suddenly, my head is full of things Scott and I don't discuss. We talk about feelings but not facts. Facts are Mark's bag. I don't have any other choice than to turn to Mark if I want answers.

'I'd like to have been consulted,' I say shortly.

'He's going to be crowned King of America, Fern,' says Mark.

'America doesn't have a king,' I say, somewhat tetchily.

'They've been waiting for him.' Mark laughs and his

cigar smoke billows in my face. 'You've heard the album. We have to get on the road asap. That's how albums sell.'

'At the cost of his health?' I ask, by which I mean sobriety.

'This album needs to sell at any cost,' says Mark steadily. 'Scott knows that. Scott wants that.' Then he asks, 'Is this about you not getting a honeymoon? I'll see he makes it up to you.' I hate Mark implying I'm being a sulky spoilsport when in fact I'm seriously worried about my fiancé's health and with good reason.

Ben is standing shoulder to shoulder next to Mark; he beams at me, reassuringly, and says, 'I'll come on tour too. It'll be fun.'

I wish Ben had warned me to expect this. I could have given the matter more thought. I feel exactly as I did when presented with the pre-nup; everyone says it's all OK, but it doesn't feel OK. Deep down, somewhere in my gut, something feels off. It's the oddest sensation. I remember having it as a little girl when I was playing hide and seek with my older siblings and their friends. I didn't really understand the mechanics of the game. I'd cover my eyes and think because I couldn't see them they couldn't see me – that I was well hidden and safe. But they could see me as clear as day. I was the one standing alone and exposed, blind because I was covering my own eyes. Everyone around me kept playing and winning the game. It's a creepy comparison; one I don't enjoy making. I push the thought away.

I sigh, confused, beginning to doubt myself. Am I being a spoilsport? Scott's happy with the decision, Mark says it makes business sense and even Ben's in favour. Maybe the tour is a good idea. Maybe I'm over-reacting. What do I know? Perhaps going on tour will be fun. Besides, it's pretty clear it's a done deal. I have no idea how they arranged everything in just a few weeks but I bet it was expensive and I know it would be even more expensive to undo.

'Come on Fern, cheer up,' says Ben. 'Don't be grouchy. You, more than anyone, know Scott's full of surprises.'

Yes, I do. I do know that much.

62. Fern

The wedding guests start to arrive. Unable to suppress their excitement, they burst through the double doors at the airport arrivals; behaving much like popping corn in the microwave, they bounce in every direction. At first I go to greet friends and rellies at the airport, but it soon becomes apparent that picking up in person is impractical when my great-aunt Liz is knocked over by an over-zealous photographer. He was clamouring to take a photo of me with greasy hair. I complained to Mark about the scrum of photographers; he said I shouldn't leave the house without full makeup ever again. The majority of my guests are staying at one of the flash hotels on Sunset. They all 'oh' and 'ah' at the glamour and fantasy of the enormous rooms with glowing glass walls and white furnishings. Saadi has booked the penthouse for my mum and dad.

Everyone is excited to meet Scott and to see our home. I was concerned about how he'd respond to me trailing ten parties of eight through the house but he rose to the occasion beautifully by suggesting we throw one big pre-wedding party, around the pool, so that both families can get to know each other in a relaxed way. I worried that arranging another party just days before the wedding would be an impossible task but Mark assured me every-thing could be attended to without giving me extra stress.

He suggested we throw the party on the eve of the wedding, which is the day the chart positions are released so that we can celebrate *Wedding Album*'s position. He's clearly confident and so he should be; the album is awesome. I know all my cousins will still queue for Scott's autograph, but I agree that on balance one big get-together will be less painful than multiple introductions.

The party is scheduled to start at about lunchtime. We're serving Scott's speciality, barbecued prawns marinated in lime and coriander, the meal he cooked for me the first night we arrived here – which is a really romantic touch. Although Scott isn't going to do the barbecueing himself – obviously, we have two hundred to feed – so we've hired caterers instead. The expectation is that we'll celebrate through the afternoon and into the evening. I have three outfits for the day. I plan (by which I mean Colleen has planned for me) to start by wearing a purple velvet beaded mini dress with taffeta sleeves; it's Gucci. She said it will make a stunning but hip first impression, plus Scott loves purple. As it happens, I'm still in a dressing-gown with a towel wrapped around my head when my mum and dad arrive at 8.30 a.m. Not the dramatic first impression I wanted to present.

One of the pretty girl organizers shows my parents into my room and while my dad immediately wraps me into a brief, self-conscious hug, my mum is too busy falling over herself to be nice to the pretty girl and seems momentarily to forget I'm here at all. She actually bobs a small curtsey as the girl leaves.

'You should have tipped her, Ray,' my mum scolds my dad.

'No, really, there's no need,' I say, wrapping her in a big hug. I can see she's tense and agitated; she's made the effort though, she's had her hair coloured and she's had a blow-dry.

'It's tips left, right and centre, over here. I'm bleeding cash,' mumbles my dad.

'I'm sure we should have tipped her,' argues my mum.

'She works for me, Mum, you're in my home. Dad, put your money away, there's no need for a tip.'

'I've gone blonde.' Mum fingers the edges of her hair shyly. I think she's telling me she's blonde because there is a level of uncertainty, the shade is open to interpretation; I'd say it has the same hue as rice pudding – the sort with sultanas and nutmeg in.

'Our Fern will have someone who can do something with it,' says Dad. 'Fix the colour.' He's said what I'm thinking but the anxiety that floods into Mum's face stops me backing him up.

'You look fantastic,' I smile.

She repays my solidarity by commenting, 'You're too skinny.'

'Do you like your hotel?' I ask.

'Your father struggled to get into the bathroom for thirty minutes. There's no handle on the door. You just give it a gentle push and then it sort of springs back at you.' Mum looks smug, as she was clearly the one who conquered that particular Everest.

'Too bloody clever for its own good,' mutters my dad. I remember feeling just as helpless when I struggled to turn on the taps that first night I arrived here. 'And your mother isn't keen on the enormous tangerine-coloured mirrors; she says they make her look overcooked.'

'It's very spacious though, dear, very elegant,' adds my mum. 'And those lovely long terraces! Oh, the views, city wide! Stunning. Shame about your dad's vertigo, though.'

Clearly they are bewildered and uncomfortable. I bet my mum hasn't dared use the soap or disturb the towels; she probably brought her own with her. Saadi should have put them in a more traditional hotel. What was she thinking?

'You could stay here,' I offer, not for the first time.

'We don't want to be in the way,' says Mum, gazing around my vast bedroom, which is the size of their house.

'You wouldn't be.'

She shakes her head and I know her decision is final. She's a proud woman and I understand her reasoning. If it's going to take them thirty minutes to open a minimalist door, they'd rather do that in privacy.

'Listen, how about I get dressed and show you around?' I offer.

Mum and Dad are overwhelmed by Scott's place. They are, in fact, flabbergasted, a word my dad uses to describe his reaction to the snooker table, the gym, the extensive gardens and the Jacuzzis (we have one indoor and one outdoor). My mother repeatedly asks, 'What will they think of next? A cinema in your house?' When I show her the cinema in our house, she resorts to Dad's response of choice; she too is flabbergasted.

I've lived in Beverly Hills, Hollywood, in Scott's home, for six weeks now and I have already become entirely accepting of luxury. The funny thing about luxury is that it turns out to be more or less the same everywhere and it's possible to stop noticing it's there at all, thus defeating the very point of luxury, surely. In just six weeks I've started to expect nothing less than perfection. I'm no longer amazed by translucent fabric walls that screen glamorous and outlandish goings-on. I barely register frosted glass furniture that changes colour with the beat of the music (a challenging indigo at the beginning of the evening when lounge music drifts through conversations, then – shifting through the rainbow – a cool blue as the beat intensifies, then an invigorating green as people start to party and then finally a sinful red as the bodies and thoughts flail around the dance floor). I expect every object I encounter – whether it's a shopping bag or a hotel lobby – to be tasteful, modish, kitsch, discreet, flamboyant or stunning; I expect everything to be, in some way, notable. Nothing is ordinary any more, so in an odd way, once again everything is. Just a different kind of ordinary.

My family are not similarly acclimatized. I realize that Fiona has arrived as I repeatedly hear her yell at her children, 'Don't touch that, you'll break it!' or 'Be careful of that, it will be worth a fortune.' I pour her a large G&T as quickly as I can. My younger cousins, nieces and nephews quickly strip off and dive into the pool. Most of them have had the sense to bring swimwear but a few haven't and dive in wearing just their underwear. My mum is outraged and keeps apologizing to Scott. Scott just smiles and assures her he's seen much worse in his pool. Thankfully, he doesn't feel the need to elaborate.

Scott's family are indistinguishable from mine. That shouldn't surprise me, he's told me all about his ordinary beginnings, but somehow I was expecting them to be in some way more extraordinary; after all, his mum gave birth to *him*. His mum is fussing with my mum about kids running around with bare feet and his brother is talking websites and journey lengths with my big brother. If it wasn't for the pool, the staff and endless buckets of chilled bottles of champagne I could think we were all in Mum and Dad's back garden having a barbecue. I ought to add that just because his mum is normal doesn't mean meeting her has been any less terrifying. Quite the reverse. As a normal mum she's exercised her right to treat me with polite distance and a certain amount of suspicion; after all, I am about to marry her amazing son, after the most brief of whirlwind romances – of course she's suspicious. No matter, I'm sure we'll become far more comfortable with one another. I'll have to get Ben to let slip that I signed a pre-nup; that ought to allay some of her fears. I want her to know that the gold I'm digging for is commitment and a happily ever after; a grown-up life with a husband and kids. All the things Adam wouldn't give me.

Adam? Why is he in my head? Even as an unfavourable comparison he's unwelcome. I blame Jess for insisting on bringing him to the wedding as her guest; it's pretty difficult to ignore his existence under those circumstances. I've been dreading seeing him ever since Jess asked if she could bring him here. The very thought of us meeting up fills me with cold terror, I've hardly been able to swallow a bite all day and yet I find myself constantly searching for even the briefest of glances of him. So far there's been no sign.

I drift through the gentle din of polite laughter and clinking glasses and breathe in the heady perfume of fat, waxy lilies and creamy roses. I'd wanted to arrange the flowers for the party myself, especially since it was agreed that I couldn't manage the ones for the actual wedding (I'll be too busy), but in the end Saadi's third assistant hired someone else to do them. It was decided that I shouldn't run the risk of scratching my hands on rose thorns before the ceremony. The magazine that's got the exclusive to cover the wedding specifically asked for shots of our rings (hands clasped). Colleen said that they wouldn't like it if my hands were grazed. I can hardly complain – the florist has done a fantastic job, as good as anything I could have done. It's silly of me to want to be so controlling; I should let go more.

The entire party looks amazing. There are über-fit waiters, dressed in surfer shorts, carrying trays of mojitos and Alabama slammers. There are dozens of all-weather pink and purple light bulbs strung in every tree; it's still too early and warm for them to be anything more than pretty and eye-catching, but they are most definitely that. There are ice sculptures and chocolate fountains dotted between the loungers and enormous scatter cushions. Someone has removed the cream loungers and replaced them with cerise ones. There are giant scarlet inflatable ducks floating in the pool. The place screams excitement and fun.

It's a joy to turn and see familiar faces everywhere. My friends and family beam at me as I float between them to ask if they have everything they need. As it's my party it's frustrating that I don't manage to actually talk *talk* to anyone. We settle for pithy and pertinent exchanges; a variation on the theme.

'Bloody hell, Fern, you are such a lucky cow' (said with a beam – a few of which are unconditional – most are tinged with envy or disbelief).

I smile back (careful not to gloat or boast). 'Aren't I? Now can I get you a drink? Something to eat?'

Most of my friends are happy to get blathered on cocktails and munch the tasty treats provided; a couple of the cheekier types test the reach of my dream world by asking for Cristal champagne or caviar and oysters, although I seriously doubt they have a real fondness for either. Whatever is requested can be found and in the end my guests tire of trying to catch me out. They grudgingly accept my life is perfection and simply try to scoop up a bit of it instead.

While the party was originally intended to be an intimate get-together for family and close friends, inevitably it has grown. I spot a number of people I've come to recognize as 'the cool people', who somehow always appear out of nowhere when there's a gathering of any significance. Mark has invited *all* the cool people to our wedding. He insists their beauty lends an authenticity to a Hollywood party; without them it would just be a regular party – full of loved ones and mates having fun, which (he explained seriously) isn't enough for a Hollywood party. Mostly the cool people in LA are actors in their twenties and sometimes thirties (although none of the women are in their thirties, no matter what their birth certificates say). I recognize everyone and am momentarily lulled into the belief that the party really *is* full of friends but then I realize I recognize them from the silver screen and, despite the fact that they are coming to my wedding and are currently eating and drinking in my home, they couldn't pick me out in a police line-up. Still, it's exciting having all these amazingly beautiful and talented people splashing in my pool. No one could think anything else. I don't know why I have to keep reminding myself that this is the case.

Besides the actors, musicians and models are liberally scattered too. While the actors exude good health (muscled bodies, light tans, white teeth), the musicians and models are wan and pale. Generally nocturnal species, they look startled and ever so slightly nauseous in daylight. I also spot famous photographers, famous movie producers, famous record producers, famous chefs and famous dogs. I recognize nearly everyone from the briefing notes Saadi has thoughtfully supplied for the wedding. She's provided a photo and three pertinent facts about every one of our influential guests. I'm supposed to have memorized the notes by tomorrow but to be frank I'm struggling. I find one multi-million-dollar deal merges into the next and it's hard to stay focused on the specifics. I'll wing it tomorrow; I'm assuming that on my wedding day most people will want to talk about my dress and shoes and I won't be grilled too closely about how Guest A made his enormous fortune or what film Guest B most recently directed.

It's odd, but in this rich blend of guests I've yet to spy

Lisa or Jess. It's not until around 2 p.m. that I finally spot Lisa, Charlie and the kids arriving. Touchingly, Lisa has brought a cake and Charlie is carrying what will no doubt be a very nice bottle of wine. I fling myself into her arms, almost causing her to let the cake go splat.

'Hey you,' she beams as she wraps me in a gawky, problematic one-arm hug. 'We brought gifts.'

'But what do you bring the girl who has everything?' says Charlie as he takes a sweeping glance at the party scene stretched out in front of him. He whistles appreciatively.

'Yourselves,' I beam. 'I'm so happy to see you. And cake is good too. I haven't been allowed to touch anything the least bit sinful for weeks.' I dip my finger into the gooey icing and cram it into my mouth.

'So I hear,' grins Charlie. Lisa nudges him but he can't help himself, he starts to giggle; I guess that she's told him about the chastity vow between me and Scott. It's to be expected, they tell each other everything. He manages to compose himself enough to add, 'Congratulations, Fern. This is amazing.'

The kids dash off towards the bouncy castle. I slip between Lisa and Charlie and link my arm through theirs; we follow the children at a more leisurely pace.

'It's so wonderful to have you both here,' I gush. I stare at their oh-so-familiar faces and their radiant, delighted expressions douse me. It's not until I'm with my friends that I realize just how much I've missed them.

Lisa, Charlie and I find seats and food and position ourselves close to the bouncy castle so that we can keep an eye on the kids.

As soon as we are all comfortable and sipping ice-cold cocktails I ask, 'Have you seen Jess?'

'Yes, she and Adam have the room next to ours,' says Lisa carefully. She watches me closely as she delivers this news. I'm grateful for my oversized shades and I continue to stare resolutely at the kids flinging themselves off the inflated walls. It's vital I don't react. Any reaction is open to misinterpretation; I learnt that on the media training Saadi so thoughtfully organized. They're sharing a room. Right. Fine. Right. Of course they are. That's normal for boyfriend and girlfriend.

'I can't wait to meet the man himself,' says Charlie. For a smidge of a second I think Charlie is talking about Adam; that doesn't make sense at all – they've met hundreds of times. Then I understand he means Scott. Of course. Charlie is trying and failing to hide his excitement at this treat that is within his grasp. I'm not surprised that even the usually calm and collected Charlie is a little giddy; I've seen people shake and weep as they've clasped Scott's hand. He's a sensation.

'I'll go and hunt him down and bring him over,' I say. Frankly, I'm glad of the excuse to break free of Lisa's penetrating stare. I'll find Scott and he'll join the party, entertain my friends and by doing so reassure and comfort me. The reasons for needing to be reassured and comforted are a bit blurry right now. I think it's something to do with the knowledge that imminently, I'll be coming face to face with my ex-boyfriend and his new girlfriend, a.k.a. my ex-best friend.

I can't find Scott. He's not in the pool; there's a noisy, splashy game of handball happening there. He's not overseeing the barbecue; the sizzling and swirling smoke is managing to happen quite independently of his skills. Nor is he on the dance floor; although there are lots of lithe, writhing bodies – his isn't one of them. I imagine he'll be in his den, playing on the football table with the bass guy. He loves it in there and prefers it to sunning himself on the outside deck. Yet, while I'm usually happy to indulge him, I do think that today he should be outside with our guests. I suspect he's gone into hiding until the chart position is announced. He's bound to be nervous, although everyone I've spoken to seems to assume it's a foregone conclusion the album will have sold by the bucket and will be rocketing up the charts.

As I enter the house the cool marble floors and pale walls soothe me. I shouldn't care that Adam and Jess are sharing a room. It shouldn't matter to me. But it does. I try to be rational about the situation. *I* am the one getting married *tomorrow*. I'm sharing a life with Scott, although notably not a room – not a bed. I can hear the party buzz somewhere distant. It sounds like an annoying fly that I want to swipe away. What's wrong with me? The party is the most luxurious, spoiling event of my life so far, how can I possibly be comparing it with a hideous, filthy, buzzing insect? I'm not thinking straight. I shake my head in an effort to clear it. I thought I was being steady with the cocktails but I must have drunk too much already. I have to find Scott.

63. Scott

I've taken refuge in my den. There were a few blokes hanging around playing the table football, but I sent them packing. I need to be alone. I sit in a gloomy fog of fag smoke. I'm in the habit of keeping blinds and drapes drawn, because in the UK the paparazzi used to pap me through the smallest curtain chinks; they have endless photos of me scratching my belly while wandering around in my boxers. Fern strides in, looking vexed. She says she sympathizes with the issue of privacy intrusion I have to endure but she makes straight for the curtains, flings them and the patio doors open, and mutters about letting fresh breeze waft in. She stands in the doorway, desperately gulping air.

'You should stop smoking,' she says.

My smoking gets on her tits. I smoke a lot and all my mates smoke like chimneys too, so the smell of fags permanently lies in the folds of the curtains and the squish of a cushion, in the air, on our skins and in our eyes; it doesn't bother me but Fern seems to need more air. Often, I sit in the den and she sits outside on the loungers. But cigarette smoke behaves like cats. Cats always search out the person they can freak out the most, the person with an allergy or a phobia, and then they rub against that person's leg, curl up on that person's lap. My fag smoke slinks after Fern and I watch as she tries to waft it away. It sits in the still, warm air surrounding her;

it lingers and clambers up her nose, no doubt, scratching her throat. I offer her a glass of champagne – that normally freshens her up – but she shakes her head; it's not going to do the trick today.

'I can't stop smoking, it will change my voice,' I reason.

'You'll die a horrible death,' she points out, frightening no one other than herself.

'Yeah, well, some people live a horrible life,' I say, as I throw her a devil-may-care grin.

'Are you OK?' she asks.

I could've asked her the same, except I didn't because I'm not OK. Definitely not. I'm possibly more stressed and agitated than I've ever been before in her company.

'Nervous,' I confess. I stub out my smoke and bite my already ravaged, stubby fingernails.

She throws herself down by my side and flings her arms around me.

'Are you nervous about the wedding?' she asks gently. 'There's no need. Honestly I have – well, Colleen has – everything under control. It's going to be amazing. We'll have –'

'No, it's not the wedding.' I stare at her, bewildered. I feel a bit like I imagine astronauts must feel when they step out of their shuttle; slightly wary and displaced but a little manic and excited too. The wedding? What the fu – 'I'm nervous about the chart position,' I explain.

'The chart position?'

'I'm thinking, is it unreasonable to be hoping for a top ten position? Or maybe at least a number thirteen or twelve? Have we rushed things? Do you think I'll crack America this time? Do you think this is my big chance?

Or my last chance? Will the Americans love the album?' I fire the questions at her with a rapidity she's unable to field.

'I'm sure they will,' she says encouragingly, the moment I let her get a word in. Her response seems woefully passive. 'But whatever happens in the charts this afternoon, it doesn't matter. The thing to remember is that we are getting married tomorrow. It's the biggest day of our lives. And then, after the wedding, you have the tour, you'll keep selling through. We have so much to look forward to.'

I know she hasn't got all the answers but she's giving me the impression she doesn't even understand the questions.

'Yeah, yeah,' I say. I pat her hand.

I wish I could believe that. It must be nice to be like Fern. She believes in all the good stuff. That must be great. I'm a pessimist and even so I find that being proven right isn't as much fun as it should be. She moves to kiss me but I can't be doing with that at the moment. Anything sexual with Fern is the last thing on my mind right now. I move first and give her an affectionate peck on the nose. I'm sure that instead of the sexless little kiss on the snout she'd prefer it if I was taking down her knickers with my teeth. But before she has a chance to voice her thoughts, Mark and a cast of thousands burst into the room.

'Son, son, here you are! Hiding, I might have known.' My body turns to slop. I'm unsure if my legs are holding me up. Maybe I'm a puddle on the floor. Someone might step on me. Come on Mark, spill. Shut the fuck up, Mark, I don't want bad news. Both thoughts explode into my being simultaneously. I hardly dare breathe. 'Well, step into the limelight, lad, I have the chart position.' Mark is waving a piece of paper above his head as though he's Moses just returning from Mount Sinai.

I must stand up from the couch in a hurry because I'm vaguely aware that my haste topples Fern. She slides away from me and clumsily lands on the floor. I mean to hold a hand out to help her up but I can't tear my eyes away from Mark. All eyes are on him, actually.

'Fuck,' I say, because I don't want to hear it, yet I'm aching to hear it. I pull my hands through my hair with such force I might yank out a chunk.

'Hey, calm down. Can you imagine the wedding photos if you've pulled out lumps of hair?' says Fern. She doesn't understand. Poor thing. Lucky thing. This is it. This is what it's all about. This is what it's all for. I'm twitching and jittering. I can't stay still; I look like I'm auditioning for a part in *River Dance*.

'Fuck mate, don't mess. Just tell me. Top fifteen? That would be good on the first week's sales, hey? That would be respectable? I mean we haven't had that much air time yet. The Americans are always cautious.'

I'm justifying my failure before I even know the results. I look at Fern; she pours back an expression of pure sympathy but she can't wrap me in cotton wool, no one can. I want this so much. I want this more than anything.

'Number eight, son. Number fucking eight. In your first week. You've made it. You've bloody made it!' yells Mark.

I don't remember how I reacted, no one waited for my reaction. This is gold. I'm swallowed by a mass of screaming and jumping bodies.

64. Fern

When Scott's chart position is announced to the guests, the party suddenly hikes up a notch in hysteria and intensity. People fling themselves into the pool and into the arms of strangers. I had no idea my friends and family could party so hard. The mojitos and Alabama slammers have taken effect and my nearest and dearest are no longer in awe of the movie and rock stars. They've emerged from the safety of their tight, peripheral clusters and are now sprawled among the cool people. In fact, now that the cool people are beery and leery, smudged and shining, it's pretty difficult to distinguish them from the other guests. Alcohol and sunshine are great levellers.

'I guess it's been parties like this every night, hey?'

I recognize his voice before I have to turn. I recognize it despite the fact there's something unusually hard and sneering in his tone. It sounds as though he thinks parties are a sin, which is definitely not the case; I know he likes a party.

I can't look at Adam, I don't know how to greet him. In Hollywood everyone double air kisses but that wouldn't seem right – just because it's so over-used – but a handshake would be ludicrous. In the end I settle for staring resolutely at my feet.

'No, actually. This is the first party we've had. We're more likely to go out for dinner and to bars but even then, not that often,' I say with a bright and entirely forced tone.

'Of course, Scottie is sober at the moment. Well, don't worry, things will liven up when he falls off the wagon.'

'That's really not very kind, Adam.'

Adam takes a deep breath and looks out across the scene. 'No. It's not, is it.' He sighs and adds, 'I apologize.'

I finally force myself to look up at him. It's a peculiar thing, I've been full of trepidation at the thought of seeing him but now he's stood in front of me I feel strangely relaxed, almost happy – despite his sarcasm. I suppose it's because we've been friends for so long, well, more than friends – obviously. We never had a chaste or platonic stage in *our* relationship. It was all about longing and lust and then fulfilment. The happy feeling vanishes the moment I realize what I need to ask next.

'So, you and Jess, are you an item now?' I want to sound breezy but the words catch in my throat. I hope Adam doesn't think that means something; that it means anything. He glances at me in surprise. Doesn't he think I have the right to ask?

'What makes you ask that?'

'Well, you are here together. Why else would she ask you to come?'

'I have no idea. Maybe she thought the place would be full of coked-up wankers and she needed my company.'

Fair point. But it's notable he hasn't answered my questions. He's neatly side-stepped in a way Scott would be proud of. It's frustrating. I just need to know for sure. One way or the other. There's a horrible silence that sits between us like a bad smell. I push on.

'I mean not that it's any of my business.'

'No.'

'I was just thinking about the seating plan for tomorrow.'

'Right.'

'I mean should I sit you with a bevvy of young lovelies and Jess with a throng of butch blokes or should I seat you together?'

'I see.'

'And that's the only reason I asked, really.'

'Right.'

'I mean it must be pretty intense, since you live together.'

'We've always lived together.'

'Yes, but before it was with me too. You haven't got anyone else in the flat apart from you two now.'

'And where exactly would that third person sleep, Fern? With me? With Jess? In the cupboard with the cornflakes?' Adam sighs impatiently.

Oh. I hadn't thought of that. I'd forgotten how small the flat is. I fall silent and consider what he's just said. A third person could have moved in, if Jess had moved into the double room with Adam but that is clearly not the case. Hurrah. Somewhere deep inside I'm singing and dancing an entire tap routine. Jess hasn't moved in with Adam!

Yet.

Music and dancing stop abruptly. Obviously that could change at any moment and, I remind myself, why shouldn't it?

'Oh well, at least my share of the rent will tide you over. Will you move?' I ask.

Adam looks exasperated. Funny thing is I've always thought of him as eternally laid back — too laid back. Vexation and frustration were not part of his repertoire, except when the batteries ran out in the remote control and he had to get out of his chair to change channels — that always caused him to huff and puff. But now he's snapping and sighing at me as though he's some sort of enormous steam-powered crocodile. He's changed.

'We haven't cashed your cheque, Fern. Although that was clearly a point of principle that has gone unnoticed so I'm beginning to regret it now. Especially as it's clear that for you coughing up the dough for a few months' rent is the equivalent to handing over the loose change you find down the back of the sofa. But we don't need your help, thank you, we're managing our money. We're both working a little bit longer and harder, remember that, Fern?'

I'm humming to myself in an effort to block out his sarcasm and anger but it doesn't work.

'I miss it, actually,' I confess. It's only now, when I'm articulating this, that I realize it's true.

'What, working?' Adam is incredulous, not surprisingly since he's the person I used to grumble to most when I had to get up at 3 a.m. to go to the flower market every other day.

'Well, yes. At least, I miss the shop and being surrounded by flowers. I really miss the flowers.'

'Heart bleeds for you, Fern.'

Why does he keep calling me Fern in that cross and impersonal way? But then what did I expect? Who'd have thought I'd hanker after 'Fern-girl'? Before I have to endure any more of his mockery I notice Jess approaching. I watch as she emerges from the crowd and makes her way towards us. She's hurrying but it's one of those weird moments where everything appears in slow motion. She's looking fabulous. I have time to note her gleaming hair, broad smile and effortlessly trendy jeans and skimpy top. I've always considered her the prettier of the two of us. But we are so dissimilar we never had to seriously compete or compare. I like dark-haired guys, she likes blonds. Guys who like brunettes went for her, blokes who liked blondes went for me. But, in the moment that she slips her arm through Adam's, I question whether those simple childish divisions still hold true. From where I'm standing I'd say she's quite keen on dark guys. My guy. My ex-guy, that is.

Jess and I hug one another; it would have been an awkward hug anyway – even if she had let go of his arm.

'Did Adam tell you his fabulous news?' she gushes.

'No.' I smile and look at Adam expectantly.

'Well, it's not just *your* man who was desperate to hear the chart position today. Adam was too. His band is number forty-eight in the singles chart,' squeals Jess. She jumps up and down and hugs Adam tightly. Her boobs squash against his arm – is that really necessary? He allows her to hug him for a moment or two before he gently disentangles himself and tries to shush and calm her.

'Band?' I ask, confused. 'You're not in a band.'

'He's *managing* a band. They're called the Deputies. The hottest thing to come out of Wigan since, well, *ever*. Adam discovered this band and now he's managing them!' Jess is burbling delightedly. 'He's been brilliant for them. Changed everything around. Changed their lives – imagine. They've got gigs and a deal and everything,' she prattles. I don't think I've ever seen her as excited before, not even when she was reading someone else's paper over their shoulder on the tube and she thought her numbers had come up on the lottery (they hadn't, she just needed new glasses).

Adam is fighting a slight reddening of the cheeks – I don't think it's the sun.

Instantly I forget the sniping and griping and I'm just thoroughly, intensely, unequivocally pleased for him.

'Really? Wow, that's amazing!' I fold Adam into a big hug too, just as Jess did. It's freaky because my body seems to sort of remember his and smudges a fraction closer into him – a fraction closer than I was planning. I leap away quickly. My body shouldn't be feeling like that. *I* shouldn't be feeling like that.

But I am.

Oh God. I feel weak as my legs turn to liquid. This isn't right. This isn't good.

I rally. 'Hey, but don't you know the rules, though? All exes ought to have the good grace to be abject failures or at least not stunning successes.' I make myself grin and then I add, 'Seriously, this is brilliant news. Listening to all those demo tapes, knocking on all those closed doors of record companies has finally paid off. How fantastic,' I gush. I mean it, this *is* amazing. I can't actually believe that Adam is managing a band; organizing gigs and record contracts. This is Adam we're talking about.

Adam shrugs; he's trying to hide his jubilation. 'Yeah,

well, I said it was only a matter of time. What did you think? That I was going to be a rigger for ever?'

Yes. The thought punches me in the gut. I can't respond and I'm grateful when I discover he's not expecting me to.

'They are good guys. With a great sound. This first single of theirs is pretty much a statement of intent. It's full of beautiful chiming guitars, pop sensibilities and a hint of their widescreen ambition. We've nearly finished the album, it's going to need just a few more weeks, I think.'

'My God, that's brilliant, Adam. So will your boys be fighting Scott for the number one slot?' I joke excitedly.

'They won't ever get to number one, you know. I'm saying that as their manager. I'm not being modest, I'm just being realistic. They're not commercial in the right way, the way that sells at the moment. We'd be delighted to get to the top thirty and to see a few more gigs. They'll have a year in the sunshine. They'll have fun and it will be long enough for them to get some money together, you know, make a start in life.'

'I can hardly believe you're saying this, Adam. You, who used to make veiled references to a non-existent drug habit, in a desperate effort to appear more rock and roll.'

'Yeah, well, I was stupid,' he says, with a big easy grin which makes me think maybe it was not just him who was stupid. 'I've decided I'm going to be the sort of manager who tells his bands to put their earnings into property, not to let them go up in smoke.'

'Is that what you are going to do? Buy a house?'

'Oh, Fern.' Adam sighs. It seems as though I've irritated him by bringing up purchasing a property. Is he still so allergic to a commitment of any sort – even to a mortgage? That doesn't make sense in light of what he's advising his band members. I stare at him puzzled. He opens his mouth as if he's about to say something more but then he snaps it shut again and shakes his head. After a pause he adds, 'You know what? I'm going to care about my band. Radical, hey?'

Very.

'Besides, looking around here today at all this, I'm not sure if this is what I'd want for them. They are all really young, I'm not sure they could handle it. I'm not sure anyone can and this is it in the end, isn't it? This is rock and roll. This is success.'

I follow his gaze. It's weird, everyone has been having a fabulous time for – I don't know how long – hours? But suddenly the stylish and exciting party is morphing into something vaguely unpleasant and unwieldy under our gaze. Probably everyone should pack up and go home. I've only had a couple of cocktails but I'm dizzy and confused. Nothing seems clear-cut; nothing is as I thought it was.

I look around for my mum. Last time I saw her she was wandering around collecting over-full ashtrays and used glasses. I asked her to come and sit down and relax with me and told her we have people who do that stuff but she just replied that I'll get a big bum if I sit on it all day. Now, I'm relieved to note that my mum and Scott's mum have retreated into the kitchen; I think my mum is washing up, Scott's mum is drying. I don't waste time considering whether this is appropriate or not, I just count my lucky stars Mum won't witness the joints currently being rolled on the expensive side-tables. Not that she'd suspect there's anything more than tobacco in the rollies, nor would she understand why all the bathroom doors are suddenly locked. I'm grateful to note that Saadi and her assistants have rounded up all the kids and packed them safely away somewhere but I'm irritated there are drugs in our home at all. How will Scott manage? Where the hell is Mark? I know he'd soon have this lot out on their ears.

It also comes to my attention that the fit semi-clad waiters are now wearing more clothes than pretty much anyone else. The roaring temperatures have encouraged models, groupies and desperate starlets to throw off sarongs, T-shirts and bikini tops. Near-naked bodies rub up against one another in a way that seems to me unnecessary and unseemly. I'm no prude but I want to ask people to get a room. There's nothing remaining of the ice sculptures or the delicious chocolate fountains – except sticky, dark pools. The light is fading but the pink and purple all-weather light bulbs are casting vaguely menacing hues, not the lovely girly ones I expected. Someone is in the pool trying to have sex with one of the scarlet inflatable, giant ducks.

This is success.

Jess beams at me. 'We're going to go back to the hotel now. We might hit the bar and celebrate. We'd ask you along but no doubt you need an early night. Big day tomorrow, hey?'

'Yes, big day.' I plaster on my broadest smile. The Mondrian Sky Bar, in the hotel where they are staying, is stunning but I know my friends well. 'You ought to go to the Standard if you're peckish. They do the best fat chips ever,' I advise.

'Perfect, just what I fancy.' Jess gently tugs on Adam's arm and there's a glint in her eye that makes me understand that chips aren't *just* what she fancies.

We hug each other briefly and as Adam leans in to me he says, 'For what it's worth, I hope Scott stays sober and I hope you're happy.'

I watch Adam and Jess weave through the drunken crowds. They make a really attractive couple. I take a deep breath but it's like breathing in glass shards. I gasp and try to understand why Adam's good wishes hurt more than any of his barbed comments or sullen monosyllabic answers. I guess he's found closure if he can be so generous. Well, that's good. Isn't it? Surely. I don't want him to fly into a jealous and angry rage. Surely.

Oh I do, I do, I do.

No I don't, I don't, I don't.

I know what I need. Or rather who I need. I need Ben. If I ask him to, Ben will confirm that I was right in thinking Adam and I were treading water. Ben'll remind me that I was fed up with Adam. That *I* left *him* because right now – and I'm sure that it's the cocktails and wedding nerves – but suddenly I'm baffled as to how I could ever have thought Adam unchallenging and lacklustre. I've even started to look back at his magpie clutter with affection.

As I pick my way through writhing bodies I hope to

hell Ben doesn't have one of his honesty bursts and insist on reminding me that, up until about a week before my thirtieth birthday, Adam and I were perfectly happy. It's bad enough that I've remembered this myself.

65. Fern

The house is no longer cool and calming, the party has spilt into here too; it's noisy and chaotic. In the hallway I bump into a woman throwing up in our umbrella stand. I console myself with the fact that I never liked it much anyway. I call for one of the maids and ask her to get the girl a cab and hurl the hurl bucket. I also track down one of Saadi's assistants and instruct her to get my mum and dad back to their hotel as quickly as possible. I suggest she uses blindfolds to get them into the car. She laughs but I'm not joking. Then, I wade through the grunts and moans of copulating couples and snorting singles as I start my hunt for Ben.

I haven't seen him all day. He told me that he was going for a wax this morning; he said it was essential prep for the wedding. I thought he meant he was going to wax his car but in fact it transpired he meant he was planning on waxing his back, sacks and crack. Not an image I care to dwell on, no matter how much I love him. I'm at a loss as to why that is essential prep for the wedding; I suppose he's hoping to get lucky.

I check his room but he's not in there. A couple I've never met are making out on the pile of shirts he's left sprawled across his bed; he's going to be furious. I check the den but he's not there either. Another couple are shagging on the footie table, Scott is going to be furious,

I hope it holds their weight. I move on. I open door after door and soon discover that while there were plenty of semi-naked writhing bodies around the pool, many more *have* actually got a room, as there are endless naked bodies indoors too. At first I'm flustered and embarrassed but after a while I become anaesthetized to hairy bums moving up and down or bare breasts jiggling from one side to the next. It's actually quite boring.

After a fruitless thirty-minute search I decide to find Scott, or Mark, or Saadi, anyone who can bring this party-stroke-orgy to an end. I want to go to bed. It's been a long day and the skin around my eyes feels as though it's been stretched on a rack. I'm getting married tomorrow morning and I desperately need my beauty sleep. I check the kitchens, the drawing-room and reception rooms, then I check Scott's bedroom. I can't find any of them. Where the hell are they? Have they gone out partying without me? It's possible and irritating. Weary, I decide I'll have to forgo Ben's pep talk and take myself off to bed.

I left *him*. It's none of my business what Adam does or who he does it with. The fact that the first surge of unfettered affection I've felt, or given, all day was when I folded him into a congratulatory hug is neither here nor there. The fact that I was actually excited to hear that his band was number forty-eight in the singles chart and in contrast relieved to hear Scott's album was number eight in the album chart, isn't significant either. I just know the wedding would be maudlin if Scott hadn't made it to the top ten. I'm excited for Scott, of course. It's just a different sort of excitement. I shake my head but Adam won't slip from it.

I take a deep breath and remind myself that I'm very tired. And a bit drunk. And very emotional. I'm getting married tomorrow. Every woman thinks about her ex the night before her wedding; it's tradition, like wearing something old, new, borrowed and blue. It's simply what happens. It doesn't mean *anything*.

Exhausted, I open my bedroom door. Immediately I sense there's someone else already in here. Great, just what I need, a fornicating couple on my bed. I'll have to change the sheets. There is no way I'm going to sleep on sheets used by strangers on the eve of my wedding. It's probably bad luck or something. At the very least it's unhygienic.

Sure enough, through the flickering candlelight (randies with a romantic streak, they've taken the time to light every one of my thirty-odd Molton Brown candles) I see another naked white bum.

'Ben?' As Ben makes a grab for a sheet to protect his modesty (and mine for that matter), I see who is in the bed with him. 'Scott!'

66. Fern

I'm actually sick. I make the woman I just caught puking into my umbrella stand look restrained – I haven't even got the self-control to find a receptacle for my vomit. It splashes on the marble floor. And when I run, my designer-clad foot slips on my own up-chuck.

'Fern! Wait!' It's Ben's voice I hear call after me down the corridor and I hear Scott say, 'I'll get Mark.'

Bastard.

Bastards.

Both of them!

I hate them!

I run through the house and out of the front door. The gravel of the drive scrunches beneath my feet. It's a sound I've always associated with wealth and luxury but I will for ever more associate it with betrayal and pain. I look around me. Drivers are helping drunken guests into their cars; the party is well and truly over. I don't know what to do. I'm surrounded by dozens of faces but I don't know anyone well enough to ask if I can go home with them or even ask if they'll give me a lift, and besides, where can I go? I just found my fiancé in my bed with my best boy mate, on the eve of our wedding. The thought causes my insides to turn to liquid again. I need to sit down or I'll fall down. I start to stagger towards the lawn when I hear Barry, the driver who has ferried me on countless shopping trips in the last few weeks, call out to me.

'You all right, Miss?' His respectful question is part and parcel of service in the USA. Even checkout servers are polite here but even though I know that, I'm overwhelmed by the generosity of his enquiry and the quiet sympathy that seems to lie behind it.

'Not really,' I mutter.

'Little too much celebrating perhaps?' he asks kindly, as he offers an arm to steady my progress while I lower myself on to a step. My legs are shaking. My whole body is shaking. My whole world is. I crave something sweet but then maybe not, I think I'm going to be sick again.

'No, not celebrating,' I assure him.

Barry must catch something in my voice that explains more than I'm capable of understanding.

'I've just driven some of your English friends to the Standard. I understand they are getting some chips. That's what you guys call French fries, right? I'd suggest, Miss, that chips are just what you need.'

I don't chat to Barry as he efficiently speeds off to Sunset Boulevard. I'm incapable of making small talk – usually my default setting. How could Scott have done that to me? How could Ben? I don't know who I'm most angry or shocked with. I don't know if I'm more furious or hurt. Let's face it – I don't know anything at all. A whole bundle of hideously painful thoughts are assaulting my mind and heart. I honestly thought Scott was going to try to make it work between us. I thought he wanted to be faithful. Is he gay? Am I just a beard? And Ben? How could he do this to me? Helplessly I run through the scene I've just witnessed and wonder, is it possible I've misinterpreted events? Were they actually having sex? Maybe they were just hanging out together. Maybe they were waiting for me. They were, after all, in my bedroom.

Aaghhh. They were in *my* bedroom. With candles. There's no mistake; I haven't misinterpreted anything. Ben got a wax today. His best Paul Smith boxers were discarded on the floor – his lucky pants. Oh God, this is all too vile to think about.

Barry drops me off outside the Standard and says he'll wait for me until I instruct him otherwise. At this time of night I expect the restaurant to be quiet. Usually by now most of the action has moved downstairs to the Purple Lounge, the hotel's chic but mellow cocktail bar; it has space for dancing and space for hanging around being hip. The restaurant is more of a coffee shop by design, the service is quick and efficient and the cuisine is renowned as comfort food. It's the perfect hide-out. I imagine wandering into the restaurant and scanning the booths for Jess and Adam. I need a friendly face more than I've ever needed one in my life. The place will be deserted and I'll spot Adam instantly, even though his back will be to me. I'll fall into the booth and plonk myself down opposite him; without ceremony I'll say, 'Ben is sleeping with Scott.'

As I push open the door I am hit not by intense and meaningful silence but by exuberance and cheer. Far from the semi-deserted scene I imagined, I'm faced with a party, which in terms of energy and liveliness could rival the one at Scott's place earlier on today. The difference being

I can't see any semi-clad waiters or wanabees, nor can I see any lines of powder on the tables – although there are lines of dominoes snaked across them – they belong to my dad, he's playing with Uncle Ted. My mum, Aunt Liz and my sister, Fi, are gossiping with Lisa. They are huddled into one of the booths, ferociously guarding a large bowl of steaming, fat chips. I watch as one or two of my cousins swing by and try to pinch a chip; they are swatted away like flies. Adam and Charlie are sat in a second booth; they are deep in conversation too. I think they are talking about the beer because they keep holding up their bottles and examining them as though they contain all the answers to the mysteries of the universe. I can't see my brother Bill and his family, I think they palled up with Scott's brother; Bill isn't one to miss a networking opportunity. Rick and a handful of cousins fill a couple more booths. They are drinking Coke, which seems deliciously innocent after this afternoon's antics, when the only coke being consumed was quite another sort and I'm not talking caffeine-free. I needed a friendly face and here they all are. All my friends and family, and yet suddenly I feel peeved and lost.

'No one said there was a party going on,' I say petulantly as I squeeze into the ladies' booth. Lisa budges along to make room for me. I try to shake the nagging feeling I've been left out, that I'm missing out.

'Oh Fern, lovely to see you, do you want a chip?' asks Aunt Liz, proffering the previously greedily guarded bowl of temptation.

'She's not allowed,' says Mum, whipping away the bowl with unusual dexterity. 'I was talking to her personal trainer this morning. I don't want to be blamed if she can't get into her dress tomorrow.'

'Unlikely,' says my aunt, dropping her gaze to my now flat stomach. 'There's not a picking on her. If she eats a chip, we'll probably see it.'

'I think she's too thin,' calls my dad from the next booth; I hadn't realized he was listening.

'Well, *I'm* having chips,' says Lisa, 'I'm starving. As lovely as canapés undoubtedly are, they don't do much of a job at lining your stomach or quelling alcohol-infused munchies.'

'That's the problem with posh food, it's always tiny portions,' adds my uncle. 'I'm knocking, no sixes, no fives and no threes,' he adds, returning to the game of dominoes.

'Lovely party though, dear,' says Mum, no doubt noticing my silence and assuming I'm offended by their analysis of my party food.

'Wicked,' yells Rick. My cousins all nod their agreement.

'So much champagne and cocktails, it must have cost a fortune,' says my sis.

'Great band,' says Charlie. 'It's been years since we danced like that, hey Lisa?'

'You are so off the scale lucky,' says Rick.

'You are living the dream, no doubt about it,' adds my sister.

'Who could have imagined such a thing?' asks Lisa.

'Ben is sleeping with Scott.' That's me.

'What?'

It's gratifying that everyone else seems as shocked as

I am (although no one else throws up). On the drive over here I've been haunted by the idea that everyone knew about this, everyone other than me, that is.

'I've just found them together, now, after you all left,' I explain.

'Ben wouldn't do that,' says Lisa. Notably, she does not put up a similar defence for Scott.

'I caught them in the act,' I say. Then I start to cry. Well, cry suggests an element of restraint – I sob actually, and howl.

'I'll get you a drink,' says Charlie.

I gratefully gulp down the whiskey. I enjoy the warmth swirling around my stomach; it offers me some sort of comfort. Not enough comfort. Not as much comfort as beating Scott and Ben with a spiky pair of Jimmy Choos until they beg for mercy – but some comfort.

'How long do you think it's been going on?' asks Charlie.

'Do you think it was the first time?' asks Lisa.

'Do you think Scott is gay or experimenting?' asks Rick.

'Is this a fling or the real thing?' asks my sister.

'I don't know,' I wail. These are exactly the questions that have spurted around my mind on the journey over here but I haven't got any of the answers. Another whiskey appears from nowhere. I register murmurs assuring me that 'It's good for the shock.' I down it. It has a calming effect or at least a numbing effect and that's as good as, right now. I still can't process what I saw half an hour ago. I can't begin to tackle the enormity of the situation.

'I'm supposed to be getting married in the morning!'

I wail, placing my head on the table. The cold surface soothes my hot head. Mum bustles around to my side of the booth and evicts Lisa. She grabs me and pulls me into a hug. I close my eyes tightly so I can't glimpse her appalled and aggrieved face. It's bad enough dealing with my own disappointment.

'What am I going to do?' The whiskey loosens my tongue and I start to blather, giving voice to thoughts I hadn't allowed to blossom fully. All my secret, difficult thoughts, that I've been working so hard to keep entombed.

'Sometimes when I'm with Scott, I think that we are made for one another. At least, I did in the beginning. I really did. It was so exciting, overwhelming. I thought it was *it*, you know, everything you ever read about or dreamed about.'

Everyone is gathered around me now; all my loved ones, they nod and murmur their understanding. Only Adam has stayed in his seat and is silent. While every other face is twisted with concern or blazing with a ghoulish astonishment, Adam doesn't change his expression from neutral. I keep peeking at him but I have no idea what he is thinking. Most likely he's using every iota of self-control to resist yelling, 'I told you so!' In my effort to be honest, I'm probably really hurting him. Hurting him again. Which is shaming. Now I have a hint of how Adam must have felt when I left him. I try to explain my actions to him, under the guise of telling the whole crowd. I stare at the sticky condiments on the table and mutter, 'I wouldn't have left like that, unless I believed Scott was everything, do you see? That's why I cut all strings. I'm sorry I was so – insensitive.'

The word is inadequate. No doubt Adam thinks so too but he still doesn't move or respond. Everyone else bursts into another round of sympathetic grunts and someone orders more whiskey, I *think* it's my third. I dip a chip into a small pot of ketchup. It splits and the fluffy white innards are exposed. I gobble it down in one bite. It tastes fantastic. I carry on talking.

'But that feeling that we're made for each other, that somehow we were destined for one another, I haven't been getting it too much recently,' I confess. How long have I known this? Why haven't I said something earlier? At least to myself? 'Truthfully, I don't think I've had that feeling since we came to LA,' I admit. 'And we are never alone. It's hard to stay connected when you have to shout above thousands of people just to ask him to pass the salt. And I don't think I care enough about his records and his ambitions. And I don't think he cares about anything else.' And I do care about Adam's band. I also care about where Adam is sleeping and who he's sleeping with. Sensibly, even in my distraught state I'm aware I can't confess this. I am however prompted to ask, 'Where's Jess?'

When I first came in I assumed that Jess was in the loo but she can't possibly still be in there.

'She's downstairs, in the Purple Lounge,' says Adam. It's great that he's finally entered into the conversation, although he still doesn't budge from his seat.

'Alone?'

'No, this guy asked her to join his friends. He seemed really cool.'

'You don't mind?'

'Mind? Why should I?'

'Because. Well –' I don't know how to finish the sentence. Adam understands perfectly, without my having to do so.

'I thought I told you Jess and I are just friends,' he says with a shrug.

Oh thank God! Thank God! No, no, he hadn't told me. Not as such. Not clearly. I wasn't sure. Suddenly (and no doubt improperly) I'm filled with a dreamy sense of delight and relief. It swooshes around my body, causing my knees to shake.

Charlie claps his hands together and looks delighted. 'Jess hoped you might think that there was something going on between her and Adam. Didn't she, Lisa?' Charlie has never been known for his subtlety and he's had far too much booze today to compute whether his revelation is going to embarrass anyone. He lunges on. 'Jess has this crazy idea that you and Adam shouldn't have split up and she thought that if she could make you jealous you'd come to your senses. She bet Adam a tenner you'd beg him to come back to you; she was *that* certain.' Charlie is suddenly struck by another thought. 'Not that her view seems so crazy now. I mean, I was all in favour of you running off with a multi-millionaire, we all were.' If that's the case, my friends and family now look extremely unsure. They are clearly mortified at being made accountable for their opinions in front of Adam. 'But since he's playing for the other team, it doesn't look like such a smart move, does it?' finishes Charlie. The silence is deafening. Adam rescues us all from the awful embarrassment.

'Jess has been a really good friend to me when, you

know, I needed a friend,' he says. The delight and relief are rapidly replaced with something more like shame and regret. I feel like the cow I undoubtedly am.

Rick asks, 'Should I go and get Jess? She'll be pleased to know that you were taken in by her little ploy. Even though it didn't pan out exactly as she hoped. Part A worked at least. You did think she had the hots for Adam, even though you never begged him to come back to you.'

Why wouldn't she have the hots for him? I ask myself this as I sit staring at Adam. Why wouldn't Jess or any other woman, come to that, have the hots for Adam? My fingers are itching to scuttle through his long, scruffy hair. His heavy eyebrows are knit in concentration and his dark brown eyes ooze concern. His cheekbones are sharper than I remembered, his shoulders are broader.

'No, don't interrupt her fun,' I mutter. She'll hear about my nightmare soon enough.

It's only just dawning on me but I realize now that Adam is unique in his ability to be so laid back in this hectic and frantic world and he is not at fault. He's a man with a quiet certainty that everything will be all right. He lives without fear. He isn't afraid of people not liking him, or of being a failure, or even normal things that everyone is a bit afraid of, like being mugged, lost or unloved. He sees all that as pointless worrying. He's not even afraid of missing the last train home. That's why he wasn't prepared to bow to the deadlines I, or anyone else, imposed. He was not afraid of time passing because he knew he'd have his time. I'm afraid of lots of things and Scott is afraid of everything. Now, being with Adam seems like a freedom. He's unafraid, he's not even worried. His quiet confidence is unusual and deeply, deeply attractive.

Oh God, if only I *could* beg him to take me back as Jess was hoping or, better yet, turn the clock back so that I'd never left him. That's got to be the whiskey thinking, doesn't it? Maybe not. Or the shock of finding Scott with Ben. Maybe not. I don't know. All I know right now is that I want to push past my mum and all the other confused and concerned faces and throw myself on the floor, wrap my arms around Adam's legs and plead with him to have me back. I think I wanted to do this the moment I saw him by the pool this afternoon, I just couldn't admit it to myself. What a nightmare. What a total idiot I've been. Suddenly, I'm awash with startling, overwhelming memories. We were happy, Adam and I, once upon a time. We were happy in each other's company and we didn't need movie premieres or Rodeo Drive or infinity pools. We were happy waiting for a bus, sharing a stick of chewing-gum, finishing the Sudoku, guessing the outcome of a *Coronation Street* plotline. We were ordinary. Why didn't I see that ordinary isn't so bad? It's actually rather nice when on the other hand you consider that the extraordinary includes your boyfriend having sex with your boy friend.

Dad gently tries to bring me back to the matter in hand. 'Would you like me to go and tell Scott the wedding is off?' he offers. He stands up and draws himself to his full height. He's not enormous but his beer belly is quite impressive; in my eyes he's never looked so heroic.

'Someone will have to go and say something,' says my

mum. 'There are so many people making plans, the sooner we start to unmake them the better.'

'You think I should call off the wedding?' I'm actually just confirming I've understood their intention, rather than questioning the sense of the plan. It's an important nuance.

'Of course!' Everyone choruses at once. Everyone, except one person, that is. I'm staring at Adam and he's silent.

'I know it's going to be hard giving up all that wealth: the designer clothes, the mansion, the jewellery,' says Lisa.

'The helicopter, the private jet,' adds Charlie.

'But you have to,' says my sister, flatly.

'Money never brought anyone happiness,' adds my aunt. I don't actually think she's right about this but I know what she's getting at, besides it's impossible to argue with her when she adds, 'I mean, Scott isn't actually happy, is he?'

'You can't buy love,' notes my dad.

'I know, I know all this,' I snap. I don't think I can bear to listen to another one of their platitudes. Of course I know what I have to do. I have to dump Scott and walk away from the wedding of a lifetime. I have to say cheerio to the most glitzy future imaginable – I know that. It's just a hard thing to do. I wanted my life to be exquisitely special, distinctly not ordinary, but now I realize that the only way it can be that is by being honest with myself. I used to wonder, if I could have anything what would I ask for? A bath full of M&Ms to sit in? A room full of actors to chat to? A wardrobe full of designer clothes to lounge in? None of the above. Being with Scott is not what I want. I look at Adam, Adam is what I want. I smile at him gently, sure that he'll communicate his support. With a single glance he'll make it easier for me to walk away from all that glitters and towards what's truly golden. Easy.

Abruptly he stands up, grabs his battered leather jacket and walks towards the door. In a flash I push past my mum and everyone else, and follow him out of the restaurant.

67. Fern

'Hey, Adam.'

My voice cuts through the warm night air. He stops and turns. He stares at me and I'm doused with feelings of almost painful tenderness. He waits for me to say something else. But what do I want to say? What can I say? This has been the most bizarre and painful night of my life. The image of Ben's bum sticking out of my bed sheets is scored on to my brain. I can't compute the level of betrayal. But that's not the only thing I'm grappling with. Suddenly, I am certain that Adam's steady solidness, his reliability and calmness out-wows Scott's front-man antics. Yes, Scott is dynamic and innovative – he's also exhausting and disloyal. Scott feasts on adulation and acts on abandon. It's all a bit much for me. I'm shrouded in the overwhelming belief that all the sorrow of tonight will be washed away if Adam just holds me. I don't know what I'm hoping to gain from his touch, where I'm hoping it will lead, but I know that I definitely don't want Adam to walk away right now; I have a feeling that will be more of a loss than chucking away the jewels and the helicopter. Way, way more. I used to *believe* that Adam proposing would make my life more luminous, glorious and triumphant. Now I'm *sure* that being with him, married or not, would be just that.

But Adam didn't join the rest of my family in their

resounding calls for me not to marry Scott. Is it possible that Adam is past caring what I do?

'Do you think I should marry him?' I ask.

'That's a stupid question, Fern.' Adam sighs and pulls his hands through his hair. He looks weary.

'Could you take me back?' I blurt. 'I'd give it all up for you – the fame and money and stuff. I'd give up the mansion with the pools and the cars and the store cards and the –'

'No, Fern. I'm sorry. No.' Adam stares me full in the soul. 'You can't go backwards. I don't want to be the guy you ran back to.'

My ears start to buzz as a burning heat creeps through my body. Humiliation seeps into every pore, leaks into my bloodstream and carousels through my body. Humiliation and sour, sour, disappointment. What was I thinking? Did I really expect Adam to fling his arms open and say, 'Come back, Fern-girl, all is forgiven'? How stupid of me. How pathetic.

But then, yes, yes, that is exactly what I was hoping for.

I scrabble around for the tiniest shred of poise that might have survived detonation of my dignity. I wobble on my feet. 'Fine.'

Then quickly I walk towards Barry and the waiting Mercedes. My walk is neat and purposeful. I don't indulge in a regretful glance over my shoulder. He doesn't want me. He doesn't want me.

Understood.

68. Fern

Barry drives me back to Scott's. I don't have anywhere else to go. I don't know who or what to expect when I arrive there. I wonder if Scott or Ben, or both, will be waiting for me on the steps or will I be greeted by a more formal damage limitation group? Mark, Saadi or Colleen? A combination of the above? I have no idea. The car creeps up the long drive and I see that in fact no one is waiting for me on the steps. I'm relieved and furious at once. Shouldn't Scott be pacing up and down on the forecourt, fearfully awaiting my return? Surely in a normal relationship the bastard, deceiving fiancé would be waiting on the steps – but there's nothing normal about our relationship. There never has been. How could I ever have thought being ordinary was dull?

Most of the guests have gone now; I spot only one guy comatose on the front lawn, all the other stragglers have been seen off the property. An army of industrious staff is already returning the magnificent house to its former glory. Dirty plates have been cleared, waste food has been dumped, the bouncy castle is deflated, vomit has been mopped and broken glasses have been swept up. The guts and gore of the party have been effectively removed and dealt with.

Mostly.

I wander into the house and towards my room. I don't

actually want to go to my room, the scene of the crime, but I can't think where else I could go. There's an eerie calm swirling through the entire house. I imagined everyone would be on alert, rushing about to discover my whereabouts, desperately trying to find me in order to calm me down and establish whether or not I intend to go to the press. But, in fact, there is no drama. It strikes me that while I think the world has imploded, Scott may simply view his infidelity and my discovery of it as an inevitable part of our relationship and Mark will remind me that there is a contract in place laying out protocol for exactly this situation.

Carefully I push open my bedroom door and sneak a peek before entering. The bed has been remade with clean sheets – very thoughtful, I think sarcastically. All the candles have been extinguished but through the darkness I can just about make out Ben. He is sat bolt upright in the chair at my dressing-table. The moonlight streaming through the slats in the blind cast shadows that make him look as though he's behind grey bars. I flick the light switch.

'Hello.' He jumps to his feet, upsetting a couple of cosmetic bottles and sending a hairbrush skidding across the floor; neither of us moves to pick it up.

I nod an acknowledgement but can't bring myself to speak. What can I say?

He says, 'I'm sorry.' The apology falls like a tiny rain-drop into an enormous sea of misery; it hardly matters.

I walk into the room, closing the door behind me. This has been the longest day of my life and all I want to do is flop into bed but I stand next to it and stare at it. I know it can't be, but I imagine the bed is still hot from their betrayal. Ben follows my gaze and stammers, 'I am so, so sorry, Fern. We didn't plan for you to find out.'

'You were in my room,' I point out. 'Exposure was predictable – some would say inevitable.'

'We lost track of time, we –' I hold up a hand in an effort to silence him. Any level of detail is too much detail. Those six words alone tell me that Scott and Ben have reached a level of passion Scott and I never reached; a state of oblivion when everything else, including time, chastity vows and loyalty, was forgotten.

'Why?' I ask. Ben knows it's an all-encompassing 'why' and that, right now, I'm too frail and battered to be specific.

'Because when I'm walking next to Scott I feel drenched in this feeling of success and possibility,' says Ben simply and quietly. His explanation rolls off his tongue. It doesn't sound rehearsed – it's heartfelt. I know the feeling he means, I once thought it was mine alone. I don't feel it at all any more.

'Was that the only time?' I ask.

'It was the first time.' Is he making a distinction?

'Did you seduce him or did he . . . you know . . . chase you?' It's a stupid question to ask. It doesn't matter and yet at the same time it's vital that I know. Ben looks away, he's reluctant to satiate my curiosity. No doubt he's guessed he can't; one question will lead to the next, and the next, and then to another, and no matter what he confesses, he can't explain things to me. This level of betrayal can't be rationalized, or justified or even apologized for. 'Who made the first move?' I demand.

'I, I don't remember.' He had his bits waxed, he was wearing his lucky pants – I think I can assume Ben took the initiative. I can't decide if this is a comfort or the cause of further distress. Who do I want to have betrayed me the most?

'Was he drunk?'

'A bit.'

'How could you let him drink?' I demand angrily.

'Not slaughtered, if that's what you are implying. I didn't have to get him drunk to get him to agree.'

'Was it planned?'

'I –'

'Did you plan it?' I insist.

'Maybe on some level.' My breathing is fast and shallow. So are my friends, it appears. Ben turns to me and pours a complicated expression my way. I can't decide whether he pities me or hates me. Then he asks, 'What if he's gay, Fern?'

'He's not gay, Ben. He likes experimenting. We all know that. He's slept with thousands of women. He was trying you on for size.'

'Yeah, well, I think I fitted. I think he's gay,' says Ben firmly.

'That's just your wishful thinking,' I reply sharply.

'I've thought it for a while now. I had no idea how to tell you.'

I remind myself that before I met Adam I firmly believed sex wasn't in any way tied up with responsibility, reliability or even love. As far as I was concerned sex was all about hedonistic pleasure, meaningless delight. This is what Scott thinks too. I tell myself that what he's just done – what *they've* just done – doesn't have to matter; Ben seems insistent on proving otherwise.

'So you decided shagging him in front of me was the best way.'

'No. But let's face it, whatever I'd have said you would have ignored. You've become an expert at burying your head when faced with inconvenient truths.'

'That's not true,' I say forcefully but I know that it is. I'm an ostrich, it's an essential survival tactic, especially as I know now for sure that I'm still in love with Adam and he doesn't want me. Scott's my only option, that's an inconvenient truth.

'Women haven't made him very happy and he didn't even want to sleep with you. Is that the behaviour of a heterosexual man? You look as delicious as a –' Ben searches for the right words – eventually he comes up with, 'a strawberry low-fat smoothie. Even I fancy you a bit. Shouldn't he have shagged you?'

'He wanted us to be special,' I reason.

'That's just *your* wishful thinking,' replies Ben.

Ben has betrayed me so entirely that I'm finding it hard to stand in the same room as him without clawing out his eyes, but then, there's something that's pulling me towards him. He's been a great friend for four years now. He recommended the only hairdresser I've ever trusted, he introduced me to M&S sushi lunches, since we met I've never bought an item of clothing or (lord forbid) a pair of shoes without consulting Ben's impeccable taste first. He was the one who gave me my first decent job, he sent me on expensive training courses when he could barely afford them, he gave me pay increases before I even had to ask for them – he has always been fair and honest with me. I don't understand.

'Why did you sleep with him, Ben? Just to show me he might be gay?'

'No, sweetheart. I slept with him because I'm in love with him,' says Ben sadly.

'Oh please.' I can't keep the scepticism out of my voice.

'I am. I'm not saying he's in love with me. I'm just telling you why I couldn't help myself. I slept with him because he's delicious. He's irresistible.' Ben starts to walk towards me but thinks better of it as I shrink back towards the door. 'I am so, so sorry that I hurt you, Fern, but you more than anyone know how irresistible he is. You left Adam for him. And what's more, I won't be the last one to demonstrate this weakness. There will be better and worse men than me who will feel the same. *Do* the same. Men and women. Anyone he wants. That's the way it is.'

'No, there won't. There won't be opportunity,' I say firmly. 'Once we are married and having sex, Scott won't need anyone else.'

There's a stunned silence and then Ben splutters, 'You can't still be thinking of marrying Scott.' He looks sick and horrified, he sways a little and then sits back down.

'Yes, I can and I am,' I say determinedly. Truthfully, I'm not one hundred per cent sure I mean this. I'm saying it aloud to make it seem more real. In the moment I saw Ben and Scott together I said goodbye to the dazzlingly glamorous and beautiful Jenny Packham wedding dress and all the associated dizzy, glitzy fabulousness that was to be my future. I assumed that wasn't going to be my route any more. But what else is left for me now? Adam doesn't want me. I discovered how much I love him too late in the game. There's no future there. He said it; you can't go back. I have to go forward. At least Scott wants me. He chose me. He could have chosen anyone and he chose me. That has to mean something. That has to stand for something because that's all I have.

'Fern, you can't marry Scott. You'll be living with constant infidelity. I know his millions are attractive but you have to see what you are getting yourself into.'

I shoot poisoned darts from my eyes; if looks really could kill, the undertakers would be measuring Ben up right now. How dare he? How dare he! This isn't about Scott's money.

'You can't marry Scott,' says Ben again.

'I can, if he still wants me to.' I'm in the habit of being full and frank with Ben, so before I realize how stupid my honesty is, I add, 'I asked Adam to take me back and he said no.'

'And that's *it*? That's the reason you are marrying Scott?' Ben leaps to his feet dramatically once more. He flings his arms in the air and then places them heavily on his hips. He scowls at me. 'Well, why am I surprised? Let's face it – that was the reason you got together with Scott in the first place, because Adam didn't want you. If he'd proposed on your birthday you'd never have been here, there's no doubt in my mind about that. You just want to be married! For fuck's sake, Fern, enough with this obsession of getting married because you are thirty. These are real people with real lives you are talking about. Mine being one of them.' He's yelling now, which I think is unfair – surely I'm the one entitled to do all the yelling tonight.

'This isn't about Scott's money and it isn't about my obsession with getting married. I just need something. I need a future of some sort. This is the only offer on the table.'

'You're panicking. You're rushing things.'

'Scott *wants* to marry me. Scott loves *me*. This thing you two did tonight –' I gesture towards the bed '– it doesn't have to mean anything. People get through these things.'

Ben looks suffocated with rage. His chest is heaving up and down as he tries to catch his breath. He makes a huge effort to recapture some calm. He's silent for a moment and then he adds, 'Fern, Scott wants to win over the American market, he thinks you'll help him do that. You are part of that deal.'

'What are you talking about?'

'He doesn't love you, he needs you, or some bride at least – to guarantee *Wedding Album* will resonate with the Americans. They demand sincerity and you are the nearest he could come up with.' Ben's face is granite.

'No, no, that's not true.' I cower away from Ben as though he might hit me. But I already know that no physical blow could hurt me as much as the words he's just spoken. Everything is unravelling, like knitting stitches, and I'm the wool, I'm left knotted and damaged. 'You were a fling. He was drunk. I'm his true love,' I insist. 'He's written songs about me. *Wedding Album* has my name in three tracks.'

'He wrote most of those songs before he even met you. He dropped your name in and changed the odd word. You are not essential to this. You are just a small part of a big show, a member of his supporting cast. He'd already decided he needed to marry someone or other, you just came along at the right time. The engagement announcement, the presentation of the ring, the date for the wedding and the album release were all choreographed.' Ben says this formally. I'd have been less frightened if he'd bawled at me. His serious, calm tone is more convincing than hysterical rage.

'How long have you known this?'

'A while.' He looks at his feet.

'Why didn't you tell me before?'

Ben sighs and clasps his hands over his head, elbows touching as though cradling his thoughts. 'At first I thought it might work, that he might make you happy. You seemed happy. You left Adam for him. You made your choice. You're a big girl, I assumed you knew what you wanted.'

'So why tell me now?'

'I'm in love with him. You're in love with Adam.'

'Adam doesn't want me.'

'But two wrongs don't make a right.' Ben's tone is pleading but I can't be sympathetic.

'You just don't want him to marry me because you want him to yourself,' I argue, lamely.

'You know what, Fern? I think I could make him happy, at least for a while, because I know him, faults and all. You think you do, yet you don't. But I'm not trying to stop this wedding to save Scott for myself. I'm trying to stop this wedding to save *you*. You are my friend and you are throwing your life away.'

69. Scott

What is it with these people? The more you tell them you are unreliable and unstable the more they cleave to you and then they are disappointed. I *told* Fern I wasn't to be trusted. I *told* her addicts are fucking terrible people to care about and pop stars are worse. I *told* her I could resist anything other than temptation and now she's all surprised because I slept with her best friend.

OK, I admit it, not my wisest move ever, nor the kindest. I am genuinely sorry I hurt her but what could I do? Ben made a pretty determined play and yes, I was curious. He's a bright guy; he's funny, interesting and, well, he's hot.

'You shouldn't have been doing this abstaining from sex thing,' grumbles Mark. 'You were pushing yourself too hard, testing yourself too severely. No drink, no drugs and no sex, it's not rock and roll. You're straight back in the clinic, as soon as we get this mess straightened out.' He scowls. 'Although how the hell I straighten this one out, I don't know. There's a real danger that everything is properly fucked now. If this gets out, you have *so* lost the American market. Who the hell is going to buy the records of a cad who swaps teams for his fiancé's best man the night before the wedding?' Mark looks really stressed. He's sweating and pacing and swearing by turn. 'You're going to have to go on a full charm offensive and win her back, son. Quickly. And I mean quickly. You're supposed to be getting married tomorrow.'

'I hadn't forgotten.'

In a way he's right, it is properly fucked now. I can't see a happy way out of this. If I don't marry her, if I tell her how I'm feeling about Ben, then my career is over, but if I do marry her I'm only going to continue hurting her and that's not right. I don't want to hurt Fern. We should never have picked an innocent. I am surrounded by women who would rather die than imbibe carbs but would swallow the sperm of an influential stranger faster than you could say 'coke or poke'. I should have got engaged to someone like that. Someone robust enough for this life. But I liked Fern, still do. Love her, perhaps. What I feel for her is a lot like love. Yes, sometimes I can go as far as to say that. But it's my experience that loving one person doesn't stop you loving another and it certainly doesn't stop you having great sex with someone else. And the sex with Ben was excellent. Mark must catch me smiling to myself, and he probably catches the drift as to why I'm smiling because he hitches his anger up a notch.

'This isn't a fucking joke, Scott.' He's a total guttersnipe when he's under pressure. 'Do you know how much bloody money is riding on this? Besides the cost of the wedding – a limitless, dazzling exhibition, a multi-million-pound trifle – there's all the money we stand to lose if *Wedding Album* sinks. How could you have been so fucking stupid?' Neither of us actually expects me to respond to that, so he just carries on. 'Well, we'll get her posh mate in. What's her name?'

'Lisa.'

'Yeah, Lisa, she seems a bright girl, she'll point out what side Fern's bread is buttered. She'll talk Fern into going ahead. She likes nice handbags. And Colleen and Saadi, they can have a word too. Do you think between them they might be able to persuade her to go through with the wedding?'

'No.'

'You don't?' Mark was grey before; now he's so pale he's practically transparent.

'I think I have to go to her. I have to be honest.'

'We are dependent on you being honest?'

'It's our only hope.'

'Well, it's like I said then. We're fucked.'

70. Fern

I tell Ben to get out of my room. I don't expect to sleep, but I need some time to think. My body is aching with tiredness and so, despite my squeamishness about lying on the scene of their treachery, I flop on to my bed. What to do? What to do?

Scott has the decency to look terrible when he turns up in my room. I don't want to look at him. I don't want to see him. I can't imagine a time when I gaped at his image on a calendar, let alone ogled him in the flesh. I wonder whether he's going to tell me to leave the wedding dress in my closet because he's coming out of his. After one sneaky glance at him, to check he looks genuinely remorseful, I stare at the ceiling. He sits down on the end of the bed, leans forward and lets his head fall, like a tonne weight, into his hands.

'Have I a hope of getting back in your heart?' he asks.

I think about what he's just said. It sounds oddly familiar and I can't help but worry whether it's a lyric from one of his songs, or, worse – someone else's song. I don't answer. He moves up the bed towards me. Gently he places his arms around me and I'm so in need of comfort that I allow myself to sink into his chest and start to cry. He rocks me backwards and forwards, patiently waiting for my tears to subside. He thinks it's the least he can do because he thinks he's the cause of my tears. But he's not. I'm crying for Adam. I'm crying with regret at my own actions, not Scott's.

He whispers, 'I can't love you any more than I do right now.'

And that might be true. But it's not the comfort he wants it to be.

He says he's sorry. He says it over and over again. He says it so often his voice is hoarse. He hums his songs to me. He kisses my tears away as they fall down my cheek. He asks how he can make it up to me and in the end I start to feel bad about allowing him to shoulder all the blame for my sadness. He talks about his inadequacies and frailties; he reminds me that he warned me he was weak and stupid, he warned me weeks ago.

'You didn't tell me I was part of your plan to conquer America,' I point out.

'Don't be like that. Don't think of it like that. Don't think of it,' he pleads. 'You understand. You understand me.'

'Maybe,' I mutter. And maybe I do. Maybe I understand how you can want something so, so much that you fail to notice the consequences it might have on the people around you. Because isn't that what I did when I backed Adam into a corner with that damned ultimatum?

'Don't go, Fern, don't leave me on my own,' he begs.

'You won't be on your own, Scott, you'll be with this ocean of people who wash up every morning. You'll be with Ben,' I point out.

'Ben,' he mutters. He rolls my friend's name on his tongue like a delicious sweet. I glance up at Scott and I think I see indisputable regret in his face. What I can't be sure of is whether the regret is that he slept with Ben or that he won't have the opportunity to do so again.

Somehow we wiggle about and I find that he's no longer holding me, I am holding him now. His head is resting on my lap and, as I stroke his hair, it's easy to forget that he was unfaithful to me, on this very bed, just hours ago. It's possible to overlook the fact that he's a mega pop star who needs me to launch his career here in the States. It's almost feasible to submerge all recollection of the fact that I too have been unfaithful tonight; I begged Adam to take me back. To take me.

I remember being out-of-this-world giddy and irreparably starstruck by Scottie Taylor when we first met, but now I see him for what he is. When he's lying with his head on my thighs, all I see is a man. A man who is actually a bit boy-like. I try to remember everything we have talked about in the last six weeks. I remember how he described his ambitions and his addictions. He warned me. And I remember that he's given me the ride of my life, although not quite the ride I was expecting – but at least he wanted me to hitch along. I remember moments when he trusted me, defended me and, right at the beginning, spent lots of time with me. True, we don't play cards much now, but then I think I know all there is to know about hearts versus diamonds and clubs versus spades. On Santa Monica beach and at the premiere we had a blast.

I think maybe we might manage. There's enough affection to see us through and although this isn't exactly the fairytale ending I was hoping for, I could do worse than marry Scott. He could do worse than marry me. It could be worse.

'It's not exactly like I've been unfaithful,' he points out carefully. 'You and I haven't actually had sex yet and tomorrow, after the wedding, we will and it'll be like starting again.'

'Ben thinks you are only marrying me as a PR stunt. Is that true?'

'This is why I like you, Fern. Other women wouldn't care. They'd take me any old way,' he replies, neatly side-stepping the issue.

I force the point by remaining silent; after what seems like a millennium he admits, 'It's part of the reason I wanted to marry you but I could have married anyone. You are a gorgeous girl from a flower shop, but I'm always going to be meeting gorgeous girls from flower shops or clothes shops or some sort of bloody shop – I chose you.'

It is some reassurance, yet we are not in the clear. 'Ben thinks you're gay.'

Scott sits up, puts his hand up and cups my chin. 'Honestly, I don't know whether I'm gay or straight.'

And I see it there with absolute certainty – he's telling me the truth. We might not be one another's first choice but, miles away from where we both started, we certainly seem like we're all we've got. He wants a home, he wants a family, he says that hasn't changed. Weeks ago, I gave up on Adam. I threw him away. I can't risk making the same mistake twice.

An orange glow is squelching into my bedroom, the sun is getting up. It's my wedding day. Or is it? I'm too fractured to think clearly. Too shattered to stand alone. I can't reason, and with every sunbeam that sneaks through the blinds I'm conscious I'm running out of time. I feel a lot like I did when I was presented with the pre-nup and again when I heard about the tour. I can't stop the bulldozer. Do I really have a choice?

'I don't really care. I just want you to be faithful. Mine. Just mine,' I admit.

'Really?' He looks surprised.

'Forget the labels. Gay, or straight, or bi, or experimental.' I offer a minute smile. 'Or, if you must wear a label, wear one saying "Happy".'

He smiles. It's his slow, irresistibly sexy smile. 'What's yours say?' he asks. 'Doc?'

I sigh and tell myself I'm doing the right thing. 'I don't mind as long as it doesn't say Dopey.'

71. Fern

Scott falls asleep on my lap. Before I know it my entire room is bathed in bright light and birds are singing outside my window. As I haven't managed a wink of sleep, my eyes sting and my head is pounding, the birds' gleeful twittering sounds like nails scraping down a blackboard. At six Scott slips away and at six thirty Colleen raps on my bedroom door and bursts in. My personal trainer is with her too.

'You look terrible,' says Colleen. 'I don't suppose you got any sleep last night – too excited, huh?'

'Something like that,' I mutter.

'Well, don't worry. The wedding isn't until eleven, we can fix *everything* by then.' I doubt it, but can't bring myself to squash her enthusiasm. 'Let's forget the three-kilometre run, you can have a massage instead. I'll call Linda and Natalie. Then a bath, exfoliation, a power shower, manicure, pedicure . . .' She consults her clipboard. She has a plan that is timed to the nearest thirty seconds and accounts for the next four and a half hours. I'm grateful to be swept along by her momentum.

My room is like Piccadilly Circus at rush hour; even though the place is enormous it's soon jam-packed, there's little room to breathe out. Hot on the heels of Colleen and my personal trainer, Saadi and her assistants arrive. Saadi discreetly calls Lisa to update her on my decision to go ahead. She asks her to inform my family and to urge everyone to attend as planned. 'It's important for the press,' she says. The assistants are quickly despatched to complete various essential tasks – such as checking the beading on the napkin rings, measuring the distance between the tealights on the stairwells and ensuring that cones of lavender buds have been placed on the back of each and every seat in the reception room. Linda, Natalie, Joy and a hair stylist arrive to give me a massage and do my makeup and hair; between them they carry enough boxes of hair product and cosmetics to open a chain of salons. I dip my fingers into buttery creams and slosh velvet lotions on to my limbs. It's somewhat soothing. Two people from Jenny Packham's studios arrive to help me into the dress. They hang the gown from the top of the wardrobe and everyone pauses for a moment to sigh in reverence. It's exquisite. Swathes of oyster-hued silk overlaid with vintage organza swish in a relaxed and feminine bias cut. The dress is made unfeasibly glam due to the addition of intricate beading and crystals, hand-embroidered around the hem and neckline. It's so beautiful I want to cry. Mark pops by and gives me a rare hug. The florists, vicar and jeweller squeeze into my room too – to deliver my bouquet, advice and the two million dollars' worth of jewellery I'm borrowing for the day.

It's not until nearly ten that Jess and Lisa finally arrive; I was wondering whether they'd decided to stay away. They look pale and fraught but they dutifully start their own preparations for the wedding. I'd wanted them to get dressed with me. I'd imagined the scenario for ages; I'd thought we'd elegantly sip champagne through solid silver straws and chatter excitedly as we scrambled into our dresses. In fact they both desperately glug from bottles and huge silences stretch awkwardly between us, like unsuppressed yawns at a recital. I'm glad the jeweller insists he has to stick around until my hair is finished so he can examine the drop of the stones in relation to the curve of my neck; it makes it impossible for my friends to speak their minds openly. Instead they have to confine themselves to hissed, panicked whispers.

'You cannot be going ahead with this wedding,' says Jess.

From the look of disbelief and horror on her face I know Lisa has filled her in on the gory details.

'Yes, I am.' I keep my eyes on my own reflection and pretend to be totally absorbed in what Joy is doing with my makeup. Quite brilliantly, she's managed to hide the black shadows around my eyes. I make a mental note of what cosmetics she's using, it might be useful to know for the future.

'You must really love Scott,' murmurs Lisa. I doubt she means this, she probably thinks I'm marrying him for his money, but as it's my wedding day she's too polite to say so.

Colleen continually runs through a checklist of the details of the day; she's clearly suffering some sort of verbal incontinence. She yells, 'Has anyone seen the crates of customized silver foil white chocolate coins? They're monogrammed! I said *heart*-shaped marshmallows, these are more oval. The candelabras are all wrong. The ribbons and crystal butterflies should create a sweeping effect, this is more of a swooning effect!'

I don't involve myself with any triumphs or disappoint-
ments but concentrate on remaining calm as I dress. I
think about putting on my stockings without laddering
them. I focus on straightening my hair-clips and I think
about whether my mascara is waterproof. Waterproof
enough.

The room begins to settle. I'm told that guests have
arrived at the venue where the service is taking place; I'm
assured Scott is already waiting for me. The people who
have fussed and fawned over me all morning vanish;
suddenly I'm alone with Lisa, Jess and Colleen.

'You look beautiful,' smiles Lisa. As she fiddles with
my veil for the hundredth, unnecessary time.

Jess nods, her eyes brimming with tears. She leans close
to me and for a moment I think she's going to whisper
something urgent and profound; maybe something like,
'You don't have to do this.' But she doesn't, she just drops
the lightest kiss on my cheek and says, 'Yeah, you look
really gorgeous.'

I gather my veil and my thoughts, buckle up the most
dainty, most beautiful strappy, diamanté sandals and step
outside where I find a waiting horse-drawn carriage. All
six horses are white; their coats are sleek and worthy of
an appearance in any fairytale. The carriage is entirely
covered with colourful peonies, gerberas and fat, loose
roses, as I specified. The road is strewn with petals, as
I'd dreamed. Crowds of Scott's fans line the streets, as I
could never have imagined. Most are screaming their good
wishes, some girls are sobbing or their mouths are twisted
in disappointment and fury. I don't know whether to wave
at them or ignore them. Lisa and Jess are sat opposite

me but they don't look at me; they stare at the flowers and the crowds but neither makes any comments. I suppose I'd always thought Mum and Dad would escort me to my wedding ceremony but Colleen didn't think they'd look as good as Jess and Lisa in the photos; besides, I'm not even sure they are still coming to my wedding now and I daren't ask.

After a few short minutes, we pass the media scrum and leave the press and disappointed fans behind security barriers. The horses' hoofs stop click-clacking as we draw to a halt.

'This is it then.' I beam at my friends. They nod and force smiles that bunch up their cheeks but they can't push the smiles as high as their eyes. This *is* it. Or at least, this is as near *it* as I'm ever going to get.

Lisa helps me out of the carriage; she still looks unusually white and drawn, the professional makeover doesn't seem to have done its job. I turn to Jess. I always imagined my friends giggling and beaming and making jokes about the wedding night. I guess that's a tricky one now, under the circumstances.

Jess stares resolutely at the floor and blurts at the gravel, 'You are so obviously still in love with Adam.'

'He didn't want me. Nothing's changed there.'

'Yes, it has.' Now she does meet my eye but I can't see happiness or confidence, just concern and sincerity. 'He's grown up such a lot. He has the band and he's bought a —'

'I know he's changed and grown up in many ways but he still doesn't want me. *That* hasn't changed.'

'I think he does want you.'

'No, he doesn't. I asked him.'

'Oh.' Jess and Lisa look crushed by this news. The hems of their dresses flutter so prettily in the light breeze. We look gorgeous. I wish it was a more gorgeous moment.

I spell it out. 'I don't have a choice.'

'There's always a choice,' insists Jess. I love Jess in this moment because she is taking an enormous risk. She's being brave and honest. I'm breaking her heart by making what she considers to be the wrong decision. I feel duty bound to cheer her up.

'Scott's not a bad man. He's just complex,' I assure them.

'Gay?'

'Maybe.'

'Oh, Fern.'

'Don't, Jess.' I hold up my hand. I can't hear any more from her. I can't give up Scott. And it's not the clothes, shoes and lifestyle that are pulling me. He's my only option. 'You've been great, Jess. You've done everything you could. You brought Adam here. You tried to make me jealous. You've pointed out how he's grown and his new successes. You've been the best friend. But –'

The 'but' is swallowed by a click of the camera as the reportage photographer captures the moment.

'I love the moment the bride soars into the service,' he calls with a grin. 'It's a moment of such exquisite loveliness, a moment of intense possibility and unblighted hope. Isn't it?'

No one answers him.

72. Fern

I glide up the aisle and it is all so breathtakingly beautiful. The pews are packed with faces I recognize and even one or two people I know. As I get closer to the altar I smile and nod to neighbours, friends and family. My family have turned up, after all. I wonder whether they have accepted and approve of my decision to marry Scott or have just decided to support me because that's what family do – and besides, they all like a good party. I have no time to decide, as in a few short steps I'm face to face with Scott.

He looks wonderful. He's wearing a tailor-made Versace suit; it's a deep aubergine colour with a lime green lining. I'm not sure whether I knew this and had forgotten or whether I've ever shown much interest in what Scott was going to wear today. This man, this beautiful and complicated man, is about to become my husband and I'm so lucky. I really am. Ask Amanda Amberd.

Saadi stands up to do a reading. I'm surprised – it was supposed to be my sister, Fiona, who was going to do the first reading; she must have stage fright. I know she's here. She's sitting a few rows back in a pew to the left; I heard her crying when I walked down the aisle. Scott chose the reading and it's been kept a secret from me. I did insist that it wasn't Corinthians chapter 13. It's not that I have anything against that reading, it's just that I've heard it one hundred times and know it so well I no longer know it. I wanted Scott to choose something meaningful and unexpected so that I'd listen fastidiously. As Saadi painfully enunciates every word, in that overly precise way people do when they read aloud in church, I take careful note. The reading is called *Why Marriage?*

She coughs and looks my way. '*Why Marriage*, author unknown. *Why Marriage? Because to the depths of me, I long to love one person, with all my heart, my soul, my mind, my body.*' Saadi glances at her notes; she clearly hasn't been given much notice about doing the reading – I bet she's irritated. She's a professional; I know she'd have wanted to read this fluently and without prompts. She coughs and then carries on.

'*Why Marriage? Because I need a forever friend to trust with the intimacies of me, who won't hold them against me, who loves me when I'm unlikeable.*' The words are shockingly poignant. I prick up my ears. Scott chose this reading. Scott wants this from me. He's talking to me. '*Who sees the small child in me, and who looks for the divine potential of me.*'

I do, I do. I glance at Scott and we lock eyes. His green, sparkling, soul-slicing eyes are drilling into mine. I care for him, so much.

'*Because marriage means opportunity to grow in love, in friendship. Because marriage is a discipline to be added to a list of achievements.*'

Even if he'd written these words himself they could not have been more appropriate and moving. The aching disappointment that he did not write the *Wedding Album* songs for me is some way salved. He does care. So much.

'*I promise myself to take full responsibility for my spiritual, mental and physical wholeness, I create me.*' That part is a bit new age-y for my tastes, but it's still good. '*Why Marriage? Because I take half of the responsibility for my marriage. Together we create our marriage because with this understanding the possibilities are limitless.*'

Saadi sighs with relief at getting through the speech and then quickly returns to her seat. I play the words over and over in my head. 'I take half of the responsibility for my marriage. Together we create our marriage.'

Two of the little bridesmaids start to whisper and giggle. I don't know who the culprits are – maybe my nieces. Scott flashes an indulgent grin in their direction; even so, Saadi's third assistant leaps up and whisks them out of the service. I bet she's gutted to miss out on the ceremony.

The vicar is talking about how sure he is that Scott and I will have a marvellous day today, supported by all our guests. A prayer is said. A hymn sung. I float above all this. Breathing in the heavy scent of lilies and lavender, catching the odd, muffled 'oh' or 'ah' from the congregation, feeling the weight of my bouquet and my friends' concerned glances.

I take half of the responsibility for my marriage.

The vicar calmly intones on and on. He talks about the peace Scott and I have found in one another, but it doesn't resonate. Scott is offering me many things – peace isn't one of them. The vicar talks about hope and about life's quests – that makes more sense. I'm going to need buckets full of hope, and quest is another word for hunt, expedition or mission, isn't it? He goes on and on and on until –

'If any one of these people here present today knows of any reason why these two may not be joined in lawful matrimony, may they speak now or forever hold their peace.'

And I stop breathing.

I wait. I wait and I wait. I wait for my brain to make the connection as to exactly what it is I am waiting for. What? Am I waiting for the nail-biting moment to pass so that we can carry on and seal the deal? Or, truly, am I waiting for an interruption? Suddenly my head is full of sizzling messages that somehow won't compute; instead they scream mindlessly, causing greater confusion in my spaghetti-like mind.

I know.

I know what I want but I can hardly bear to acknowledge it – to feel it, even. I take half the responsibility for my marriage.

I know. I want my mum to stand up and tell them she never saw me living the kind of life where you can't find the loo door and you have to clap your hands to turn on the taps.

I know. I want Ben to stand up and tell them he loves Scott and that maybe Scott's gay and the wedding shouldn't go ahead. I look for Ben. He's nowhere to be seen. Where are you, Ben? I need you.

I know. Above all, what I want, what I really, dearly want is for Adam to stand up and tell them – tell me – that he loves me and that the wedding can't possibly go ahead. Is Adam even here? I couldn't see him among the bobbing heads as I walked down the aisle. I turn a fraction and try to sneak a glance at the congregation out of the corner of my eye. He's there! I see him sat next to Charlie. He's wearing a smart suit and a grim expression. But he's not standing up. He is not crying, 'Stop, this can't happen.' He's resolutely staring at the ceiling.

No one stands up for me. I look around and everybody looks beautiful. Everybody looks buffed and gleaming, and preened and pampered, if not a little uncomfortable.

Mark coughs; he wants the vicar to carry on but the vicar's noticed I'm crying and we're not talking a quiet little tear sailing gently down my cheek. An elegant single tear is expected from a bride, almost *de rigueur* for a Hollywood bride – quite fetching – but I'm sobbing. I'm sobbing hard and heavy tears are starting somewhere deep in my gut and exploding out over the vicar and through the congregation. I'm sobbing because this *isn't* my dream. I am not living the dream. At least not the one I wanted. I didn't dream of a thousand-guest wedding, I was going to do my own flowers.

I turn to Scott. And what does Scott want? Scott longs to love one person, with all his heart, his soul, his mind, his body. That's what was said in the reading. He wants this despite the odds, despite his pleas that he can't control himself, that he has intimacy issues and that infidelity is part of his makeup. Secretly, he wants one person. I'm *not* that person. Ben thinks he might be.

'I'm sorry,' I mutter. I do love him even when he's unlikeable, I do see the small child in him, just like the reading asked. But the love I feel is all about friendship. And while he's my only offer on the table and he's a very good offer, he's not the offer I want. He's not the one.

I have to take responsibility in and out of a marriage. I manage to squeak again, 'Sorry.'

Then I turn and run. I do the whole Cinderella thing, except I don't even leave a shoe. I dash from that church and I just keep running.

73. Fern

No one tries to stop me. The congregation is frozen with shock and confusion and I'm determined to escape, so despite my precarious heel height, I'm nimble. Besides, even in a moment of extreme crisis Mark has the sense to assess the situation; no doubt he realizes a bundle of hefty security guards tackling me to the floor is not going to help this PR disaster.

Frantically I search for a vehicle to get me away from this nightmare. The horses and carriage I arrived with won't cut it. I spot one of Scott's security guards in a black BMW.

'Change of plan,' I yell as I pull at his arm and drag him from the car. Terrified by my crazy, irrational behaviour he gives up the fight – and the car – immediately.

I drive and drive. I'm unsure where to go and initially I have no plan. I can't go directly to the airport, I don't have a passport and I'm wearing my wedding gown – that sort of thing causes quite a stir at airports. I don't want to go back to Scott's; I've just dumped him at the altar. I don't want to check into a hotel or go anywhere people might recognize me and call the press. The last thing I need now is a howling pack of paparazzi on my trail. I think of the places where I've been happy in LA. The Getty Center? Disneyland? I think I'm a little overdressed to merge into the crowds at either of those places. Suddenly, it comes to me. I know where I should go. Not somewhere I've visited yet but somewhere I've ached to see: the Los Angeles flower district – home of the most enormous flower market. Flowers soothe. Flowers heal. I desperately need to be among dozens and dozens of fresh, therapeutic, calming blooms.

I haven't done much driving in America since I arrived here, I've always had Barry to ferry me around, but, from the passenger seat, I've managed to pick up the majority of the city's geography. I thank God for the US grid pattern; their roads are so logical and uncomplicated, it doesn't take long before I am heading downtown towards the flower district in Wall Street.

I park the car as close as I can to the block-long row of stalls. The attendant notes my attire and asks laughingly whether a delivery failed to show. I don't find the words to answer but instead start to float towards the beautiful scent of lush blooms that signposts what I anticipate to be a staggering array of flowers.

I spot a huge, open warehouse. I can already see stall after stall of colourful amaryllis, hydrangeas, chrysanthemums and gerberas; the sight of them is the equivalent of seeing a good friend holding a glass of wine and a bar of chocolate. A plump, smiley lady asks me for a two-dollar entrance fee. I mutter that I'm not carrying any money. She shrugs and says, 'Well, it's late, we're closing up anyways soon. You might as well go on in there.'

I try to smile to convey my thanks.

'Nice dress,' she adds. 'Don't get it wet.'

The bustling activity I normally expect to encounter at a flower market has started to subside. No doubt most of the day's trading has been completed; growers, shippers, wholesalers, distributors, floral designers, event planners and retail florists will have poured through these doors this morning, even earlier than Colleen surged into my bedroom. Now there are just a few non-commercial customers wandering around. Women who are throwing dinner parties this weekend looking for deals on the flora for their centrepieces and some guys buying bouquets for their mothers and lovers. There are a few couples; most look newly engaged. Brides-to-be can be easily identified because they are generally stressed but determined; the grooms-to-be are romantic but clueless and together they search for floral inspiration for their big day. More than one bride-to-be looks at me with horror and suspicion, then takes a wide berth as though I'm bad luck. Admittedly, I must be a sight. I'm wearing the most exquisite wedding gown ever created and I'm wearing my mascara in panda bear patches. I probably do look unlucky.

On the other hand, the burly men who are closing up their stalls barely give me a second glance. Perhaps they've seen other brides wander among their flowers like lost ghosts. I watch the stallholders' efficient and confident actions as they pack and stack empty crates, hose the floor and load up their vans. I'm soothed by the familiarity of their simple, uncomplicated work. I've missed the clank of trolleys, the thud of plastic buckets clunking on wet cement floor and the noisy blaring radios pulsing in the background. LA flower market has its own flavour. In

Covent Garden I used to be surrounded by robust, cheeky cockneys; here there is a melody of languages, Spanish, Chinese, Singaporean – the effect is mystical and exotic.

I wander aimlessly around the vast market, concentrating on nothing other than breathing deeply. I cross my arms in front of my body and frantically rub my hands up and down my arms, over and over again, in a hopeless effort to warm up. I'm freezing because I'm wearing a scant, shimmery number and there are dozens of huge fridges, introduced to keep the flowers cool on piping hot days, but this slight physical discomfort hardly matters. What have I done?

I realize I've probably ruined Scott's career, although I know I haven't broken his heart – it doesn't belong to me. By running out on the wedding I've wasted hundreds of thousands of pounds and I've passed up the opportunity to enjoy millions more. As soon as the world's press gets hold of the story everyone will agree that I am the most stupid, ungrateful woman on the planet.

But the more I stare at orchids wrapped like newborn babies – with tenderness and padding – and the deeper I breathe in the elegant fragrance of radiant ranunculus, which refreshes my lungs after so many dark smoky days behind closed doors, the more I think I've just done the bravest and best thing in my life. I thought my future was all about a wedding but it's not. When I saw Scott on stage he seemed to offer an escape route. I should have recognized it for what it was; a stonking great crush. I got carried away. No, I ran away. There's a difference.

I watch a group of voluble and raucous Mexican guys

selling irises; they are wearing a uniform of chunky gold jewellery, tight T-shirts emblazoned with slogans and baggy pants. They don't look poor but they are a long way from wealthy. Ordinary. They look happy. Which makes them extraordinary. I wonder what my ordinary will be?

The question pops into my head, despite my resolute efforts to block any soul-searching. I concentrate hard on the startling amaryllis and the delicate dendrobium orchids. But the harsh realities won't go away. I have no boyfriend, no job, no home, no future. These facts are icy cold and can't be softened, even by confident lisianthus. The flowers begin to swim in front of me. I realize I'm crying when I almost fail to recognize the peonies that are laid out in rows, ranging from the palest, most tender pinks to hot, urgent crimson.

I slump down on the cold floor and practically hug the nearest crate of blooms.

'Good God, Fern, that was quite an exit. Haven't they taught you anything here? It's a dramatic *entrance* that a girl is meant to make.' His voice pours through the noise. He's found me.

74. Fern

'Oh Adam, I've fucked it up,' I wail.

'I dunno. I think that was the most sensible thing you've done in six weeks — well, that and the new hair, it really suits you.'

I splutter a laugh despite the overwhelming misery that's ripping through my gut. It's not a good idea as it happens, because snot comes out of my nose — never a great look. 'I don't mean leaving him. I mean —'

I mean leaving Adam but I can't tell him that. I did leave him and now he doesn't want me, he said so last night. Quite clearly. Unequivocally. I have to avoid talking about us. I don't want to frighten him away. I need a friend right now. I'd hate it if he became embarrassed or offended and left me here alone. I put him on the spot yesterday and it didn't work, there is no point in going down that route again. Ever again. You can't go backwards, he said that. I don't finish the sentence. My face flushes with mortification and regret. I clear my throat and scramble around for something neutral to talk about — a pointless exercise in the circumstances, not unlike making polite small talk at a wake.

'How did you find me?' I ask.

'Everyone is searching for you all over the city, but I knew you'd need flowers. You always said they help you think. And once I got here I thought I'd find you near the peony stall.'

'Because they're my favourite flower?'

'No, because legend has it that mischievous nymphs like to hide in the petals of peonies, causing this magnificent bloom to be given the meaning of shame or bashfulness in the language of flowers,' he replies.

Is he calling me a mischievous nymph? And if he is, is that a good thing? I shake my head. This is not the moment for innuendo and analogies; we're confused enough. Another thought strikes me: since when did Adam know so much about flowers? I stare at him, dumbfounded. 'How do you know that?'

'You told me,' he says, looking awkward.

Did I? I'd forgotten. 'When?'

'Forever ago.'

I blush again, newly doused with shame and regret. Is it possible we once talked about the meaning of flowers? How could I have forgotten that? How did I let that slip away?

Adam notices I'm scarlet and comments, 'You look like one of these peony flowers, right now. You know, the same colour.'

He's looking at me with an intensity that is making me wilt. I scramble about my brain for something neutral to say; something that won't betray regret or wistfulness. Something that is impossible to misinterpret; a comment which cannot have a deeper meaning read into it. Some plain speaking.

'Peonies tend to attract ants to the flower buds. This is due to the nectar that forms on the outside of the buds,' I say authoritatively.

'Are you calling me an ant?'

'No!' Failed there then – he still read more into my comment than I meant him to. I try to explain. 'I'm just saying that however perfect they look there's always a drawback.'

'Are you talking about Scott?'

'No! I was trying to talk about nothing!' I sigh, defeated.

'Really?'

'Yes.'

'Oh, yeah, that'll be right, you don't do talking. You run, don't you,' says Adam. Oh bugger, didn't see that coming. Adam glares at me. Any compassion I thought I detected has been swallowed by anger. He shakes his head wearily. 'I didn't know what I'd done wrong, Fern. I *still* don't know what went wrong. I woke up one day and that was our last and I never even knew it. We were doing fine, Fern, weren't we?'

I can't answer. I want to look away from him because his pain is burning in his eyes and it's obvious in the small, tight lines around his mouth too. But I don't look away, it would be too selfish, I should see what I've caused. He continues.

'Well, I thought we were and then you left. You just weren't there any more. People shouldn't just bale out when the going gets tough. People should stay put and work stuff out. People should talk things through.'

'I tried to talk to you,' I offer gently, weakly.

'You gave me one ultimatum and you didn't even stick around long enough to see how I'd respond.'

'I'm sorry.'

'Well, that's good to know,' he says sarcastically. 'And now you've run away again.'

'I thought you approved of me running out on Scott.'

'I'm glad you're not marrying the man but there were better ways to tell him.'

'I'm sorry,' I repeat.

'Yeah, I'm sure Scott will be stoked to hear that.'

'He slept with Ben,' I point out.

'You knew that yesterday. You could have called it off yesterday before the cameras were rolling.'

'It's complicated.'

'Life is.' Adam spits out the words and stares in front of him. He looks irritated. Nearly all the flowers and stalls are packed away now; the warehouse looks bleak. I get the feeling that pretty soon someone is going to brush us up with the bits of stray foliage and sweep us into the bin. 'Why didn't you finish it yesterday?' asks Adam.

'Because you didn't want me,' I reply with a heavy sigh. I'm not delirious about admitting this but what is the point of trying to save face at this stage? 'And I didn't have the courage to leave without you. Or, at least, I thought I didn't.'

We sit silently side by side. Him in a smarter suit than I have ever seen him wear – in fact, the only suit I have ever seen him wear – and me in a gown that cost six months' salary, but we don't look as grand and refined as we ought. We look bizarrely out of place in among the empty trestle tables.

Adam looks nervous but strangely elated. I can almost

see his thoughts whirling around his head. I wonder what he's thinking? I wonder whether he'll let me move back into the old flat, just for a while, just as friends; I could sleep on the sofa. But even as the plan begins to take shape in my head I know this idea is hopeless. I could never sleep near Adam without sleeping with him. We'd never have managed a chastity vow. My limbs are stiff with the cold now and my eyes are stinging from lack of sleep and the constant drip of tears but I know that sooner or later I'm going to have to pick myself up and brush myself down.

I'm going to have to start all over again.

Alone.

Adam coughs. I think he's thinking the same thing. He's probably cold too and suffering from pins and needles because he's scrunched down next to me. I wait for him to tell me I have to get on with it.

'You know yesterday, when I was talking about my band and I said that they'll never make number one because that stuff doesn't happen to me, I'm not a number one sort of guy?'

'Yes, I remember.'

'The thing is, Fern, that sort of stuff doesn't happen to me because, truthfully, I don't want it enough. I don't want it at the cost of everything else and that's how much you have to want it in this business. That's how much Scott wants it. He deserves his success and all that comes with it.' His tone is slightly scathing. I don't think there is any love lost between Adam and Scott. 'But you know, maybe they might get into the top forty. Maybe number twenty-six or something around that mark.'

'Yeah, you said.'

'I'm just saying it again, so that you are clear. I'm not going to be a stonking, raving, unequivocal success. I'm more average than that.'

'I know, Adam.'

And that's why we could have a chance, if he'd allow it. I look at him and try to understand exactly what he's saying. I listen very, very carefully. Is he saying what I think he's saying? Is he managing my expectations? That would mean he is at least allowing me to have expectations. How far away is starting again? Millions of miles or just around the corner?

I lean closer and closer towards him. He stops talking and I stay silent. My mouth is just inches away from his. I can feel his warm breath heat my being. Just an inch apart now. His delicious lips are right there, a nose length away.

He pulls back. The space he leaves between us is a world. Or should I say, the space I put between us is a world. He doesn't want me. If he did, that was his moment. He could have kissed me here, among the buckets of flowers. I've blown it. I start to cry again. I wish I wouldn't. It's girly and weak and messy but I can't stop myself. I don't know how I'll make it through this.

'Why are you crying now?' he asks with a touch of impatience. It's agony that even his impatience thrills me; everything about him is familiar and straightforward.

'Because I've lost everything. I've thrown away everything.' I give in to the big, ugly sobbing once again.

'You don't know what the future holds, Fern. You never know, in a year's time you might look back at all of this and, well, laugh about it.'

I stare at him as though he's insane.

'OK, maybe not laugh exactly,' he concedes. 'But it might not seem like the end of the world if you were sitting in your lovely two, maybe even three, bedroom home in – I don't know – let's be realistic, the wrong end of Clapham. Not a bad place for a starter home.'

'Not at all.' I sniff, momentarily giving in to this fantasy he's describing.

'And you might be pregnant and my band will have made a bit of cash, maybe I'll have more than one group to manage by then.'

Pregnant? How? That's stupid. How could I have met and fallen in love with someone and decided to have a child with them in that short time? Looking at Adam right now, I can't imagine doing even the first part of that scenario. How could I meet anyone else when I'm in love with Adam? And I am in love with Adam. What I feel for him is not a three-day infatuation, ignited behind closed doors in Wembley, already cooling as I flew across the Atlantic. What I feel for Adam is not a fairytale, it's a love story. There's a difference.

'And you know what else? Scott and Ben will have invited us to their wedding. They'll be our best friends again.'

Us to their wedding. *Our* best friends. Did I hear that right?

'Us? But yesterday, I asked you if you would take me back? And you said no. You said you can't go backwards.'

'I said I didn't want to be the guy you ran back to, but being the guy you ran towards, well, that's a different thing.' Adam isn't looking at me; he's still staring straight ahead. This level of emotional chat is clearly more than he's comfortable with. It's not his fault, it's his Y chromosome. To his credit, he battles on. 'I couldn't ask you to give it all up for me, Fern. All of that. I couldn't risk that one day you'd turn round and hate me for making you do that. But then you gave it up because it didn't suit *you*. If you'd been the type of girl who could have gone through with that farce then I had you all wrong and I didn't want that, Fern. You had to work it out on your own, girl. I was so proud of you back there. You looked so brave and strong, telling the hottest rock singer and songwriter Britain has ever produced, the world press and your thousand guests to fuck off.' Adam's smiling now; it's a broad, uninhibited smile. The best smile I've seen from him, or anyone for that matter, in months.

'I didn't say that exactly,' I say with a small, shy grin.

'You sort of did.'

Once again we lapse into silence. I don't know exactly what to say. I don't want to rush at him, force anything, move too quickly or set any deadlines. None of these things would be right. Instead we both sit and enjoy the moment. I breathe in the smell of foliage and peonies.

'Hey guys, we're closing up now. You have to get on your way,' calls out the guy who owns the peony stall. Adam and I scramble to our feet and splutter apologies for inconveniencing him by delaying his packing-up. The guy shrugs, not worried, not bothered.

We start to walk out of the warehouse and towards the bright LA streets. Adam puts his arm around me. It feels just the right weight.

'Tell me some more about how it might work out,' I say. 'You know, the future you imagine, tell me more about that. Do you really think Ben and Scott might make it?'

'OK, well, let's imagine Ben is right that Scott is gay, and you are wrong to assume he was just experimenting or indulging.'

'But Ben still doubts Scott's ability to be faithful,' I point out.

'Ah, but *you* might be right about Scott there. You've always maintained that as soon as Scott finds the right person he'll settle down. Maybe he'll be content and complete with Ben. Other people might catch Scott's eye but they won't turn his head.'

'And the American market? Is his career over?'

'No way. *Wedding Album* will go to number one. First, he can really play the jilted lover bit. That will get the sympathy gushing in and then he will tell the world he's gay. The Americans will love Scott's sincerity, you know, especially if he comes out on *Oprah*. He'll storm America.' I smile, delighted with this idea.

'And Jess will meet someone really special and live happily ever after?' I add, just to tie up loose ends.

'Yeah, she will. It might be that guy from the Purple Lounge last night. She didn't get back to the hotel until four a.m. and she was wearing that crazy grin of hers.'

'I know the one. So, it will all be all right,' I confirm.

'Most of the time,' says Adam.

He pulls me towards him and we hold on to each other, enjoying our quiet moment in the baking sun. We stay like that for an age and then we break apart and set off towards the car.

'Do you have any money on you for the parking lot?' I ask.

'Yes.'

'Is it too soon to start scrounging off you?'

'No,' says Adam. 'I'm a manager of a band now, I can slip you a few dollars. As long as you pay me back, with interest,' he jokes.

'I'm broke,' I point out. 'And I don't have a job.'

'Maybe you can buy the B&B off Ben. If not, you'll have to pay me in kind,' he grins suggestively, and I feel a faint fluttering against the lining of my stomach as excitement and hope hiccup back into my soul.

'Sounds good.'

'It's too soon to propose, though, yeah?' he asks.

'A bit,' I admit.

'OK, I'll ask you tomorrow,' says Adam with a satisfied smile.

'You do that,' I beam back, smug in my ordinary ever after.

Acknowledgements

Enormous thanks go to Linda Di-Marcello for her generous support of Sparks, the children's medical research charity. Their sole remit is to fund research across the entire spectrum of paediatric medicine. Their goal is for all babies to be born healthy and stay healthy.

To learn more about Sparks, visit www.sparks.org.uk

Enormous thanks also go to Fern and Jim Dickson for their generous support of the Helen Feather Memorial Trust. The aims of the Trust are to support people with cancer and raise money for carefully selected Cancer Research projects.

To learn more about the Helen Feather Memorial Trust, visit www.helenfeathertrust.co.uk

LOVE LIES

Bonus material

Reading Group Questions

- In Chapter 10, Fern describes Scottie Taylor as 'the perfect fantasy man'. To what extent do you think this is true? Does this change as the story progresses?

- 'He showers me with stunning compliments in a way that seems casual and yet authentic.' How big a part do you think this played in Fern's attraction to Scott?

- Scott describes himself as having 'an addictive personality'. Do you agree?

- 'I need America. I have to have America. Above everything.' Looking at Scott's behaviour throughout the book, to what extent do you believe this is true?

- The papers described Fern as being very ordinary. Do you agree? Do you believe that Fern becomes, as she herself believes, 'no longer ordinary', once she is engaged to Scott?

- Scott describes some of his stories as 'painfully predictable'. How far do you think Scott has been seduced by fame?

- Fern claims she tried to talk to Adam before leaving. Do you think she was in the wrong to assume Adam was not going to propose, and too rash in her decision to leave?

- At the end of the book, Fern once again decides to go out with Adam. What is her main reason behind reigniting the relationship?

Have you read all of Adele's fabulously addictive novels?

ABOUT LAST NIGHT

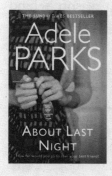

There is nothing best friends Steph and Pip wouldn't do for one another. That is, until Steph begs Pip to lie to the police as she's desperately trying to conceal not one but two scandalous secrets to protect her family. Her perfect life will be torn apart unless Pip agrees to this lie. But lying will jeopardise everything Pip's recently achieved after years of struggle. It's a big ask. How far would you go to save your best friend?

LOVE LIES

It's a girl's ultimate fantasy – being swept away by Prince Charming and living a life of luxury, wealth and celebrity. But after a whirlwind romance with pop star Scottie Taylor, modern-day Cinderella Fern must ask herself if love is telling the truth. Can she find her Happily Ever After in a world where there isn't much room for fairy tales?

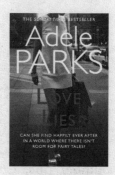

YOUNG WIVES' TALES

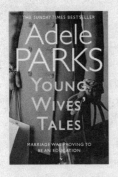

Lucy stole her friend Rose's 'happily ever after' because she wanted Rose's husband – and Lucy always gets what she wants. Big mistake. Rose was the ideal wife and is the ideal mother; Lucy was the perfect mistress. Now neither can find domestic bliss playing each other's roles. They need more than blind belief to negotiate their way through modern life. And there are more twists in the tale to come . . .

HUSBANDS

Love triangles are always complex but in Bella's case things are particularly so as she is *married* to both men in her triangle. She plans never to reveal her first marriage to husband number two Phillip – after all, Stevie is no longer part of her life. That is until, inconveniently, her best friend introduces her new man to Bella and it's none other than husband number one. Could things get more complicated? Well, only if Bella and Stevie fall for one another again . . .

STILL THINKING OF YOU

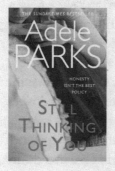

Tash and Rich are wild about each other; their relationship is honest, fresh and magical, so they dash towards a romantic elopement in the French Alps. However, five of Rich's old university friends crash the wedding holiday and they bring with them a whole load of ancient baggage. Can Tash hold on to Rich when she's challenged by years of complicated yet binding history and a dense web of dark secrets and intrigues? Does she even want to?

THE OTHER WOMAN'S SHOES

The Evergreen sisters have always been opposites with little in common. Until one day Eliza walks out on her boyfriend the very same day Martha's husband leaves her. Now the Evergreen sisters are united by separation, suddenly free to pursue the lifestyles they think they always wanted. So, when both find exactly what they're looking for, everybody's happy . . . aren't they? Or does chasing love only get more complicated when you're wearing another woman's shoes?

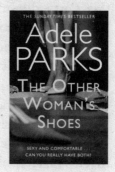

LARGER THAN LIFE

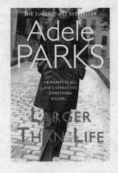

Georgina fell in love with Hugh the moment she first saw him and she's never loved another man. Unfortunately, for all that time he's been someone else's husband and father. After years of waiting on the sidelines, Georgina finally gets him when his marriage breaks down. But her dream come true turns into a nightmare when she falls pregnant and Hugh makes it clear he's been there, done that and doesn't want to do it all again. Georgina has to ask herself, is this baby bigger than the biggest love of her life?

GAME OVER

Cas Perry doesn't want a relationship. When her father walked out on her and her mother she decided love and marriage simply weren't worth the heartache. Cas, immoral most of the time and amoral when it comes to business, ruthlessly manipulates everyone she comes into contact with. Until she meets Darren. He believes in love, marriage, fidelity and constancy, so can he believe in Cas? Is it possible the world is a better place than she imagined? And if it is, after a lifetime of playing games, is this discovery too late?

PLAYING AWAY

Connie has been happily married for a year. But she's just met John Harding. Imagine the sexiest man you can think of. He's a walking stag weekend. He's a funny, disrespectful, fast, confident, irreverent pub crawl. He is also completely unscrupulous. He is about to destroy Connie's peace of mind and her grand plan for living happily ever after with her loving husband Luke. Written through the eyes of the adulteress, *Playing Away* is the closest thing you'll get to an affair without actually having one.

She thought he was definitely the one.
But what about the one before?

Read on for a preview of
Adele Parks' novel
MEN I'VE LOVED BEFORE

1

Nat picked up her BlackBerry. Its smooth, cool, shininess was instantly soothing; once again she ran through the 'Birthday To Do List'. It wasn't that she was a neurotic controlling type, she told herself; it was just that it was important to her that Neil's birthday was absolutely perfect. Actually, she was a neurotic controlling type but luckily her husband rather liked it in her, he recognised that her organisation skills propped up his tendency towards the chaotic.

1) Confirm cake has been delivered to restaurant. Check.

She'd already called the Bluebird restaurant and verified that the moist chocolate cake with lavish marshmallow stack had safely arrived in the kitchen. It had been delivered by a neighbour of her parents who, coincidentally, had been coming into town to see a new exhibition at the Tate Modern and (according to her mother) really didn't mind making the diversion to drop off the cake. It was true people tended to like doing things for Nina. It had taken some negotiation to convince the restaurant chef to allow Nina's home-made cake into his inner sanctum in the first place. But Natalie was very persuasive when she needed to be and she considered her husband's thirty-fifth birthday such an occasion. Neil would not think his birthday complete without a cake baked by his mother-in-law.

The Bluebird restaurant on the King's Road in the heart of Chelsea was undeniably stylish, but the obvious sophistication and daring modernity was not at all intimidating because some clever interior designer had chosen warm, rich colours and subtle lighting which created a relaxed and intimate ambience. Nat had thought it the perfect place for cocktails and dinner with friends. Neil would appreciate the modern British menu; he always had to stop off at the chippie if they ate at a nouvelle cuisine restaurant or at a sushi bar.

While she'd been on the phone, Nat had also checked that the reservation was for 7.15p.m., *not* 7.30p.m. She'd once read a tip in a magazine about how to ensure great service in a restaurant and she'd been struck by the suggestion of making a booking for quarter past or quarter to the hour, as the vast majority of the general public arrived at restaurants on the hour or half past. Nat had never bothered to follow the tip before, but tonight she was keen that everything (including service) was heavenly.

2) Confirm time of reservation. Check.

Whilst on the phone she'd also changed the reservation for eight people to six. Neil's brother's wife, Fi, had called this morning to cancel – again. Babysitting issues – again. Nat was disappointed, for herself and especially for Neil. She knew he'd have loved to have had his big brother there tonight, not least because Ben was always rather good at discreetly mediating between Tim (Neil's oldest friend) and Karl (Neil's most fun friend). Despite the fact that Neil, Tim and Karl saw each other socially at least once a week, from what Nat had witnessed over the past seven years, it was clear that, other than a deep and enduring affection for Neil, Neil's best mates didn't have that much in common. Neil appeared to be unaware of the slight tension and tussle of their being a threesome, or at least he did a damn good impression of seeming so. He was happiest when everyone just got along.

After Nat had informed the restaurant about the alteration to the number of guests she was expecting, she'd also made sure that the sommelier's selection still included Chenas Cuvée Quartz, Piron & Lafontthe. She was quite nervous about her pronunciation of the wine's name but the last time she and Neil had visited Bluebird (well, the only other time, in fact) he'd commented how much he liked the wine and she'd taken note of it so she could try to track it down in a supermarket.

3) Confirm availability of Chenas Cuvée Quartz. Check.

She could almost feel the maître d' rolling his eyes in exasperation through the telephone. No doubt he thought she was horribly painful and was probably contemplating instructing the kitchen staff to spit in her soup. Nat didn't care. All she cared about was giving Neil a great night. Nat never got so excited about her own birthdays; actually she preferred to ignore them altogether, that date wasn't much cause for celebration, but Neil's birthday was something special. The day Neil came into this world was really important, at least to her. Not that she was given to saying such sloppy things; she preferred to show her feelings through her actions. That's why she wanted tonight to be wonderful.

The sun had cooperated, which was a bonus. It had been a hot and hazy day, the warmth still snuggled in the London pavements and brickwork and in the smiles of people who spilled outside pubs, beer bottle and fag in hand. Nat loved the lively sun-induced chatter that erupted between strangers, she loved the brightly coloured clothes that, like butterflies, could only be spotted in London for a fleeting summer moment, and she loved blasts of the smell of suntan lotion on warm skin. Despite Neil's birthday landing in late August, there was never an absolute guarantee that they'd enjoy sunshine on the day. The likelihood of a British BBQ summer was about parallel to actually spotting a UFO or that of a woman over forty being complimented on her beauty without the compliment being accompanied by the deadening caveat, 'for her age'. Nat remembered Neil's thirty-third birthday with horrible clarity. She'd arranged for them to enjoy a gourmet picnic in their local park, Ravenscourt; they'd practically had to use the hamper as a lifeboat because of flash floods. Then there was the year that she'd thought it might be fun to go to Brighton and eat fish and chips on the front. In her mind she'd imagined them wandering, hand in hand, along the pier. She'd expected bare, sun-kissed shoulders and flip-flops. In fact they'd needed to wear wellington boots as they bravely strode along the pebbles and, ultimately, they were driven back inside the hotel because of the bitingly cold sea wind. Still, the hotel had been cosy, there were compensations. Nat started to think fondly of the fireside loving they'd enjoyed in their Brighton suite – which brought her to item four on the 'Birthday To Do List'.

4) Wear matching underwear.

Nat reached into her underwear drawer, rummaged around and then pulled out a flesh-coloured bra and knickers set which was edged with cream lace. Perfect. Dressy enough to show that she'd made an effort but comfortable and wouldn't show through her blouse. Check.

Natalie wanted to look her best. Dressing up was fun and she always believed preparing for a night out was part of the joy of the event. During her lunch hour she'd dashed to the hairdressers for a blow dry and last night she'd squeezed in a quick visit to the local beautician and undergone the masochistic act of having a bikini and half-leg wax. She'd thought longingly of the wonderful pampering treatments on offer. She'd have loved an Indian head massage or a rehydrating facial but Nat was aware that no matter what beauty miracles might be achieved through an hour in the floatation tank or a quick rub-down with hot stones, Neil would be more impressed by a tidy vadge and, after all, it was his birthday.

Despite the fact that Nat had an important and nerve-wracking meeting with her boss in the morning she'd slipped out of work at exactly 5p.m. today; an unusual occurrence as Nat loved her job at the world's largest pharmaceutical company and often worked much longer hours than those specified on her contract. She was happy to run the extra mile whenever asked (or even without being asked) as she believed what she did was life-changing and contributed to society at a profound level. Although, obviously, this was not an opinion she often voiced as she was aware that doing so would, at best, make her sound self-consciously worthy (which was unfashionable) and at worst make her sound self-congratulatory and smug (which was unattractive).

She'd dashed home to shower, slather her body in moisturiser and pull on a fresh outfit. Home was a modest but stylish two up, two down terraced home in Chiswick, west London. Nat and Neil both loved living in Chiswick, a leafy, villagey sort of place, awash with bistros, trees, arty types and, less romantically but quite certainly, stuffed with commuters, Starbucks franchises and estate agents. They embraced both aspects of Chiswick life, the cool chic and the convenience. Proud and thrilled to have got on the property ladder at all, they were both delighted to be living in such a desirable part of London. They'd chosen to live in Chiswick because it was so convenient for both of their places of work. Nat's office was in Brentford, less than three miles west of Chiswick, and Neil's office was right next door to Goldhawk Road tube station, just two miles east. Neil had argued that the extra they spent on rent was offset because they barely had any commuter costs, they could even walk to work, he'd said somewhat optimistically. They rarely did so, they usually opted to stay in bed for an extra ten minutes and catch the bus. His figures didn't add up but Nat also desperately wanted to live in Chiswick and so was prepared to pay the inflated rents if they had to.

They had rented the house from the relative of an elderly woman who had been seeing out her days in a residential home. She died six months before their wedding and her relatives, keen for a quick sale, gave Nat and Neil first refusal on the property and offered it at a knockdown price. Nat and Neil had snapped it up; after all, for months they had been imagining and speculating as to what they would do with the property if it was theirs. As soon as they had the deeds, they started to strip the pink flowered wallpaper and painted the walls in taupe and beige shades. They ripped up the tatty carpets and varnished and polished the floorboards that secretly lay below. They painted the front door an imposing black and Nat spent a week online choosing a new knocker and letter box. Instead of a conventional wedding list, they asked their guests if they'd mind giving B&Q or Ikea vouchers, and before their first anniversary they had the kitchen and bathroom replaced. They had potted plants on the window sills and blinds rather than curtains in every room. They had their perfect home.

They lived in a small, thin road, south of Chiswick High Road. True, they could always hear the A4 traffic whizz or chug by (the speed of the traffic was time-dependent, but it was safe to say there were snarls during most daylight hours) yet the noise was more than compensated for by the fact that they were a short walk away from Ravenscourt Park, if they ever craved greenery, a stone's throw away from countless trendy bars and cute chichi shops, if they ever needed to buy anything pretty, tasty or luxurious, and for Nat, the best thing of all about Chiswick was that it was nestled right next to one of the long, lazy loops of the River Thames. She often dragged Neil out of bed on a Sunday morning so that they could amble along the Chiswick Mall, a road lined with elegant and shockingly expensive houses, which had the pleasure of overlooking the Thames. The houses ranged in style from Georgian to gingerbread; the thing they had in common was that all the residents enjoyed tremendous views of the river.

She had hoped to meet Neil at home this evening so that they could go to the restaurant together. Truthfully, she had thought that maybe, somewhere between applying the body moisturiser and picking out what she'd wear tonight, they might have the opportunity to make love. It wasn't that Nat was expecting to swing from the chandeliers on this hot evening; she would have been extremely content with something more straightforward, something satisfying in the missionary position, perhaps. Neil invariably left his office the moment the clock struck five. He loved his work too, he worked as a video games designer, an ambition he'd had since he was a kid and discovered Pac-Man and Donkey Kong in a seaside arcade when he was on a family holiday in Blackpool, but he never saw the need to linger in the office. He could play games at home and call it research. Nat had thought he'd be home early enough for them to enjoy some lovely birthday sex and still get to the restaurant on time. Sex before the birthday dinner was preferable to sex after the birthday dinner because the important meeting with her boss tomorrow meant that Nat wanted to avoid a very late night if at all possible.

Nat was aware that it was a thin line between being organised and squashing all artless and joyful spontaneity. Everyone knew spontaneity was a great thing to have in a relationship – in a personality, come to that – so she really wished that she didn't think through every last detail with such precision but she found she couldn't help herself. She was such a worrier. She had responsibilities, lots of them; responsibilities to her husband, to her boss, to her family, to her friends and to the maître d' who was expecting them at 7.15p.m. precisely. She found that careful planning minimised the opportunity for disaster and disillusionment. However, extensive planning could not cancel *all* risk of disappointment, as was proved when Neil called her and said she was not to expect him home as Karl had insisted that they go for a birthday drink straight from work, to kill the time between work finishing and their reservation at the restaurant.

'Do you mind?' asked Neil with concern. He was aware that Nat liked to plan things and he didn't want to mess up anything she might have arranged.

'Not at all. It's your birthday. The important thing is you have fun,' Nat replied honestly. She didn't think it was fair to say she was lying on their bed in her scanties; what would Karl do with himself when Neil made a dash from the pub?

'You're sure?'

'Certain. I'll see you there. Has Karl arranged to meet Jen there too?'

'Dunno, I'll ask him.'

'Do. You know what he's like, he might just have a beer too many and forget that he has a girlfriend who is supposed to be joining us.' Nat had introduced Jen to Karl about this time last year and she tended to feel responsible for their relationship staying on track; quite an undertaking as Karl was a consummate flirt and Jen was an absolute romantic. Neil often said that they were all grown-ups and that Nat shouldn't feel she had to manage them but she couldn't shake the habit.

'Will do,' said Neil. He glanced towards Karl, who was at the bar ordering drinks. Karl was chatting up a very beautiful redhead but Neil decided there was no point sharing this information with Nat, it would stress her out. Best thing he could do was go and drag his mate back to the table. 'Better go. Love you, see you there. Thanks so much for arranging tonight, Nat. I'm really looking forward to it,' he added sincerely.

'You're welcome. Love you too.' Nat hung up and considered how she could best use the unexpected hour she now had to herself. She could tie the helium balloons to the bedposts, at the moment the balloons were just drifting around the house willy-nilly, or she could reread her notes for the morning meeting, or she could paint her fingernails. She decided that she would reread her notes and then arrange the balloons. Neil would be so excited when he saw the thirty-five balloons (various shades of blue and purple) as he was such a big kid. So there wasn't to be birthday sex, at least not yet.

That probably meant they'd have to miss out or she would have to stay up late. Nat put the issue to the back of her head and reached for her laptop. Oh well, Nat thought to herself. After all, sex isn't everything.

2

Neil clawed through the fuzzy mess that was his mind and tried to grab on to the point his friend, Karl, was making.

'Say that again.'

'A man can never hope for, think about or indeed actually have too much sex. Sex is *everything* it's cracked up to be and more,' Karl said with absolute, unwavering conviction. Then Karl closed his eyes and pursed his lips. He probably wanted to communicate certainty and confidence, but Neil thought his mate had only managed cool and smug. Karl liked to play the sage, even when he was pissed – especially then. Yet Neil and Tim had to grudgingly admit that Karl could afford to be cool and smug because, as his freshly relayed story about his recent antics with a Dutch air hostess proved, he was clearly still enjoying the sort of sex that *is* everything, although admittedly not always with his girlfriend, Jen.

Sex is *everything* it's cracked up to be and more. How profound was that? Neil stared at his empty wine glass, probably his fifth empty wine glass that evening, and two pints before that. The empty glass provided the answer to his question: his mate was *deeply* profound.

'You're right. It's bigger than football and even video games by a long shot,' Neil agreed with drunken enthusiasm. He nodded his head so vigorously that his eyes disappeared, up and away, somewhere behind his forehead. His smile was slack and accepting but, even through his drunken haze, Neil recognised a prickle of discomfort spike his conscience. By agreeing with Karl he was tactically condoning his illicit affairs, but in fact he didn't agree with Karl's behaviour. Besides, Neil knew that Nat would be disgusted if she got so much as a whisper of Karl's exploits and he knew she'd want him to be dismayed by Karl's vulgar, careless bragging. And so he was. Appalled by it. Mainly. But the horrible truth was, he was also just a tiny bit curious and a smidgen envious.

Neil and Natalie had been married five years now and in all that time Neil had been completely and utterly faithful in deed and mostly faithful in thought. Naturally, after years of sex with the same woman (usually in the same bed, at the same time of the week, initiated in the same break between TV programmes) it tended not to be the sort of sex that could be described as *everything*. Neil found that he often stole some illicit, gratuitous pleasure from listening to Karl's stories. Neil sneaked a look at Tim, who had been married to Alison for three years. Were they still having the *everything* sort of sex?

Tim was trying to look bored with Karl's conversation; he hadn't had a drink and so could not find it in him to indulge Karl's loutish conceit. In the past there had been occasions when he, too, had enjoyed living vicariously through Karl's escapades but now it all seemed infantile; he was simply irritated by it. He would have liked to tell Karl that he was spouting crap but it was Neil's birthday and to celebrate the fact they were here at the Bluebird restaurant on the King's Road in posh Chelsea and so it would seem rude; dissent would hinder the digestion of the gorgeous grilled organic rib-eye steak. Besides, a condemnation of what Karl was saying might reveal that he was not having the *everything* sort of sex and he'd rather stab himself in the eye with a steak knife than admit as much to Karl.

Karl and Tim had always been furtively competitive. Tim knew it was something to do with the dynamics of their respective relationships with Neil but he couldn't put his finger on exactly what (not without sounding gay) and he'd rather admit to Karl that he wasn't having the *everything* sort of sex than say something that might make him sound gay. Neil and Tim were each other's oldest friend. They'd been buddies since primary school.

They'd grown up on the same sprawling housing estate, just a few miles south of Nottingham town centre, in identical, modest 1970s semis. Houses that Tim's mum and Neil's parents still lived in, although both families had since added a porch and Neil's parents had gone the whole hog, they'd built an extension which provided a fourth bedroom. They had been able to afford this at just about the time Neil, his brother and sister had left home, rendering the longed-for extension useless except for every other Christmas when Neil and his siblings, their spouses and families visited home for three tense days of overeating and mild squabbling. Neil had once told Tim that he didn't mind Christmas squabbles; he believed them to be inevitable. He thought of his family as a very close family and he was pretty sure that things like his mother's continual insistence they all eat just one more mince pie, his sister's doggedness that they opened their Christmas presents in size order, his father's resolve that they each discuss (at tedious length) the route they chose to travel home (and then all alternatives!), and his brother's competitive nature, which sprang like a well throughout charades, Monopoly and even when answering the quiz questions in the crackers, were all signs of their closeness. Families were supposed to be comfortingly habitual; that was the point of them.

Neil and Tim had attended the same small and earnest primary school and the same sprawling and indifferent comprehensive. At both institutions they had frequently stood side by side, silently encouraging and supporting one another whenever they faced their headmaster or mothers (after being caught in the inevitable scrapes that kids are caught in) and then, as teenagers, when they'd faced down Dave-built-like-a-brick-shithouse and his gang of thugs (both of them refusing to hand over their lunch money which was a stand neither could have made alone). They went to separate universities, Tim studied mathematics at Bristol and Neil studied computer graphics at Cardiff, but they called and visited one another frequently throughout those three years and then after graduating they moved to London and shared a dingy flat and numerous cheap curries. For nearly three decades now they'd stood shoulder to shoulder for various team photos, at bars, in ski lifts, before exams and job interviews and at the altars where they'd been each other's best man. There was no doubt that Tim was Neil's *oldest* friend but at the risk of sounding like a girl, Tim could never shake off the nagging feeling that Karl was Neil's *best* friend.

Of course Neil and Karl both worked in video games, they had that in common, Neil as a designer, Karl as a marketer. This instantly transformed them into hipper types than Tim could ever hope to be. Tim was a computer programmer. He liked his job well enough, it paid nicely but it hadn't been a childhood ambition, he wasn't passionate about it like Neil was about his work. Neil had always been mad about video games and manga illustrations and superhero comics and all sorts of other cool stuff. Since Neil had been a teenager he'd been determined to become a games designer and he didn't give a damn that career advisers, teachers and such were forever telling him there was no real money in it.

Neil and Karl had met twelve years ago at an industry event but cut the seminar to go to a lap-dancing club. Tim had had no idea that Neil had ever wanted to visit a lap-dancing club; he probably hadn't wanted to until Karl had suggested it. It turned out Neil also wanted to go snowboarding in Le Corbier, quad biking in the Cadiretas Mountains and mud wrestling with naked girls in Bratislava. Everything Karl suggested was fun, enticing and irresistible; everyone found this to be the case. Especially women. Karl was sickeningly successful with women. The mystery was, Karl wasn't actually that good-looking. He was trendy and had an expensive haircut (artfully sculpted to look as though he'd just got out of bed and never gave styling any thought) but it had long since occurred to Tim that all of Karl's features just missed being extremely handsome by a smidgen. His eyes were blue and he had thick, long lashes (the type that girls craved) but the eyes were small and too close together, his top lip was disproportionately thin in comparison to the bottom one, he had a fine nose but it was a fraction too long and gave the illusion that it was about to crash into his chin. He was tall, which was a plus, but he hadn't bulked out in his thirties as most men did and he'd been described as lanky as a teenager and it was just as accurate a description today. And yet, charismatic Karl was and always had been a colossal hit with women, with his bosses, with his mates, with footie refs, even with the men who came to install his cable or read his meter.

It was sickening, really.

When he burst into any room or gathering, he radically elevated the mood. There was never any embarrassing hiatus in the conversation, just plenty of hilarious jokes and interesting stories. He was amusing, razor-sharp, poised and he seemed to have a limitless stream of spellbinding anecdotes. He was happy with his lot: his job, his girlfriend, his disposable women and his flat. He didn't seem to take himself or anyone else too seriously. Many would say he was the perfect twenty-first-century man. The truth was that Karl was more amusing, astounding and controversial than Tim. In short, Karl was more compelling. Tim thought it was hard to keep up.

'Do you know what, if everyone understood and *accepted* that sex is everything *and more*, the world would be a far, far happier place to dwell,' said Karl. 'There would be less war, less theft, less violence, less lying.'

Tim wondered if Neil was simply too drunk to notice that the stuff Karl was spouting was just plain old bollocks. The sort of sex that Karl was having (the sort with air hostesses and other strangers he met on business trips) inevitably led to more lying, not less. Actually, Neil was not paying that much attention to what Karl was saying now; he'd tuned out. Neil was thinking about the fact that he really had quite a good chance of getting laid tonight even though it was Wednesday. After all, it was his birthday and Natalie was not an unreasonable woman. When he'd called Nat this evening and discovered she was at home he had considered going straight there from work, rather than going for a beer with Karl, just in case he caught her in the mood. But then he'd reasoned that she'd probably dashed home from the office to search out some quiet privacy, to prepare for her meeting in the morning, and he didn't want to get in the way, so he hadn't suggested it.

Karl carried on. 'Sex is the ultimate secret to happiness.'

'What evidence do you have for that?' asked Tim with an irritated sigh.

'Well, mate, I understand and accept that sex is, you know, massive and I'm a very happy man.'

'You sound like a sex addict,' Tim said, not bothering to hide his annoyance. Mostly Tim was annoyed because Karl, with his slack morals and careless cruelty, *was* happy whereas Tim, who had always done his best to be a decent human being, was often barely content, let alone happy. Not recently. Not since he and Ali had been *trying* for a baby. Trying and failing, that was. It didn't seem fair. Tim swept his eyes around the restaurant. It was buzzing even though it was midweek. He liked it here. Despite its lofty size, the place felt intimate. If only Karl would stop going on about sex, he'd be really enjoying Neil's birthday dinner. Natalie had chosen well. The restaurant was decorated with warm chocolate browns and deep, rich reds which subliminally suggested bitter chocolate brownies and ripe raspberries. What else was on the dessert menu? Oh yes, sweet melon jelly with poached pear, walnuts and chocolate sauce. He stared up at the stunning skylight, gilded with glimmering metallic chandeliers, and wished the women would come back from the loo. Not only could he order pudding but they'd put a halt to this infantile conversation. Why did women need to go to the loo in packs anyhow?

He knew the answer and it was not a comfort. They went in gangs to gossip. Right now, Alison would be issuing the fertility update to Nat and Jen as though she worked for the BBC World Service. She'd be discussing the exact quality of his sperm, or more accurately the lack of quality. She just didn't see any reason to keep this sort of information to herself. 'It's nothing to be ashamed of,' she'd insisted when he'd asked if she could possibly be a tad more discreet. 'It's just biology.' She'd be explaining that for most men each millilitre of semen contains literally millions of spermatozoa (technical name for sperm and the one she preferred to use right now), but this was not the case for Tim, his sperm count was 'significantly below average'. That's why he wasn't allowed to get pissed tonight which was making this conversation about filthy, flirty, dirty sex all the harder to endure. Apparently, his sperm had a better chance of hitting the jackpot if it wasn't pickled in alcohol. It was astounding to Tim that Alison had insisted that they go to a doctor to have that choice piece of information suggested and confirmed. He'd have thought years of living together and seeing how getting lashed affected his ability to aim piss into the pan would have been evidence enough for her, but no, Alison needed to hear it from the men in white coats. It had been a mortifying exercise. Ali wasn't herself just now. Baby-making had become all-consuming and over a period of about eight months he'd watched his wife change from a happy and intelligent woman to an angry and irrational beast. He really hoped that if (when, he self-corrected; he always had to think positively, Ali insisted on it) *when* she got pregnant, she'd revert back to her rational and reasonable self. Otherwise any child they might have would certainly end up in therapy. Suddenly Tim felt rebellious.

'How about I get us a bottle of champagne, to go with pudding?' he asked. 'I'll get it from the bar then it won't go on the bill. My treat.' Tim stood up abruptly.

'Nice one, pal, very generous of you,' said Neil with a grin.

'My pleasure.' Anything rather than listen to Karl's bragging or at least if he had to listen to it, then he'd rather be slightly numbed. Off he strode in the direction of the bar.

'I wish Tim would just leave his car here and he could pick it up in the morning,' said Neil the moment he was out of earshot. 'I think he could do with a real drink. He's not himself tonight.' Neil was disappointed this was the case. Birthdays, by necessity, only came round once a year and he wanted all his mates to be in the right mood to celebrate. He knew Nat had put a lot of effort into arranging tonight for him. She'd been coordinating diaries all summer. Tim's jittery mood and refusal to get wasted wasn't very celebratory.

'Have you noticed that if you mention the word sex, Tim reacts as though he's just been snapped by a speed camera,' commented Karl.

'What?'

Karl leaned towards Neil conspiratorially. He actually tapped his nose which was only excusable as they were both drunk. 'The thing is, to him sex and speeding are a bit similar at the moment, a mix between occasional necessity and genuine compulsion, but if you're caught, you have to cough up big time.' Karl laughed at his own witty metaphor. Encouraged by a booze-induced belief in his own brilliance and a sneaky, somewhat pleasant, suspicion that he knew more about this subject than Neil, he continued to explain. 'Tim is drowning in domestic responsibility and being beaten by procreation issues.'

'What?' repeated Neil. He was none the wiser.

'They're doing the baby-making thing. He only gets it at certain times of the month now. He's not even allowed to shake hands with his old fella. Plus, when they do actually get down to it, it's all a bit perfunctory,' explained Karl.

'*He* told *you* this?' Neil asked in disbelief. It was generally acknowledged that friendships between boys are sustained (indeed blossom) only if all the concerned parties are careful never to talk about anything too personal which might embarrass any one of them and, besides, if Tim was ever to behave out of type, he'd confide in Neil, not Karl. Neil was pretty sure of that.

'No, you silly sod, of course *he* didn't tell me this. Alison told Jen, who told me. Alison must have discussed it with Nat. I'm surprised she hasn't filled you in. I think this conversation about me getting it up the Dutch bird is reminding Tim of what he's no longer enjoying.'

Karl and Neil both turned and watched, with some sadness, as Tim tried and failed to attract the attention of the chic barmaid. Tim used to be quite the man about town although he'd never been aware of it. In the past, he was the one they always sent to the bar because he was the undisputed looker of the gang. Since a pair of red-blooded males noticed and acknowledged he was hot, how could barmaids – mere women – resist him? They'd practically slithered in his direction if he so much as nodded. But that was then, this was now.

'He's never going to get that fucking champagne,' said Karl impatiently. 'You know what the problem is, don't you? He's fading. The receding hair, and "dad uniform" of pale chinos, pink shirt, slight paunch mean he's faded into the background and Alison's not even up the duff yet. By the time their kid is attending nursery school, he'll be invisible.' The phrase 'poor sucker' flitted in and out of Karl's mind. 'Hell. He might call me a sex addict but I'd say I'm just a normal man and he's forgotten what being a man is,' he added.

Suddenly they were swamped by an anxious, slightly despondent silence. Neil didn't like it, Karl couldn't stand it. Despondency was not their thing. Karl made an effort to claw back the former mood of irreverence, a mood more fitting for a birthday celebration. 'And as a normal man it's my given right to think about sex every thirty seconds,' he joked.

'Every thirty seconds, are you sure?' Neil looked alarmed. Instantly he felt inadequate. Hearing this statistic was a bit like finding out that your best mate understands all aspects of the quantum theory; you feel left behind.

Karl appreciated the insecurity. Even he considered every thirty seconds an unsustainable and unlikely goal. 'Don't sweat it, mate. This dubious statistic, which has seeped into modern culture as fact, originated from nothing more substantial than a women's magazine. It's ironic that it was women who gifted this particular carte blanche to us lads by publishing an article claiming pathetic single-mindedness is true of all men. The article was probably little more than an elaborate joke, initially intended to highlight men's inability to multitask, or emotionally engage, or some other bollocks. Well, that apple pie back-splattered, didn't it, mate?'

'Why's that then?' asked Neil.

'Well, if a bloke were to think of sex, say, once an hour, he is considered moderate, not deviant or imbecilic,' Karl explained.

'And do you? Do you think about it once an hour?'

'I do.'

'What are you talking about?' It was Nat who asked this question. Neil and Karl jumped guiltily as they registered that Tim had returned from the bar and was holding a chilled bottle of house champagne and six glasses and the girls had returned from the loo. As the women sat down, they rolled their eyes at one another conspiratorially. They hadn't caught the conversation but they took an educated guess as to what the blokes would be talking about.

Football. Again.